· THE ·
SOFTWARE
· BOMB ·

Also by Steven Womack

Murphy's Fault
Smash Cut:
Dead Folks' Blues

·THE·
SOFTWARE
·BOMB·

STEVEN
WOMACK

ST. MARTIN'S PRESS

NEW YORK

THE SOFTWARE BOMB Copyright © 1993 by Steven Womack.
All rights reserved. Printed in the United States of America. No part
of this book may be used or reproduced in any manner
whatsoever without written permission except in the case of brief
quotations embodied in critical articles or reviews. For information,
address St. Martin's Press, 175 Fifth Avenue, New York, N.Y.
10010

Design by Basha Zapatka

Library of Congress Cataloging-in-Publication Data

Womack, Steven.
 p.   cm.
 "A Thomas Dunne book."
 ISBN 0-312-09390-X
 1. Computer crimes—Louisiana—New Orleans—Fiction.
 2. New Orleans (La.)—fiction. I. Title.
PS3573.O576S67   1993
813'.54—dc20   93-10338
                                                     CIP

First edition: July 1993

10 9 8 7 6 5 4 3 2 1

to Mr. Bill,
still the Best Man

▪ *CHAPTER 1* ▪

I f Fred Astaire had been born with two left feet, and bad acne to boot, he would have looked exactly like Martin Brown.

The young man's straw-colored hair was badly in need of a good washing. He'd been in the same pair of khakis for a week. His pin-striped cotton shirt was old, smelled slightly, and hadn't seen the flat side of a hot iron in months.

But on the graveyard shift, it didn't matter.

Martin Brown shivered in the dry, icy midnight air of the glass-enclosed computer room. The offices outside were deserted, the cleaning crew having emptied the wastebaskets, the ashtrays, and dusted a little before calling it a night.

Back in Brown's tiny uptown apartment, on Lowerline Street down from where the streetcar line turns, his wife, Patí, an aerobics instructor at a health club in Metairie, lay in bed staring at the ceiling. Patí Brown's naturally blonde hair was as pale as winter wheat, usually moussed, and teased in the style known back in her Jefferson Parish home as "Big Hair." She was tanned to a copper sheen. Everything about her was tight. Fit. She imagined herself, as did many, a Venus in Spandex. She and Martin had been married only two years. And Patí Brown was beginning to think she had married beneath herself.

Martin's degree in computer science hadn't gotten him

very far. Perhaps, Patí thought as she lay there sleeplessly, her husband's personality was beginning to stand in the way of his climb up the corporate ladder. He should be a lot further along than night-shift lead operator in the computer room of a New Orleans bank.

The same things that led her to marry him in the first place were sinking him now. The incredibly dry, sharp wit that was so funny at parties and among their friends had earned Martin Brown a reputation as a smartass in the corporate environment. His refusal to play by the rules, combined with his minor eccentricities and his total refusal to suck up to anyone, would have served him well in many occupations. But not this one. Nuances of personality—in fact, any personality at all—were anathema in the world he had chosen for himself.

The hard truth was that Martin Brown just didn't fit in at the First Interstate Bank of Louisiana. His career had taken up lodgings in the last house on a dead-end street.

He was in charge of four other operators, each in his or her own way an out-of-place corporate dweeb in the harried world of the Data Processing Division. Every night, his crew prepared a stack of computer printouts nearly fourteen feet high for distribution among the bank's forty-seven officers;—forty-seven little Hitlers determined to make Martin's life miserable. If an operator called in sick, or if one of the five massive printers broke down, or if a storm came over and an emergency shutdown was called because of the threat of lightning, then Martin Brown was in for a long, whacked-out night. The adrenaline would rise in his veins like floodwaters. The nervous sweats would permeate his already gamy shirt, and he would run about shouting orders and screaming obscenities like a banshee.

Understaffed, underpaid, overstressed. . . . Martin knew Patí was frustrated at their failure to move into a larger apartment, trade up to a better car, take that cruise she'd been talking about for months. But what could he do besides mutter obscenities and fight back as hard as he could?

This night, thankfully, had been fairly quiet. One operator was running the decollator in the printout room, another was hanging magnetic tape reels on the massive, floor-to-ceiling steel racks in the tape library, and two others were delivering printouts.

Martin Brown stood at the master console, typing instructions to the computer in a form of Pidgin English called Job Construction Language. Above him, to his right, a 27-inch monochrome monitor displayed a screen full of status lines. On the left of the screen, a column of user IDs let the operators know who was on the system at any given time. Another series of columns described the task being performed, the tape drive in use, certain flags indicating when magnetic tapes should be loaded, a number that told the amount of core memory in use, and a last column indicating the amount of core memory still available in the system.

The First Interstate Bank of Louisiana had a huge mainframe computer. The CSS 9600 Series II had enough memory to support more than one hundred users at a time. A row of eight mag tape drives on one wall of the computer room ran constantly, while twelve hard disk drives with removable diskpaks lined the other wall. It was nearly impossible to tie up the CSS 9600 II. Occasionally, during periods of extremely heavy use, the monitor indicated up to eighty percent busy. Martin Brown had never seen it any higher than that.

This night, there were only two other users on the entire system, both of them young vice-president workaholics who felt compelled to work until at least one A.M. a couple of nights a week.

Martin and his crew had the rest of the system all to themselves. The line in the lower right hand corner of the monitor read:

IN USE - 20% / AVAILABLE - 78%

Martin knew that with a click of the keyboard here and another click there, he could cause the bank more problems than a sport dog could jump over. Then they'd wish they'd been nicer to him. But he never did. It was too easy to get caught.

Below the console where Martin stood lay a 2400 baud

external modem sitting under a black telephone. The modem was set to automatically answer the phone, then ask for a user I.D. If the caller typed a legitimate user number, the computer would ask for a password. Each programmer, systems analyst, and operator picked his or her own secret password. No one except the boss knew anyone else's password. At least that was the way it was supposed to work.

Martin Brown's password was WEASEL, his college fraternity nickname.

As the huge printers behind him churned printout at the rate of five thousand lines per minute, Weasel began to wish he were home in bed with Patí. Their sex life had suffered greatly since he got transferred to the graveyard shift, working six at night until three in the morning. His mind wandered and he began to feel pressure below.

The clock approached 1:30 A.M.; Martin's fantasies grew kinkier. Suddenly, the printers stopped. The abrupt silence was like a hammer stroke, smashing Martin out of his reverie.

"Dammit." He punched the silent console. "What the hell's going on?"

The printers had stopped mid-line.

Martin examined the printer ribbons in both printers. They were okay, on track, still plenty of cloth left. He hit the red restart button on each one.

Nothing.

He turned and looked up at the monitor. The user lines had all gone blank, except the top one.

EXT1

the display read, indicating an outside user, and down in the bottom corner:

IN USE - 99.9% / AVAILABLE - 00%

The system was full, maxed out completely. Martin had never seen that before.

"Holy shit," he muttered. He reached for the master console keyboard and typed STATUS VERIFY, then hit the ENTER key.

Nothing. The keyboard was dead. Martin stared at the idle

tape drives. The only sound was the whirring of the diskpaks and the hum of the air-conditioning system.

Martin jumped as the phone rang.

"Computer room," he barked into the phone.

"What's going on down there?" a voice demanded. It was one of the obsessive-compulsive vice-presidents. "My keyboard's dead."

"I'll have to call you back," Martin said rudely, hanging up on the veep.

EXT1 the monitor read.

One of the programmers, Martin thought.

They did that sometimes, worked from home, called in to make corrections in programs or to troubleshoot. A couple of them were pretty weird; they never slept. They'd work twelve, maybe fourteen hours all day long, then Martin would see them logging on at three in the morning as he was checking out.

But who the hell was it? Martin typed USER ID - EXT1 - VERIFY into the console and hit the ENTER button. Nothing. The keyboard was as dead as David Duke at an NBA picnic.

The phone rang again. Martin let it ring.

Then, without warning, the tape drives spun to life. The printers behind Martin exploded into a pounding din. The monitor now read:

IN USE - 15% / AVAILABLE - 85%

"Whoever it was," Martin said out loud, "they hung up."

The internal phone next to him rang again.

"Yeah," he said nastily, holding the phone to his face.

"Never mind," the vice-president said. "It's working now."

Martin slammed the phone down.

Who the hell was that on the modem?

Thank God it was nothing serious, Martin thought. Before he went home, he had to start the program to generate the monthly checking account statements for the banks' 125,000 customers.

■ CHAPTER 2 ■

Trevenia Royale was the youngest and last surviving daughter of the man who once owned the largest rice plantation within fifty miles of Golden Meadow. That had been eons ago, however, and now Trevenia lived alone in a deteriorating "shotgun"—a nineteenth-century house with one room behind another five deep, no hallway—on Freret Street near Broadway, just up from the Tulane campus.

She was sixty-seven and had been widowed just over a year. Her husband had smoked "Home Runs," the Grade B Mississippi cigarettes he'd been buying since before the war, until they finally killed him. The old S.O.B. hadn't left her much; most of what he'd saved had been eaten up by medical bills. But Trevenia had his social security and a small widow's pension from the asbestos factory where he had worked.

Only it wasn't enough. Not near enough. Trevenia Royale, like Johnny Rocco in *Key Largo*, wanted *more*. Her husband's death had brought their staid marriage to an end; and with that end came a release of something wild, unpredictable, and completely inappropriate for a woman her age.

Take the boys, for instance. Her face was wrinkled and her scraggly hair was graying fast, but she was still thin, still tight in the places that counted. If the light hit her just right, she could get the boys in.

And if she could get them in, she could have them.

Like last night, with that Tulane boy who lived down on South Carrollton, the one with the short hair in the Marine ROTC. She'd been watching for weeks as he strolled past her house on the sidewalk every day after his last class. She had his schedule memorized, even on Sunday nights, when he walked past her house on the way to the library at precisely seven o'clock, and then again on his way home at precisely ten-fifteen.

Those military types. So precise, and always on time. . . .

At ten minutes after ten that Sunday evening, Trevenia walked outside onto her front porch wearing only a sheer silk gown and a pair of slippers. In the subdued light of the front porch, she looked perhaps fifteen years younger than her actual age.

She slammed the door behind her as hard as she could, locking it. Then she sat down on the front porch, looking to the left and right. It was dark, with long shadows cast across the street by the orange glow of the streetlights. The neighbors were safely inside, out of her way.

At 10:13, she glanced again to her left, down the street toward the traffic light at Broadway and Freret. A lone figure, tall, carrying an armload of books, crossed the intersection and headed her way.

Trevenia smiled. Then she reached way down deep inside her, to some dark and hidden part of herself, and began to cry.

Her sobs grew louder as the boy approached. He slowed, carefully at first, and continued walking. He was almost in front of her now, barely a few feet from the steps.

The boy hesitated, and looked at Trevenia as she sat on the top step of her porch with her knees pulled up around her, sobbing. He started to walk on without saying anything. Trevenia caught him out of the corner of her eye.

"Excuse me, sir," she said quickly, before he could get away.

The boy stopped, hesitated at first, then turned toward her. He seemed a Greek god crowned in orange, as brilliant as the sun, as dazzling as the heavens. His shaved head and wide shoulders were outlined starkly in the sulfureous glow of the streetlights.

Trevenia licked her lips.

"Yes, ma'am," the boy said, stepping toward her.

Oooh, and polite, too.

"I'm sorry," she sobbed, drawing out her words like a true Southern belle with an impending case of the vapors. "I hate to bother you, but I seem to've jammed my front door. Would you mind helping me? I'm so very fearful of the night."

The boy smiled, relieved that it wasn't anything serious, and set his books down on the first step of the porch.

"Sure, ma'am," he said, flashing her his perfect, square, white-toothed Marine smile. He took the steps two at a time and was at the door in a second.

"Ma'am," he said, "this door isn't jammed. It's locked."

"Oh, dear," Trevenia said, breaking into fresh sobs. "Whatever shall I do now?"

She stood next to the boy, between him and the streetlight. She saw him look at her. He was unaware that she had found this spot months before, the exact spot where the streetlight would be behind her, shining through the thin gown, her naked silhouette as much on display as if she'd been a Bourbon Street stripper.

The boy stared. Trevenia pretended she didn't notice.

"You could call a locksmith," the boy said, after a moment. He looked away quickly, afraid that she would catch him gaping.

"I can't afford that," she said. "Whatever shall I do?" she repeated.

"Gee, ma'am," he said. "I don't know."

"Wait. I think I left the side window cracked a bit. But it's too high for me to climb. Would you take a look and see if you could get in? I'd be glad to pay you. I know this is a terrible bother . . ." Trevenia reached out and brushed the boy's forearm ever so slightly. She felt the hair bristle.

"Sure," he said, smiling. "Let's take a look. But you don't have to pay me, ma'am. I'm only too glad to help."

The boy led the way around the side of the house. He was six feet tall if he was an inch, and built like the Marine officer he'd someday be.

The window was five feet off the ground and opened just a crack. With one hand, the boy pushed the sash up as high as it would go. The muscles in his arm rippled like waves pounding against a sandy beach. In a second, he leapt up to the window and into Trevenia's house with the grace of a cat. Trevenia watched in awe as the boy's rump disappeared into the house, followed by his powerful legs.

He beat her around front and had the door open by the time she could get there. She reached down and picked up the boy's books and carried them into the house.

"I can't thank you enough," she said, gratefully, hungrily, as the boy held the door for her. "Close the door."

The boy stood there awkwardly for a moment as Trevenia walked through the front room and into the dining room. The door clicked shut behind her. She put the books on the table and came back to him.

"If you won't let me pay you, at least let me fix you a drink," she said.

"No, ma'am, that's not necessary. Besides, it's getting late."

"Nonsense," Trevenia said, "it's not that late. Indulge a lonely old lady and let her show how grateful she is. You're a college boy, aren't you?"

"Yes, ma'am," he said, shyly.

"Well, in my day, all college boys liked beer. I think I have a can or two in the refrigerator. It's been in there so long, I hope it hasn't gone bad. Does beer go bad, boy? Sit down on that couch over there and make yourself comfortable."

"Well, okay, ma'am," he said, sitting down. "If you're sure it's not too much trouble."

"Of course not," she said, walking lightly back to the kitchen, where she had a fresh case of Bud in the icebox. She poured two glass mugs full of beer, put them on a tray, and carried them into the living room. She stood in front of the coffee table and leaned over to set the tray down, letting her gown fall open. She knew the boy would be staring down the front.

They were midway through the second beer when Trevenia opened the drawer of the table at her end of the couch. She pulled out a small wooden box and set it on the coffee table in front of her. She opened the box and pulled out one perfectly rolled, bulbous joint.

"Would you like to share this with me?" she asked, smiling. "I don't do this often, but my late husband used to keep a little around. To ease the nausea from his chemotherapy. If you don't mind, that is . . ."

The young future Marine looked down at the old lady sitting next to him. You couldn't tell she was that old, at least not in this light. The beer was starting to get to him; he didn't drink much. He'd gotten a good look down the front of that slinky thing she was wearing. *Not bad, not bad at all.*

"That's fine with me, ma'am," he said, smiling, relaxed.

"Don't ma'am me, boy," she said, teasing. "Call me Trevenia."

"That's a pretty name," he said.

"I'm named after my grandmama," Trevenia smiled. "The prettiest belle in Terrebonne Parish. What's your name?"

"Dudley, ma'am," he drawled. "Dudley Boudreaux."

An hour later, Trevenia stood up in front of the couch and reached down to take Dudley Boudreaux's hand. The tie around the robe was open now, the cloth barely hanging onto her shoulders. Her stomach was flat, her breasts still firm, high, with only a few traces of gray in the thick, long hair between her legs.

The boy took her hand.

Inside her bedroom, Trevenia had him naked in two minutes. When she pulled the last of his clothes off, she let loose with a deep gasp. A knot the size of a crabapple tightened in her stomach.

The boy was a real pony; rock hard and hung like an army mule. In all her sixty-seven years, she'd never seen anything like it.

"*God,*" she thought, in a momentary flash of fear, "*you ain't putting that in me!*"

Then something else took over, and Trevenia reached out and grabbed the boy between his legs, barely able to get her tiny hand around him, and pulled him toward her on the bed.

By lunchtime the next day, Trevenia could almost walk normally. They'd been at it for hours; the boy, it turned out, was every bit as hungry as Trevenia. She soaked in a hot bathtub now, floating lazily, sleepily, in the steamy water as she thought back over the past evening.

Trevenia smiled to herself and stretched. At one point, she'd had to stuff a pillow in her mouth to keep from screaming.

She heard the clap of metal hitting metal on her front porch, then the heavy bootsteps of the mailman stomping off her porch.

As she lay there, she remembered that today was the fifth of the month. Trevenia was, as usual, worried about money. A delay in the last check from her husband's company had caused her to run short. The bank was no longer patient with Trevenia's chronic rubber-check writing. If she bounced any more checks, she'd have to run for Congress. Daddy's money had been gone a long time.

If she'd gotten the deposit to the bank on time, she'd be okay. The balance in her checkbook, $248.65, would be correct. If not, she'd have to subtract $15.00 for each overdraft.

Too concerned to savor the warm bath any further, Trevenia stepped cautiously out of the bathtub and towelled off, being careful to pat gently between her legs. *Which hurt worse,* she wondered, *the friction burns or the stubble rash?* Then she threw on the robe and walked through the house.

The small metal mailbox nailed to the door frame held her bank statement. She jerked it inside and tore it open before sitting down.

The statement was unusually long, a full two pages. She scanned down the list of activity on the left side of the first page. No overdrafts so far.

She turned to the second page. Great, no overdrafts, only

the usual service—no, wait. There wasn't even a service charge this month.

"What's going on?" she asked aloud.

Trevenia Royale scanned down the numbers on the page until she came to the box labeled "End Of Month Balance."

Crammed into the tiny little printed box were a whole string of numbers, which, when Trevenia was able to read them all together, read $646,897.66.

The next-door neighbor heard Trevenia's yelp over the sound of *General Hospital* on the TV.

"Goddamn, Trevenia," he muttered. "You gonna wear that thing out, you don't give it a rest."

▪ *CHAPTER 3* ▪

The Fiat began smoking just west of Albuquerque. By Houston, a steady stream of blue-black was trailing out behind the small convertible. When Lynch made his last stop for gas just before Causeway Boulevard and I-10, only the faintest drop of thick black sludge hung on the bottom of the dipstick.

"Damn," Lynch muttered. He pulled out his Texaco card and hoped it would slide through one more time.

He filled the tank, placed two quarts of thirty weight on the counter, and smiled nonchalantly as the young Asian girl in the brown uniform slid his credit card expertly through the slot scanner. The digital clacking of the printer spewing out his receipt told him he'd made it past the computer one more time.

The traffic on I-10 slowed to a crawl as Jack Lynch crossed the Orleans Parish line for the first time in three months. During those months, he had watched his mother die slowly in a Southern California nursing home, buried her, settled what was left of her estate, and then driven aimlessly, yet relentlessly, for days until his money ran low. The lawyers in California would forward him a check after the estate got out of probate—minus their fee, of course—but that might take months. Until then, cash was going to be tight.

The Fiat shook and backfired as Lynch slowed toward the

City Park Avenue exit ramp. He glanced down at his watch: 4:30 on a Wednesday afternoon. The traffic would be as thick as flies on an open garbage truck. Despite this, Jack Lynch felt an unusual calm.

Perhaps, he thought, it was the death of his mother.

After years of having that hanging over his head, it was finally over. Maybe it was just coming home, knowing that after all the chaos of the last few months, he would be able to slip the city back on like an old glove. He would lie up in his apartment for a few hours, then cross Esplanade and walk to Jackson Square through the back side of the Vieux Carré, through the residential part where only the most adventurous tourists ever ventured. He looked forward once again to coffee and beignets, then a breezy stroll on the Moonwalk, as long as it wasn't too late. Even Jackson Square wasn't as safe at night as it had once been; crack cocaine and a failing economy had seen to that.

He was glad to be home.

The traffic was backed up at the City Park Avenue light nearly onto the freeway. Lynch braked the car and slipped the gearshift into neutral, feeling the setting sun full on his face. He had driven only about seven hours that day, but seven hours driving across Texas and Louisiana in a convertible could take a lot out of a man. Especially a man who had spent the night before celebrating his fortieth birthday at a Motel Six in Galveston, Texas.

Lynch leaned his head back against the seat and waited for the traffic to crawl through the light a few cars at a time. His face was windburned, chapped, but his hangover had finally gone away somewhere east of Beaumont. Once he got through that light, he knew he was less than twenty minutes from home.

He coasted down the ramp until he was next in line, then shot through the intersection as soon as the light changed, back left under the interstate, then through the yellow light on the other side and onto City Park Boulevard. This was Lynch's usual highway interchange, the easiest one to get to from his apartment, and he thought it probably meant something in his life that his first real impression of the city after leaving the highway was a sense of being surrounded by cemeteries. As he sped along the wide boulevard, the mausoleums, the crypts, and the above-ground graves to his left and right loomed like movie sets. He'd always speculated that the rule about burying bodies above ground because of the water table was just an excuse. It was just as plausible, he thought, that it was more a reflection of dramatic sensibilities than maritime logistics.

He drove on past Delgado College, past the huge gnarled oaks of City Park and the art museum, then right across Bayou St. John onto Esplanade. He felt home again for real now, the sunlight skittering through the canopy of trees in a shower of sparkles. The oaks and palms arched above him, their branches joining above the neutral ground, making a kind of natural bridge over the avenue. One day, he thought, he'd like to live further out Esplanade toward Bayou St. John. The area was up and coming, with young professionals and urban pioneers seeming to mix in effortlessly with the poorer families who had been there for generations. Chic new restaurants sprang up over night; coffee houses and natural food markets dotted the neighborhood. People strolled along the wide sidewalks as Lynch's clattering Fiat bounced by on its bald tires.

He crossed North Broad into the inner city. Groups of sullen blacks and whites gathered at bus stops eyeing each other suspiciously. A gang of black teenagers in Chicago Bulls jackets hung around outside under the bright purple sign of a Katz & Bestoff drugstore, looking simultaneously bored and threatening.

Lynch stopped at a traffic light, ignoring the movement around him, and stretched his arms out to the side to pull the knots out of his shoulders. He reached across the passenger's seat and opened the glovebox. He searched in vain for a fresh pack of cigarettes. He thought of pulling into the K & B. Then the light changed.

He crossed North Rampart and was on the backside of the Quarter. He smiled, thinking of the hot shower and cold beer that lay in front of him just a few minutes away. Several blocks farther down, he turned left off Esplanade and pulled to a stop in front of his apartment house. He turned the key and the engine coughed to a rumbling stop. His head buzzed, and he realized as he shifted his weight that his butt was numb and his legs had gone to sleep.

He took off his sunglasses and rubbed his eyes, sitting there a moment listening to the relative silence. Behind him, a block away on Esplanade, he could hear traffic passing by. Somewhere off to his left, a radio played loudly from a window. A voice yelled in the distance above the faint roar of a lawn mower.

Lynch opened the door and climbed out. Then he reached into the tiny back seat and pulled out a canvas bag and a small suitcase. The rest of his gear was locked in the trunk. For now, he would leave it there. He would come down later and lock the car up in one of the empty garage spaces that occupied the first floor of the building. He wondered how dusty his apartment would be.

He climbed the stairs and opened the front door of the building, checked his mailbox and, as he expected, found it empty. Mr. Pelias, the building owner who occupied the largest apartment on the first floor, always held his mail for him. He continued down the long, dark hallway, then up the curving steps to the second floor. At the end of the hallway, he stopped in front of his apartment door and stared.

It was padlocked.

A stainless steel hasp had been screwed into the dark wood. Above the hasp, two ugly gashes next to the deadbolt had been ripped out of the jamb. Lynch muttered an obscenity under his breath, then dropped his bags on the hall floor. He held the padlock in the palm of his left hand and stared at it as if he weren't quite sure it was what it appeared to be. The lock was cold, heavy, painfully real.

He left his belongings in the hallway, then marched downstairs to the landlord's apartment and rapped on the door. Inside, he could hear the local news blasting loudly on the television. He knocked again, harder. There was a shuffling inside, then the rattling of a doorknob. Gus Pelias opened the door a crack, a thin silver chain providing the illusion of security.

"Mr. Pelias, hi. It's me, Jack Lynch."

A bloodshot eye above an unshaven cheek glared out. A voice thick with Greek accent said: "Oh, it's you." Then the door closed.

Lynch stood uncomfortably waiting for the unchaining of the door. There was no unchaining, though, only the sound of the television. He raised his knuckles to rap again when the door clattered open. Mr. Pelias stood there in an old undershirt, a ring of keys in his hands.

"Where you been?" he demanded, brushing by Lynch and stomping toward the stairs.

"Out of town. Out west, to California. My mother was ill, she—"

"Somebody broke in your apartment," Pelias interrupted.

"Oh, hell," Lynch muttered as he followed Mr. Pelias's jiggling backside up the narrow stairs. The man smelled of garlic, cheap wine, and cigars.

"When did this happen?" Lynch asked.

Mr. Pelias stopped midway up the stairs, turned, glared down at him. "Six weeks, maybe two months ago. You should have called me."

He continued on up the stairs, pulling himself up the rail an arms' length at a time.

"You got my rent checks, didn't you?"

"If I hadn't, your stuff would have been on the sidewalk."

Pelias shuffled down the hall toward the door, stopped in front of it, then held the key ring toward the bare hall light and flipped through the keys. He selected one, held it between two fingers on his right hand as his left held the lock, then slipped it in.

"How bad was it?" Lynch asked, his gut tightening at the thought of what he was about to see.

"Bad enough," Pelias said. His thinning, greasy salt-and-pepper hair dropped down on his forehead.

"Jesus," Lynch whispered.

Pelias lifted the padlock out of the hasp, then pushed the door open. He stepped in ahead of Lynch and fumbled for a light switch.

"Jesus," Lynch whispered again as he stepped into the apartment. To his left, a shattered china lamp still lay on the floor in pieces. The sofa cushions were thrown end over end across the room. An already battered easy chair was on its side, the stuffing ripped out of it, one leg broken off.

A clump of dusty, discarded wires was all that remained of Lynch's stereo. The faint outline of dust on a shelf was the only trace left of a nineteen-inch color television and a VCR.

Lynch stepped in quickly, past the man who stood sheepishly in front of him, almost embarrassed at the unveiling of what was once a man's safe and secure home.

"I'm really sorry about this," the older man muttered. But by then, Lynch was already in the kitchen staring at the spot on the kitchen counter where his microwave oven used to be. Pelias followed into the darkened room, the musty smell of a closed off kitchen filling both their nostrils.

"Did you call the police?" Lynch asked quietly. He was standing in front of Pelias, back to him, ramrod straight, with only his fists clenched at his side to give him away.

"Yeah, they took a report. But you know the cops. They said they couldn't do anything. It's just a burglary, that's all."

Lynch turned and scowled at the man. "Just a burglary?"

"Hey, dis's New Orleans. You's lucky you weren't here when they broke in."

"Dammit, man, I *live* here. This is my home!"

Pelias dropped his eyes to the linoleum floor and shuffled his feet. "Well, actually, Mr. Lynch, that's another thing I got to talk to you about."

Lynch put his hands on his hips, bent down and unsuccessfully tried to meet the man's eyes. "What? What is it, Gus?"

"Well," Pelias said uncomfortably, "it's the old lady. She says I got to get you out of here. The last couple years, she ain't happy with you living here."

Lynch's jaw dropped. "What are you talking about? I've lived here almost ten years."

"Yeah, but the last couple of years, you been coming and going all hours of the night. All that mess with the bank— what, a year-and-a-half or so ago—when we had the TV news trucks here. . . . You screaming in the middle of the night—"

"Hey, Gus, I was having nightmares for awhile. It was a bad time. That's over now."

"And now this. You disappear for three months, don't tell nobody where you're going."

"You got your rent, didn't you?" Lynch's voice dropped. His hands fell to his side. "Every month."

"Yeah," Pelias said, voice firmer, "but we never knew for sure whether we were going to get it or not. Not 'til it came in the mail."

"But you got it."

"That don't make no never mind, the old lady says you got to go. This break-in was the last straw. We need a tenant that's going to live here, be here. So the place looks lived in and the creeps'll stay away."

Lynch paced across the kitchen floor. "Gus, I got a lease."

"You *had* a lease," Pelias answered. "You ain't signed a lease here in years."

"Hell, I didn't think I had to. I've lived here for so—"

"I know, Mr. Lynch, and up until the last couple years, you been a pretty good tenant. But the old lady says you got to go, and believe me, buddy, when the old lady says it in the tone of voice she's been using lately, she means it."

"Maybe I could talk to her." Lynch felt like he was pleading, a sensation that made him profoundly uncomfortable.

"That won't do no good. All you're going to do is make her more upset, which is going to make me more miserable. No, that won't do at all. I'm really sorry, Mr. Lynch. . . . Jack. But you got to go. That's all there is to it."

Pelias looked up at him; their eyes finally met. And when they did, Jack Lynch knew this was a done deal. The fat lady had sung. It was time to move on.

"How much time can you give me?" Jack asked wearily.

"It'd be best if you could do it by this weekend."

■ 19

Lynch shook his head, resigned. "Three days, thanks a lot. Okay, Gus, I'll take care of it."

Pelias turned to go, relieved to have delivered the bad news. "I got a copy of the police report downstairs with your mail."

"Okay," he sighed. "I'll stop and pick it up in a few minutes."

"You got renter's insurance?"

"Yeah, I think so. I mean, I think I paid the premium. I'll have to check."

"I hope you did, Mr. Lynch. Maybe get a little cash out of this to help you start off right in your new place."

"Thanks, Gus. I appreciate that."

Pelias left the kitchen. Lynch started to follow, then slid down into a kitchen chair instead. He listened as footsteps echoed through the living room, then stopped.

"I'm really sorry about this mess, Mr. Lynch," Pelias called.

"Yeah," Jack muttered. "Me, too."

Lynch straightened the furniture and brought the rest of his bags in from the car. He tossed them on the bed and unzippered them, then sorted them into two piles. Those that needed laundering went on the floor; the few clean clothes left from the last time he'd done laundry in California went into drawers.

He was pushing aside hangers in his tiny closet to make room for his suits when he saw—or rather didn't see—what the burglars must have gotten in addition to the rest.

"Damn," he spat, slapping the wooden door. His favorite leather jacket was gone, one his ex-wife had given him while they were still married. Her last Christmas present to him. To think that they'd even gone through his clothes sent a chill up his back. Suddenly, the walls of the apartment felt like shrink wrap.

To make matters worse, the shoe box where he kept his Smith & Wesson .38 was empty as well. Disgusted, Lynch left the apartment, oblivious of the fact that with the padlock gone, there was no way to lock the door behind him. If he had noticed, it wouldn't have mattered. He was determined to find another apartment as quickly as possible.

The car was locked up; no point in getting it back out. Lynch walked to Esplanade, then down the avenue toward the river. The shadows were deepening across the wide lanes and the broad expanse of the neutral ground. The city was settling in for the evening. Music came at him from a dozen different directions. The sounds of partying and laughter filled his ears.

He turned right on Decatur, the sidewalks increasingly crowded the closer he got to the heart of the Vieux Carré. The promise of a warm evening heavy with smells and humidity wafted past him. In any other time of his life, Jack Lynch would have felt a building excitement within him; now he felt only fatigue.

Ten minutes later, he came to the intersection of Decatur and St. Ann, at the corner of Jackson Square nearest Cafe du Monde. To his right, from the other side of the square in front of the cathedral, a motley brass band was pounding out "When The Saints Go Marching In" to a small group of picture-takers. Just up St. Ann, past the tarot-card readers and the watercolor artists, a juggler with forearms as thick as channel cats had two flaming batons and a meat cleaver in the air at once. The smells of fresh horse manure, auto exhaust, frying beignets, and hot coffee whirled about into an earthy assault on the senses. Lynch's head swam with it all, and he suddenly realized he was ravenously hungry. He fought the urge to get a drink; even for Lynch, it was too early for cocktail hour.

He crossed the traffic between two horse-and-buggies filled with pale, grinning tourists and stepped through a gap in the wrought iron rail around Cafe du Monde. In the far corner, a table sat empty with a discarded copy of the *Times-Picayune* on it. Lynch headed straight for it and beat out two college students wearing T-shirts proclaiming the joys of beer drinking.

He flipped the paper open and straightened it, then refolded it neatly. The lead story was on the impending startup of the Louisiana Lottery. The state government, desperate for revenue and afflicted with a populace that simply refused to bear any more tax burden, had turned at last to the savior of governments in the last two decades of the twentieth century: legalized gambling. The lottery would commence in September, with talk of computerized video lottery and casino gambling in its wake. Offshore gambling was already allowed in Mississippi and riverboat gambling in several other states. One faction of politicians had warned that the state better join the parade before the floats were all taken; another proclaimed the immediate wrath of the Almighty upon us all. A third, much quieter group, was no doubt licking its chops in anticipation. It was, Jack thought, a sad commentary on the times that governments had come to depend on the weaknesses of its citizenry in order to survive.

Lynch ordered a cafe au lait and two orders of beignets—thick fried doughnuts dusted in powdered sugar—and settled back to check out the classifieds. Finding an apartment in New Orleans in this economy would not be hard; the hard part would be finding a decent place he could afford. He pulled a pencil out and began circling possibilities as his order arrived.

A half-hour later, Lynch left the cafe, fortified by strong coffee and with a half-dozen or so apartment candidates. He was feeling better, less shell-shocked at being back in the city only to find himself ripped off. He decided to take a walk along the river, along the Moonwalk and Woldenberg Park.

He climbed the steps to the top of the levee, which had been turned, over the past twenty years, from an earthen wall lined with rock into a prime tourist attraction. He crossed the tracks of the Riverfront Streetcar and onto the Moonwalk. The evening was evolving into a gorgeous, moonlit night. Silver shimmered off the river in a billion sparkles; the lights from traffic still streaming across the bridge danced and flickered above like fireflies. Lynch smiled despite himself, stretched in the heavy night air, and folded the newspaper under his arm. He strolled down among the tourists and the locals, the rabble and the roused, effortlessly streaming together in a faceless blend.

Ahead of him, a concrete bench sat next to a few steps that led down to a short pier out over the river. A middle-aged white couple in shorts, running shoes with white knee-length socks, and matching French Quarter T-shirts stopped and walked down the steps. The man leaned against a pillar, the river a backdrop, as his wife struggled to focus the camera and get a light reading.

Suddenly, out of the corner of his eye, Lynch saw a young black man in calf-length checked shorts, a white T-shirt, and opened-laced Air Jordans shoot by him toward the couple. The man was not much more than twenty-five, if that, with a closely shaved head, no facial hair. Lynch instinctively tensed as he watched out of the corner of his eye.

The man hopped down next to the husband and threw his arm around his shoulders, his hustle a singsong rap as smooth as the river slipping by, and with just as dangerous an undercurrent.

"Hey, ya'll, where ya'll from?" he began. "Welcome to Nyahluns. Let me help with that. Ya'll both get down here and let me take ya'lls pitcher."

The man smiled uncomfortably. "No, that's all right. We're fine, really."

"Hey, c'mon, man, be cool. Where ya'll from now?"

The woman looked down toward him over the top of her camera. Her hair was jet black, pulled back and tied. Lynch eyed her; she was attractive, pale, shapely. Nice legs, he thought. Husband looked like a dork.

"Lexington, Kentucky," she said, with more intensity and less discomfort than her husband had mustered.

"Lexington, Kentucky, now," the black man chimed, "horse country. That's beautiful. I love that. Say, why don't you c'mon down here and let me get the pretty lady's pitcher with her man."

"No, that's okay. We're fine really."

"Yeah, I know you fine. You told me that already. Let me introduce myself," he said, taking his arm from around the man's shoulder and backing away. "I'm Fast Eddie, that's what my friends call me. You heard it before, but I say it again. Fast Eddie, glad to meet you."

Fast Eddie stuck out his hand, fingers spread. The middle-aged geek from Lexington was fool enough to actually take it. Lynch smiled broadly as the two shook hands, watching the take unfold before him.

"People tell me I got magic, you know that," Fast Eddie continued. "Lemme give you'an example. Just by looking at them, I can tell you exactly where you got yo' shoes. You don't believe me, do you?"

The man looked down at his shoes. "No, how can you do that?"

His wife's face was a mixture of irritation and confusion. "Harold," she said, "let's go. We'll take pictures later."

Harold, Lynch thought, *do what your wife tells you.*

Harold, though, was feeling a little more confident now. "No," he said forcefully, "how can you tell where I got those shoes just by looking at them?"

"You don't think I can do it?"

"No, I don't."

"You're sure, now?"

"Yeah," the man insisted, sealing his own fate. Lynch didn't know how this was going to end, but he could hear the whine of fishing reels being cranked.

"Well, sir," Fast Eddie said, dropping down to his knees and pulling a rag and a small bottle of sneaker cleaner out of his back pocket. "You got these shoes right here, sir, right cheer on yo' feet."

He squirted a thick blob of white goop on each shoe, then began furiously wiping the man's toes before he could back away.

"Wait, wa—" Harold sputtered.

"What are you doing?" Harold's wife snapped.

Fast Eddie buffed the shoes like putting out fires. Then he stood up, snapped the rag in front of him smartly, and looked Harold straight in the eye.

"Sir, you've just learned something. A valuable lesson in this day and time. Never assume anything, and never play the game if you don't know the rules. Right?"

Harold pursed his lips until they disappeared. "Yeah. Yeah, sure. Thanks."

"My usual fee, sir, for that lesson is twenty-five dollars. But since you're only wearing running shoes, that'll be ten dollars. That's five for the shine, sir, and five for the line."

Lynch grinned broadly. Harold's face went numb with shock, as if he'd just been mugged. Only he hadn't been. He'd just been taken. Lynch knew an honorable man would accept being taken and pay the man; he wondered what Harold would do.

"Now notice, sir," Fast Eddie continued, "I could be out here robbing people. I could be out here selling crack. You see a switchblade in my hand? Did I pull a gun on you?"

"No," Harold answered, still unable to believe this was happening . . . *and in front of other people.*

"Five for the line, and five for the shine," Fast Eddie said, holding his hand out palm up.

Harold reached into his back pocket and extracted his wallet.

"Harold, you're not giving him *money!*" the wife exclaimed.

"Well, honey, I—" Harold held out a ten. Fast Eddie had it in his fingers like a lizard snapping a fly off a leaf.

"Thank you, sir." Fast Eddie smiled broadly, a huge row of clean pearl-white teeth spreading across his thick jaw. "Have a nice evening."

"Harold, you—" It was the wife's turn to sputter as she turned toward Fast Eddie. "Give that back, you. . . ."

"You what, ma'am?" Fast Eddie asked coldly, yet politely.

Harold reached out and took his wife's arm, still dazed. "Honey, let's just go."

"But he—"

"Let's just go, honey," Harold said.

Fast Eddie turned and started down the walk away from the couple, who stood there for a moment arguing before turning to head back to their hotel as quickly as possible.

Lynch put his head down just a little as Fast Eddie walked by the bench.

"Five for the line, five for the shine, buddy," he said as Fast Eddie walked by. Fast Eddie stopped.

"You gots a problem, mister?" he asked, all the slick gone from his voice now.

"Yeah, why don't you get a freaking job, work for a living?"

There was a moment of long, dreadful silence. Lynch sensed that people on either side of them had stopped everything they were doing, preparing to run from whatever fulminate was about to be ignited. Lynch kept his head down, staring only at the flapping neon green tongues of Fast Eddie's Air Jordans.

"What you want me to do, mister?" Eddie said, his voice low, threatening, deep. Lynch wondered if he'd gone too far, but then Eddie's voice went high, sing-song again, the slick back in. "Go back to work in that damn mailroom?"

The two broke out laughing hysterically. Lynch threw his hand out; Fast Eddie slapped him a high five.

"You knew it was me all along!" Lynch panted.

"Sheeyit, I'z watching you the whole time," Fast Eddie chirped. "I put on a extra good show for you."

"Park it here, Eddie, and tell me how the hell you're doing."

Eddie sat, threw his legs out on the sidewalk and cradled his hands behind his head. "Aw, man, I'm fine. Ever since I got outta that damn mailroom. I ain't never working in no bank again as long as I live. Give me the fresh air and the pigeons."

"Yeah, I saw you with the pigeons just now. You know, Eddie, you just messed that man's karma up bad. His wife's going to be mad at him the rest of the night. You might've screwed up their whole vacation."

"I did that man a service, Jack. This is a tough town, and the gapers that come down here expecting genteel living in the deep south don't know what they getting into. I did that man a favor. The rest of the time he's down here, he'll be looking over his shoulder. And that's the way it should be."

"Besides," he continued. "Think of it as Zen destiny. It was that man's fate in life to be reeled in by the one and only Rapid Edward."

"Yeah, maybe," Lynch said. "All I know is it ain't likely

poor Harold's going to be celebrating his first night in New Orleans by getting any of the good thing."

Lynch crossed one leg over the other and looked up river to where a brightly lit freighter was just rounding the bend. The steamboat *Natchez* had just pulled away from its dock, the nighttime party-boaters already on their way to laissezing the bon temps rouleeing. The steamboat let loose with a blast of its horn that snuffed out all other sounds. A moment later, the freighter responded.

"So how you doing, my man?" Eddie asked. "What you been up to? Ain't seen you down this way in a while."

"Been out a town for awhile. Couple, three months. Out in California. Got back to town this afternoon only to find out my apartment's been ripped off and my landlord's throwing me out." Lynch counted off the disasters on his fingers like he had a fistful of them. "I got to find a place to live quick."

"Ripped off? Man, what drag. This city ain't safe no more. You want to come crash with me, my man?"

"Thanks, Eddie, but the sooner I land someplace, the better off I'll be. So how's life treating you?"

Eddie smiled, his huge white teeth shimmering in the moonlight. "Super. I finally found me a good, honest clean hustle. No heavy lifting. Hundred, maybe a hundred-and-a-half on good days."

"You doing okay, huh?"

Eddie turned on the bench, pointed down behind them over the wall to a parking lot. Lynch turned to follow his gesture.

"See that Dodge pickup down there, the green one?"

"Yeah," Lynch answered. "Good-looking truck."

"Paid cash for it," Eddie said.

Lynch leaned back on the seat, stared out at the *Natchez* as it pressed downstream past the bridge. "How'd you like to make an honest buck? Say, fifty bucks for a couple hours work?"

Eddie smiled. "What you got in mind?"

"Nothing that exciting," Lynch answered. "I could use a hand moving my stuff into a new place. Not that I've got that much stuff left, and not that I've got a new place yet, you understand."

"You mean lifting furniture?" Eddie asked, gasping. "Physical labor?"

"C'mon Ed, it'll be one pickup full. That's all. The rest I'll carry a bit at a time in the Fiat."

Eddie stood up, stretched, yawned. "About quitting time for me. Tell you what, I'm working the Moonwalk starting about eleven every morning. Saturday's the busiest day of the week for the geek harvest. If you have to do it on the weekend, though, you come on down. I'll knock off a couple hours, come move your shit. Long as we don't scratch the truck."

Lynch smiled. "Thanks, Eddie. I'll catch up to you."

"One thing, my man. I'll need the fifty in advance. My usual retainer fee."

"In advance? C'mon, Eddie, get real."

"You don't trust me, bro', find yourself another stooge."

Lynch hesitated, frowned, took out his wallet. He only had thirty-two dollars on him. He pulled out two tens, two fives.

"I only got thirty on me. The rest when we do it. If you don't mind, I'll keep a couple bucks. Just for emergencies."

Eddie laughed, snatched the bills in a flash of brown. "You white guys are funny, man. What kind of emergency's two bucks gonna cover?"

Lynch stood up. "About the only kind I could afford. . . ."

■ CHAPTER 4 ■

Martin Brown was in a sleep so deep the ringing of the telephone seemed like another element of his dream. Martin was still young; his dreams were mostly erotic. Some part of him separated itself from the dream, stood back, and tried to figure out how a ringing telephone fit into the movie showing on the backs of his eyelids.

The phone rang again. Martin was passionately making love to a young blonde not unlike his wife, and she was screaming how good he was, how he was the only man that had ever made her feel this way.

Then the damn telephone rang again.

Martin came up out of his dream like a diver coming to the surface. He fumbled with the phone and knocked it off the nightstand. He swore and tried to untangle himself from the covers. He was sweating, erect, confused, irritated.

"Yeah," he said nastily, finally getting the handset somewhere close to his ear.

"Brown?" a voice answered.

"Yeah."

"Harold Gupton here," the voice said, "from the bank."

Gupton identified himself unnecessarily. Martin knew who he was without introduction, even if Gupton never gave him the same courtesy.

"Yes, Mr. Gupton," Martin said, rubbing the sleep from his eyes.

"We need you down here," Gupton's cold voice instructed. "Right away."

Martin turned his head painfully and stared at the clock. It wasn't even eight in the morning yet.

"I worked overtime last night. I just got to sleep three hours ago," Martin complained.

"We've got a problem," Gupton stated, flatly, professionally. "We need you down here right now."

"Shit," Martin said out loud as he hung up the phone. "Goddamnit."

He reached for his khaki pants, then put on the same wrinkled shirt he'd worn the night before. He walked painfully into the bathroom, stiff and fuzzy-mouthed, and looked into the mirror. His eyes were bloodshot, his dirty hair matted down on his head, his teeth scummy.

He scrubbed his face as best he could, brushed his teeth, combed his hair, and threw on a sweater to cover the wrinkles on his shirt. He left the small apartment and walked out into a weekday morning, which was something he hadn't seen in months. Patí had the car at work, so Martin grumbled silently to himself as he walked up Lowerline Street to St. Charles. Just as he got to the wide avenue, with its grassy median—referred to locally as the "neutral ground"—separating the two lanes of opposing traffic, the olive drab streetcar pulled away.

Martin started to jump into the traffic and go for it, but a carload of teenagers cutting school sped past, horn blaring, barely missing him. Martin swore out loud as the teen-aged boys turned and laughed. His complaints were met by a chorus of raised middle fingers.

He crossed, finally, and walked over to the concrete slab that was the streetcar stop to await another car.

Forty-five minutes later, Martin Brown stomped off the streetcar a block down Carondelet from the bank and glared like a madman at passersby as he battered the concrete. The streetcar had shaken and tossed him from side to side the whole way downtown. He'd waited twenty minutes for another car to come along; then it had taken twenty-five more minutes to cover a distance Martin could have driven in less than ten.

Exasperated, Martin stomped into the crowded lobby of the bank. He made his way through the crowds to the row of polished brass elevators at the rear. He went down, two floors below street level, to the sanitized, dehumidified air of the computer room and the data-processing division.

No one spoke to him as he walked past the modular cubicles where the programmers and analysts sat hunched over glowing amber video screens day-in and day-out like urban, technologized moles.

Gupton's secretary sat at her desk to the left of the closed door to Gupton's office. The sign outside read: HAROLD GUPTON, VICE-PRESIDENT, DATA PROCESSING.

The secretary picked up the phone, punched the intercom button, and spoke into the handset. She was silent for a moment, then placed the phone back in its cradle.

"Have a seat," she instructed. "Mr. Gupton will be with you directly."

"What's going on?" he asked, trying to hide his irritation and a swelling uneasiness that made him feel sick at his stomach. The office had never called him in like this. He wished he'd had time for a cup of coffee.

"Just have a seat," the secretary repeated.

"*Bitch,*" Martin whispered under his breath.

He fidgeted in the chair, unable to sit still. One of the younger programmers walked by him, over to the secretary's desk, and laid a handwritten yellow page on her desk.

"I need this typed up before the two o'clock meeting," he said, more a request than anything else. "Can you get to it?"

"Sure," the secretary said, without looking up.

The programmer walked by Martin and stopped.

"What's going on?" Martin asked, very low.

"You don't know?" the programmer asked, raising an eyebrow.

"No, what the hell is with all you people today?" Martin said, a little louder, a little more tense.

The programmer put his lips together to mimic a whistle

■ 31

and rolled his eyes back. He walked off, leaving Martin with an even bigger ball of fur in the pit of his stomach.

The door to Gupton's office opened. Buford Adkins, the Senior Analyst, stuck his head out the door. Adkins was okay, Martin thought, a bit dull but an all right fellow.

"Martin," he said, "c'mon in here." Martin got up and walked slowly into Gupton's office.

What is this, a firing squad?

Gupton, his face deeply lined from too many years working on his tan and too many packs of Marlboros, sat behind his massive oak executive's desk. He radiated power, ruthless power, to the people whom he perceived as being under him. But his eyes were dull and lifeless, like an old dog's. In fact, when Gupton relaxed in his chair, and his head sank down into his shoulders, the skin on his face wrinkled up into loose folds, giving him a marked resemblance to a Shar Pei.

Adkins sat down on a couch against the far wall of the office. Next to him sat Kenneth Cook, the chief programmer. Cook was a bastard, Martin thought, a petty little shit who stole credit and glory from his staff when they did well but refused to take the blame when anything got screwed up. Martin and the two other lead shift operators reported directly to him.

"Sit down," Gupton said, staring at a spot on the wall two feet over Buford Adkins' head. One of Gupton's more acute eccentricities was his inability to look anyone directly in the eye.

Martin took a seat. He tried, nervously, to seem jovial.

"So what's happening, guys?" he asked brightly. The stone looks he received in return sent something cold through his veins.

There was a moment of awful, dead silence. Finally, Gupton removed his stare from the wall and planted it on a pile of computer printout on his desk. He picked up the stack and moved it to the front of his desk, inches from Martin.

"Can you explain this?" he asked.

Martin picked up the inch-thick report. His heartbeat accelerated; his breath came in short, quick gulps. He felt himself in the grip of an impending full-blown anxiety attack.

The paper felt heavy in his lap. He numbly picked the first quarter-inch or so of paper up and flipped through it.

"It's a standard second shift report," Martin said softly.

"Not quite standard," Cook interrupted, in an accusatory tone.

Martin's unease melded smoothly with his confusion. "What's the matter with it?"

"Go to page one-twenty-seven," Cook instructed.

Martin flipped to the appropriate page. It was the beginning of a section entitled "Summary of Branch Operations: Daily Transactions."

"Okay," Martin said.

"What normally precedes that section?" Cook asked.

Martin thought for a second. "Uh . . ." he hesitated, "should be the CD summary."

"Right," Cook said, accusing him. "Do you see it?"

Martin flipped through the pages preceding 127.

"Okay," he said, "it's not here. I forgot to punch it up. What's the big deal?"

Gupton sighed, disgusted, and settled back in his chair, his gaze fixed on a spot of dirt on the ceiling.

"The big deal is *not* that you forgot to run a report," Cook said, his voice rising. "You've screwed up like that before. If that was all, I'd have just had a memo for you when you came in tonight."

"So what's wrong," Martin asked. His relief from what he thought was a minor problem evaporated quickly.

"The problem is, Martin," Buford Adkins said, his tone calmer and softer than Cook's, "is that when we were notified that the report wasn't run, we put in a ticket to have the first shift run it over."

"Okay," Martin said, after a moment. He was still anxious, confused.

"Don't you know what happened?" Cook asked. "You should."

"What are you talking about?" Martin demanded.

"Stop playing games with us, Martin," Cook said.

"Dammit," Martin said. "The only games being played around here are the ones you're playing with me."

"Martin," Adkins said, again calmer, "when we went to run the report, we couldn't."

"What do you mean, you couldn't?" Martin asked.

"When the operator tried to run the job, he couldn't," Adkins said. "So he came in and got Ken. When Ken tried to raise the program to see why it was hosed up, it wasn't there. It was gone."

"Gone?" Martin asked, almost in a daze at what he was being told, with the as-yet-unspoken accusation hanging frozen in midair.

"The program was gone," Adkins continued. "Ken came and got me. We ran a directory on the database. That portion of it, with all the CD Resident Programs and information, had been erased. Wiped clean. The Certificate of Deposit records for the entire bank are gone."

"We shut down the system to do a diskpak refresh," Cook said. "To try and recover the data. It was gone."

"Wiped clean?" Martin repeated. "That's impossible. What about the backups?"

"That portion of the database is maintained on Diskpak three and backed up on Diskpak seven. We chained the inquiry to backup and it came up clean, too," Cook said.

"What about the tape?"

"The last tape backup was done Friday night. You know that. That means everything since then, three days worth of bank transactions, is lost forever," Cook said. "It can be recreated from the paper trail, but that'll take a helluva lot of work."

"And time," Gupton interjected. "And money."

"Can you tell us what happened?" Adkins asked gently.

"Yeah, Brown, why'd you do it?" Cook demanded.

"I didn't do anything," Martin protested. "I don't know what you guys are talking about."

"C'mon," Cook said, "it happened on your shift. What do you think happened? One of your operators do it?"

The tone of his voice made Martin's ears burn, and he was very close to telling Cook exactly what part of his anatomy the overbearing S.O.B. could kiss.

"I didn't do a damn thing to the database," Martin said angrily. "Why would I do that? It's stupid!"

Sweat ran down Martin's sides, from his armpits to his waist beneath the sweater.

"We've got to bring up all those programs from archival storage and reload them out to the disk," Cook spat. "My programmers will be here all night. Some of those programs will have to have fixes rewritten."

"Well, hey, listen," Martin said in his usual smartassed tone, "if you don't archive your fixes, that's not my problem."

"Well, I'll tell you what is your problem!" Cook said, practically yelling at him in the close confines of the office. "We can't prove you did anything. But in all my years in this business, I've never seen a computer instruct itself to erase a database. Even if there'd been a hard disk malfunction, the data would have still been there."

"The data itself was physically gone," Adkins interrupted, trying to soothe the tension. "Not just an erased directory. Martin, that takes somebody who knows what they're doing. Somebody that can program in assembler, if not machine language. An operator wouldn't know how."

"But—" Martin said.

"Just shut up!" Cook barked. "I can't prove you did this, but you can bet that I'm going to be watching you from now on out. You won't be able to go to the bathroom without one of us tagging along with you."

"That's not fair, dammit," he protested. "I didn't do this."

"Are you sure you didn't make a mistake, Brown?" Gupton asked, staring at a spot in the middle of Martin's forehead.

"No sir," Martin said. "There's no way. Maybe it was one of the programmers—"

"My programmers don't sabotage their own work," Cook sputtered.

"Calm down, Ken," Adkins said. "That's not going to get us anywhere."

"For now," Gupton said, "we're going to let this slide. We

can recover the work a little at a time and be caught up in about a week. Maybe this was just one of those gremlin foul-ups that everybody in this business encounters at one time or another. I'll have the data entry people go on mandatory overtime until we're caught up. Until then, gentlemen, I hope we clean out our nest before the people upstairs find out what kind of operation's going on down here."

Martin massaged his temples as a ferocious, maddening headache began to overtake him. He knew he'd have to stay at the office to begin work on the data recovery. He also knew that the next couple of weeks were going to be hell.

Then Martin remembered Monday night, when the computer had suddenly and mysteriously locked up for almost a half-minute. He hadn't thought anything else of it after it started working again. But maybe. . . .

"Anything else, gentlemen?" Gupton asked, his eyes focused on a spot on the ceiling.

"Wait, last Mon—" Martin started.

"No more excuses," Cook interrupted. "Just get back to work, Brown."

Martin's ears burned. To hell with the upper management types, he thought. If there was something weird going on, it was their worry. That's why they got the big bucks. Right now, he had a long day to get through.

■ *CHAPTER 5* ■

Carlton Smith, chief counsel for the First Interstate Bank of Louisiana, was thumbing through a stack of papers on his desk when his secretary buzzed him. Grateful for the interruption, he picked up the phone.

"Yes, Gloria."

"Mr. Smith, Mr. Gupton from Data Processing is on line one."

Carlton thought for a moment. Gupton . . . had they ever met?

"Did he say what he wanted?"

"No sir, but he did say it was very important."

"All right, I'll take the call." Carlton reached over and punched the blinking light.

"Carlton Smith, here. What can I do for you, Mr. Gupton?"

The voice that answered was gruff, but nervous, on edge.

"We haven't met, Carlton. I'm in charge of the computer division. We have a problem I think you should know about. I spoke with the division vice-president, my immediate superior, just now. He suggested I call you."

"Okay," Carlton said cautiously. "I gather this is some kind of legal problem, then."

"Not exactly."

Well, are you going to tell me what it is or do I have to keep guessing? Carlton remained silent.

"It's kind of sensitive. Hard to explain. Would you mind coming down here?"

"To the computer room?"

"Yes."

Carlton stared at the briefs on his desk. At least two hours of review were needed, and the papers had to be filed today. "I'm kind of busy right now. Can't you tell me what the problem is over the phone?"

There was a long silence, then the voice came back, this time more tired than anything else. "Someone's planted a bomb down here."

Carlton stiffened, sat up quickly. "A bomb! My god, man, why call me? Evacuate the building and get the police."

"It's not that kind of bomb."

Carlton scowled. "What does that mean?"

"It's in the software. I've never seen anything like it. My chief programmer says it appears to be real. The ransom note came in this morning's mail. Whoever planted the bomb wants five million dollars to tell us how to defuse it."

Carlton thought for a second. His heart rate rose slightly; he felt his palms moisten.

"I figured I'd better kick this one upstairs," Gupton said.

"I'll be right down."

Carlton had never descended that deeply into the bowels of the bank building before. The air was heavier down there, stale, cold, dense. He pushed through two heavy glass doors into a huge expanse of white room, sterile and frigid and filled with people hunched over computer terminals. His heels clicked on the uncarpeted floor as he made his way to the far end of the room, where a few closed doors led to executive offices.

A dyed-blonde secretary sat in front of the farthest closed door. "May I help you?"

"Harold Gupton, please. I'm Carlton Smith."

Painted-on eyebrows lifted. She stood, stepped over to the door, and held it open for him.

"Mr. Gupton's been waiting for you."

Carlton stepped in quickly. The secretary closed the door, leaving the two men alone.

"What's this about a bomb?" Carlton asked.

"Have a seat, Carlton," Gupton said, raising his head from the desk. He stared at something beyond Carlton's left shoulder, behind him. Carlton swung his head around to see what it was, confused, then took a seat. Gupton's neck seemed immobile, as if his head was anchored to a camera mount that could only pivot on one axis. He unfolded a sheet of paper, shook it loose, and handed it across the desk, then fixed his eyes on the brass doorknob. Carlton fought the urge to turn around again. Instead, he took the letter and held it spread open in his hands.

His eyes scanned the neatly typed words. The paper was cheap copy paper, available anywhere. The letters were printed on a dot matrix printer. Carlton wondered if printers worked like typewriters, with each machine having a unique, and traceable, type.

THE SOFTWARE BOMB HAS BEEN PLANTED IN YOUR MAINFRAME. YOU HAVE FORTY-EIGHT HOURS FROM 4 P.M. TODAY, FRIDAY. AFTER THAT, THE SOFTWARE BOMB WILL DETONATE ON ITS OWN AT A RANDOM TIME PICKED BY THE BOMB ITSELF. I CANNOT STOP IT. NEITHER CAN YOU. ANY ATTEMPT TO REMOVE THE BOMB WILL CAUSE IT TO GO OFF. ANY ATTEMPT TO FORMAT YOUR DISKS OR REMOVE DATA WILL CAUSE IT TO GO OFF. ANY ATTEMPT TO ARCHIVE YOUR DATA AFTER 12 P.M. FRIDAY WILL DETONATE THE BOMB. UNLESS YOU ACCEDE TO MY DEMANDS, THE ENTIRE COMPUTER SYSTEM OF THE FIRST INTERSTATE BANK OF LOUISIANA WILL CEASE TO EXIST.

IF YOU DON'T BELIEVE ME, EXAMINE THE CONTENTS OF YOUR NUMBER ONE DATA DISKPAK FROM THE LOCATIONS 43FF25B TO—

"What do all these numbers mean?" Carlton asked.

"They're locations on the disks, in hexadecimal," Gupton answered, staring at the wall. Carlton found Gupton's eye movements an irritating distraction. "They correspond to a physical area on the hard disk that was wiped clean some-time in the last couple of days. We lost some data regarding our Certificate of Deposit records. We thought our night shift lead operator had done it. He's a bad apple. But we questioned him and couldn't trace it to him. Now it seems that he's innocent." Gupton seemed almost disappointed.

Carlton returned to the note, finishing the rest of the typed page quickly.

"Five million dollars," Carlton sighed. "Who knows about this letter?"

Gupton thought for a second. "My secretary and I. The division vice-president, Phil DeWitt, upstairs. That's all."

"That's all you know of."

Gupton laid his head back on the chair, his eyes to the ceiling. "Okay. All I know of."

"What does DeWitt say?"

"He's panicked. Says we have to pay up. Says above all else, no publicity. The bank can't take it."

Carlton thought for a moment. "He's probably right. Do you know for sure that this person can do what this note says?"

"No, not really. I think we can find out. I haven't told my lead programmer about it, yet."

"Will you have to?"

"Of course," Gupton said. "For one thing, we start archiving in—" He looked at his watch. "Six hours. I'll have to order the archive stopped. I'll have to explain why."

"Do your programmers have to know?"

"At least a couple of them. I also want permission to bring in an outside computer security firm. We'll need to beef up our security once we get past this."

"And as soon as they know," Carlton said, "somebody else will, too. Somebody's bound to tell a wife, a girlfriend. A buddy in the gym. Something. There's the rumor mill, too. As soon as word gets out that something strange is going on down here, there'll be no end to the speculation."

"Right, and in the meantime, we have to be careful not to do anything that will set the bomb off."

Carlton looked at Gupton, a question on his face. "Can this person really do this? I mean, do we have to have the computers? What will happen if this guy sets his bomb off?"

Gupton rested his focus on the tip of Carlton's nose, as close as he would allow himself to meeting anyone's eyes. He folded his hands in front of him, shrugged his shoulders.

"What's this bank's capitalization, Carlton? One-point-six, maybe seven, billion? This guy sets his bomb off, you may as well take all that cash up in an airplane and drop it over the city. Because without computers, we can't track a dime of it."

"My god," Carlton whispered. "And if word of this gets out to the public. . . . The panic. We'll be overrun."

"The best thing that could happen would be to shut us back down," Gupton said. "That's a best-case scenario."

"If this bank closes its doors twice in a year-and-a-half, the government will probably revoke our charter."

"You know what the worst thing is?" Gupton asked.

"What?" Carlton asked, wondering what could be worse than what had already been laid out for him.

"It's probably some greasy little fourteen-year-old genius working a five-hundred dollar IBM clone out of his parents' den."

"We need a meeting," Carlton said. "Everybody involved. Strategy session. This afternoon. Set it up for one o'clock."

"We need to decide what we're going to do with the media," Gupton offered.

"There's not going to be any media," Carlton said. "That's all there is to it."

"But what if there is? These things have a way of breaking loose on us," Gupton insisted.

"If we can't defuse the bomb," Carlton said, "we've got to cover our asses. We need somebody discreet, somebody who can go behind the scenes. I don't even want the regular public relations people in on this. They're all idiots, anyway."

Carlton looked at Gupton, subconsciously trying to catch his eyes if even for a moment. No luck.

Carlton stood up. "I know somebody who may be able to help us. If he's available. May I use your phone?"

Gupton slid it across the desk. Carlton punched four buttons on the console.

"Gloria? Carlton. Get me Jack Lynch's phone number."

Carlton reached into his pocket and pulled out his fountain pen. As his secretary dictated, Carlton scribbled down the number. "Thanks, Gloria. Oh, wait. Better get me his home phone as well. He's not always in his office."

He scrawled the numbers down, then pressed the switchhook to end his call. He released the hook a second later, then dialed "9" to get an outside line. Staring at the pad, Carlton shakily punched in seven more numbers.

The line's silence was broken only by the staccato burp of electronic ringing. The line rang three times, then a computerized voice came on the line.

"I'm sorry, the number you have dialed has been disconnected or is no longer in service. . . ."

Carlton slowly placed the phone back in its cradle. "Oh, hell," he muttered.

▪ *CHAPTER 6* ▪

The three days he'd been back in the city had been hell. He'd looked at nine apartments: six he wouldn't house his dog in; three he couldn't come close to affording. The weekend started at midnight, and Pelias wanted his space back.

Lynch gathered the penciled classifieds and a handful of change and headed out the door for another day of apartment hunting. Mr. Pelias was in the front yard, pulling weeds from a flowerbed.

"Gus, this time I'm going to find one."

"Good luck, Mr. Lynch," Pelias said without looking up.

Lynch walked two blocks down to a pay phone on Esplanade. He fumbled with his change, dropped a quarter in the slot, hoped the phone still worked.

"Hello," a male voice answered.

"Hi, I'm calling about the apartment in the classifieds."

"The two-bedroom's already gone. The one-bedroom's still left."

"Great," Lynch said. "That's the one I'm interested in. Can I come by, take a look at it?"

"I'll be here 'til noon," the voice answered. "Then I got to run out for awhile. Can you make it?"

Lynch read off the number from the ad. "Which block of Esplanade is that?"

"Almost to City Park. Corner of Esplanade and Mystery. Diagonally across the street from the St. Louis Cemetery."

"I can be there in fifteen minutes."

Lynch hung up the phone and trotted the two blocks back. Pelias was still in the front yard digging. Lynch went past him without speaking, to the row of garages facing the side street. He fumbled with the lock, then slid the heavy wooden door aside.

Ten minutes later, he pulled to a stop in front of a two-story Victorian house on Esplanade. The sidewalk by the gate in front had been pushed up into a crest of split concrete perhaps a foot high by the roots of a convoluted, towering oak just to the right. A half-flight of steps led up to a front door. A gallery accented by ornate carved gingerbread ran the entire width of the house on the second story. Lynch stepped out of the car without opening the door and gazed at the old house. In a moment, he knew he wanted to live there.

A wave of anxiety washed over him. *What if they won't let me have the place?* He thought of Pelias's unbending stance toward his living situation.

He ran his fingers through his windblown hair to straighten it, then tried to calm the butterflies in his gut. He needed a haircut, but at least he'd shaved that morning. He tucked his shirttail in neatly and walked calmly along the brick walk up to the steps, then took them two at a time up to the front door. He knocked twice on the glass and saw through the sheer curtain a body walking down a long hall toward him.

A thin man, about Lynch's height but younger, opened the door. He had thinning blond hair, pale blue eyes, and his lips were open just enough to reveal a mouthful of graying teeth.

"I'm Jack Lynch. I called about the apartment. Hope I'm not too late."

"No," the man said in a low voice. He seemed, Lynch thought, almost shy. He held the door open. "Come in."

Lynch stepped through the door frame onto a highly polished wooden hallway that led toward the back of the house. The ceilings were high, at least eleven feet, and the uneven plaster walls were painted a light, pastel rose. Lynch guessed the house was turn-of-the-century at least, perhaps older.

"This is a beautiful old house," Lynch said. "Looks like it's been well taken care of."

The blond man turned and led the way down the hallway. "1896," he said. "It was single family until the twenties, then broken up into four apartments. My wife and I bought the place three years ago. We live down here."

He pointed to the right as they walked past an ornate painted door with frosted-glass panels. "The other three apartments we rent out for now."

"For now?" Lynch asked.

"One of these days," the man continued, "my wife and I are going to convert the place back to single family. That's a couple years away, though. We can't offer you more than a year's lease. As we get closer to the renovation, you'll have to go on month-to-month."

"But you are offering a year's lease?"

"Yeah. By the way," the man said, stopping at the top of the stairs, "I'm Henry Hill."

The two men shook hands, then Henry Hill opened the apartment door. Lynch stepped into a large sitting room with a mantel over a bricked-up fireplace, polished wooden floors, floor-to-ceiling windows looking out over Mystery Street.

He gulped. The place was too good to be true.

"Kitchen and bath's down there off to the right. Bedroom's to the left and looks out over Esplanade. Only bad thing is, you've got to walk through the living room to get to the bathroom. There's no bathroom off the bedroom."

Lynch followed into the bedroom. A small closet off to the right was, as in many old homes, the only storage space. No matter.

"You didn't put the rent in the ad," Lynch said. "And I forgot to ask while we were on the phone."

"Four-ninety-five a month, but that includes water and gas. You pay electricity and phone."

Lynch's heart dropped; the rent was a full hundred a month more than he was paying with Gus. He only had about twelve hundred left in his checking account, with no job, and no prospects of new clients any time soon. He was also two months behind on his office rent, a matter that would have to be settled first thing Monday morning.

What the hell, he thought.

"I'll take it. Can I write you a check?"

"Whoa, hold on. I need to know a little about you."

"I'm single, no pets. I smoke, but if it bugs you, I'll only do it on the gallery. I haven't had a party at my house in years and for now, I'm not even dating anybody."

"Where do you work?"

"I'm self-employed, have my own company. P.R. agency. Down on Carondelet."

"Well," Henry Hill hesitated.

"Listen, Henry. I'm a good tenant. I can give you a reference. I've been ten years in my last apartment. I'll be a good tenant, and I *really* love this place."

"I usually run this stuff by my wife first."

"I tell you what," Lynch offered. "I'll pay the first and last month's rent in advance. You don't cut me a lease until your wife approves. She doesn't like me, then I leave after my rent runs out. What do you say?"

Five minutes later, a grinning Jack Lynch went in search of Fast Eddie and his pickup truck.

The next morning, Saturday, Lynch pulled to a stop at the intersection of Esplanade and Mystery. He looked across the street in disgust; the place where he needed to be in front of his new apartment was taken up by a United American Van Lines moving truck. The tractor-trailer rig was parked as close to the curb as it could get, but the oncoming traffic on Esplanade practically had to climb onto the median to get around it.

"Dammit," Lynch muttered, then turned in his seat and looked behind him.

A sweating Fast Eddie, with a truckload of furniture barely tied down in the bed of his pickup, shrugged. "What you want to do?" he yelled out the window.

Behind the Dodge, a tight-lipped man in a gray sedan laid on his horn. Eddie's brow wrinkled.

"I don't know," Lynch yelled back to him.

The man in the sedan hit his horn again. Eddie's eyes blazed and the driver's door of the pickup flew open.

"Yo!" Lynch yelled. Fast Eddie took two steps toward the sedan behind him, fists coming up. "Don't start no shit now, Eddie! Just pull in here."

Jack pressed the accelerator and eased out the clutch. The heavily-loaded Fiat strained, belched a puff of blue-black smoke, then shot left across traffic onto Mystery Street. He pulled far enough down to leave room for Eddie's pickup, then braked and looked behind him. Thankfully, Eddie was back in his truck now, instead of thrashing the man with the itchy horn finger.

"What are we going to do?" Eddie asked, as the two stood on the sidewalk on the wrong side of the house.

Jack turned around and faced the truckload of furniture. "I'm getting too old for this shit, Eddie."

Eddie laughed. "I was too old for this shit when I was ten."

"Hell of a place to park a moving truck."

"Yeah," Eddie offered. "Let's go kick some booty and get 'em to move it."

"I don't think that would be the best way to impress my new landlord. Remember, I don't have a lease yet."

"Hey, Jack, how come you're moving into a place without a lease?"

Lynch turned. "Wait'll you see the place, Eddie. I got a good feeling about it."

He put both hands in the small of his back and arched backward. "Well, buddy, we may as well get to it. And since it's taken so much longer than we thought it would, you just tell me what else you need for your time."

"Don't worry," Eddie said, unlashing the rope that was barely holding the couch upside down on top of the truck's load. "You'll get my bill."

Lynch realized, as he backed up the steps holding one end of the couch, that his back was just as old as the rest of him. Pains shot across his belt line in quivering shocks. He only hoped he wouldn't embarrass himself by dropping the couch on Eddie.

The two sweating amateurs made it slowly up to the front door, then carefully down the hall to the winding staircase leading to the second floor. Halfway up the stairs, Lynch was seriously puffing, sweating, and wondering how they were ever going to get the rest of his stuff in without him having a heart attack.

"You okay, man," Eddie asked as the couch approached the landing on the second floor.

"Yeah," Lynch panted, "I'll make it."

Jack stepped backward into the hallway, careful not to bang into either side of the clean plaster walls.

"Hey, man, look out," Eddie warned. Jack started to turn, but it was too late. The backs of his legs hit a packing case about three feet on each side and he went over backwards. He yelled as he dropped the end of the couch and it went scraping down his shins to the floor.

"Dammit," Lynch barked as he glared upward toward the ceiling. "Who the hell left that—"

Lynch's voice locked in his throat as he stared up at a burly, sweating, bearded redneck in overalls, a United American Van Lines cap pulled low over his forehead.

"You got a problem, man?" a gruff voice demanded.

"Uh, oh," Eddie muttered.

"Yeah," Jack said, scrambling to his feet. Then he saw that the hall was full of furniture and packing cases. "How am I supposed to move into my apartment when you guys've got the hall full of this crap?"

"I'd watch my mouth if I was you," the mover warned.

"Well, you're not me and get this stuff moved out of the way."

A hand shot out and grabbed Lynch's collar. . . .

A voice behind the hand, high and strained, shouted: "Hey, what's going on out here?"

The burly mover eased his grip on Jack's shirt. Jack took a step back, clear of the man's grasp, and shifted sideways to look around him. A woman stood there, early thirties, thin, tight jeans, blue work shirt. Her hair was pulled back in a dusty scarf.

Lynch looked at her for a second. "I'm moving in today, and I can't get my stuff in because the hallway's jammed up."

"I'm sorry," the woman said, taking a step toward him, wiping her hands on a dirty rag. Jack could tell by the accent she wasn't from New Orleans, but he couldn't place it. "But I'm moving in, too."

"Oh," Jack said sheepishly. "Sorry about barking at your movers here. My friend and I—we're kind of strung-out already."

"Moving's terrible, isn't it?" the woman offered, holding out her hand. Jack stepped beside the mover and took her hand. It was small in his, warm, delicate. Behind her, a black man with a body builder's torso stepped out into the hallway and stood there with a T-shirt stretching across his chest.

"Yeah, it's pretty awful."

"I'm P.J. Campbell," she said. "Looks like we'll be living across the hall from each other."

"Jack Lynch. Glad to meet you."

"Well, Jack Lynch, how are we going to work this traffic problem out?"

"How's this," he ventured, "Eddie and I'll take a break— by the way, this is Eddie—"

"Hi, Eddie."

"Hey, P.J., what's happening?"

"And we'll wait for these guys to get the hall cleared out. Then we'll just work on our timing and try not to get in each other's way."

P.J. Campbell smiled brightly. "Great, that'll work. Okay fellows," she instructed, "let's get moving."

The brooding redneck in the overalls turned to his mate and gestured toward a wardrobe box, disappointed that he wasn't going to get to finish smearing Lynch all over the walls. Lynch stepped gingerly around his own couch and caught up with Eddie on the stairs.

"What'd I tell you, Ed? This a great place or what?"

"Oh, yeah," Eddie answered, grinning. "There's just something about this place, and I can't think of what it might be. . . ."

* * *

By ten the next morning, it was as if he had always been there. Lynch awoke to a steady rain, the air as cool and thick as crushed velvet through the open door onto the gallery. He wallowed in bed for nearly an hour, his head buried in the thick pillows, a comforter fluffed up to his chin. Finally restless, he got out of bed, made a pot of coffee, and carried his cigarettes and a steaming cup out onto the gallery. Rain hung off the tree leaves like teardrop crystal.

A calm had come over him the last few days that was as unexpected as it was unfamiliar. The last few years had not been good. He was forty now, alone in the world, virtually penniless. But it was as if in his loneliness and his poverty, he could start over. Circumstance had wiped his slate clean. He had lost a secure and lucrative job; had survived the murder of his fiancée, Sally; had kept himself intact through both struggle and scandal. He had somehow managed to come through that which might have destroyed him. With the death of his mother, he was now free, or at least that's the way it felt for the time being. Starting tomorrow, he would begin the long climb back, and this time, he thought, he would get it right.

The painted gray wooden floor of the gallery tilted toward Esplanade Avenue, the result of generations of settling. The gallery ran the width of the front of the house, but a wooden partition had been erected in the middle, in effect to separate his part of the porch from the apartment next to his. Lynch's apartment was on the front corner of the house closest to downtown, and the wooden partition dividing his part of the porch blocked his view of the cemetery from where he was sitting. That was fine, he thought. He had seen enough of cemeteries in his life.

He heard a metallic scraping as the rain slowed to a sprinkle and the sun began to force its way through the clouds. He got up to get more coffee and leaned out over the rail facing Mystery, the small side street that ran diagonally off Esplanade. Henry Hill was down by the street, scraping a shovel along a storm drain to clear it of debris. Farther up Mystery, two teenage boys on rollerblades struggled to stay upright on the cracked and uneven street. Lynch smiled as he watched them. He knew he would never be that carefree or that adventurous again, but he could, he thought, salvage what was left.

He finished the coffee and made a plate of scrambled eggs, then shaved and showered. He felt like moving, like getting out, so he went downstairs with an extra towel, blotted the seat where the rain had leaked through the ragged top of the Fiat, and headed for the Central Business District.

He drove down Esplanade two blocks until he hit City Park, then wormed his way through the intersection onto North Carrollton. It was an easy, slow Sunday in New Orleans. People strolled back from late brunches in neighborhood cafes. With one hand, he reached up and unlatched the top and pushed it down behind him as he drove. The wind blew rain spray over him, chilling him, invigorating him.

He made an illegal left turn onto Tulane Avenue, ignoring the horn blasts from more righteous drivers, and drove past the Criminal Courts Building and, further down, past the ornate silver-and-green dome of the Dixie Beer brewery. He made a right on Loyola at the public library, down to Poydras Plaza, then left on Poydras to Carondelet. The traffic was thin, the driving pleasant in the cool morning air.

He pulled to a stop in front of his office building for the first time in three months. Lynch had a feeling he knew what was coming, and as he walked up the sidewalk to the front door of the building, he steeled himself.

His front door key to the building still fit. He opened the heavy glass and chrome door, then locked it behind him. The old elevator creaked and shook up to his darkened floor. He padded down the polished, silent hallway to his office door, slid the key into the door lock, and turned.

Nothing. As he feared, the lock had been changed.

He suspected that if he called the building manager directly, there might be hell to pay. It was not so much that Lynch intended to be a deadbeat; it just sort of turned out that way. He felt certain that he'd eventually make good on the rent debt, but it was going to take awhile, and some doing.

Lynch left the building not knowing if it was for the last time. He drove around the block, down St. Charles, passed a streetcar on Lee Circle, tires whining and slipping, and headed out toward the Garden District and the Uptown area of the city.

Maud Pelletier still had the plastic Virgin Mary shrine in her front yard, or what passed for a front yard in this part of town. It was more a small patch of dirt on either side of an aggregate walk that led from the front porch, down the tiny passageway between Maud's house and that of her neighbor, to Maud's garden in the back.

Lynch had been eager to see her ever since California. Maud had become one of his last trusted friends, perhaps the last. She was his safety net. They had known each other a decade now, ever since she started accepting his little gifts in return for access to the newspaper morgue she ran. One day, she'd been caught taking one of his gifts, and it had cost Maud her job. Jack felt responsible after that, and had tried, without much success, to help her since.

He looked up at the sky; the clouds seemed to be breaking up. He left the top down on the car and walked through the creaky iron gate, up the rotting wooden steps, the front door. He rapped gently a few times, then stood there. Through the curtain over the front window, he saw a light come on in the living room. A moment later, he heard the rattling click of a door being unlatched. Maud Pelletier opened the door and stood there staring through the screen at Jack as if he were a ghost come back to haunt her.

She was dressed from head to toe in black.

▪ *CHAPTER 7* ▪

Lynch could feel her warm tears soaking through his shirt. His arms were around her thin, bony shoulders, pulling her close into him, the smell of her graying hair flowery and heavy. Her gaunt body was wracked with sobs and she could barely get words out. Maud had held the door open for him as he stepped into the living room, but once inside, she all but collapsed in his arms.

"Maud, when did it happen?" he asked, after finally realizing what she was trying to tell him.

"Last Monday," she stammered. "They didn't even find him until Wednesday. After two days in the Gulf, we had to bury him quick."

"I'm so sorry," he said, rubbing her back and pulling her to him.

"They did a autopsy on him Thursday night. They said he wasn't drinking or nothing. He might've had a heart attack or something, but falling off a eighty-foot rig into the Gulf's what killed him."

Lynch closed his eyes, rested his head on top of hers. "Aw, honey, that's awful. . . ."

She sniffed and brought her head up off his chest, her face glimmering, her skin pulled sallowly across her strong cheekbones.

"I'm sorry," she said. "I swore I wouldn't do this in front of anybody else."

"Oh, Maud, c'mon—"

"No, I mean it. My sister was here 'til this morning. I had to put her on the bus back to Shreveport. She has to work tomorrow, and I just couldn't see making her miss work on my account."

Maud pulled away from him and walked through the living room into the dining room, then down the hall to the kitchen.

"So you were just going to tough it out alone, right?"

"That's what I've had to do all these years," she said over her shoulder. "It's not like Pelletier was ever around very much anyway. It's not even like we was all that happy together."

"Yeah, but he was your husband, Maud. And you guys were married, what?"

"Thirty-five years," she answered. She opened a kitchen cabinet door and pulled out a coffee mug. "I just made another pot. You want some?"

Lynch sat down at the small kitchen table. "Sure."

Maud poured two cups and brought them to the table. "I'm sorry about your mother, baby."

"You got my letters?"

"Yeah, I got them. I feel bad now. Here I am peeing and moaning and you've just lost your mama."

Lynch stared down at his cup. "I lost her a long time ago. Long before she ever got sick."

She reached across the table, took her hand in his. "We're both alone now, ain't we?"

Lynch sighed. "Yeah, I guess so. But for some reason or other, I don't feel so bad about it. Course, I've had a little longer to get used to it than you have. What're you going to do, Maud? Stay here, move?"

She thought for a moment. "I don't know, really. I can get Pelletier's social security, and the oil company'll pay me a widow's pension, I think. I don't know how much."

"Maybe you should sue the bastards."

"I'd like to," Maud said. "But Myrtle Bouche did that when her Henry got killed on a rig and the oil company tied it up so long she settled for next to nothing. Lawyer's got most of it."

"He have any insurance?"

"Ten thousand," she said, then chuckled. "He took the policy out twenty years ago. Cheap bastard always hated insurance companies. Said by the time he retired, the house'd be paid for and we wouldn't need much. If anything happened to him, it'd take care of me for the rest of my life, or so's he said. We never figured on things getting the way they are these days. And with him laid off so much these past few years, we sure couldn't afford to buy any more."

Lynch leaned back in the chair, his head against the wall. "We got to go back to work. You know that? And not just for the money."

"Yeah, you're right," Maud answered. "You knew they changed the locks on the office?"

"Yeah. I stopped there on my way over here. I'm not too surprised. Problem is, I can't pay the back rent."

"Maybe you don't have to," Maud said. "I got all the files out, the answering machine, the lamps."

Lynch brightened. "How the hell did you do that?"

"I knew what was going down. The building manager's secretary and I got to be pretty good friends, especially since our bosses were never around very much. She told me on a Friday that he'd ordered the locks changed the following Monday. I came in Saturday and cleaned everything out I could. I even got the two smallest chairs."

Lynch whistled. "You're amazing."

"I could'a told you that." Maud smiled. "The only thing left there's the two desks and chairs and that one large filing cabinet. The phone belonged to the building in the first place. You don't want the furniture back, you ain't ever got to talk to the guy again."

"You don't think they'll come after me."

"Shoot, in that building? You know how many of their tenants have skipped out in the past year? Mazie—that's the building manager's secretary—she told me nearly thirty of those offices got vacated in the middle of the night last year. One guy bankrupted on them. Owed six months rent, and he had a suite of offices that was costing three grand a month."

"So our lousy little four-hundred-a-month two-room office was no big deal."

"Ain't worth coming after you over it."

"Still," Lynch said, "I hate to skip out on the guy. I get back on my feet, I'll send him the money."

"You do that, you be one of the few that ever does. This economy done ruined people. They don't give a damn no more. They got articles in the paper now about people who look like they know they're going under, so they go out and charge anything they can. I guess they figure if they going down anyway. . . ."

"May as well go down in flames," Lynch said. "Voodoo economics in action."

"We had voodoo down here for centuries, but ain't never been nothing like this." Maud picked up her coffee cup, blew across the top of it, then put her lips to the edge and slurped.

"It *is* crazy. You knew I got thrown out of my apartment?"

Her eyes grew wide. "Get out of here."

"That's what the landlord said. The apartment got burglarized, and it must have pissed the old guy off. I guess he'd have been happier if I was there when the guys broke in."

"And maybe got yourself killed in the process."

Lynch shrugged. "Who knows what he was thinking? Anyway, I found a new apartment quick and moved in yesterday. There's a ton of stuff to do tomorrow. Get the utilities transferred into my name. Go pay my back phone bill so I can get the phone turned on in my new place. Kind of overwhelming."

"Where you going to be living?"

"Got a piece of paper? I'll write it down."

Maud stood up and walked over to the kitchen counter, then shuffled through a kitchen drawer for a pad. Lynch stared at her back, noticed she was walking kind of bent over, and looked as if she'd lost weight. Or maybe, he thought for the first time, Maud Pelletier was starting to show her age.

"You're walking kind of funny, Maud. You okay?"

She turned, forced herself to stand up straight. "Back's

been kind of hurting me lately. I haven't been sleeping too well since Pelletier got killed either. Funny, I always slept better when he was gone than when he was here. Now that he's not coming back at all—"

"You can't sleep for shit."

"That's an indelicate way of putting it. But yeah, that's about right."

"Maybe you should see a doctor?"

"I will," she said. "As soon as I get old enough for Medicare. Right now, I ain't got no health insurance."

"No health insurance? Maud!"

"Well, the company cut back on Pelletier's hours and he lost his. We couldn't afford none on our own, so—" Maud sat down, slid the pad toward him. "Don't look at me that way. I'll bet you ain't got any either."

"That's different, Maud. I'm . . . well, I'm younger than you are."

"So you don't get hurt as bad, a car runs you over?"

"Hey, we still got Charity Hospital," Lynch offered.

"No, we ain't. That's the Medical Center of Louisiana now, and I hear their charity ain't what it used to be."

"God, the Kingfish would turn over in his grave." Lynch rubbed his eyes. "Okay, okay. As soon as we can afford it, I'll take a group plan out on us. I'll join the American Society of Public Relations Executives or some crap like that."

"You got to get business, first. You got to find another office and you got to bring in some cash. I'm serious about that. I'm not even sure I can work for you without a paycheck. At least not for very long."

Lynch scribbled down his new address on the pad and handed it to Maud. "Okay, I'll tell you what. I won't have a phone for at least a few more days. There's only one person I know of who might be able to feed me a few table scraps now. Carlton Smith over at the bank."

Maud rolled her eyes. "You going to get involved with that bank again? You are desperate."

"Maud, it's the only chance I've got to pick up a few quick bucks. I can crank out a few press releases, maybe consult on the annual report. Maybe some ad work. Hell, it's got to be better than nothing."

"I want to see you climb back out of this as much as anybody, Jack. But I hope they ain't got nothing for you."

Lynch paused, then found himself smiling at her. "I kind of hope that myself. But I feel like I have to try."

He stood up, pointed toward the living room. "The phone this way?"

"You going to call the bank on Sunday?"

"I'm going to call Carlton at home. I think it'll be okay. Maybe he can talk freer there."

"Next to the couch," she sighed, disgusted. "Phone book's under the nightstand."

Lynch dialed the number and sat through three rings. Then a voice answered, one Jack hadn't heard in months.

"Hello?"

"Carlton, this is Jack Lynch."

"Jack! Is it really you?"

"Yes, Carlton. Good to talk to you." Lynch prepared to go into his pitch. "Listen, I'm back in town now, and I—"

"I've been trying to get in touch with you since Friday morning," Carlton interrupted. "Where in blazes have you been?"

"California, my mother—"

"Never mind about that. I have to see you today. Can you make it over to my house?"

"Your house?" Lynch said, surprised. "Well, sure, I can . . ."

"Good, dinner then. Be here at six. You have the address?"

"The one in the phone book right?"

"Yes. Six tonight. Be on time. I need to talk with you."

"Sure, Carlton, and hey listen, thanks, I—"

But Carlton Smith had hung up. Lynch turned with the phone in his hand, a blank look on his face.

"Well?" Maud asked, leaning against the hall door jamb.

"I just got a dinner invitation," Lynch explained. "Sounds like a hot one, too."

▪ CHAPTER 8 ▪

Carlton Smith's house was closer to Tulane than Maud Pelletier's, and in a considerably more upscale neighborhood. Lynch knew the area well, had visited professors in that neighborhood while an undergraduate himself, but had rarely gone back since then.

He hadn't known that Carlton lived there. In all the years that he had known Carlton Smith, had worked with and for the bank's senior lawyer, he had never been to his house. It struck him as both odd and urgent that Carlton would have demanded that he show up at his house on such short notice. Even though it meant driving all the way across town, then back again, Lynch decided to return to his new apartment, shower, and put on a coat and tie.

At five minutes before six that evening, he stood at the top of a flight of concrete steps leading up to a screened-in porch and pressed the buzzer. A voice above him called out his name.

"Yes, Carlton, it's me," he responded.

The door in his hand buzzed and he felt it move slightly as the lock disengaged. He opened the door and stepped up onto the porch. Huge ferns hung from hooks in the ceiling, with pots of brightly colored plants dotting the floor between black wrought iron antique lawn furniture. The walls of the porch were waist-high, painted in earth tones, with screen extending to the top of a twelve-foot ceiling.

Lynch looked around, impressed. "C'mon in, Jack," Carlton yelled from somewhere inside the house. Jack pulled the heavy wood- and bevelled-glass door open and stepped into the house.

Carlton Smith may have been a life-long bachelor, but he had the taste of a seasoned and discriminating interior decorator. A thick Persian rug filled the front part of the sitting room, with a sofa and easy chair on one side of the room facing a floor-to-ceiling, built-in bookcase. In the center of the room was a black metal fireplace with a gas log sitting dormant, a polished black and chrome vent leading up to the ceiling and outside. The house had an air of opulence and wealth, the easy and comfortable kind that came when one was born with it, had nurtured and protected it, and knew how to live in it with serene grace.

Lynch walked toward the back of the house, from where he'd first heard the voice calling him. He heard the sound of running water and pots clanging.

Carlton appeared at the door, wiping his hands on a kitchen towel and wearing a canvas apron. He smiled, tossed the towel behind him onto the counter, and came forward with his hand extended.

"Jack, it's so good to see you, boy," he said, smiling broadly and with a relaxed air Jack had never seen him display at the bank. "Welcome, welcome."

Jack took the older man's hand in his and was surprised at his zeal. This was a side of Carlton Smith he had never seen.

"I hope you like crayfish," he said, pronouncing it "crawfish" like a good native. "I found a deal on live ones out River Road and couldn't resist."

"It's been awhile since I've had any," Jack said, following Carlton into the kitchen.

Carlton led him over to the kitchen sink. As Lynch approached, he could hear the water splashing. In the sink, covered in about six inches of cold water, hundreds of gray, shiny crayfish thrashed about, trying to escape over each others' backs.

"Sixty-five cents a pound," Carlton said, beaming. "I could

have gotten them for less if I'd bought a whole sack, but I figure five pounds apiece is plenty for the two of us."

"Five pounds?" Lynch asked.

"You'll be amazed how quickly we'll go through them, especially the way I cook them. I've also got a pot of gumbo on simmering."

Lynch sniffed; the smell of okra and spices cooking in broth filled his nose. He wasn't all that fond of gumbo—to him, boiled okra sliding down the back of his throat felt like something he should take an antihistamine for—but that was the sort of thing one *never* admitted. He'd force the stuff down and hope for the best. He was already hoping he'd be offered a drink.

"Funny, though," Carlton continued, "when I was a young boy, you could get crawfish for three cents a pound, five if it was a bad season. Lots of people ate 'mudbugs' because they couldn't afford anything else. Now they're a delicacy. You can't buy them certain times of the year because we ship them all off to Boston and New York."

"They look wonderful," Jack offered. "I really appreciate you asking me over like this."

"We'll see if you still feel that way at the end of the evening," Carlton said. "Here, let me get this started, and we'll fix ourselves a couple of drinks and go into the den."

"Here—" he pointed behind him. "Open that cupboard door. The liquor's in there. Pour me two fingers of Jack Daniels in one of those tall glasses with ice and about two fingers of water. And fix yourself whatever you want."

Lynch opened the door and pulled out a half-gallon of Jack Black. He glanced across the row of bottles in the dim light and found a bottle of Johnnie Walker Red and a quart of club soda.

"Have you got a weak stomach," Carlton asked.

"Not particularly," Lynch answered, hauling the bottles out of the closet and onto the counter.

"Well, watch," Carlton instructed. He held a box of Morton table salt over the sink and glanced at Jack with a twinkle in his eye. "My mother taught me this when I was eight years old. You know how big a pain it is to devein shrimp?"

"Yeah," Lynch said, pouring the whiskey into a tall glass.

"To begin with, it's not a vein at all. It's a very tiny, very full alimentary canal."

"Yuck," Lynch commented.

"Right. This way, you don't have to devein them." Carlton turned his eyes to the sink and tipped the container of salt. A steady stream of white poured out of the box and into the sink.

A terrific thrashing churned the water. "They hate salt," Carlton explained. "Cleans them out completely."

Lynch stared in revulsion as the cold, clear water in the sink turned jet black. "Disgusting," he said. "All that's inside those little buggers."

"Not any more it's not. And we'll let them sit there for a few minutes. After they've cleaned themselves out, they go into a kind of shock. They'll get another bath after that. Then into, as we say down here, the 'crawfish berl.' "

Lynch exhaled a deep breath. "Okay, sure. Why not?"

He handed Carlton a drink, then the two clinked glasses. "To old friends showing up again," Carlton said.

"It's been too long, pal," Lynch said. "Good to see you again."

Carlton took a long sip of his drink, then set the glass down on the slate counter. He rolled up his right sleeve, then sunk his arm up to the middle of his forearm in the black slurry.

Lynch wrinkled his nose. "Won't those things pinch you?"

"Not right now, they're too preoccupied." Carlton found the drain plug and pulled it. Slowly, the thick water receded. Carlton pulled the sprayer hose out and began showering the tiny lobsterlike creatures. In a moment, they were back to life, grabbing and clawing each other to try and get at the gargantuan monster who had entrapped them in this ceramic hell.

Carlton turned the tap on and rinsed his dirty hand, then left the water on, running slowly into the sink. "C'mon, let's go into the den while we wait for this to boil."

He turned the flame on under the large black enamel

kettle and checked the fire under the gumbo. Lynch followed him through the dining room into a large room off to the side. A tiger skin rug filled the center of the room, the stuffed head with mouth opened, fangs glaring, pointing toward the door like a guard dog.

"That for real?" Lynch asked.

Carlton stepped around the head, with the outstretched legs pointing like a large X in the middle of the floor, and took a seat in a well-worn chair. Across from him, a four-foot television monitor dominated a wall, with a stereo and shelves full of compact disks next to it.

"I shot that in Burma in 1949, after the war. I was with the Far East Command, as a judge advocate general stationed in Tokyo. We were on leave, a tiger hunt with MacArthur. He was furious when I bagged one bigger than his."

Lynch sat in a chair opposite him. "You mean Douglas MacArthur? *The* Douglas MacArthur?"

"Dugout Doug, himself," Carlton said. "Man was a real prick. Never thought much of him."

He leaned back in the chair, sipped the drink, savored it, then reached for a pack of Turkish Ovals on the smoking stand next to him. "Of course, nowadays," he continued, "it's considered politically incorrect to go around shooting beasts like that. But things were different then."

Jack stood up, reached for his cigarette lighter, and leaned toward Carlton. "Thanks," he said, inhaling. "You too, if you want. Smoke 'em if you got 'em."

The two men sat silently for a moment, then Carlton spoke abruptly, as if he'd just had a sudden thought he needed to relay before it left him.

"I'm leaving it, Jack. Giving it up."

"Leaving what?"

"I'm retiring. End of this year."

"Great, Carlton." Jack smiled. "Congratulations."

Carlton scowled at him. "Congratulations, hell. You think I want to quit? A man quits working, he starts to die, to atrophy. One should work every day one can. Then, when you can't do it anymore, it's time to die."

"If you don't want to quit, then why are you doing it?"

Carlton leaned forward, cigarette in one hand, drink in the other. "Because I just don't see things ever getting better down there. At the bank, I mean. You know what it's like. One crisis after another. I don't see how we've managed to limp through as well as we have. It's gotten worse since Mr. Jennings died. When he was around, there was always control. Now it's all committee, no leadership at all."

He shook his head, his voice trailing off. "I miss the old man, too," Jack said. "Since he died, it's like . . . well, it's like nothing's been the same since."

"Nothing has been the same since. Now this new mess. . . ."

"What new mess?"

"This mess that started Friday," Carlton said. "And by the way, where have you been?"

Lynch stiffened. "Long story," he said. "I've been in California for the past three months. Family stuff."

"Well, your damn phone's been disconnected. At your home and office both."

"Yeah, I know. I've moved. And I'll be moving my office tomorrow, I hope, and getting phone service back on after that. I'll let you know my new number."

Carlton stared him directly in the eye. "Jack, what do you know about computers?"

"Nothing," Lynch said. "Or very little. I've avoided them all my life."

"So have I. Unfortunately, that's hard to do in this day and age. I wish right now the damn things had never been invented."

"Why, Carlton? What's happened?"

"Thievery and dishonesty of a potential I've never seen before," Carlton said. "The bank is being held hostage. And if we don't transfer five million dollars to a numbered bank account in the Far East by the close of business tomorrow, the entire computer system of the First Interstate Bank of Louisiana will cease to exist. And along with it, the bank itself."

Lynch sat up in his chair, thunderstruck. "But how? How can a bank be held hostage?"

"The way it was explained to me," Carlton said, "some errant computer genius has planted a virus or something inside the bank's mainframe computer. Only it's the most advanced kind of virus ever imagined. It was described to me as more of a bomb, impossible to detect or defuse. If we don't accede to the bomber's demands, he can, and will, destroy us."

"So why not back up the computer data and tell the extortionist to go screw himself?"

"Apparently, that's not possible. The way the bomb's set up, attempting to back up the data will set it off."

"So just unplug the computers," Lynch offered.

"Don't you see, that has the same effect. Either way, the bank shuts down. Completely. He wins."

"Jesus, Carlton," Lynch muttered. "That's terrible. But why did you need to see me? I don't know a computer keyboard from third base."

"Neither do I. But there are other things at stake." Carlton reached down beside his chair, where an overstuffed lawyer's briefcase sat open, brimming with papers.

"You know about the upcoming lottery, don't you?"

"Only what I've read in the papers; that it's coming."

"This September. Less than six months away." Carlton fumbled with the briefcase and pulled out a thick file. "Let me give you a little background into what's going on here."

Carlton opened the file. "The Louisiana Lottery won't be like most state lotteries. Instead of the state government setting up an agency to run the lottery, we're going to establish a corporation to administer and run the lottery. This has several advantages. First, the lottery will have much more decision-making power. It can establish its own games, its own rules, without having to go through that morass of manure in Baton Rouge we call a legislature. Secondly, since the corporation will have a clear profit motive and no civil service protection, it will be run more like a business and less like the government—"

"Hooray," Lynch interrupted. "Maybe that means they'll succeed."

"Here, here," Carlton agreed. "But there's a downside.

There won't be as many controls as other states exercise. The corporation will hire and fire its own people, who won't have civil service protection or guidelines, and who won't be under the direct control of either the legislature or the governor. And you know what that means. . . ."

"That somebody is going to consider the Louisiana Lottery their own personal trough."

"Exactly," Carlton said. "And that's got the stew scared out of everybody. So the political powers-that-be are struggling to keep this as legitimate and straight as possible, while at the same time maximizing the potential for profit. Jack, this state is nearly bankrupt. If the lottery doesn't succeed for us, we could very well see the state of Louisiana be the first state government in American history to declare insolvency."

"I didn't know it was that bad," Jack said.

"It's worse," Carlton emphasized. "Where do you think men like David Duke come off doing so well? These are conditions that breed demagogues like heat and humidity breed mold and mildew. Things are so bad that the state can't even afford to set up the lottery that's going to bail its financial ass out. Which is where the bank came in."

"The bank?" Lynch asked. "What's the bank got to do with this?"

"Since the death of Mr. Jennings," Carlton said slowly, "the bank's—my—level of political influence has waned considerably. But that's the nature and dynamics of power, my friend. It ebbs and flows, waxes and wanes. But I still have a few friends in B. R., and New Orleans still swings a lot of weight in this state.

"So I put together a deal whereby the First Interstate Bank of Louisiana will set up a ten-million-dollar line of credit to start the lottery, with another ten in reserve. We're on the line for up to twenty million here, Jack."

Lynch whistled.

"After the money laundering scandal that sent our dear friend Sheriff Murphy to Angola, I thought we were finished in this state. But this was our way back to credibility and influence," Carlton continued. "I could retire knowing that the bank was back on solid footing, a player once again in the state power game. Now its all at risk."

Lynch thought of Civil Sheriff Murphy for the first time in months, of the scandals that had resulted in the deaths of four people he loved. He felt a knot of tension at the back of his neck and brought his hand up to squeeze it. "What about the ransom?" he asked.

"That can be handled," Carlton said. "We'll have to hide it from the auditors, but that can be done with a minimum of trouble. The problem is that if it comes to light that the bank financing the computer-based Louisiana Lottery was just hijacked for five million by a . . . a *hacker*, for Christ's sake, then the question of credibility and influence, and indeed the very fate of the lottery itself, might be at risk. I've seen the numbers, Jack. The real numbers, the ones the news media and the citizenry don't have access to. This state is a house of cards in a hurricane, my friend, and it's all fixing to come down around us."

"Carlton," Jack asked after a moment, "have you been to the police?"

The older man groaned. "Did you see the paper this morning? A two-year-old girl was murdered and raped last night, not ten minutes from here by car. This city is a war zone. There are pockets, enclaves, of relative safety. But the police aren't able to handle the perverts and the crazies, let alone computer criminals who can't even be traced."

Lynch settled back, stared at the rotating ceiling fan spinning slowly above. "Any chance of it being an inside job?"

Carlton shot forward. "I've already thought of that, and that's what's got me worried. You see, Harold Gupton, the director of our data processing division is a consulting member of the Louisiana Lottery Commission. I don't trust the man any further than I can throw him. He won't even look you in the eyes."

"Could he have anything to do with this?"

"Nothing would surprise me, Jack. But I think this is one area where you could help. I've got a discretionary account in the legal department. I can access the money without having to explain to anyone what it's for. What I'd like to do is put you on retainer, have you do a little background on several of these guys in the department. Start at point A and see where getting to point B takes you. Are you available?"

Lynch brightened. "Am I available? Does David Duke wear a white sheet?"

"Good," Carlton said, standing up. "There's a meeting set up for one o'clock tomorrow down in the data processing division's conference room. I'll get an update from the computer people, and then I'll take it upstairs to the chairman. He'll make the final decision, but for all intents and purposes, it's a done deal already. Can you be there?"

"You don't have a lot of choice, do you? On the ransom, I mean."

"None," Carlton said flatly. "The best we can hope to do is to track this down and snuff it out, so that it never happens again. We also need to make sure none of our own people are involved. But most importantly, no one must *ever* find out about it."

"Okay, I'll be there. I'm not exactly sure what I can do, but I'll give it my best shot."

"Truthfully, Jack," Carlton said somberly, "the reason I called on you is that you're one of the few people I feel I can really trust these days. You break rules, you step on toes, you get yourself in trouble. But you're persistent as hell, and I value that. I'll also back you to the hilt. Whatever you need, you name it."

"I appreciate that, Carlton," Jack said.

Carlton stared down at his drink, lost momentarily in thought.

"You know, this isn't a mugging or a rape or some other dramatic and violent incident that would play well on the six o'clock news. But it is crime, and it's crime on a scale that's frightening, not because of the dollar value alone—money comes and money goes and what the hell, we all die penniless anyway—but because of the insidiousness of it. You can't fight what you can't see, what you can't feel or smell or hear coming at you in a dark alley. The people who trust banks and depend on the system to keep them safe will keep on thinking everything is intact and whole until it fragments and collapses. No one understands the implications, how terrible this is. . . ."

Carlton's voice was almost plaintive now, as if he felt helpless and old and vulnerable. Jack stared at him a moment, then reached over and patted him on the back.

"You convinced me," he said. "I'll do anything I can to help you."

"Good," Carlton said, shaking his head as if to clear the fog. "Right now, our glasses need filling and I'm starved. Let's go boil some crustaceans alive."

Carlton stood, threw his arm around Jack's shoulder and the two walked into the kitchen. The boiling pot on the stove had filled the air in the entire back of the house with sharp, acrid, overwhelming clouds of steam. Lynch coughed; his eyes ran. His nostrils burned all the way back to his ear lobes.

"Hell, Carlton, what're we boiling 'em in, battery acid?"

Carlton laughed. "It will clear your sinuses, won't it? My mother's old recipe. Don't worry, boy, you'll get used to it."

As Carlton ladled the squirming crayfish out of the sink and dropped them a scoop at a time into the boiling water, it occurred to Lynch that during a number of periods in his life, he had known exactly how the mudbugs felt.

▪ CHAPTER 9 ▪

Lynch was already awake and stirring when his alarm went off at seven the next morning. He sat at what passed for his kitchen table—a card table and two folding chairs—and drank his coffee while scanning the Sunday classifieds for office space. The way he figured it, the best thing he could do was take his last clear credit card, a gold card he always kept in reserve for emergencies, and get a couple of thousand in a cash advance. He would repay it the next month when the money came down from either his mother's estate or Carlton's mysterious slush fund.

He circled two good prospects, both either within or a few blocks from the Central Business District, then climbed in the shower. He shaved, shampooed his too-long hair, and dressed as neatly as he could. He made a mental note to get a haircut as soon as possible, then glanced around his apartment one last time to make sure he had everything. He slid the folded newspaper into his briefcase, held his key ring in his right hand, and opened the door.

Across the hall, the metallic clatter of door hardware caught his attention. The door opened just as he was locking his, and P. J. Campbell stepped into the hallway.

"Oh, good morning," she said. Lynch turned; she had on a bright turquoise blouse with matching black silk pants and a jacket. Now that she wasn't sweaty and covered in dust, Lynch was struck by how classically attractive she was.

"Hi," he said. "P.J., right?"

"Yes. And you're Jack?"

"You got it," he said, motioning for her to step ahead of him. "How do you like your new apartment?"

"Just fine. I think I'm almost settled, though sleeping in a new place still feels strange."

"I know what you mean," he agreed as they started down the stairs. "It always takes me awhile to get used to new surroundings. What part of town did you live in before?"

"I didn't. I moved here from New York City."

"New York City?" Lynch asked, surprised. "You don't sound like you're from New York City."

"Well," she turned, "you don't sound like you're from New Orleans."

"Touché," Lynch conceded, then switching into a deep Southern drawl, "but if ah have to, ah can just fine."

"You certainly can, sir. But I do a terrible New York accent. Comes from being born in Illinois, I think."

"Illinois to New York to New Orleans. My, you've been around. How'd you wind up here?"

The two stepped through the front door into the bright morning sunshine. A few clouds still hung off in the northwest, toward the lake, but the morning heat was rapidly burning them off.

"What a beautiful day," P.J. said. "Say, I'm still getting my bearings. What's the easiest way to get to I-10."

Lynch pointed to his left. "Go down Esplanade a block or so until you get to City Park. Go left at the light, then bear right at the next light. That's City Park Avenue. It'll take you straight to the entrance ramp. You'll go by a bunch of cemeteries."

"That's one thing I've noticed about New Orleans," she said, opening the driver's door of a late-model, copper-brown Toyota. "You can't go anywhere here without passing a cemetery."

"Well," Lynch commented, looking down at her from the curb as she started her car, "the living and the dead mix in real well around here."

"Thanks, Jack, I'll remember that." P.J. Campbell put her car in gear and pulled away from the sidewalk. Lynch stared after her for a moment, then it came to him.

She never answered his question.

The corner of Canal and Ramparts was a jumble of bodies, the pedestrian traffic mostly shoppers, mostly black. Some rollerbladers, a few "boyz-in-the-hood" types, and a sweaty, fat white guy nervously passing out Jesus leaflets. Typical day downtown, Lynch thought.

The Audubon Building was a half-block toward the river. Lynch walked past a discount shoe store, a men's clothing store, a newsstand, a drugstore, and stopped. AUDUBON BUILDING was laid out in silver art deco letters above the door.

Lynch stepped through the heavy glass doors. The building was old, but seemed well kept. A burly security guard sat at a tiny metal desk with a clipboard in front of him.

"I'm looking for the building manager."

"Fourth floor, left off the elevator, down the hall, turn right," the guard instructed. "And sign here."

He swiveled the clipboard around. Lynch signed his name and noted the time.

Upstairs, the floors were slick, polished rose marble. The doors were heavy and thick, the hallway filled with the silence of a building that was all but abandoned. Several doors were padlocked, the tenants having disappeared in the middle of the night, their possessions now held hostage to back rent. Come to think of it, Lynch thought, that's what he had just done at his last office.

He knocked once on a frosted-glass door with the name "R. Adams, Building Manager" painted on it in chipped black enamel.

"Yeah, c'mon in," a muffled voice said.

Lynch pushed the door open into a tiny office jammed with wall-to-wall filing cabinets around all four sides. In the center, hunched over a scarred wooden desk stacked with file folders and piles of paper, sat a large man with slicked back gray hair and a smelly cigar hanging wetly out of one side of his unshaven jaw.

"Yeah," the man asked, looking up.

"Name's Jack Lynch. I saw your ad in the paper and I'm looking for an office."

"Yeah? What kind of work you do?"

"I'm in public relations. More of a freelancer than anything else."

"How much room do you need?"

"Not much. An office for me to work in. A small waiting room for clients and a place for my secretary to put a desk."

The man raised an eyebrow. "You got a secretary?"

Lynch nodded his head. "Part time. She comes in, does some work for me now and then."

"What does a public relations person do?" the man asked suspiciously.

"I get my clients' names and businesses in the papers and on TV. It's kind of like advertising, only you're trying to get the attention paid to your client for free rather than paying for it."

"Maybe you could help us around here. This is a classy old building, you know."

"Yeah, I saw that when I came in. How old is it?"

"Built in 1928, just a year before the crash. Don't build them like this anymore, no sir. This old building's been through a lot."

I'll bet, Lynch thought. *It shows, too.*

"Yeah, but now with this new recession, we can't keep tenants any more. Only about a third of the building's even occupied. I guess that's why I'uz a little suspicious of you. Guy comes around here dressed real neat like you, wants space in a building like this, I got to figure he's up to no good."

"To be perfectly honest, I used to be in a more expensive building. But my business is off just like everybody else's. I need to cut my expenses."

The fat man laughed. "Well, by God, you've come to the right place." He stood up, reached behind him to a pegboard and took a set of keys down from the wall.

"C'mon, I've got something on this floor you might like." The man led the way down the hall, his huge behind bouncing around under his shiny suit pants as he walked. Lynch followed, trying not to inhale the stench of thin blue cigar smoke trailing out.

Down the hall, two doors away from the elevator, the man stopped.

"Used to have an astrologer in this office. Astrology, you believe that shit? If she could see the future, she shoulda seen she was going broke. Woman left in the middle of the night owing me two months."

"Jeez," Lynch said, trying to sound sympathetic. "What some people won't do."

The door opened into a dark, dusty waiting room perhaps ten feet by twelve, with an old black-topped green metal desk sitting cockeyed in the middle of the room. The wall opposite the entranceway was mostly thick, frosted glass. Light coming in through the glass told Lynch the main office had a window, although heaven knew what it looked out on.

A black phone, the old-fashioned rotary-dial type that was permanently wired into a wall socket, sat on the floor on top of an outdated, tattered white pages directory.

"Phones are here already," Lynch observed.

"Yeah. I can get one of the boys to take them out if you want to use your own."

"No, that's fine. No problem."

"I'll get one of the boys to get that old desk out of here, too." The man leaned against the door jamb, swivelling the thick green stogie around between his purplish lips, as Lynch walked around.

Lynch stepped into what would be his office. Scarred linoleum floors, dirty windows looking out onto an alley behind the building, plaster with cracks running floor-to-ceiling, rusty steam radiator against one wall. And in one window, a filthy window unit that had to be twenty-years-old if a day. Not exactly Trump Tower, he thought.

"How much?" Lynch asked, his back to the fat man.

"Hmmm," the man hesitated. "What would you say to two-twenty-five a month? That'll include utilities, but not the phone."

Maud's going to raise hell with me, Lynch said to himself. He turned. "Okay, say on a six-month lease?"

"Whatever you say," the man said. "A lease don't mean much. If you want to stay here, you'll stay. If you want out, a lease ain't going to keep you here."

"You wouldn't happen to have another desk down in the basement somewhere, would you? Maybe a couple of chairs and a filing cabinet. I'm a little short in the cash flow department."

"Well, I could have—"

"Yeah, right. One of the boys," Lynch said.

"Say, for twenty bucks?"

Lynch pulled out his wallet, handed the man a twenty. "You'll take care of it for me? See that they get it?"

"Glad to, Mr. Lynch." He handed Jack a set of keys. "I'll have your lease drawn up. Come by and sign it tomorrow and drop me a check for the first and last month's rent. In the meantime, welcome to your new office."

"Yeah," Lynch said. "It's good to be home."

Two hours later, Lynch had deposited $1500.00 into his checking account, courtesy of the gold-card folks, paid off his outstanding telephone bill, and convinced the phone company that he was a good enough risk to take a chance on turning on his new telephone. Afterwards, he pulled off Tulane Avenue behind the Dixie Beer brewery and into the parking lot of a Bud's Broiler. The smell of charbroiling beef and hickory-smoke barbecue sauce drove all traces of car exhaust and smelly cigars from his nostrils. His mouth began to water. But first, he dropped a quarter in a pay phone and dialed Maud's number.

"You *what?*" she demanded, after he explained the new deal to her. "You got an office *where?*"

Lynch got off the phone as quickly as possible, then stood in line for the cashier. Behind him, the jukebox played a lonesome George Jones tune.

"Number two with cheese," he said when he got to the head of the line. "Fries, large coke."

He took his ticket and walked over to one of the picnic

tables that passed for furnishings at Bud's. He sat down and fingered his ticket, waiting for the food.

"I knew she was going to be pissed," he said, to no one in particular.

■ *CHAPTER 10* ■

I t was a quiet measure of Jack Lynch's desperation that he even considered working for the First Interstate Bank of Louisiana again; every time he walked through the doors into the cavernous lobby of the grand, ancient building, a chill shook him to the marrow of his bones. The place had been nothing but trouble for him. As he pushed the bronze and glass doors open and eased into the blast of cold air, he came within a whisker of turning around and walking back out.

Then he remembered his client list, which consisted of one name; and the one name on that list was Carlton Smith, chief legal counsel, the First Interstate Bank of Louisiana. He had, he realized, no choice. But this time, he swore it was just a job. Just a paycheck and nothing else. Nothing to get emotionally invested in, nothing to care about.

Do the job. Cash the check. Go home.

"My name is Jack Lynch," he said to the unfamiliar young face wearing too much makeup and thick false eyelashes at the information table. Back when the Old Man owned and ran the bank, you saw the same faces, day after day, year after year. Stability, continuity; that's the way things used to be. Now, if you ducked your head once and came back up, you'd see a whole new raft of people each time. "I have an appointment with Carlton Smith."

The woman scanned a list of numbers, then phoned upstairs. She talked low into the phone for a couple of exchanges, then looked back up at Jack.

"Mr. Smith will be down for you in a minute. If you'll just have a seat over there." She motioned toward a bank of chairs beyond a low polished wooden railing.

Lynch sat nervously down in the chair with his back to the lobby. From where he was sitting, it was barely ten paces to the spot where his boss, William Jennings, had been gunned down not quite two years earlier. Lynch had written his resignation earlier that same day, ready to give up the only real job he'd ever had, and leave the bank and the city behind him forever. Then there was the popping sound, with the Old Man grabbing him and sinking slowly to the floor. And then gunfire all around, and bodies flying, and the fading warmth of a dying man in his arms—but not just any dying man, not just a boss. William Jennings had been, in fact, his father in every sense of the word but the biological one. Lynch stared vacantly ahead, a barren look on his face, the screams and the sounds of the chaos ringing in his ears once again. Behind him, a throat cleared.

Lynch shot up out of the chair and whirled, wild-eyed, at the sound.

"Are you all right?" Carlton Smith asked softly.

"Yeah," Lynch answered, shellshocked, numb. "Yeah, I'm okay. I was just think . . . faded away for a second."

"I saw you staring when I got off the elevator." Carlton took a step toward him, held out his hand and placed it on Jack's forearm. "You had the look of a man who'd just seen a ghost."

Lynch stared at the hand on his arm, then looked up into Carlton's face. "Sorry. Guess it's a little weird being back here."

"It was right over there, wasn't it? Right over there where Mr. Jennings was shot." Carlton nodded in the direction of the gunfire.

Lynch winced. "How do you come in here everyday?"

"You just do it, Jack. Like so many unpleasant things in life. You just do it and you don't think about it."

"I don't think I'll ever be able to stop thinking about it."

"You'll have to," Carlton warned. "Or it will make you crazy."

Lynch smiled. "Probably too late for that."

"I don't believe that for a second. Now," Carlton held his arm out before him to indicate the direction they were headed, "let me give you a rundown on who we'll be meeting with."

Lynch walked ahead, through the wooden gate and toward a bank of elevators against the broadest wall at the back of the lobby.

"First," Carlton continued, "there will be Harold Gupton. He's the vice-president for data processing I told you about. He's a strange bird. Deep tan. Wrinkled like a bulldog. Dark, deep-set eyes that won't look you in the face. He's quiet in meetings, just seems to sit there on high waiting for his underlings to present him with all the options, then he picks the one he likes. He's very powerful down there. His word is law."

"And he's the one who's the consulting member on the Louisiana Lottery Commission."

"Exactly, he's the one who'll have the most input about which vendors they go with, the hardware and the software and all that other stuff you and I don't understand."

"Great." Lynch glanced at his watch: 12:50. "Meeting's at one, right?"

"In the data processing conference room. Deep below where we are now."

The elevator door slid open and the two men stepped aboard. Carlton leaned over and pushed a button marked "D" on the panel. The door closed in front of them with a hiss. Lynch felt the car drop quickly, and farther than he expected. In all the years he'd worked for the bank, he'd never been down to the computer division. It was as foreign to him as an installation on the moon.

"Then there's Kenneth Cook, who I believe is the chief programmer for the division. He's the one who ought to be able to deactivate the bomb if anyone can. I've done a little checking around the bank, a few discreet questions here and there. It seems he's a bit of a tiger; runs his end of the operation with fear and intimidation. A real slave driver, generally not a nice person."

"Okay," Lynch commented. "I'm really looking forward to meeting him."

"And then there's a fellow named Adkins. Buford Adkins, I believe. He's the senior analyst. I'm not exactly sure what a senior analyst does, but my sense is that he and his team work off in a corner by themselves. He's not at all like Cook or Gupton, though. Seems very softspoken. Even, dare I say, nice."

"Good heavens, a nice guy working here? How has he managed to survive?"

Carlton turned to Jack just as the elevator settled to a stop. "I suspect by being the sort of fellow who doesn't get in anyone's way."

"What are you going to tell them about me?"

The door opened. Carlton stepped out ahead of Jack and into a brightly lit, sterile area bordered on one side by a wall of clear glass. Beyond the glass, row after row of computer operators sat, faceless drones at white plastic terminals, heads bowed to their work, fingers flying away like buzzsaws at numeric keypads.

"I haven't decided yet," Carlton answered.

"You'll have to tell them something."

"I suppose it depends on what they ask."

Lynch shrugged, happy with that if Carlton was. They walked the length of the glass wall to a heavy door, beyond which sat a middle-aged, dark-haired woman at a desk. Carlton pressed a button; the woman looked up from a stack of computer printout and recognized Carlton. She reached under the desk. A buzzer went off next to Jack's head. Carlton pushed the door open.

"Hello, Mary," Carlton said. "Are they all here for our one o'clock?"

"I believe so, Mr. Smith," the woman said brightly. She reached into a desk drawer and pulled out two blue badges with the word "VISITOR" printed in bold black.

"Does my friend here need to sign in?"

"Is he with you?"

"Yes, he'll be joining me at the meeting."

"No need then. He can go on back. Just make sure the badges show."

The air inside the enormous room was dry, cool, uniform, stale. Lynch had read articles about office pollution; he figured that most of them must have been conceived and researched in places like this. The walls were lined with white acoustical tile, which combined with the harsh white-tiled floor and the white walls gave one the impression of being in a futuristic, arid spaceship.

"These people ever look up from these terminals?" Lynch asked as they passed by a bank of operators.

"Not if they know what's good for them," Carlton said. "The computers keep track of how many keystrokes per hour the operator enters. If it falls below a certain number, the supervisor is alerted at his terminal."

"Electronic sweatshop. Real *Nineteen Eighty-Four* stuff," Lynch said.

"At its worst."

The two walked past the sea of terminals, into a smaller area. Desks on this part of the floor were separated from one another by moveable panels. To their left, in another glass-enclosed area, was the control room, the heart of the data processing division. A lone man stood at a terminal in the center of the room, surrounded by rows of tape drives, printers, and huge blinking computer hardware that Lynch neither recognized nor understood.

At the end of the room, where the walls came together in a triangular point, a tall woman sat at a desk guarding a door. Lynch read the sign as they approached the door: HAROLD GUPTON, VICE-PRESIDENT, DATA PROCESSING.

"Hello, Ms. Darman," Carlton said as they approached the desk. "I'm here for our one o'clock."

The woman eyed Lynch suspiciously. "And who shall I tell Mr. Gupton will be joining you?"

"Mr. Lynch. He's an outside consultant who's done some work for me in the past. I want him in the meeting with us."

"All right. I'll tell Mr. Gupton you're here. If you'd like to step on into the conference room, the other gentlemen will join you shortly."

Carlton led the way into a room off to the right of Gupton's office. The lights were turned down low and the air was cold to the point of uncomfortable. Carlton crossed to the other side of the room, pulled out a chair next to the head of the polished, heavy, wooden table, and sat down. Lynch scooted a chair over next to Carlton and sat.

"Now, the question becomes how long will we wait," Carlton said. "You get an awful lot of petty power stuff going on in places like this."

"So I remember," Lynch said. "It always seems like the pettier the tyrant, the more you have to put up with."

"My one bit of advice is don't let these bastards intimidate you. We may not know computers, but we know how to protect this bank. And we have a much better sense of how this bank really runs than they do. They know their own little isolated world like they know the backs of their hands, but there's a lot more to running a bank than—"

The door scraped across the carpet as it opened. A pleasant looking, slightly overweight fellow with a shock of brown hair hanging down in his face stepped in carrying a legal pad.

"Hi, Mr. Smith," he said. "Good to see you again."

"Hello, Buford. I'd like you to meet Jack Lynch."

"Hi, Mr. Lynch," Buford Adkins said, offering his hand across the table. Lynch took it and the two shook warmly.

"Please, it's Jack," Lynch said.

"Okay, Jack."

The door scraped open again and Harold Gupton walked in, followed closely in tow by the man Lynch took to be Kenneth Cook. Gupton was unmistakable, given Carlton's warning. Folds of loose, tanned skin flapped down over the man's collar. He was the only one in the room jacketless, as if to let the others know that this was his turf and he didn't have to suit up for anybody.

"Hello, Carlton," he said, looking away from the table as he entered the room. He made his way to the head of the table and sat.

"Hello, Harold," Carlton said formally. Lynch followed Gupton around the room and realized that Carlton had been right; the man never looked anyone in the eye.

"Harold," Carlton said, "this is Jack Lynch. I've asked him to join us today because he's on retainer with the bank as a public relations consultant. He's handled a number of sensitive matters for me and I want his input."

Gupton went silent for a moment, his eyes circling the room at ceiling level. "Well, I wish you'd told me earlier he'd be here. But now that he's here. . . ."

"Glad to meet you, Mr. Gupton," Lynch said.

"Yes," Gupton muttered.

"And this is Kenneth Cook, the chief programmer for the data processing division. Is that right, Kenneth, 'chief programmer'?"

"Yeah," Cook said to Carlton, then turning to Jack. "Glad to meet you."

Lynch wished he'd brought a winter sweater. This was a cold bunch.

"If I could suggest we get right into it," Carlton said. "Have you had any luck figuring out how or where this this 'bomb' is?"

"I'm beginning to think it's a hoax," Cook spat. "My guys have been over every executable program in the entire system. They're all clean."

"It's not a hoax," Gupton said. "Not with the damage he did to the system just to get our attention."

"Besides," Buford Adkins offered, "we really haven't been able to go in there and do a low-level format and reload the software off clean backups. The bomber made it clear in his note that if we tried that, the bomb would self-ignite."

Lynch had no idea what they were talking about, but realized that for now, it wasn't important for him to understand. His job now was to observe the way that power ebbed and flowed among these men and to study the dynamics of their relationships.

"The important thing, as I understand it, is that we have less than four hours to respond to the extortionist's demands or he blows up our computer system and shuts us down,"

Carlton said. "Is that correct? We haven't been able to defuse the bomb?"

The three men across the table from Carlton and Jack stared at each other stonily. Finally, Cook, the programmer, spoke.

"That's correct. The bottom line is we can't stop the guy."

"And if we do what he demands," Carlton continued, unmistakable tension in his voice, "what's to keep him from coming back here next week and demanding another five million? And what guarantees do we have that he will, in fact, defuse the bomb?"

This time, the stares among the three had an edge of nervousness, as if no one, not even Gupton, wanted to be the one to deliver the bad news.

"We don't have many guarantees," Adkins finally admitted. His soft-spoken voice had an air of resignation to it. "If he does defuse the bomb, he won't be able to plant another one. We'll disconnect the modems from the mainframe and isolate it completely. We can hook up a mini or a couple of PCs to the telephone line to handle electronic fund transfers and stuff."

"What's a modem?" Lynch asked.

"A device that let's computers talk to each other over the phone lines," Adkins said. "That's how the extortionist planted the bomb in the first place. He got our phone number, somehow bypassed the built-in security, and loaded it out there somewhere. We can't find out where."

"I find this simply incredible," Carlton Smith said. "Is this where all our acclaimed technology has brought us? We can't even see the bank robbers anymore?"

"Hey," Cook interrupted, "don't climb all over us on this. Hackers break into computer systems every day. The Department of Defense, NASA, every major government agency, every major university in the world—all of them have had problems."

"But what's the point, gentlemen?" Carlton demanded. "If the system is so vulnerable, *why do we use it?*"

"Because there's nothing else!" Cook yelped. "We can't

go back to quill pens and handwritten ledgers! It's the price of doing business."

"Well, the damned price just got five million too high. I've got to go upstairs to the chairman of this bank, who by the way, gentlemen, is still worried that the Feds are doing everything from watching his house to bugging his bathroom, and explain to him that in less than four hours, we're going to dump five million dollars of our depositor's money down a rathole. We have no idea where it's going, no idea who it's going to, and no guarantees that this time next week, we won't be doing the same thing again!

"That, gentlemen, is unacceptable!" Carlton's voice was shrill, and his eyes bulged. Lynch had never seen the man come this close to losing his composure.

"What in the hell would you suggest we do about it?" Cook hissed.

"Wait a minute," Gupton interrupted, raising his hand to silence the meeting as he stared straight down the table between the two opposing sides. "This isn't getting us anywhere. Whatever we do, we have to present a united front. We have to send a recommendation upstairs that will be unanimous."

Gupton turned to Carlton. "Recriminations aren't going to do anyone any good. It's too late for that. We have to somehow get past this situation and make sure that this never happens again. In addition to the measures we've already taken, we've hired an outside computer security consulting firm that's analyzing our network right now. They'll make recommendations. We'll implement them. This won't happen again."

Lynch glanced sideways and saw that Carlton's face was bright red. By losing his temper, he'd allowed Gupton to gain control of the meeting, despite the fact that he was technically Gupton's senior.

Gupton swiveled in his chair, the folds of skin rubbing together over his shirt collar as he turned.

"And you Kenneth, have got to assure me and Carlton and the entire senior management of this bank that everything possible has been done to find the software bomb and to defuse it. If you make your case solidly, then we can make our recommendations upstairs equally as solidly.

"Finally, whatever happens, neither our depositors nor the media must ever find out what has happened here. Too many people know of our problem already. I hate to use this term, but from now on out, we have to stonewall it. I want no dissension. We must all be in agreement on this as well."

Gupton rotated his massive head again and seemed to focus in Lynch's general direction, although in following his eyes, Lynch had the sensation that there was something going on behind him that had drawn Gupton's attention. Then Gupton laid his hands on the table, palms down, fingers pointing toward the other end of the room. The still, cold air was silent and heavy. Cook sat glaring at the two men across from him. Despite the temperature, dark circles spread out under each armpit, a thin sheen of sweat showing above the greasy fingerprints on his glasses.

Lynch stared across the table at Buford Adkins. The younger, quieter man had settled back in his chair, seeming almost to recede out of focus in the room full of angry men and one observer. Adkins had himself ceased to be a participant at that point; the corporate political world's equivalent of playing possum.

The tense silence went on for what seemed like forever to Lynch. His own palms began to sweat. "May I ask a question?" he asked.

"Of course," Gupton said, as if stating the obvious.

"I'm unclear as to how this got started in the first place. Carlton explained it to me as best he could, but we're both laymen. Can you bring me up to speed on how this . . . this 'bomb,' was planted in the first place. In laymen's terms?"

Gupton looked at Buford Adkins and subtly nodded his head. Adkins sat forward a bit, cradled his hands in front of him. "We think it happened this week. Our first clue was when we noticed that a portion of one of the hard disks, which is where information is stored in the system, had been wiped clean. Literally. It was in an area that tracked certificates of deposit. We were able to recreate the lost data from the paper trail, but it was time consuming and expensive."

"So you think the bomber planted the bomb and then messed with your computer to show he could do it?"

"Something like that," Adkins said. "But that's not all. The next week, we started getting complaints from depositors. In some cases, balances were suddenly and inexplicably lowered. The person would have cancelled checks and deposit slips to verify what they were saying, so we couldn't argue with them. In other cases, customers would come in claiming the computer was showing them as having more money than they thought they had."

"And in both instances," Cook interrupted, "our books balanced. Everything zeroed out. An auditor would have come up with nothing unusual. Except a bunch of pissed off customers complaining their balances were wrong."

"So you think the bomber did this, too?"

"You figure it," Adkins said. "Believe it or not, we're pretty careful around here. Those kinds of mistakes rarely happen. What worries me is that we still don't know how many of our customers out there have screwed up balances. It will take a full audit to track it all down. And we can't do that until we get the mainframe decontaminated."

"So you're sure there are still problems out there?" Lynch asked.

"Oh, yeah. No doubt. They'll dribble in a little at a time until they're all found. The funny thing is, this is just a taste of what will happen if the bomb goes off."

"What a mess," Lynch whispered.

"What about Martin Brown?" Carlton asked. "Are you sure he's told you everything that could have happened that night?"

"Who knows?" Cook said. "Brown's a rotten apple. Bad attitude. Classic underachiever. We ought to have gotten rid of him a long time ago."

"If he's that big a problem, maybe he had something to do with this?"

"We thought that for awhile, too. But Brown's not the

type. Besides, what could he do that we couldn't trace and undo?"

Probably a lot, Lynch thought to himself. *Jesus, if egos were airships, yours would be the* Hindenberg.

"And then when did you find out about the extortion demand? Was there a note?"

"Do we really have time for this?" Cook asked irritably. "And for that matter, does *he* really need to know all this?"

Carlton tightened in his chair. Lynch felt the need to defuse the tension, and quickly.

"If you want me to help you," he said. "I need to be apprised of exactly what's been going on here. If there's some top-secret proprietary information involved, that's one thing. But the more you keep from me, the less I might be able to help you."

"What can you do anyway?" Cook asked.

"That is not for you to ask," Carlton shot back. "This is an upper management decision—"

"Now, Carlton, let's not pull rank—" Gupton tried to interrupt.

"Quiet, Harold, I'm talking," Carlton ordered. Both Cook and Adkins looked stunned, while Gupton merely refocused his gaze on a spot in the ceiling. "You gentlemen down here have presided over one of the most massive screwups in the history of this bank, maybe in the history of American banking. Now you have two ways to play this: you can let me and Mr. Lynch try to bail your asses out or you can refuse to cooperate with us, in which case I march upstairs to the chairman and the board of directors and lay this whole mess in front of them. And since you, Harold, have chosen to use political terms like 'stonewall' here, let me throw another one back at you. Does the phrase 'twisting slowly, slowly, in the wind' mean anything to you?"

Throughout this, Carlton Smith's voice never wavered, either in tone or volume. He was secure, composed, and completely in control.

"Carlton, of course we want to cooperate with you," Gupton began.

"Then you can start by answering Mr. Lynch's question. When did the note arrive and what did it say?"

Gupton settled back in his own chair, the folds of his neck settling into a deflated position. He rotated his head, almost made eye contact with Adkins, and nodded.

"The note came in Friday afternoon. Unsigned, first-class mail, no return address."

"From where was the envelope posted?"

"This zip code."

"Right here in the downtown area?"

"You got it," Adkins said. "Could've been from within this building."

"Go on," Lynch said.

"The note had complete instructions and a description of what the bomb could do, which we've already outlined for you. We have until four P.M. central standard time Monday—today—to wire five million American dollars to a numbered account in the Bank of Bonin."

"Bank of Bonin?" Lynch said. "Never heard of it."

"Neither had we. We had to look it up. It's in the Far East, Bonin Island. Southeast of Japan. We haven't had time to do much research, but it looks like it's the southeast Asian equivalent of a Cayman Islands bank. Secret numbered accounts, no information divulged to anyone. No cooperation with authorities."

"Probably set up because of the heroin traffic in that part of the world," Cook offered. "Plenty of business for a bank that'll keep its mouth shut."

"So you wire the money halfway around the world," Lynch said. "Then what?"

"The bomber's note said we were to set up an electronic mailbox in our system for him under the name of 'Vernon Wormer.' When he confirms the electronic fund transfer, he'll simply dial in and leave instructions in the mailbox for defusing the bomb."

"Vernon Wormer." Lynch laced his fingers together in an arch and rubbed his thumbs on either side of his chin.

"Who in blazes is Vernon Wormer?" Carlton asked.

Cook and Adkins looked at each other. "We have no earthly idea," Adkins said. "No idea at all."

Carlton looked down at his watch. "It's almost two o'clock now. Have you readied everything you need to make the transfer?"

Gupton stared down at his fingernails. "We completed the preliminaries this morning. The money's ready to go as soon as we can get the satellite uplink, which will take about twenty minutes advance warning. Then it's PTB."

"PTB?" Lynch asked.

"Push the button," Adkins explained. "Five million bucks. Whoosh."

"Whoosh," Lynch said. "Just like that."

As easy as taking a cash advance on a credit card. Only this was one advance, Lynch thought, that probably wouldn't have to be paid back. Unless, of course, there was some way to catch the guy.

▪ *CHAPTER 11* ▪

Lynch paced up Carondelet oblivious to the sidewalk hustlers, the shoppers, the suits, the freaks. He was deep in thought as he stood at the light at Canal waiting for the "Walk" signal that would start the pedestrian race across the widest boulevard in America.

He tried in his own mind to lay out the order of battle at the bank, to somehow draw a mental schematic that would help him understand how the ebb and flow of power in the division affected circumstance. He also tried to grasp the full implications of what had gone down at the bank: five million dollars entrusted to the bank by people who punched time clocks, waited tables, drove trucks. Lynch wasn't at all sure that anyone at the bank, including Carlton, had any idea what that meant to the people who sweated their lives away in jobs they lived with only because they had no choice.

As the lights changed and he began the brisk walk toward the concrete median three lanes away, Lynch thought that it was kind of like the federal deficit. Silent and beguiling, no one would ever pay much attention to it until it rose up out of the muck and slime of the swamp and dragged us all back under, to devour us in its own sweet time like a gator with a poodle who happened to be swimming in the wrong place at the wrong time. The media gave more attention to routine street muggings than it did to this sort of thing. Not good copy. Not exciting enough.

He crossed to the other side of Canal, then began the two-block long walk to the Audubon Building. The cool of the morning had dissipated now, and while it was a long way from the sweltering, suffocating heat of August, it was still warm enough to shed jackets.

Lynch entered his building and nodded to the security guard, who no longer required his signature on the visitor's log. He stepped into the elevator and pushed the button for the fourth floor. A few moments later, he was passing the door to his new office.

He walked to the end of the hall and made a right. Two doors down, he knocked on Mr. Adams door. There was a grumbling and shaking from inside, then a dark fuzzy hulk blocked out the creamy light through the frosted glass.

"Yeah?" Adams mumbled, as if he'd just been awakened.

"Jack Lynch, Mr. Adams. Brought your check by."

The doorknob rattled, then turned.

"Yeah, c'mon in." Adams's clothes were wrinkled, his pants bunched around the crotch.

Lynch followed him in, pulling out his checkbook. "Two months in all, right?"

"Yeah," Adams answered. He went behind his desk and spread his massive arms out, stretching and yawning.

"Looks like I caught you at a bad time," Lynch said. "Sorry."

"Don't worry about it. It's dead around here today. I need to lock up and go on home."

Lynch scribbled the check and handed it to him. Adams opened up a black ledger in front of him and noted the date, amount, and number of the check. Then he wrote out a generic receipt, the kind available in any drugstore, and tore it loose. His huge, hairy hand came across the desk toward Jack.

"I got the boys to bring you a desk and a couple, three chairs up. Filing cabinet, too. The lease hasn't been typed up yet, though. The building owner's secretary takes care of that."

"No problem," Lynch said. "I'll pick it up later."

Adams had been true to his word: there was an old desk and three chairs shoved into the back office, along with a dented green filing cabinet against one wall. It looked like the floor had been swept as well. All in all, the place looked pretty damned dreary, but Lynch reckoned that he would have to live with it until something else opened up.

He picked up the dusty black fifties-vintage phone to call Maud and held it to his ear. The handset was silent, and like in the movies, Lynch flicked his fingers a few times on the switchhook, as if that could bring it to life.

"Oh, hell," he muttered, then remembered the telephone lady telling him it would take twenty-four hours to activate the line.

Lynch sat in one of the chairs and put his feet up on his new desk. The five million was history; that, he felt, was for sure. The only option was to shut down the entire computer system, which meant shutting down the bank. And that would be hard to do without drawing more heat than they could handle.

But that didn't mean the trail ended there. Somebody out there was about to come into five million dollars that they didn't have before. That would be equally hard to do without drawing down some heat. Lynch wondered if there were any way he could find the bomber. He was, after all, a public relations consultant, not a cop. But then again, no one else had tried. There hadn't been time yet. All they could do was pay up and hope to God it didn't happen again, like an immigrant newsstand owner in the Quarter paying protection money to the mob.

But where to start? If this was a conspiracy from the inside, Lynch had a hard time believing that Adkins would be a part of it. He didn't seem the type. On the other hand, he thought, what the hell *was* the type of person who could extort five million out of a bank?

He still didn't believe it. But Adkins was part of the team, and there was no way he could go behind Gupton's back and talk to Adkins without getting nailed. He might need to get to Buford Adkins eventually, but that wasn't the first step.

Gupton and Cook were another story, though. Lynch not only believed the two of them had the ability and capacity to pull a number like this, he figured they had the egos for it as well. They were a couple of tinhorn bureaucrats in a tiny little fiefdom jockeying for power with drones who didn't stand a chance against them. Lynch had seen men like that before, men who seemed instinctively to sense their own limitations, even in some cases, their own cowardice, and who managed to rise to their own level of incompetence by cleating the suckers who were even less worthwhile than themselves. Gupton and Cook were a couple of textbook corporate powermongers, siphoning off the work and talents of others like bottom-feeding scum suckers. If they were involved in this, Lynch fantasized, and he could bring them down, he'd do it with relish.

But none of this was helping him now. He needed to crack the loop, and he knew he was never going to crack it from inside. He needed to hammer away from the outside. That meant finding another crack.

What was that guy's name, he thought. Brown, the night lead computer operator. Sometimes the guys down in the trenches knew more than the suits in the office. Yeah, that was it. Martin Brown. Cook plainly had disliked him, which meant that Brown was probably all right. And if Cook had made life rough for Martin Brown, as Lynch could imagine him doing to almost anyone, then maybe Martin Brown would be willing to help him. But first, he had to find him. Carlton had agreed to get him a list of all computer department personnel, but it hadn't arrived yet.

Lynch dropped his feet to the floor and climbed stiffly out of the office chair. He reached down and pulled the telephone off the white pages.

"Great," Lynch muttered. "Last year's directory."

He flipped through the pages to the Bs. There were two Martin Browns and one M. Brown listed. Lynch jotted the numbers down in his notebook. If Martin Brown didn't even come on duty until nighttime, he might still be home. If he was still in the sack, Lynch thought, he was about to be abruptly awakened.

* * *

The third call found him. The first two were answering machines, but on the third, the indisputably groggy voice of a night-shift worker answered. Lynch let the voice ask hello twice, then hung up the pay phone.

Lynch glanced at the notepad in his hand: Lowerline Street, uptown. He mentally figured the blocks and estimated Martin Brown lived closer to St. Charles than South Claiborne. He shoved the notepad inside his jacket pocket and plodded off to retrieve his car.

From where he was, it was easier to maneuver over to Claiborne Avenue and head uptown that way, rather than fight the increasingly thick, near-rush-hour traffic out St. Charles. He pulled onto the overpass with the engine whining. The clutch had started slipping lately; if he didn't wind the gears out completely before shifting, the slipping was worse.

To his left, the Louisiana Superdome sat silver and gray under an overcast sky. Lynch remembered when the dome had first gone up; he had covered the construction as a newspaper story, amid rumors of graft, corruption, bid-rigging, and the padding of construction costs and budgets. But the Superdome had gone up anyway, more or less on schedule, and while it had once dominated the New Orleans skyline, the new office buildings and the towering Poydras Plaza now seemed almost to dwarf it. Nearly twenty years had passed, and neither the edifice nor Lynch had aged particularly well. Great brown streaks ran down the side of the structure that once dominated, but now merely imposed. The governor was proposing a costly renovation, but no one knew where the millions would come from.

The traffic slowed as it funnelled off the overpass. Lynch downshifted, feeling the wind on his face. Patches of sunlight broke through the clouds; perhaps the almost daily spring-time rains would skip today. Lynch felt warmth and excitement; the city was beginning to feel like home again. He hadn't realized he'd been gone so long, not in time or space, but in heart and thought. He had gone away, run away perhaps, but whatever had driven him away had also allowed him to come back. The city felt like a comfortable, yet frayed, old sweater.

Lowerline Street was narrow, with potholes and swellings that made driving it resemble riding a bucking horse. Houses on either side of him were pushed in close to the street, with lush trees and overhang everywhere. He pressed on a block at a time, until he crossed Willow and began searching for the house number. He weaved his way in between the parked cars, at times with only the thickness of a coat of paint separating him from a collision.

The house was on the right, a duplex with entrance doors on either side of a wooden porch trimmed in ornate Victorian gingerbread scrollwork. The grass was close-cropped, well-maintained. He parked the car and stepped onto the curb, then walked up the brick sidewalk. Two polished brass mailboxes were nailed directly to the house. The one to the left had a tape label which read "Brown."

Lynch stopped at the door and listened for a second. There was no sign of activity; no television or radio. He folded his right hand into a fist and rapped his knuckles on the green wooden screen door. The door was loose on its hinges, and rattled within the jamb. If anyone was home, they'd hear it.

Silence. He pushed the knuckle of his middle finger forward and banged on the door again. Inside, he heard someone coughing, then a light switch flicked on.

"Hold on," a muffled voice said from inside.

A young man, perhaps mid-twenties, rail skinny, with greasy sandy hair hanging down in his face, no shirt, khakis that looked like they'd been slept in, pulled the door open and looked sleepily through the screen.

"Martin Brown?"

"Yeah," the man said. There was a huge glop of sleep in one eye and he badly needed a shave.

"Are you the Martin Brown that works at the bank?"

"Yeah," Brown said, his voice a little more suspicious.

"My name's Jack Lynch. I've been hired by the bank to look into the problems they've been having down in the computer room lately."

Brown raised his head and squinted at Jack. "What problems? What're you talking about?"

"You know what I'm talking about," Lynch said, smiling. "C'mon. . . ."

Martin Brown looked as if he were into some serious pondering. "You got any identification?"

Lynch shrugged. "Sure, driver's license. I'm not a cop or anything. I'm a consultant. All I need is a few minutes of your time. I know you were asleep and all—"

Jack looked at his watch. "But you were going to have to get up soon, anyway. Right?"

As Brown looked through the screen, a sneer slowly crawled across his face. "You guys are something, you know. Last two weeks, I get called in early nearly every day. Work all kinds of fucking overtime. Now they're sending guys to my house."

"Nobody sent me, Mr. Brown. I'm on my own. This was totally my idea, and I think you'd serve us both well by not mentioning my visit to any of your coworkers."

Lynch could tell by the look on Brown's face that this had aroused his curiosity. He hesitated for a moment, scanning the screen door as if it alone held answers for him. He reached up and lifted the metal hook out of its eye, then pushed the door open.

"Thanks," Lynch said, as he walked in to the small, yet neatly furnished apartment.

"Give me just a minute," Martin Brown said. "I'll put on some coffee. You want some?"

"Sure." Lynch walked further into the living room. In the far corner of the room, next to a shelved open cabinet that held a large TV monitor, a stereo tuner, and a compact disc player, sat a small desk, the kind a college student would have in a dorm room. Piles of books and boxes of floppy disks were on the floor next to it. And on the desktop sat a computer next to what he assumed was a printer. Lynch couldn't tell anything about it from looking at it, but he saw that a thin gray telephone cord ran from behind the computer to a phone plug in the wall.

Martin Brown padded barefoot across the oak floor behind him. "Coffee water's on. When it boils, turn it off. I gotta brush my teeth and put on a shirt."

"Don't do it on my account."

Brown turned at the door into the hallway. "I'm not. Like you said, I gotta go to work."

Lynch surveyed the apartment. Everything was neat, too orderly. None of it fit. Guy like Brown ought to have a pile of smelly laundry piled on the couch and a cardboard container full of yesterday's dinner growing mold on the coffee table. Maybe a few empty beer bottles scattered around, or an ashtray with a roach clip in it.

From the kitchen, the slow whistle of a tea kettle grew louder. Lynch turned, walked past an oak dining room table and chairs, and into the kitchen. The light attached to the overhead ceiling fan hit the table at just the right angle, and Lynch could see a clear, recently buffed layer of shine on it. No smudges, no dust.

The sound of running water from the bathroom stopped and Martin Brown walked back into the living room, buttoning the last two bottom buttons of a sort-of-pressed shirt as he came through the doorway.

"What've you got here, instant?" Lynch asked.

"Yeah, in the cabinet above you. Pull down a couple of cups, too."

Lynch pulled the cabinet door open. "Nice place you got here."

"Thanks. My wife does most of it."

"Oh, you married, huh?"

"Yeah, almost two years now."

Lynch handed Martin Brown a cup. "I thought you looked kind of young to be long-married. How you like it?"

Brown scooped a huge teaspoon of coffee into his cup, then added boiling water. "It's okay, I guess. My work schedule, we don't see that much of each other."

The two men carried coffee cups into the living room. Lynch sat down on the couch and started to set his cup on the table.

"Oh, wait a second," Martin said, pulling a drawer open in

a dark mahogany table against the wall. "Use a coaster. My wife'll kill us both, you get a ring on that table."

Lynch thought it odd that someone married so young, for such a short time, should sound like such a long-timer.

"Sorry," Jack said, sliding the coaster over and setting his cup on it. Brown sat opposite him, in a new Queen Anne chair, cradling his cup in his hands, and gazed down at the steam rising off the surface.

"So what can I do for you, Mr. Lynch?"

"I was at a meeting this afternoon with Harold Gupton, Ken Cook, and Buford Adkins."

"I knew about the meeting. I was cordially not invited to it." There was an irritating edge to Brown's voice.

Lynch leaned forward, his elbows on his knees. "I get the feeling there's a lot of meetings like that."

"Yeah, they've pretty well cut me out of the loop. Not that I give a damn."

Lynch thought to himself that when people insisted they didn't give a damn, they usually did. "There seems to be a little hostility between you and Ken Cook."

"If you want to define hostility as ripping a guy's face off."

"I think that qualifies. Tell me, Martin, what's really going on down there. From your point of view."

"From my point of view, there's a bunch of bogus assholes running things down there and nobody knows why any of this has happened." Brown's eyes flitted around the floor as he became agitated.

"Any of what has happened?"

Brown sneered over the top of his coffee cup. "I know they've had some kind of computer sabotage down there. It's all over the rumor mill. I could have told you without the rumors, though."

"Yeah, how?"

"I've seen how screwed up things have been down there lately. The Certificate of Deposits report missing, the inquiries on checking account balances and unexplained adjustments. Hell, I know my people aren't screwing things up. Has to be something weird going on."

Jack stared at Martin Brown. Something in his eyes made him think Martin knew more than he was saying.

"Do you know how it happened? Did you plant that virus in the mainframe? If you did, maybe I can help you." Lynch spoke softly, trying to sound reassuring.

"No, I didn't plant the damned virus," Brown said. "Besides, it's not a virus in the first place."

"Not a virus? What is it?"

"You've been studying computer science by reading *Newsweek* and watching "Nightline", haven't you?" Brown had the annoying habit of adopting a tone of voice that made you want to slap him.

"Okay, I admit I'm ignorant. Set me straight."

Brown snickered. "Right, dude. I got my first computer twelve years ago. I was thirteen. I've been on one every day since. And you want me to educate you this afternoon."

"Try it, without getting too technical."

"Get real." Where had Lynch heard that tone of voice before? Oh, yeah, he thought, Jeff Spicoli, *Fast Times At Ridgemont High*.

"Listen," Lynch said abruptly, "a hacker has broken into the computer system of one of my clients and committed major league sabotage! That may not bother you. Maybe you got an attitude problem. But I'm being paid to find out whatever I can about it. And if you're not going to help, fine. Screw off."

Lynch stood up abruptly and walked toward the front door. His hand was on the doorframe, when Brown's voice came at him again, this time considerably subdued.

"It wasn't a hacker."

Lynch stopped, turned, faced the man. "What?"

"It wasn't a hacker."

Lynch took two steps toward Brown, hesitated, then sat back down on the couch.

"Then just who in the hell was it?"

CHAPTER 12

Brown stood up, set his coffee cup down on his desk, and paced back and forth.

"Hackers don't do that shit," he protested. "I'm a hacker. I admit it. Hackers are like moles; they like to see where the tunnel leads. That doesn't mean they're the ones that make your house fall down."

"You're losing me again."

"Let me explain it to you." Brown dropped to the floor, scooted over and sat cross-legged across the coffee table from Lynch.

"There's so much bullshit out there, it's hard to know where to start. Okay, look. The first thing you got to understand is that a virus is a programming technique. It's called a 'Trojan Horse,' from that ancient battle in, where was it. . . ."

"Troy," Lynch said.

"Yeah, whatever. Anyway, probably every computer program ever written has a Trojan Horse in it, a set of hidden commands, a back door to get into the program in case something screws up on the front. Maybe its an undocumented command, something only the programmer knows about. So you see, a virus is a specialized kind of Trojan Horse. It 'infects' another computer by copying itself onto a disk or going through a modem—"

"Okay, I know what a modem is." Lynch interrupted.

"Oh, great, we're getting somewhere. The virus copies itself from computer to computer, and the virus can be a set of instructions that can do harmless stuff or bad stuff. It just depends on the guy that wrote it."

"The hacker that wrote it."

"No! Hackers like to push computers to the limit. They like to maybe break in, look around, leave a few messages on the bulletin board. It's *wormers* that plant bombs."

"What?" Lynch said, frustrated. "You're just playing word games with me."

"Everything's a word game, when you come down to it. Right? Just listen to me. A virus is a program that plants itself on your hard disk and goes off when you least expect it. What got stuck in the mainframe wasn't a virus at all, it was a worm. A worm is like a virus, except that it's designed to bypass computer security and enter the software itself. It doesn't just hide on the disk. It's buried deep in a hundred thousand other instructions to the computer."

"So what's the diff—"

"If it were a virus, we could disinfect for it. You find where the virus is, you wipe that part of the disk clean. Ta-da, you're home free. No problem."

"But this . . . this worm, it becomes part of your normal system software?"

"That's usually the way it's done," Brown said. "I'm not sure what happened here, because the wormer buried it someplace we can't find it. But I know it's there."

"You? How do you know it's there?"

"I've been looking for it," Brown said. "Late at night. When the operators are gone. Trying to get my ass out of hot water. They all think I did it down there. I know more about programming than most of them, anyway. Freaking trade school graduates, all except for Adkins."

"A wormer," Lynch said, thinking. "Did you know there'd been a note? From the . . . wormer?"

"Nah, like I said, I'm too far out of the loop. I just catch the shit when something goes wrong. I don't get to be part of the fraternity." Brown pasted a look of disgust on his face, then ran a hand through his hair.

"The instructions in the bomber's note said you guys were to create an electronic mailbox for Vernon Wormer. He'd leave instructions on how to defuse the bomb there."

Martin Brown erupted into roaring laughter. His thin shoulders trembled, he rolled on his haunches onto his back, his legs still crossed in the air, and slapped at the floor.

"Oh, God, I love it!" he yelled. "I just fucking love it."

"Yeah," Lynch said. "A criminal with a sense of humor."

"You know what else?" Martin spat between guffaws.

"What?"

"He likes movies. . . ."

"What do you mean?"

"Vernon Wormer," Brown cackled. *Animal House.* Vernon Wormer was the dean of Faber College!"

Lynch thought for a moment. "Oh, yeah. Years ago, I—"

"Me, too," Brown howled. "God, my whole college career was based on that movie!"

"So we already know several things about the guy. First, he knows programming inside out. Second, he's got a warped sense of humor. Third, he's young enough to have identified with *Animal House.* You know what, Martin?"

"What?"

"He sounds like you."

Brown's laughter stopped. "Wait a minute. . . ."

"Be cool," Lynch said. "Just an observation. I don't know why, but for the time being, I'm willing to trust you. If you were the bomber, you probably wouldn't have let me in the door."

"Unless I was trying to throw you off the track."

"You're not helping your case any," Lynch said, smiling. He finished the last of his coffee and leaned back on the couch. He looked thoughtful for a moment, then rubbed his eyes. "The problem is that I don't really know where to start."

"That's okay. None of those other assholes did either."

"All I can do is start digging into backgrounds, see if it leads anywhere. May as well start at the top."

"If there's anybody on the inside that had anything to do with this, it was Ken Cook. I wouldn't put anything past that sonofabitch."

"I don't mean to pry, but as good as you are, why are you wasting your time as a computer operator at a bank? Working the night shift, no less."

Brown looked away, first at his coffee cup, then at the window. "Beats me. I hate it. Maybe one of these days, I'll break off, start my own business or something. I'd like to be in development, writing new software or something. Be the next Bill Gates or Wozniak. I got an attitude problem, I admit it. But right now, I need the money. My wife wants to buy a house. Maybe have a kid. I got no capital. We're in a recession. . . . Should I go on?"

"Yeah, life's a bitch, right?" Lynch said.

"And in about an hour, it's going to be a lot bigger bitch if I don't start getting ready for work. What time you got?"

Lynch looked down at his watch. "Almost four-thirty. I thought you didn't go in until later."

"Forced overtime for the peons. Only way we can take care of everything without our backup routines. Hell, I got to get moving," Martin said, jumping up. "If Patí doesn't get home on time, I have to take the streetcar. This time of day, it's liable to take an hour to get downtown."

"Who?" Lynch asked quizzically.

"Patí," Brown said. "My wife."

Lynch smiled. "She sounds like a New Orleans native."

"Born and bred right here in the city. Sisters of Immaculate Conception High, Class of '85; University of New Orleans, Class of '90."

"What's she do?"

"She's an aerobics instructor out in Metairie."

"Tell you what," Lynch offered, "she doesn't get here in a little bit, I'll give you a ride downtown."

"Really? You don't mind?"

"I could go that way, anyway. Besides, I have a feeling you

and I are going to be talking a lot in the next couple of weeks."

"Think so, huh?"

"How'd you like to be my eyes and ears in the data processing division?"

Brown hooked his thumbs in the belt loop on each side of his hips, then cocked his head. "A spook, huh? What the hell, I'm probably going to get fired anyway. May as well go out as a whistleblower."

Lynch grinned. "That's the spirit."

"Let me jump in the shower. Just take a minute. Here," he said, pulling a thin, saddle-stitched book from a stack on his desk, "take a look at this."

Lynch grabbed the copy in midair as it came sailing toward him.

The title read *Computer Sabotage: Viruses, Worms, Data Diddlers, and Other Boogies That Can Wreck Your Computer.* As Martin Brown turned on the shower and closed the bathroom door behind him, Lynch began turning the pages.

He was three-quarters through the book before he knew it. There was a whole world out there that he, and most citizens, knew nothing about. Computer systems are infinitely more vulnerable than people imagine. Even the government isn't safe. And the most surprising thing of all, Lynch noted, was that computer thieves steal upward of $5 billion a year, and that only about 20 percent of the crimes are ever reported.

"Particularly for banks," he read, "a successful fraud that gets exposed in the media is a public relations catastrophe."

"No kidding," he whispered.

"No kidding, what?"

Lynch jerked at the sound of the voice. He had been so engrossed in the book he hadn't heard the key in the lock. The young woman standing in front of him, hands on her hips, canvas workout bag over her shoulder, was stonefaced. She was also about five-eight, early twenties, maybe 105 pounds, with the body of a serious aerobics instructor. Except for the teased blonde pile of hair that was moussed into a high, glossy spray, she was perfect. And the hot neon pink and purple bodysuit she was wearing, with a tight pair of cutoffs rendering her almost street legal, didn't hide very much of that perfection.

"Oh, hi," Lynch stammered.

"Who are you?" she demanded. Her voice was high, tinged with that bizarre cross of Cajun and Brooklyn that marked one of the more prominent native New Orleans accents. Back during his university days, his frat brothers called them "yats," for their universal greeting: "Where ya't?"

"I'm Jack Lynch," he said, struggling not to stare at the pair of erect nipples under the Spandex. He stood up awkwardly, the booklet on his lap sliding onto the floor. "I was here talking to Martin and I offered him a ride to work because he was afraid you might be late."

Her face softened and she smiled to show a row of flawless, glistening white teeth. "Well, Jack Lynch, keep your seat. I'm Patí, I'm home, and you're off the hook."

She turned and walked away from him, her hips swaying only slightly as she walked. She slid the canvas bag off her shoulder and onto the dining room table, then disappeared into the kitchen.

"By the way," she called from the kitchen, "you're a lot more presentable than most of Marty's other friends."

Lynch felt his jaw go slack. *I'm forty years old,* he thought. *I can't take this.*

■ *CHAPTER 13* ■

I've been in that building," Maud complained. "There used to be a dentist there. He was about seventy years old and his drill wasn't much younger than that. I went in there once with a broken tooth. He tried to drill it out without giving me any novocaine."

Lynch's eyes widened. "You serious?"

"Yeah, he had this gruff voice and was real big. He was one of these old men that didn't shave every day and his breath smelled like yesterday's cigarette smoke. And he bent over me and said 'It won't hurt that much. It'll be over in a minute.' He laid that drill into me and as soon as he did, I kicked out so hard his tray of tools went flying. He said 'All right, I'll give you a shot.' And I said 'the hell you will,' and got out of there fast."

Lynch took the cup of coffee she handed him and settled back on her living room couch. Maud sat on a chair across from him and set her cup on a small table next to her.

"I can see why you wouldn't want to go to work there again."

"Oh, hell, it'll be okay. I don't know what's the matter with me. Every damn little thing seems to get on my nerves."

"You've been through a lot the past couple weeks. It'd set anybody on edge."

Maud had put away the black dress. She was wearing a

faded pair of jeans and a purple rayon blouse. Lynch had never seen her in jeans before. Every time he'd been to her house, she'd worn house dresses that some might call comfortable, others just frumpy. She looked younger now, Lynch thought, even attractive.

She looked across the top of her cup, locked eyes with him and darkened her face. "I know what it is. And I don't like it."

"What, Maud? What's going on?"

"Jack, I'm fifty-seven years old," she said. "And I been married to Pelletier since I was twenty-two. We didn't have a bad marriage, but it wasn't exactly a thrill a minute either. I missed out on a lot to stay in that marriage. Now that he's gone, I can't decide whether I'm mad at him for leaving me or—"

"Or?"

"Relieved," she said, her eyes filming over. "This is terrible, but somehow I'm almost excited at the notion of being able to start over. Get out, do things."

Lynch smiled at her. "Hell, Maud, there ain't nothing wrong with that."

"Yeah there is. I'm supposed to be missing him, grieving, lighting candles at the church for him every day."

"You've got a life, Maud," Lynch insisted. "This isn't India; we don't throw widows on the funeral pyre here."

"I feel so guilty," she said.

Lynch got up, walked over to her chair, knelt down in front of it and laid his hand on her forearm. She felt thin beneath his touch, fragile.

"C'mon back to work," he said. "Find something to occupy your time. Let this stuff ride for awhile, give yourself a little time to get used to your new situation. You feel guilty now, but my guess is you're going to wind up feeling a lot of stuff you haven't felt in a while. Just go with it."

He squeezed her arm. She smiled at him.

"How come your so damn smart giving advice to somebody else, and so damn dumb when it comes to taking it yourself."

He looked shocked. "What do you mean?"

"Life goes on, right. But what kind of life you living now? You ain't got anybody, either."

"Well, that's different, I—"

"How's it different?" she demanded.

"Well, I—"

She leaned forward in the chair, her face only a few inches from his. She held his chin in her free hand, looked straight into his eyes. "I wonder how you've managed to make it through the past couple years. I never seen a man lose everything so hard like you have. People you love, things you need. I think I got it figured out, though."

He smirked at her. "Got me figured out, have you?"

"Yeah, I think you just locked down. You're not going to let any of this get you down because you're not going to let any of it inside you. The lights in your heart are on, but there's nobody home."

Lynch's smirk faded. A pained look came across his face. "Maud, whatever's happened, happened. There's nothing I can do about it. I live with it just fine. I—"

He became silent, her hand brushed flat against the left side of his face now, his still on her arm. Her face softened, relaxed, as she stared at him. He took his right hand off her arm, found it straying onto the shoulder of the smooth, shiny blouse. The texture of the cloth was like silk, her shoulder slight and warm. His hand slid down just a bit, to her shoulder blade, and subtly, almost unnoticeably, he pulled her toward him.

They kissed. Softly at first, their eyes closing, her lips warm, wet, their heads cocked at opposing angles. Lynch found his heart racing, the question of just what the hell he was doing remaining unanswered as all conscious thought momentarily vanished.

He did not know how long they kissed, only that the feel of his lips on hers was a caress as soft as the stroke of his hand on the blouse. He felt her shake slightly, then pull away with a sharp intake of breath.

"Oh, my goodness," Maud whispered.

Lynch became instantly abrupt, backing away from her a couple of feet. "Ohmigod, Maud, I'm sorry, I—"

"No, it's, it's. . . ." She seemed lightheaded, dizzy.

"I'm really sorry," he stammered. "That was a *really* bad idea. I don't know what got into me. I, just, I don't know."

"Stop throwing clichés at me," she said, her voice back to reality. "I enjoyed it as much as you did. That's the first time anyone's kissed me like that in thirty years. My God, has it been that long? But you're right, it's a bad idea. Maybe you should go."

Jack stood up, turned his back to her as he strode over to the couch. He picked up his coffee cup and sipped at the cold liquid, then stared out the front door, wanting to say something but not knowing how to say it, or even if he really knew what it was. He heard the sound of cushions squishing and her footsteps as she came up behind him. She put her right hand on his shoulder and laid the other one on the left side of his waist. He felt her turn her head to the right and lay against his back, her head barely reaching his shoulders, the side of her face warm against him, the feel of her cheek sharp through his shirt.

"We're okay. Don't fret. But it is time for you to go."

He pulled away, then turned to face her. Her cheeks were flushed, her eyes bright. He wanted to stay with her, realized suddenly that he wanted her. Where, he wondered, do these aches come from?

"We'll still work together, won't we?"

She laughed. "Of course. I need the money and God knows you need the help."

He grinned, shook his head as if to clear thought from his mind. "No need to come in tomorrow. There's not even a phone yet. Besides, you probably need a few more days."

"I need to get busy. That'll be the best thing for me. But you call me when you need me. I'll be there."

He laid the coffee cup down, then grabbed his jacket off the arm of the couch. "I know you will, Maud. You always have been."

She patted him on the back. "You go on now. And call me when you're ready for me to come in."

Lynch pulled the door open, then threw his coat over his shoulder. "Take care, Maud. I'll call you."

As Jack Lynch pulled away from the curb, Maud stood on the porch watching him. The sun was going down; the day's heat was beginning to dissipate into a warm spring evening. The air felt lighter than usual, clearer than it had been in quite awhile.

Maud watched him until he disappeared up Freret Street, then wrapped her arms around her shoulders and hugged herself tightly. She wondered if he would call again. Nothing that boy did ever surprised her.

Jack forced himself to think about the First Interstate Bank and its multimillion dollar ransom as he turned right onto South Carrollton. He didn't know where to start. There was something bothering him about all this. He felt an uneasiness, a hint of something troublesome in the day that he couldn't quite put his finger on. He dodged cars and shifted gears as if on automatic pilot. Five million dollars, he thought. A five followed by six zeroes. More money than he could imagine, more than most people could imagine. It was chump change to a Donald Trump—or was back before he started shopping at K-Mart—or a Ross Perot, but to your average American grind, with a job he hated and kids he didn't understand and a wife that didn't feel anything when he walked through the door at the end of the day, wanting only a cold beer and a little silence, five million dollars was undeniably a hell of a lot of money.

And it was a lot of money to lose. Even for a bank, with hundreds of millions, maybe even billions, in capitalization, five million was a bleeder that would take one hell of a tourniquet to quell. Lynch drummed his fingers on the steering wheel. What would he do if he had to tell his employer: "Uh, hey, boss, I'm real sorry about this, but I just, well, I, uh, just lost you five big ones. . . ."?

And how would he feel if one of his employees strolled calmly into his office to inform him that the company had five million dollars less today than it had yesterday.

"I'd want to hold off my own heart attack long enough to

strangle the guy," Lynch said out loud over the whine of the engine. He reached down and turned on the radio, then punched the button for the public radio station that played traditional New Orleans jazz. Louis Armstrong's gravelly voice mixed in with the grinding of the engine: audio gumbo. Lynch thought of all his years in New Orleans, of all the time he'd spent here in a kind of dreamlike haze. The city promoted, nurtured, that level of consciousness. They didn't call this The Big Easy for nothing. "The City That Care Forgot" fostered, maybe even invented, the sensual stupor. It was the kind of place where a forty-year-old man could melt into the lips of a fifty-seven-year-old woman and forget everything, just let the sleaze and the corruption and the graft slide down like a freshly-shucked, still-quivering oyster.

He should have been more upset about all this. Just like Gupton and Cook should have been more upset. They were the top two men in a department that just lost an amount of money that would have fed both their families for five generations.

Jack looked at his watch: 4:02. Two minutes earlier, the five million had been zapped across land and sea and outer space with the push of a button. No filthy cash here to haul around, get one's hands dirty on, risk going through customs or an urban encounter with a less classy sleazeball. This was a twenty-first-century Billy the Kid with an IBM clone instead of a Colt .45.

Something stank. The faint stench of hidden rot was beginning to fill his nostrils. Jack Lynch's brow tightened as his suspicions grew. Carlton Smith, who was preparing to retire and wash his hands of the whole mess, had been apoplectic at the loss. It wasn't even his responsibility. But Harold Gupton, the vice-president for data processing of the First Interstate Bank of Louisiana, did not appear to be bothered by the fact that someone had just held him up for five million. Given his position with the lottery commission, he should have been purple with hysteria. And Kenneth Cook, the man responsible for maintaining the security and integrity of the bank's computer system, was not only not upset, he didn't even seem to break stride.

A man lets something like that slide off him as easy as water off a duck's back, Lynch thought, *there has to be one good reason.*

▪ *CHAPTER 14* ▪

Jack Lynch awoke to horses stampeding inside his skull. He became aware of the pain even before he was fully awake, the ache ebbing and flowing with each pulse of his heart. His mouth was dry, thick, fur-laden. A wave of nausea slid over him like a spirit passing through. He groaned, and even the sound of his own voice hurt. He opened one eye and squinted in the harsh light; the first image that formed on the backs of his eyes had a green stripe across it, and about two fingers of amber below it.

He didn't realize he'd had so much to drink the night before. He remembered parking the car and walking up the walk. P.J. Campbell had been sitting on the gallery above him in a white rattan chair, the morning's *Times-Picayune* flapped open in her lap. She'd waved, smiled down at him prettily. He waved back, brightened at seeing her. It had been a good day, given the circumstances. But his mood had darkened after that. He had gone upstairs, changed into a pair of jeans and a T-shirt, then opened a fresh Scotch bottle and a quart of club soda. The first one had been marvelous, a welcome reward for getting through the day. It was cold and refreshing in the heat of his apartment, which had not yet cooled from the day's baking. It had gone down quickly, followed by a second. By the third, he was thinking to himself that he needed to slow down, to eat something. But an old black-

and-white film noire classic had come on Channel 36, and he found himself settling into a chair with the glass in one hand and a cigarette in the other. By the time the movie was over, food was far from his mind. He didn't remember the end of the film, only that it was dark and violent. His mood had darkened further, so he had cracked open another ice tray.

As he lay there in bed suffering, Jack Lynch realized he could not remember going to bed, could not remember undressing or turning off the television or having his last drink or finishing the last cigarette in his pack.

He sweated, each attempt to move another stab of pain behind his eyes. Something came up out of the haze and grabbed him hard in his chest. He wondered for a moment if he were having a heart attack; men in their forties could do that, he knew. But then he realized that it was not his heart that was cramping up on him; the pang was lower than that. It was in his gut that he felt the spasm, and the spasm was fear. He recognized the fear for what it was, for it had been on him before. For the first time in his life, Jack Lynch was starting to be unable to remember things when he drank. That had never happened to him before. He had always been able to hold his liquor, to exercise to almost a neurotic degree absolute control over his drinking even when it was excessive. But since last year, since he'd left the city almost running, and since his mother's death, he had felt for the first time that absolute control slipping away from him.

The thought scared the hell out of him.

He rolled over in bed, determined to take his punishment. "You were stupid enough to drink that much," he said out loud, "now be man enough to take your licks."

Besides, he remembered, there was too much to do today. At least, he could remember that.

While the coffee brewed, he swallowed three aspirin with two large glasses of ice water. Then he stepped into the shower, the spray hard on his back and pounding against his skull. The noise alone seemed deafening. He cracked his neck, twisting his head from side to side to work out the kinks. Jack Lynch felt every second of his age and then some.

He got out of the shower and reached for the towel, then stood there nude and dripping as he wiped off the mirror. He'd taken a shower in the dark, the light still a bit much for his tender eyes. He flipped the switch, squinting in the white light until his sight adjusted.

He stared coldly into the mirror. In his eyes, tiny veins wandered cracked and broken in the far corners of his eyeballs, and toward the middle, closest to his nose, a solid mass of red floated beneath the surface. His skin was still smooth when he relaxed his face, but when he wrinkled his brow, the wrinkles were deep enough now to be furrows, and they spread farther out than ever before. The flesh on his face seemed to be sinking; he imagined himself being described one day as "jowly," and felt another twinge of pain at the thought.

"Jesus," he muttered to his own image, "get a grip."

He was patting his hair dry when the phone rang. He stepped out into his bedroom with an open bathrobe draped over his shoulders, like a beaten prizefighter. The clock read 9:45. Half the day was gone, he scolded himself, as he reached quickly for the phone. He didn't think his head could stand another ring.

"Yeah," he said into the phone.

"Jack? This is Carlton Smith, did I wake you?"

"Oh, no, Carlton. I've been up for awhile. I just don't sound awake until about noon."

"I just wanted to touch base with you on our problem downstairs."

Lynch sat on the edge of the bed, wishing he'd brought a cup of coffee in before he answered the phone. "Yeah?"

"The wire transfer went off on schedule and receipt was confirmed. Gupton called me a few minutes ago and said that at four this morning, a message was left in an electronic mailbox by modem containing instructions for defusing the bomb."

"Did they execute the instructions? Is everything okay?"

"Gupton said everything went according to plan."

Lynch thought for a second. "How convenient. Carlton, can you fix it so I can get into the bank after hours?"

"After hours? Why would you want to get into the bank after hours?"

"Let's say I might need some information from the people down in data processing after six. I might not want to wait for the bank to open the next morning. Can you fix it with security?"

"That might take a little doing," Carlton said, hesitating. "Besides, Gupton and all the programmers are gone at night anyway."

"So maybe I don't need the information from the programmers."

"Jack, are you up to something? What's going on here?"

"You asked me to check into this, Carlton, and to find out what I can. If I'm going to do that, you're going to have to give me room to work. I won't abuse it."

"I know that." There was a moment of silence over the phone. "All right, of course I can fix it. I'll have the memo down to security this morning. But be careful, Jack."

"I will," Lynch answered. "And I'll let you know what's going on the minute I know myself."

"That was my next request."

Lynch hung up the phone, relieved to find the aspirin was starting to do its work. He coughed heavily, the previous night's cigarettes still heavy in his chest, and walked into the kitchen. He poured a cup of hot, black coffee and made a mental note to call Brown that afternoon. In the meantime, there was plenty to keep him busy.

It was not as if Louisiana was new to the lottery game. During the last decade of the nineteenth century, the Louisiana Lottery had produced some of the most scandalous and outrageous stories ever to come out of a place and time designed by its very nature to produce scandal and outrage. When the original lottery was finally shut down, and the poor unfortunates unlucky enough to be caught with their hands in the till sent off to Angola, the black mark that was left behind lasted almost seventy years. It wasn't until 1964 that anybody else—this time, New Hampshire—decided to try again.

He turned left onto Freret and began his search for a parking space close to the Tulane campus. To his left, the Tilton Library loomed like a glass and concrete mausoleum. He drove slowly down Freret, braking for the Tulane students who stepped into the street oblivious to the fact that in a battle between flesh and steel, steel usually won. He paused at the light, then turned left and entered the campus. He snaked his way through the students, past the University Center, and parked illegally in front of the Quad.

The sky darkened overhead; a thunderstorm was percolating above. The wind shifted directions at random intervals and ever-increasing speeds. The air was burdensome, but with the clarity and beauty of a storm about to happen. Lynch made sure the top was latched on his car, then rolled the windows up and pulled out a leather case with a yellow legal pad clipped inside.

Jack Lynch looked out of place. As a Tulane undergraduate, he'd worn the campus as comfortably as an old pair of jeans. But now, his dark suit, white shirt, and tie marked him as an outsider. Even the professors didn't dress that well. At the most, he was a college administrator, which in the eyes of the students, made him a nonentity. A half-dozen students in T-shirts and knee-length plaid shorts sailed a Frisbee around in the shifting wind, running and yelling to catch it as it fitfully danced around on the currents.

It seemed to him as if his college days had happened to someone else. He was a man as far removed from these children, he thought, as a visitor from another planet. He couldn't begin to imagine what he could say to them, as if any of them would be interested in listening to the thin, serious, obviously uptight man making his way up the walk toward Newcomb Hall.

Lynch turned left, went up the sidewalk to the ramp leading to the library entrance, past the Newcomb girls with their bookbags, past the racked ten-speeds, and through the glass doors. A blast of icy, dry, stale air hit him as he walked in. He took the elevator up to the third floor and found the directory for the *Times-Picayune,* then began making a list of microfilm articles to check out.

Ten minutes later, he was in the corner of a tiny office in the microfilm room, pumping dimes into a microfilm copier as the foul-smelling, wet copies rolled out.

February, 1990: FIGHT'S OVER, one headline read. MAYOR GIVES UP ON LOTTERY.

The movement toward legalized gambling was outlined in story after story in the paper. ODDSMAKERS SAYING CHANCES GOOD FOR LOTTERY THIS YEAR:

> Baton Rouge—Ask legislators, lobbyists, even the governor, and you get a wide variety of answers. But virtually everyone in the state capitol is taking bets that a state lottery will pass this year. The only question is "how fast and how much?" How fast will the legislature move, and how much is it going to cost the taxpayers?

One by one, business groups and trade associations and local governments dropped opposition to the lottery plan. To Lynch, it had the aura of sharks joining a feeding frenzy, as if after years of shrinking budgets, diminished horizons, and outright economic disaster, the state could bail itself out only by becoming one giant office pool.

Through the thick walls of the library, Lynch heard the faint boom of a thunderclap. He stood up, walked out into the anteroom of the microfilm department, and looked out the thin slats of floor-to-ceiling glass. Outside, the sky was as dark as night; sheets of rain sprayed down the windows in flooding cascades. The cold air inside the building sent a chill through him. He returned to his work, his mood darkening again.

Apparently, he learned, the feeding frenzy wasn't limited to Louisiana. SOUTHERN STATES IN RACE TO LASSO NEXT LOTTERY, one front-page headline blared. Mississippi's governor was pushing for a lottery. A bill was working its way through the state legislature that would allow offshore riverboat gambling.

So much money, Lynch thought. *So many ways to steal it.*

He rolled through the microfilm reels, the frames flashing by in scratchy, black-and-white streams that hurt his eyes and threatened to resurrect his headache. Then, as July, 1990 zipped by, a headline caught his eye and forced him to back the reel up. He'd almost missed the most important one.

Louisiana on Cutting Edge in Plans to Run State Lottery, the headline read.

> "This is big business," said State Senator Harold LeFarge. "Not your typical arm of government. And it shouldn't be run like government. It needs to be run like business."
>
> LeFarge made this statement in committee today as he announced that the Louisiana Lottery will be run by an independent corporation.
>
> Louisiana will become only the third state in the nation to transfer control of its lottery to private business. Many lottery specialists consider this the cutting edge of lottery technology, but critics charge that in giving up control of lottery operations, government officials have set up a situation that may foster graft and corruption.
>
> "Nonsense," LeFarge charged in answering his critics. The New Orleans senator, who heads the subcommittee in charge of drafting the rules for the lottery's operation, said that if the governor signs legislation enabling the state lottery—which he is expected to do—government officials will have no trouble controling any graft or corruption that might arise.

Lynch laughed softly in the harsh light of the microfilm reader. "They'll control it all right," he whispered. At the reader next to him, a blonde twenty-year-old coed cleared her throat, as if to remind Lynch that he wasn't alone in his living room, that other people could hear him talking to himself. He looked over at her blankly, stared momentarily at her bronzed legs, then returned to his work.

He finished that article, then rolled and copied his way through a half dozen more. Finding the articles was tedious, almost painful on the old, overused machines. The governor signed the legislation creating the state lottery; the members of the newly formed lottery commission then reversed an earlier decision to serve on a volunteer basis and decided to accept pay for their services. Two weeks later, a headline read: LOTTERY COMMISSION MEMBERS AMONG HIGHEST PAID. In January, 1991, barely a year earlier, Lynch read that the Louisiana Lottery Corporation was seeking a manager, and that bids were about to be let out to vendors of the computerized games. On that same page, a sidebar headline read: LOUISIANA LOTTERY DESPERATE FOR CASH—SEEKS CREDIT GUARANTEE.

Lynch read the article and compared it with his mental notes from his first meeting with Carlton Smith. This must have been right before the bank set up the line of credit. There was no other mention of the lottery being short of funds.

INSTANT LOTTO TO START THIS SUMMER the next article read. The plan was that the lottery would first offer the shiny scratch-off tickets with smaller prizes in the first few months. The next step would be a full-fledged lottery, complete with air-blown ping-pong balls on a weekly television program, and then after that, online computerized games featuring everything from poker to bingo. Ultimately, political wags were saying, Louisiana would wind up legalizing casino gambling.

Jack squeezed his tired eyes, felt the rumble in his empty stomach. He'd been at this over two hours, and he wondered if it was doing any good. Jack felt as if he were grabbing at straws, and not very solid ones at that.

There was one more article to locate. He put on the last reel of microfilm and threaded it through the pulleys under the dirty glass lens. He held the button down to spin the rotors and tried not to stare at the flickering lights charging by in front of him.

The article he was looking for was buried deep in the Metro section, apparently not considered worthy of much attention by the editors.

LOTTO CORPORATION AWARDS COMPUTER VENDING CONTRACT, the headline read, and below that, a short article:

> The Louisiana Lottery Corporation awarded a multimillion dollar contract yesterday to a new company founded last month for the purpose of developing computerized games for the next stage of the Louisiana Lottery.
>
> Gaming Corporation of America, located in Metairie, has been named the sole vendor for computerized gaming terminals. GCA President Terry Hanover announced at the press conference that a team of designers and engineers is already at work on the next phase of lottery games.
>
> According to Hanover, the first games offered will be video poker. Gaming terminals will have the capacity to play as many as twenty variations of poker, and will have the capacity to communicate with the Louisiana Lottery Corporation's centralized computer system on a daily basis without operator intervention.
>
> Hanover also said the terminals will have the capacity to report income, payouts, number of plays, as well as built-in security measures to ensure system integrity.

Lynch settled back in the chair and waited for the thermal copy of the article to tumble out of the side of the machine. He tried to lay out in his mind the schematic of the Louisiana Lottery. The legislature created a state lottery commission to form a lottery; the lottery commission formed a lottery corporation to oversee the operation, hire employees, and create, in general, another layer of bureaucracy; the lottery corporation subcontracted to every little mom-and-pop grocery store and gas station in the state to sell the tickets and run the terminals, then hired the Gaming Corporation of America to design and build the lottery terminals themselves.

It was a complex, deceptively multilayered system, he thought as he stepped through the doors and out of the building. The rain had stopped, but the trees were heavy with dripping water. He dodged puddles and drizzling branches, thinking that the more layers, the more troughs. There were a lot of mouths to be fed; you could never set a table that bountiful without making sure there was room enough for everybody.

It wouldn't, Lynch thought as he started the Fiat and began the drive to the district attorney's office, be very polite.

▪ CHAPTER 15 ▪

Jack Lynch left Tulane University for Tulane Avenue, a contrast that could not be more pronounced. The university was lush, shaded, with expensive, landscaped buildings and well-scrubbed students. Tulane Avenue was urban New Orleans to its potholed core: cheap motels, greasy diners, bail-bonding agencies, storefront law offices, gravel parking lots, and sinister neighborhoods one was better off steering clear of in the daytime, let alone at night.

Lynch pulled to a stop in front of 2700 Tulane Avenue and eased into a parking space. He hoped that by parking in front of the Orleans Parish Criminal District Courthouse, with its attendant squads of New Orleans police on the list for court appearances, he might discourage all but the cheekiest car thieves.

The rain had started, then stopped again, in successive rows of squall lines moving in from over the lake. He locked the car door and walked back up the block to South White, then turned down the short side street, at the end of which sat the new facade and the old back of Orleans Parish Prison. Fortunately, he thought, he didn't have to go that far.

Lynch walked quickly up the few short steps to the entrance of the Orleans Parish District Attorney's office building. He swung wide the glass doors and stepped into the humid lobby.

"I'd like to see Fred Williams," Jack said to the receptionist at the long table in the lobby. "My name's Jack Lynch."

"I'm sorry, Mr. Williams is in court this afternoon," the receptionist said.

"Oh," Lynch said, disappointed. "You wouldn't happen to know which division, would you?"

"No, but he's somewhere over in Criminal Court right now. You might try over there."

"Okay, thanks."

Jack walked back out into the sunshine, which seemed finally to be winning its battle over the clouds. The air was heating up now, water evaporating off street puddles in thin wisps of steam. He took off his jacket and loosened his tie, crossed the street and walked by the construction at the Orleans Parish Medical Examiner's Office.

The Orleans Parish Criminal District Court was built in 1929, and showed every moment of its age. Paint peeled from cracked plaster walls that towered so tall over the scuffed second floor that voices echoed as if in a cavern. Cobwebs as thick as broom handles hung from a ceiling so high no one could get to them. The building was once grand Art Deco, but age and use has worn it down. Like all courthouses, it was populated by hordes of police, suited lawyers, and crowds of poor blacks and whites awaiting the dispensation of justice. Lynch had been in the courthouse before, more times than he cared to remember, and each time the aura of decay seemed more pronounced, the sense of weariness overwhelming. As in so many other parts of the city, whatever meager reserves had once existed to buffer and shield from the worst ravages were long gone.

A crowd of young black men wearing satin pants and a mixture of New Orleans Saints and Chicago Bulls warm-up jackets crowded around the side entrance. The tallest one in the center of the group faced down a younger, shorter man, his voice low and sinister, his index finger in the younger man's chest. The confrontation stopped immediately when Jack opened the door and stepped into the building.

Lynch muttered "Excuse me" and walked around them.

They all stared at him, scoping him out, trying to decide if he was lawyer, plainclothes, or just ordinary citizen.

He walked quickly past them and into the long hallway of the courthouse. It was an enormous building; his chances of finding Fred Williams were not worth figuring. But, he decided, as long as he was in the neighborhood, he'd give it a try.

He walked toward the information desk at the main entrance of the building. From his left, a sharply dressed woman with a briefcase in one hand and a pile of bound papers under her other arm entered the building and turned toward him. Her head was down, dark hair in her face. As if walking down a deserted street on Saturday night, the woman was intent on getting where she was going as quickly as possible without having to make eye contact with any of the regulars.

Lynch remembered her as one of Fred's assistants. He stepped quickly over, blocking her path. She stumbled to a halt in front of him.

"Excuse me," she mumbled, stepping around him.

"I'm sorry," Jack said. "My fault. Oh, you're. . . ."

The woman looked up at him. From beneath red-framed glasses, bloodshot and stressed eyes stared at him.

"From the D.A.'s office," Lynch continued.

"Yes, and I'm—"

"Say," he interrupted, "I'm looking for Fred right now. You wouldn't happen to know which division he's in, would you?"

The woman sighed, irritated, then screwed up her face. "Let me see, Fred should be Division III this afternoon. He's got arraignments all day. Try him there."

Jack stepped out of the way as the woman slid by him. Division III was on the second floor, Judge Harvey Cole's courtroom. Cole, Jack remembered from his newspaper days, was a crusty old S.O.B. who could be a holy terror to defense and prosecutor alike. This ought to be good, he thought.

He continued down the hall, past the crowded hallway of the juvenile processing division, then up the back stairs to the second floor. Judge Cole's courtroom was the second thick wooden door to the left. The hallways of the courthouse might be peeling paint and cracking with age, but the courtrooms themselves were spotless, dark, cool, formal.

Lynch set his feet and pulled the ten-foot-high door open, stepped through the anteroom, and pulled the lighter inside door open as well. Inside the courtroom, a few spectators watched as one-by-one, men in orange jumpsuits with "OPSD" stencilled on the back were brought before Judge Cole, who sat behind the bench a full two feet higher than anyone else in the courtroom, the absolute master of his little piece of the world. At a table to the right, Fred Williams and an assistant sat in front of a stack of file folders. At a long table across from Fred, three attorneys from the Public Defender's Office pleaded the men through as quickly as possible.

As Jack sat down, a stocky black man was being led out a door to the judge's left. Judge Cole muttered something to a thin woman who sat in a chair to his right. She stood.

"Case number 43-77654, Orleans Parish versus Odell Roster," she called.

Fred Williams and a lawyer at the defense table rose simultaneously as another orange jumpsuit was led into the courtroom from a door to Judge Cole's right.

"Your honor," the P.D. said, "we have a witness we'd like to put on the stand for this one. Mr. Roster has been charged with aggravated assault and attempted murder. We can establish through this witness that Mr. Roster was nowhere near the alleged crap game where the assault allegedly took place."

"Judge," Fred replied, "the New Orleans police arrested him at the scene. He beat a man with a crowbar. When the police got there, he was trying to clean the blood off himself."

"Your honor, our witness will establish that Mr. Roster arrived on the scene after the assault and got blood on himself as a result of trying to aid the victim."

"Judge," Fred said, exasperated, "this is nothing but an attempt to delay these proceedings once again."

"I couldn't agree with you more, General Williams," Judge

Cole intoned. The judge's voice was as deep and malevolent as Lynch had remembered it, although the man's hair was now snow white and his face covered in wrinkles. "On the other hand, the man has to have his day in court. How long do you need, Mr. Johnson?"

"Ten minutes, your honor. Our witness is somewhere in the building."

"Very well," Judge Cole tapped his gavel. "But let's make it quick, gentlemen. Ten minutes doesn't mean a half-hour."

In a flurry of black robes, Judge Cole disengaged himself from his chair and disappeared through the door behind him into his chambers.

Lynch stood along with everyone else, then stepped up to the rail separating the visitor's gallery from the tables and jury box.

Fred Williams stood and stretched tiredly, his shoulders slumping as he brought his arms back down. He looked, Jack thought, like he'd been at this all day.

"Fred," he said. Williams turned, squinted his eyes at Jack, then smiled.

"Well, I'll be damned and driven to hell in a chauffeured limousine. Jack Lynch, you old son of a bitch, how are you?"

Lynch reached across the rail and took Fred's offered hand. "I'm fine, old buddy. Good to see you."

"Where the hell have you been? It's been months."

"Out of town for awhile. Out in California. Got back to town a week or so ago. I've moved, got a new place. I'll have to have you and Janey over for dinner one night."

"We'd like that, fella. Sounds like fun. Now, is this a chance encounter or have you had to hunt me down for a reason?"

"I know it's a bad time for you, Fred. I just need some information."

"Tell you what, let's go downstairs and let me get a cup of that black syrup they call coffee here. We've been at this all day long, and I swear I'm about to fall asleep on my feet."

The two men walked to the elevator and took it down to the basement. Lynch pumped thirty-five cents into a machine and handed Fred the paper cup.

"Hope nobody construes this as a bribe," Fred said, blowing across the top of the cup.

"Don't worry. You can't be bought that cheaply," Lynch said. "Looks like you guys are running 'em through today."

"This is still the overflow from yesterday. We haven't even gotten to today's arraignments yet. Monday's always the worst. Especially the Monday after the first weekend of the month when the welfare checks come in. It's like cleaning up after the O.K. Corral. So, buddy, let's cut to the chase. What can I do for you?"

Jack reached down, pulled his own cup out of the machine. "I'm working on a research project for a client," he began. What the hell, he thought, that's not a complete lie. "I'm researching computer crime, electronic theft, that sort of thing. I wondered what kind of work you guys do in that area."

"You came all the way down here for that?" Fred asked. "You ain't got enough to keep you busy, boy."

Lynch smiled. "The problem is, you got too much to keep you busy. The last time I left you a message, it took a week to get you to return the call. Hell, I figured it was faster to track you down."

Fred grinned back at him. "Fair enough. Okay, walk me back upstairs. That's about how long it'll take for me to explain to you what the Orleans Parish District Attorney's Office and the New Orleans Police Department know about computer crime."

Fred Williams led the way out the door and down the hall to the elevator.

"Truth is," he said, "there's not much we can do about it. We don't have the resources or the technical know-how. State laws are real vague in that area, anyway. I know it's the cutting edge of crime and all that bullshit, Jack. There's billions being stolen out there, very quietly and very expertly. And there ain't a damn thing we can do about it. I wouldn't admit that to a news camera, but I don't mind telling you."

Fred took off his tortoise shell glasses and wearily rubbed his eyes as the two men waited for the elevator.

"You mean there's nobody to investigate white collar computer crime?" Lynch asked, disbelief in his voice.

The elevator door opened and the two men stepped on. The doors creaked as they came together in front of them, and the decades-old cables flapped in the shaft above them as they strained to pull the car upwards.

Fred Williams leaned against the back of the car, as if it were the only thing keeping him upright. There was an edge of weariness in his voice that bordered on despair.

"Jack, I arraigned a dope dealer this morning who got in a gunfight over in the projects Friday night and picked up a two-year-old girl to shield himself. The girl took four nine-millimeter slugs for this guy and died in his arms."

"Jesus," Lynch sighed. "Welcome to the nineties."

"Oh, that's damn near routine. We had another house invasion Saturday night."

"A what?"

"Latest thing with roving gangs. They hit a neighborhood, five or six in a car, bust into a house. Like an army. This time, thirty-year-old woman was home by herself. Opens the door to see who it is with one of those little two dollar security chains connected. Guys busted in, gang-raped her for at least two hours, strangled her with one of her husband's neckties, then stuffed that two-dollar chain inside her as a calling card. Cops popped 'em when a neighbor saw them leave in their brand new Ford Bronco, got suspicious, and copied down the license plate."

"Rough weekend," Lynch said.

The door opened in front of them and the two stepped out into a crowded hallway.

"Routine weekend," Fred said. "Everybody gives the media a hard time for focusing on urban violence. Hell, the media don't get half of it. It's a war zone out there, bud. And the good guys are losing. Somebody does something as benign as commit a crime with a computer, the reality is we're just about willing to write them a free pass. The day comes when we get the animals off the streets, then we'll turn to the crooks with the taped glasses and the pocket protectors. But that day ain't likely to come in either of our lifetimes. You remember when we were in college together, when the movie *A Clockwork Orange* came out?"

Lynch shook his head.

"Well, that was just the beginning," Fred said. "That movie was prophecy. The only part that's never going to come true is the part where the bad guys get the emotional lobotomies and quit being criminals."

Lynch's voice rose. "So even if the criminals with computers are ripping off millions, you guys can't do anything about it because the muggers and the rapists and the guys who hit the Seven-Elevens make more noise than they do."

Fred stopped at the door to Judge Cole's courtroom and turned defensively. "Yeah, that's about it, hotshot. When the guy with a computer makes it unsafe for you to walk the streets at night or a computer rapes your eight-year-old daughter, then they'll get our attention. But right now, you put out the biggest fires first. And the teenage boys who have zits and can't get dates, who break into computers while their parents are downstairs watching 'Wheel Of Fortune,' aren't my worry, goddammit."

"Okay, Fred, I didn't mean to pee in your Cheerios. I'm just blown away that this kind of thing goes on and the government won't do anything about it."

"Can't, my man. Can't. The Feds have the resources to make a big bust every now and then to make an example of some poor schnook. But local governments? No way. We can't even make the streets safe."

He paused for a moment. "So what are you up to, Jack? You uncover some kind of big computer heist somewhere? Or are you looking for a new line of work to go into?"

"Same line of work, Fred. Like I said, I've got a client who's got some concerns about computer security. I told them I'd do a little research, find out what gets done about it."

"Two word answer for you, guy. 'Nyet Much.' Now if you don't mind, I've got to go try and put some bad guys away. What a joke. The only capital punishment these guys'll ever see is if they die laughing at the system."

Fred Williams slammed back the last of his coffee as if it were a Stoli shooter. He crumpled the paper cup, tossed it toward a heavy smoking stand a few feet away against a wall. It missed, and fell to the floor in a wet mess.

Fred stared at it. "Oh, the hell with it," he sighed as he pulled the door open and walked into the courtroom. The door rolled slowly shut, leaving Jack standing alone in the cavernous hallway.

CHAPTER 16

Lynch pulled the door of the phone booth closed behind him and fumbled with a quarter. Surprisingly, the phone worked. He dialed the number and started to lean against the glass, but got a glimpse of the slime coating the inside of the booth and pulled himself upright. Behind him, two senior citizen tourist-types walked nervously out of the lobby of the Airlane Motel onto Tulane Avenue, wishing with their eyes that they'd paid the extra money to stay at a nice place in the Quarter.

"Yeah," a tentative, not-quite-awake voice answered.

"Martin, Jack Lynch here."

"Oh, yeah. What's happening?"

"Listen, do you get a dinner break on the night shift?"

"Yeah, why?"

"Meet me somewhere. I'll buy you dinner. Someplace close, maybe on Canal Street."

"I usually eat in the building. Just brown bag it."

"I need to talk to you, but I can't do it there. C'mon."

Martin hesitated. "Sure, what's going on?"

"I'll tell you tonight. Where can I meet you?"

"You like Spanish food?"

"Sure, whatever."

"There's a place couple blocks into the Quarter, on Bienville. Behind the back of the Woolworths. You know where I'm talking about?"

"Yeah, I think so."

"Cafe Cuba Libre, it's called. Best Cuban and Guatemalan food you've ever had. Meet me there at eight-thirty. Should be almost empty then. I'll be at a table in the back. We'll get served quick, cause I got to go back to work."

"Right. Eight-thirty, Cafe Cuba Libre. See you then. And Martin—"

"Yeah?"

"Let's keep this between us, okay?"

"I don't say nothing to nobody at this place. Don't worry."

Lynch hung up the phone, fiddled with his free hand to get another quarter into the slot, and dialed a second number.

"Mr. Smith's office," Carlton's secretary said.

"Hi, this is Jack Lynch. Is he in?"

"Hold on, Mr. Lynch."

Lynch watched through the filthy glass as the two tourists, the gray-haired man a full head taller than his frail wife, walked arm in arm down the street in matching Bermuda shorts and white pullover shirts. He shook his head, hoping the fact that they were two blocks from the police station might keep the vultures from swooping in too quickly.

"Jack, this is Carlton."

"Hi, Carlton. Hope I didn't catch you at a bad time."

"Not at all. What are you up to?"

"I've just been doing a little digging. Trying to learn what little anybody else knows about this stuff. I need you to do me a favor, though. I'd like to see a copy of the instructions the extortionist left in the electronic mailbox. Presumably, they're still on a disk somewhere and they can print off a copy. Okay?"

"I'll do it right now. I've raised enough hell with Gupton and his troops that there's not much fight left in them. They'll pretty well do what I tell them."

"Good, if you could take care of that, I'd appreciate it. I don't exactly know where it's going to lead, but I'd like to follow whatever trails exist for as long as I can."

"Jack, tell me. Have you found any proof that anyone down there had anything to do with this?"

"I have nothing whatever that indicates that," Lynch said,

choosing his words carefully and truthfully. "But I have found out one thing."

"What's that?"

"Even if we were inclined to go to the authorities, there's not much anyone can do about it. At least on the local level."

"Of course, the fact that the money was transported across state lines would bring in the feds," Carlton said. "And even Interpol, since it's obviously an overseas transaction. But we cannot do that, Jack. We can eat five million in cash easier than we can eat a hundred million in bad publicity."

"I know that, Carlton. Whatever I do, it'll be very quiet."

"It will have to be, my friend. It will have to be."

Lynch hung up the phone and stepped out of the booth. Blocks ahead of him, the matching senior-citizen targets were shrinking into invisibility.

Lynch parked illegally just down Decatur from the Jax Brewery Mall. He walked up the sidewalk, dodging the ambling tourists who seemed to have nowhere to go and the crowd of blitzed college students hanging around outside the Hard Rock Cafe. He cut right past the mall, crossed the Riverfront streetcar tracks, and climbed up a row of concrete steps to the Moonwalk. The bright sun had burned off the last of the clouds, and the sky was a great brilliant blue over the sparkling river. It had, Lynch admitted despite himself, turned into a gorgeous day. He was too preoccupied to enjoy it, however, and the thought buzzed through his brain as only a temporary interruption in the flow.

Behind and below him, crowds of people were strolling through Jackson Square amid sunbathers and readers. Lynch felt a twinge in his chest. He wondered briefly if he'd ever relax enough to enjoy himself that much again, then decided he didn't have time to think about that either. He scanned the crowd of people upriver toward the Aquarium, then downriver toward the point at Algiers. It was a good day to be a tourist, and hundreds of people were taking advantage of the opportunity on this one short stretch of concrete alone.

"He's got to be here," Lynch muttered.

He strained and squinted his eyes, struggling to focus as far to his left as possible. The *Natchez* let loose with a deafening blow of its steam whistle, and as heads turned to watch, Lynch found his quarry.

He moved quickly down the walk, past the steamboat dock, and made eye contact just as a tourist with an expensive-looking camera around his neck turned to his wife with a look on his face that asked "What do I do now?"

"That's five for the shine and five for the line," Lynch heard a voice say as a close-cropped head rose in front of the unfortunate man.

"Ten dollars for that?" the man piped in a high voice.

"You'll notice, sir, that I'm not carrying a knife or a gun. You see a knife or a gun here, sir? I don't sell no dope, I don't rob nobody. I just deliver one of life's lessons. Never assume anything, sir. Never assume anything."

The man looked at his wife, exasperated and nervous at the same time. "Oh, Billy, just give him the money and *let's go,*" the wife said.

The man pulled a ten out of his front pocket, slapped it in the smiling Fast Eddie's palm, and quickly walked off, his new Nike's carrying a dirty smudge on each toe where Fast Eddie had done his work.

"Never assume anything, sir," Fast Eddie said as the man and his wife bolted out off the walk at just short of a dead run.

"Yeah, and never eat at a place called 'Mom's,' and never play cards with a man called 'Doc,' " Lynch said, coming up behind Eddie.

Eddie turned with a broad smile on his face. "Jack, my man, what's happening?"

"I thought there was a recession on, Eddie. How do you continue to make such a good living?"

"Because," Eddie said, leading the two over to a concrete bench and sliding into a seat, "there may be a job shortage, but there is never a sucker shortage."

Lynch reached up and loosened his necktie. Around the Algiers point, the bow of a towering cargo ship stacked high with truck-sized containers plowed slowly upstream. Great streaks of red rust ran down to the waterline.

"Listen, Eddie, how'd you like to do something a little different every now and then?"

Eddie kicked at a pebble. It skittered across the concrete and into the grass. "What you got in mind?"

"Well, I'm sort of switching professions for awhile. I'm investigating some guys. Trying to find out if a certain crime that was committed could have been an inside job." Lynch turned to Eddie on the bench. "Hell, maybe I need to get a private investigator's license."

"Don't need one," Eddie said. He leaned down and swatted a mosquito against his bare leg. "Not in this state."

"Why does that not surprise me? Anyway, the guys I'm checking into know what I look like. I might want to keep an eye on them. Somebody I can trust. Somebody who's streetwise."

Fast Eddie turned to Jack and pasted a sneer across his face. "Well, dude, money talks and bullshit walks. Make me a offer I can't refuse."

"Same as your making now, hundred a day. In cash. If I can get my client to help me with the expenses, I'll bump it up to hundred-and-a-half."

"Well," Eddie said, hesitating, "I hate to lose my place on the walk out here. This is a very competitive business I'm in. A great deal of stress involved in this line of work. On the other hand, I could use a vacation. Do something a little different for awhile. When you want me to start?"

"Coupla' days," Lynch answered. "I need to get a few ducks in a row. Truth is, Eddie, I don't really know what the hell I'm doing yet."

"Why should you be any different from anybody else?" Eddie said. "Tell you what, my man, you know where to find me." He stretched his legs out, extended his arms behind him and pulled his body taut. Then he turned his head to the left and focused on something far down the walk.

"Ah, man, meal ticket, eight o'clock low."

Lynch followed Eddie's eyes. Down the concrete walk, a

man maybe twenty-five-years old with windblown hair was walking hurriedly down the sidewalk, his young wife in tow, his head buried in a New Orleans guidebook. He was reading out loud to her as they walked. Her camera bounced crazily around her chest as she struggled to keep up with her husband.

"Gotta run. Job responsibilities, you know." Eddie turned back to Jack, put his hands on his hips. "You know, it's tough being the best at what you do."

"I wouldn't know about that. See you tomorrow, maybe the next day. Okay?"

"Check you later," Eddie said, hopping off the bench and moving in warily for the kill.

"I got to see this," Lynch whispered to himself. He thought a moment, then: "Naw, maybe later."

He'd seen enough vultures at work in his time.

The ninth race at the Fairgrounds had just been run as Lynch headed out Esplanade toward his new apartment. The traffic overflow from Gentilly Boulevard snaked around and onto Esplanade, filling the asphalt beneath the great oaks with smoking cars.

Lynch parked in front of his apartment house and sat there a moment. He found himself filled with a restlessness whose origins he could not trace, a frustration he could not define. The day had not been, by his standards, a bad one. He felt he was making progress, albeit slow and haphazard.

There was something else, and he couldn't quite put his finger on it. He had spent so much time alone over the past months, with only his own thoughts to keep him company, that the continuous inner monologue that exists in every human brain began to seem to him like background noise.

He sat there silently in the still automobile, staring out through the smudged windshield at a group of young children bouncing a worn basketball in the middle of the street a couple of blocks away. He was surprised to find himself aching to be around people tonight. He did not want to, was in fact almost afraid to, spend another night alone in his apartment. *The drinking,* he wondered. If left alone once again with a bottle of scotch and an old movie on television, would he lose another evening?

He stepped out of the car, the metallic grinding of the door hinges breaking the silence and sending a pair of jays in an oak branch above him scurrying for greater heights. He watched them fly away, then dug out his briefcase and coat from the back seat. He flung the jacket over his shoulder and walked down the sidewalk toward the front corner of the house. Beneath his white shirt, he felt his own sweat turn clammy as he began to cool.

He rounded the house and stepped gingerly over the grass to the front sidewalk. His foot was cocked to hit the first step when a voice above him said: "Hello, there."

He stopped, looked up. P.J. Campbell was on her side of the porch, above him, leaning over the rail with a glass of wine in her hand.

"Hi," Lynch said. "How're you?"

"Great. What a gorgeous day," she said. "It's even cooling off."

"Yeah. I heard on the radio it may rain again tonight. Maybe even storm."

"That's always good for a lightshow." Lynch bent his head fully back to get a better look at her. She had on black jeans, a pullover shirt. Her black hair hung down over her face, sparkling in the fading afternoon light.

"Makes for good sleeping." Jack felt awkward. For a guy who'd spent his entire adult life in public relations, he seemed suddenly unable to make small talk.

"Can I offer you a glass of wine?"

Jack scuffed his feet against the moss-covered brick walk. He had to meet Martin Brown at 8:30, he was tired, he didn't feel up to socializing with anyone.

"Oh, I really need to—"

"It's a fantastic Australian Chardonnay," she interrupted. She smiled, her eyes bright, uncomplicated. Lynch stood there for a moment.

"I'd love to," he said. "Let me get out of the monkey suit and I'll knock on your door."

▪ CHAPTER 17 ▪

Jack raised his curled fist, hesitated for a moment, then knocked gently on the wooden door. He reached up and quickly buttoned the next-to-top button on his blue shirt. He had changed into jeans, washed his face, combed his hair. He wondered why he had agreed to come over.

The door seemed to fly open in front of him. "Hi, neighbor," P.J. Campbell said brightly.

Lynch stepped in. Art prints in expensive frames covered the walls. A large oriental rug dominated the center of the room, with a polished cherry table centered precisely on it. Several vases of cut fresh flowers dotted the room as well, with furniture that was classic in design, simple in arrangement.

"Love your apartment," he said, mustering some good cheer of his own.

"Thanks," she said over her shoulder as she walked back to the kitchen. "It took a few days, but I think I'm about to get settled."

He followed her into the kitchen. A maple breakfast table with tile inlay and four polished white wood chairs filled one corner.

"I still can't figure out what to do with this," she said, pointing at the table and chairs. "It takes up too much room in here, but I like it too much to get rid of it."

"Yeah, it's lovely," Lynch said truthfully, remembering his own scratched and scuffed table, the one with the cigarette burns. The mental image of those burns made him long for a cigarette, but he had decided to leave the pack lying on the table.

P.J. opened a cabinet door and stretched on tiptoe to retrieve a wine glass.

"Here, let me help you with that," he offered.

"I've got it." She handed him the glass and picked up a wooden cutting board that held slices of cheese laid symmetrically.

He followed her back through the living room onto the gallery overlooking Esplanade. The sun was disappearing behind the oak grove in City Park. The traffic had thinned to a trickle. The air was heavy with the oncoming evening and its threat of rain. Lynch felt himself relax as he stood next to her.

"I hope you like this. I found it at the natural food market over there." P.J. pointed down Esplanade toward Cafe Degas.

"I haven't been in there, yet."

"They've got a remarkably good wine section. Really good stuff. I was surprised to find wine in a health food store."

"Only in New Orleans," Lynch said. She motioned for him to sit in a wrought-iron patio chair padded with a pale rose and blue cushion, then reached into an ice bucket and pulled a pale green bottle out. Icy condensation dripped down the back of her hand, rolling onto her wrist. Lynch held out his glass as she filled it. The wine was pale yellow, clear and cold. Lynch tipped his glass in her direction and put it to his lips. Dry, almost buttery, wonderful.

"Oh, God, that's great," he sighed. "Here's to getting through another day at the office."

She sat down across from him and raised her glass. "And to whatever comes next."

Jack sipped again, savoring the wine, resisting the impulse to down the whole glass in one gulp.

"This is wonderful. I wasn't looking forward to coming home and facing an empty apartment anyway."

"I'm glad you decided to come over. You're my first house guest."

"An honor, ma'am, as we say down South. Now tell me, what brought you from the Big Apple to the Big Easy?"

She picked up a slice of cheese and placed it on a cracker, then handed it to Jack. He took it gratefully. She did the same for herself.

"A job," she answered.

"Okay. What do you do?" Lynch asked, biting off an edge of the cracker.

"I'm a psychiatrist."

Lynch choked, spraying cracker crumbs sloppily toward the direction of City Park. "Oh, God, I'm sorry, excuse me," he stammered. She handed him a napkin.

"Wow, you must have a thing about shrinks."

"No, it's not that. I just, well, you surprised me, that's all. You don't look like a—"

She raised a mock-critical eyebrow. "Oh, and what does a psychiatrist look like?"

"I don't know, and I have a feeling I'm about to have a mouth full of boot. I didn't mean anything about it beyond my surprise that someone so young could be so accomplished."

"My, how diplomatic. And what a recovery. You ought to be in public relations."

Lynch's smile broke into a laugh.

"What?" she asked, confused.

"I am in public relations."

"Hmmm, good guess on my part," she said, raising her glass to her lips and draining it. She reached over, pulled the wine bottle out of the ice. "Cool that off for you?"

Lynch held the glass out. "So you came down here to take a job? Where?"

"Ochsner Clinic," P.J. answered. "I'm the new director of the substance abuse unit."

"Oh, great," Lynch joked. "I'm sitting here swilling down wine with a shrink who's a substance abuse expert. What the hell, you can tell me when I've had enough."

"I suspect you'll know that well enough on your own," she said.

"I usually do. So how'd you wind up here? I mean, weren't there lots of jobs in New York?"

"There are lots of jobs everywhere for substance abuse experts. It's a booming business in this day and age. Actually, though, I needed to get out of New York. I did my residency at Bellevue. Believe me, that was enough New York to last me the rest of my life."

"I'll bet. So you decided to leave one looney bin for another."

"We in the profession eschew terms like 'looney bin,'" she said. "I prefer to think of American cities as giant urban funny farms."

Jack Lynch was beginning to like P.J. Campbell.

"Besides," she added. "I got divorced last year. Left a bad taste in my mouth."

Lynch cleared his throat. "Yeah, it'll do that."

"I gather you've been there."

"Oh, yeah."

"Any kids?" she asked.

"Oh, no. I mean, I was divorced what . . . ten, maybe twelve years ago. We didn't have any kids. How about you?"

"No. We were waiting until we both got out of residency."

"Your ex-husband was a doctor, too?"

"Yes. He was in obstetrics."

"Oh," Lynch commented. "I would imagine that could put a strain on a marriage."

"No worse than a man being married to a female proctologist."

"Oh, don't say that," Lynch said, laughing. "That hurts."

"So I'm told," she said. "No, that wasn't it. We met in medical school. We were both on scholarships, loans. Working eighty, ninety hours a week. Got married during our third year, then worked it out to do residencies in the same city. Things were going well for us. We finished our residencies, six weeks later filed for divorce."

"You mean after all you'd been through?"

She smiled, tipped her glass toward him. "Go figure. I think the lack of stress killed us."

Lynch scooted around in the chair facing her and crossed his legs. He was enjoying the conversation, intrigued by her. He had always recognized, somewhere inside himself, that the thing that most attracted him to women was intelligence.

"I've heard of stress breaking up marriages. I never heard of the lack of stress doing it."

"I think it's pretty rare. Lucky me. So tell me, what do you do in public relations? Who do you work for?"

Jack settled back, let his body slide down just a bit in the chair. "I have my own company," he answered, "although for the past couple of years, I've mostly been a glorified freelancer. I used to work for a bank here in town, but I lost that job a while back. Decided to strike out on my own."

"The past few years have been rough in corporate life, I hear."

"That's one of the reasons I decided to hang out my own shingle. And it's been tough. My income's taken a big whack. But I had some savings that lasted for awhile, and slowly I'm building a client base."

"What kind of work do you do? I mean, what's a P.R. person actually do when he goes into the office?"

"Usually, you write press releases, try to use your contacts in the media to get exposure for your client without having to actually buy advertising. That sort of thing. It's somewhere between being a publicity flack and an advertising exec.

"But," he continued, "I don't really do much of that kind of work anymore. I have kind of a specialized practice."

"Specialized?" P.J. asked, interested. "Like how?"

"Well, I take on kind of unusual cases. I used to do a lot of work in politics. My boss at the bank was sort of a power broker. And I did a lot of, how do I say this—troubleshooting. Say a company's got some problems that, if it gets out, would mean some real bad publicity. I help put the best light on it possible. Spin control, the politicians call it."

"You get out there and represent the company and take the heat for them?"

"Sort of," Lynch answered. "Only I'm never 'out there.' I work very much in the background. When I do my job right, nobody ever knows I've been there."

"It sounds interesting, and terribly clandestine."

Lynch reached over and pulled the wine bottle out of the bucket. About three inches, enough for two short glasses, remained. He motioned to P.J. and she held her glass out.

"It's interesting work, but it's real uneven. Seems like I go forever without getting much work, and then all of a sudden, I'll find myself in the middle of a hurricane."

She took the wine glass and sipped slowly. "So which was it today?"

Lynch looked over the top of his glass at her. "I think there's a storm a-brewin'."

"Who knows? You could be right. Say, that bottle is empty. How did that happen?"

Lynch looked down at his watch. It was almost 7:30. "And how'd it get to be so late?"

"How time flies when you're . . ."

"Yeah." Lynch smiled, sat for an awkward moment. He felt a pleasant glow from the wine and was completely unwound for the first time in days. He hated to see the evening end. "P.J., do you have any plans for dinner?"

The words rolled off his lips suddenly, abruptly. P.J. Campbell looked thoughtfully at him for a few minutes. "I've got an idea. Let's do something special. I haven't been to a really nice New Orleans restaurant yet. My ex-husband was down here for a medical meeting last year and a bunch of doctors went to Galatoire's. Let's try that. I feel like doing something outrageous in the middle of the week."

Lynch winced. "P.J., you won't like Galatoire's."

"What do you mean?" she asked, aghast. "It's supposed to be one of the best restaurants in the world."

Lynch leaned forward and planted his elbows on the table. "They don't take reservations. So we go to Galatoire's, we're going to stand out on Bourbon Street thirty, forty minutes, maybe an hour, watching the drunks go by and listening to the flies buzz us. And some polyester-clad, half-snockered judge from New Iberia or someplace like that'll get pulled ahead of us because he knows the maître d'. And we'll get all pissed off. Even though the food'll be great, by the time we get in there, we ain't going to be in the mood to enjoy anything. And since we don't know anybody and we aren't regulars, we'll get stuck with whoever's turn it is to take care of the tourists."

"My goodness," she sighed. "I get the feeling you don't much care for Galatoire's."

"It's just not the real New Orleans to me. Not anymore. I used to be part of the crowd that got pulled out of line and taken in ahead of the others, but that was a long time ago. It's blasphemous to say this, but it's just not that special. To me, the real New Orleans is a muffaletta and a couple of beers from Central Grocery, then go eat on the Moonwalk. Then we stroll over to the Napoleon House and sit in the back room and drink Drambuie on the rocks and listen to Prokofiev. Maybe I'm weird, but to me, that's New Orleans."

"I know, but I've always wanted to try Galatoire's. Tell you what, it'll be my treat."

"You don't know what you're getting into."

"That's okay. We'll wing it. C'mon, we'll try it both ways. Galatoire's tonight, Central Grocery the next time."

Lynch stifled a smile. "Next time, huh? Okay, Dr. Campbell, you got a deal. Two things, though?"

"Yeah?"

"One, we got to dress up a little. No jeans. Second, make sure you've got plenty of cash. They don't take credit cards."

P.J. grinned slyly. "Oh, yes they do. I called. They started taking credit cards a couple of months ago."

Jack's eyes widened. *"Galatoire's takes credit cards!* Jeez, it's a whole new world out there, isn't it?"

"Welcome to the nineties, Jack Lynch."

Lynch stood. "I'll run next door and crawl back into a coat and tie. Knock on your door in about twenty minutes. That be enough time?"

"And then some," she said. She rose from her chair and crossed the table to stand next to him. The wind had picked up as the evening darkened, blowing in from the north, over the lake at a steady pace. The wind draped her hair across her face; with her right index finger, she reached up and hooked one side, pulling it across her face and behind her ear. At that moment, with the streetlight behind her and her face in shadow, Lynch's gut felt like a burlap bag full of live ferrets.

"Good," he said. "See you in a few."

She motioned for him to step ahead of her. He went into her living room from the gallery and squinted in the brighter light. Then, he remembered his other obligation for the evening and turned abruptly.

"One thing," he said. "Are you starving?"

"No," she said. "Another hour or two, I will be. Why?"

"I need to make one stop on the way. It's close by Galatoire's. That okay with you?"

"Sure," she said. "I'm game."

"Great," Lynch said. "I appreciate that."

She pursed her lips, teasing him in mock suspicion. "Hmmm, what kind of a stop is this?"

Jack opened the door and stepped into the hallway. He turned to her and leaned against the doorjamb.

"Let's just say I have to check in with my mole."

■ *CHAPTER 18* ■

Don't you worry about leaving a convertible on the street like this at night?" P.J. Campbell pushed her windblown hair off her face as Jack slid the Fiat into a space on Decatur Street.

"It's a risk. But if you're going to drive a ragtop in the city, it's one you've got to take. But notice, my dear, we have a cheap radio in here and nothing worth stealing."

"All the same," she said, "in New York, it wouldn't last five minutes."

Lynch opened the door and climbed out onto the sidewalk. "It may not here. But you live with it."

P.J. Campbell opened the door, held her knees together, and swiveled around carefully to get out of the car. The sleek black tube dress she was wearing inhibited movement. She pulled herself up onto the street and closed the door behind her. Lynch bent over and unhooked the strap that held down the cloth top, then extended the top out toward the front of the car. He doubled over back into the car and latched the top against the windshield.

"I don't mind thieves," he said as he stood back up, "but I'd hate like hell to have it rain in my car."

P.J. crossed behind the car and stepped onto the sidewalk. Her bare arms were long and thin in the dim streetlight, her hair down on both sides of her face, her legs lean and muscular beneath black stockings with some kind of shimmering glitter woven into the fabric.

She's lovely, he thought. Then the ferrets went back to work.

"Do you have any idea where we are?" she asked.

"That's Iberville up there." He pointed toward Canal Street. "I'm meeting my . . . associate in a restaurant just a couple of blocks down. It's on the way to Galatoire's."

P.J. smiled. "Oh, so now he's your associate. Promoted from mole?"

Lynch grinned and checked his watch. They still had maybe ten minutes before Martin Brown was due at Cafe Cuba Libre. Just enough time for a stroll in the cool, windy evening. Lynch stepped forward, away from the car. P.J. Campbell laced her arm in his. The two walked slowly down the dark street.

"Funny, I'd always heard how hot New Orleans is. I never expected anything this pleasant."

"It's been a remarkably cool spring," Lynch said. "Just wait, though. Another three months, nights like this will only be fond memories."

They strolled on in silence, enjoying the night. This section of Decatur was closer in toward Canal than the heavily touristed area. P.J. and Jack were alone on the sidewalk. They turned off Decatur onto Iberville. Two blocks down, the blue-and-green flashing neon sign of the Cafe Cuba Libre illuminated the street.

Lynch pointed with his free hand. "That's where we're meeting my—"

"Your whatever. . . ." she said. Lynch smiled.

"Yeah, Martin the Whatever."

The cafe was open in front, with a long bar down the left wall of the building, and tables crowded around haphazardly. Ancient ceiling fans stirred the air. The smell of cooking grease and fried food hung in a gray pall throughout the back of the room near the kitchen.

"Hmmm, I'm getting hungry," P.J. said as they took the one step off the sidewalk into the open cafe.

"Can I get you a table, sir?" a young, dark man in white shirt and black bow tie asked.

"We're supposed to meet someone. Young guy, sort of blond hair."

"Sí," the waiter said. "He's in the back."

Jack turned to P.J. "I don't mean to play James Bond on you, but this is just some business stuff that won't take more than a couple of minutes. Can I buy you a drink at the bar?"

She hesitated. "Sure, I guess that's okay."

"Thanks. I appreciate your being so understanding." Jack took her arm and walked with her between the tables to the bar.

"What can I get you?"

"Maybe a white wine spritzer."

Jack motioned for the bartender, a short, chubby woman with dark skin and the thin shadow of a moustache.

"Can you make the lady a white wine spritzer?"

"No problem, mon," the woman said, Jamaican accent as thick as the kitchen aroma.

"I'll be right back. Thanks, P.J."

"I'll be here." She settled herself on a barstool and smiled sweetly at him again. He promised himself not to keep her waiting, then turned and ran his eyes down the line of booths on the opposite side of the restaurant. At the last one, facing the front, sat Martin Brown hidden in shadow.

Lynch walked quickly over, then slid wordlessly into the booth across from him. He eased over as close to the wall as possible, completely hidden in shadow.

"Who's the babe?" Martin asked.

Lynch's jaw tightened. He was not in the mood to spend a great deal of time around Martin Brown's mouth, especially not with P.J. waiting for him.

"My new neighbor," he answered.

"Damn, man, I can see why you moved." Brown held up a hot taco and leaned into the table to bite into it. Trickles of shiny grease ran down his fingers. Martin Brown ignored them.

"That's not why I asked you here."

"Okay," Martin mumbled with a mouth full of tortilla shell and ground meat. "Why did you ask me here?"

Lynch pulled out one of his business cards and a fountain pen. He scribbled something down on the card and passed it across the table to Martin.

"Here's my card with my new business line and my home phone number. How'd you like to go to work for me?"

"I already agreed to spook for you." Martin's hand paused dripping in midair.

"I'd like to make it official," Lynch said. "I need somebody on the inside I can trust. I'll pay you. Not sure how much yet; depends on how much I can get out of Carlton Smith for expenses. But they'll be something in it for you, and I'll try to make it worth your while."

"Yo, bro," Brown said, his voice dripping with sarcasm now as well as taco grease. "Are you going to give me a permanent job when they find out I'm getting paid to snoop for you and fire my ass?"

"Nobody's going to fire you," Lynch insisted. "At least not as long as you're reasonably cool. If you get yourself in a jam, call me. I'll get Carlton to bail you out."

Martin Brown sat back on the booth seat and sloppily tossed the remains of his taco onto the plate.

"What the hell am I supposed to be looking for?"

Lynch leaned forward, careful to stay out of the light. "You know about the software bomb, Martin. But there's some other stuff you don't know. The letter I told you about, the one from Vernon Wormer? It was a ransom note. The person who planted the bomb wants five million to defuse it."

Martin's jaw dropped. "Get the fuck out of here!"

Lynch nodded. "Five million. Some serious money."

Martin stared off, shocked, as clumps of brown, greasy hamburger fell out of his taco and splattered on the table. "So that's why Gupton and Cook and Buford have been so closed-mouthed."

"Yeah," Lynch agreed. "Apparently after you left Monday night, the extortionist called in on the modem and down-loaded some instructions. Either that or he defused the bomb himself. Hell, I don't know. But the bank paid the ransom and then got its mainframe back in one piece."

Martin whistled softly as he dropped the messy taco onto his plate and wiped his hands with a napkin. "Man, we're in the wrong business. Five million bucks, just like that."

"Something stinks, Martin. I want your help finding out what it is."

Martin picked up his half-empty can of Tecate and drained it. "I guess I should say 'thank-you' for deciding that I didn't have anything to do with it."

Lynch waved his hand. "No, the only thing you've got is motive and ability. For the time being, Carlton has arranged it so I can get into the bank after hours. Can you fix it so your people on the night shift will keep their mouths shut if they see me?"

"I can fix it up so they don't see you at all."

"Great." Lynch pulled out another business card. "You got a number where I can reach you at night?"

"There's a direct line into the computer room. From about ten o'clock on, I'm the only one there. The rest of the people are decollating printouts and delivering them."

"Write it down for me," Lynch instructed. "I'll be in touch with you as soon as I figure where we're going on this. Now if you don't mind, a young lady is waiting for me at the bar. We have a dinner engagement."

Martin Brown finished scribbling on the card and pushed it across the table toward Jack.

"Thanks," Jack said. "You're now officially a co-conspirator."

"Yeah," he said, "and if you don't get over there soon, somebody else is going to conspiracy your date away."

Lynch turned and looked over the top of the seat. A well-groomed twenty-five-year-old wearing a Tulane pullover shirt was standing next to P.J., smiling and leaning in toward her in the classic chatting-up position.

"Oh, hi," P.J. said brightly as Jack walked up behind the young man's back. "Did you finish your business?"

The man turned, disappointed. "Oh, hey, I'm sorry. I didn't know you were with anybody."

"No problem," P.J. said, as she stepped around him and took Jack's arm. "Thanks for the conversation."

"Yeah, anytime," he said awkwardly.

"See ya' around," Jack said over his shoulder as he led P.J. through the tables and into the street.

An hour and a half later, Lynch sipped his second weak scotch and soda and tried to conceal his irritation. They had stood in line for almost an hour on Bourbon Street, in the intermittent sprinkle, as the jacketed maître d' pulled people ahead of them in line and guided them through the polished wood and glass doors of Galatoire's.

"Hey," a tourist behind Jack complained. "I thought it was first come, first serve."

Jack turned and shrugged his shoulders at the man. "I recognized that last one. He's on the Mayor's staff."

"I don't care if he's Bill Clinton," the man said. "It ain't fair."

Finally, Jack and P.J. were next in line, crowded close in on the door with a long line of people behind them who probably wouldn't get in at all. They stood ten minutes, P.J. chatting and smiling amiably, Jack fighting the urge to get really sullen, when the maître'd opened the door and stood there a moment staring at the line. He glanced at Jack and P.J., then scanned the rest of the line.

"Looking for a better deal?" Lynch asked.

The man looked at him with barely concealed contempt. "Welcome to Galatoire's."

He held the outer doors open for them, then reached ahead of them to open the curtained inner doors. He led P.J. and Jack into the crowded restaurant. P.J. looked around at the white tile, mirrors, chrome, and tiny tables jammed tightly and haphazardly throughout the room.

She turned back to Jack as the maître d' led them, twisting and turning, through the maze of tables. "This is Galatoire's?" she asked.

They sat at a table another ten minutes before a tuxedoed waiter with an Italian accent and slicked-back hair tossed a couple of menus on the table in front of them and abruptly asked: "Can I get you any-zing to drink?"

"What are your specials tonight?" P.J. asked.

"Let me get your drinks first," the waiter instructed.

It went downhill from there. The waiter returned with their drinks and slopped wine on the tablecloth in front of P.J. Jack's drink was watered down to the color of Coca-Cola and melted ice. They never did learn what the specials were; the waiter rattled them off so fast they couldn't understand him. There was no way they were going to ask again. It became an exercise in intimidation. The waiter scribbled their orders and disappeared. And disappeared. And disappeared. Finally, Jack snagged another waiter and begged for a second drink.

"I'm really surprised," P.J. said as their own waiter angrily set the drink down on the table in front of Jack with instructions that if he needed anything else, he was to let him know and not just anybody in a tuxedo who happened to be standing by.

"It's a bad night," Jack said.

"I mean, I feel like we're *bothering* them or something."

Jack took a long sip of the drink. This one, at least, tasted like it actually had scotch in it.

"By the way," he said, "I meant to tell you earlier how lovely that dress is."

"Thanks," she said, almost shyly. "It's the first time I've ever worn it. It was the last dress I bought in New York."

Behind them, three men in polyester pants, checked shirts, without jackets or ties, were led in by the maître d' and seated next to Jack and P.J. The three were already drunk, laughing uproariously, slapping backs, out for a night's good time in the Vieux Carré.

"I thought you said men had to wear coats and ties," P.J. whispered.

Jack shrugged. "I thought they did."

Moments later, the maître d' returned with three loaner coats over his arm.

"Here you are, sir," the maître d' said to the largest man,

the one who appeared to be hosting the other two. "This one should fit."

The man broke out in a loud, rumbling laugh. "Man, you're kidding. Get that thing away from me."

"I'm sorry, sir. House rules."

"C'mon, Earl, let's put the damn jackets on. At least they ain't gonna make us wear ties."

Earl grinned and slapped the table. "Hell, I guess a buncha ignorant ol' rednecks like us don't make it into town often enough, do we?"

Lynch shook his head.

"Oh, boy," P.J. whispered across the table. "This is going to be interesting."

The three men ordered vodka martinis, neat, and continued their disruption of the evening. The snotty Italian waiter brought their food. Jack leaned over and motioned for the waiter to come close.

"Can't you get those guys to quiet down a bit?" Jack stage-whispered.

"I'm sorry, zey are friends of zee owner's," the waiter said coldly. He walked away and was gone.

"Well, you were right about one thing," P.J. said as she gently ran her fork into a plate of pompano meunière.

"What was it? I'd like to be right about something tonight."

She smiled broadly, the fork a couple of inches from her lips. "The food's delicious."

They ate silently, the noise from the next table effectively drowning out all conversation. As far as Jack could deduce, the three men were childhood friends. The one who called the big one Earl lived in Denver now, and was just in town for the week. All three were in the oil business, part of a dying breed of wildcatters. They were having a combination business–reunion. The business consisted largely of arguing over where the best whorehouse in the French Quarter could be found. From the intensity of their discussions, Jack figured the winner was the old carriage house on Ursulines, between Burgundy and Dauphine.

The Italian waiter came and handed Jack the check.

"Good thing we didn't want any dessert," Jack commented.

"We're out of everything good," the waiter said. "It's very late."

"You're telling me," Jack said. "By the way, Armando, I think the check goes to the other side of the table."

The waiter looked at Jack as if he'd just walked into the restaurant wearing checked bellbottoms. He picked the check back up, as if to comment upon the character of any man who'd let a woman pay for his dinner, and handed it across the table to P.J.

Across from them, the waiter for the oilmen's table brought their check. Immediately, an uproar ensued as the three fought for control of paying rights.

"It's mine," Earl yelled, snatching the ticket out of the Denver oilman's hand.

"No, give it to me, goddamit," the third man yelled, drunkenly reaching across the table.

"Earl, give me that damn check, boy, before I get up from here and whup you!"

"Wait a minute, I got it!" Earl yelled. "Let's play C-note poker for it."

In a flash, three one-hundred dollar bills were waving in the air.

"I got four nines," Earl yelled.

"Beat you," Denver yelled back. "Five of a kind. Deuces!"

"I got all three of you beat," the third man yelled. "Five sevens! Lucky Lou wins again."

Denver yelled and tossed his hundred dollar bill in the air. The other two men joined. Three bills went up in the air and floated gently down. Two landed on the table.

One didn't.

"Hey," Denver said. "Where'd mine go?"

P.J. looked quizzically at Jack. "What's going on?" she whispered.

Jack shrugged. P.J. went back to signing and totaling up her credit card slip.

"Where'd what go?" Earl asked.

"My money. My hunnert, where'd it go?"

The three men looked around. The third man reached over and slapped Earl on the arm. "Oh, it's the ol' 'hey, guys, where'd my hundred-dollar bill go?' game."

Earl howled. "Hell, he probably thinks we're going to cover his losses!"

"No, boys, I ain't funnin' here," Denver said seriously. "I done lost my money. That's a hunnert dollars, Earl."

Earl howled louder. "Listen to this crap. Lost a hunnert dollars, my ass!"

"Earl, I'm telling you. That bill's gone." He turned completely around in his chair and faced Jack. "Hey, mister, ya'll didn't see a hunnert-dollar-bill go flying by, did you?"

Jack looked at the man in amazement, then decided he'd better treat the situation seriously or he'd wind up in a brawl.

"No sir, I haven't seen it."

"You seen it, ma'am?"

P.J. smiled sweetly at him. "Not since you threw it up in the air."

"Well, hell," Denver mumbled drunkenly. "It's gotta be here somewheres."

"C'mon," Earl said, standing up. "Let's get out of here. Me and Billy Bob here'll pick up the drinks the rest of the night. Don't worry about it."

Denver stood up, the look of a scolded puppy on his face. "Hell, Earl, that'uz a hunnert dollars. Time was a hunnert dollars was a lot of money."

"Well, old buddy," Earl said, throwing his arm around his companion's shoulder, "it ain't no more."

The three men shed their jackets and left the restaurant. Over in the corner, a table with two couples applauded quietly.

"What an adventure," P.J. said. Lynch grinned widely for the first time all evening.

"Actually, I thought it was great fun," he said. He reached for his last sip of wine and knocked a fork onto the floor. "Oh, excuse me. I'm getting clumsy in my old age."

He leaned down under the table to retrieve it, then polished off the last of his wine.

"How'd you like to take a walk?" he asked.

"Love it. Let's go."

He stood and pulled her chair out for her. They snaked between the mostly empty tables and stepped quickly out of Galatoire's into the street.

"Well," Jack said, rocking back and forth on his feet and taking a deep breath of fresh air. "Thanks for dinner, P.J. It's my turn next time."

She broke out laughing. "Oh, God, you were so right. Next time we eat out, let's get that muffa—what did you call it?"

"Muffaletta."

"Yeah, what you said. And a couple of Dixies."

The two began walking down Bourbon Street, oblivious to both the late-night street stumblers and the billowing layer of clouds roiling and tumbling above them. The air was thick with the threat of rain, but as yet, none fell. They continued down Bourbon until it became a street for automobiles again, then transferred their stroll to the sidewalk. P.J. took Lynch's arm, and the two meandered slowly down a few blocks, most of the time silent, then crossed over to Royal Street. They continued down a few more blocks, then crossed over to Chartres Street and came to a huge structure surrounded by unlit scaffolding that looked almost ghostly in the darkness.

"What's that?"

"The Cabildo," Jack said. "It's supposed to be one of the oldest buildings in the country. It burned a few years ago. 1988, I think. The state's just now getting the money to rebuild it."

"This state's in terrible shape, isn't it?" she commented.

"Funny you should say that. You know, we're going to have a state lottery here soon."

"We have one of those in New York," she said dreamily, the heavy meal and the drinks leaving her relaxed and sleepy.

"You ever play it?"

"No," she said. "Too busy. Besides, I think it's wrong for the state to exploit the weaknesses of its citizens."

"Sure, it's much better to have the Mafia exploit them."

She nudged him in the ribs. "Smartass. I still don't like it.

The government ought to bring out the best in its citizens, not encourage the worst. Next thing you know, we'll be legalizing drugs to get the tax money."

"Already are," Jack said. "What do you think liquor and cigarettes are."

"Precisely my point. We legalized those two and look where it got us. We're a nation of abusers."

"Yeah," Jack smiled. "Ain't it great?"

"That was a great Semillon, wasn't it?"

"Was that the first or the second bottle?"

"Mmmm, the second . . . I think."

They crossed into Jackson Square. Even this late at night, tourists and locals intermixed in a seemingly endless parade of walkers.

"I have a confession to make," P.J. said, as they approached the front door of St. Louis Cathedral.

"This is the place to do it," Jack said.

"I was so angry at that sexist, pseudo-European snotty waiter that on a seventy-five dollar bill, I tipped him exactly ten cents."

Jack cackled with laughter. "Oh, that's great. I tell you what, right now we both need to make some adjustments in our karma. C'mon."

"Where?"

"Just c'mon," Jack took her hand and pulled her toward the front door of the Cathedral. He opened the front door; the church vestibule was open, but the doors into the cathedral nave were locked.

"What are you up to?" she asked.

"I think we need to make a donation to the poor to atone for our sins."

P.J. Campbell looked puzzled. "But wha—"

"Say a *hunnert* dollars," he chirped, whipping a C-note out of his coat pocket.

P.J.'s jaw dropped. "Jack, that's very generous, but don't you think it's kind of impulsive? I mean, shouldn't—"

Her voice stopped, hanging like icicles in midair between them. Her eyes grew big, and her jaw fell open again.

"You didn't. . . ."

Lynch smiled. "I did."

"Jack, you took that man's money."

"I did not," Lynch insisted. "He dropped it on the floor. Six inches behind my right heel. I let it lay there. If he'd seen it, he could've had it. I didn't even lie to him. When he asked me if I'd seen it, I answered him truthfully. I saw it later, and decided he needed a lesson."

P.J. began giggling. Her breath came in short gasps. Her shoulders heaved and she wrapped her arms around herself. "Oh, god, that's great! What a bunch of jerks!"

"I don't want it for myself. Let's give it to the poor."

"Oh, that's wonderful," she said, between bursts of giggling. "You're wonderful."

"Thank you," Lynch said. He folded the bill neatly in half and stuffed into the slot of a wooden box mounted on the wall. "I think you're pretty wonderful, too."

She stopped giggling, her thin arms still wrapped around her shoulders. She seemed very slight to him, almost frail, certainly vulnerable, in the dim light of the cathedral anteroom. Lynch stepped toward her slowly; her eyes rose to meet his. Outside, rolling thunder bounced end over end from the north, over the city, and rain began to fall. Slowly at first, then in the space of a few seconds, it began falling in glittering silver sheets. The sound of rain hitting the roof created a low level din above them that seemed to drown out all thought, all outside sensation. Her arms fell slowly to her sides as he came closer. Jack Lynch felt his insides go silent, the eternal neurotic monologue that played endlessly in his head derailed, at least for the moment. All he saw was her face growing larger in front of him, filling his vision, the scent of her perfume and hair dizzying him. He leaned into her slowly at first, gently, and kissed her. She shuddered slightly and he put his arms around her loosely, then tighter, until they were wrapped together. As the storm raged outside, their lips pressed closer, the shadow of their embrace dancing on the narthex back wall of the St. Louis Cathedral.

In his mind, he saw Sally, the first time he kissed her. It was raining then, too, and they were wet, together, sheltered. She was so slight, so thin, that she felt delicate in his arms. For the first time since her death, he fought to push her image away, as if it had filled his vision long enough.

It was someone else he felt now, someone else who made him feel alive. He pulled away from her slightly, said: "P.J., I—"

Then, suddenly, P.J. Campbell went limp in his arms.

■ CHAPTER 19 ■

Jack opened the door of his apartment and stepped out into the hall. He held an overnight bag in one hand, his briefcase in the other. He locked the door carefully behind him, stopped, hesitated a moment, then turned and set the bag down. He stepped over to P.J.'s door, stood in front of it a moment, then knocked gently.

There was no response for perhaps fifteen seconds. After the late night they'd had, it was no surprise to him that she would still be asleep. He turned to pick up his bag.

The door opened, just a crack at first, then wider. P.J. leaned against the doorjamb in her bathrobe, hair in an electric blaze of disarray, bloodshot eyes struggling to see past heavy lids.

"How can you look so well-put-together after the night we had last night?" she moaned.

"I'm very good at faking it," Lynch said.

"What's the bag for?"

"I'm going to Baton Rouge. I may be there overnight. Depends on how quickly I can conclude my business. Sorry if I woke you up."

"Oh, I've been up. Just doesn't look that way. I'm going to be late for work. Wonder how my secretary will feel about the head of the substance abuse unit showing up for work hungover."

"Listen, P.J., I'm real sorry about last night."

She straightened up, brushed a splay of hair out of her face. "You don't have to take responsibility for last night. I'm a big girl."

"I know that. But I can't help but feel responsible, anyway. We drank too much, stayed out too late. I don't know, I . . ."

She stepped out into the hall. "I appreciate you taking such good care of me. That's the first time that's happened since high school. I guess I got kind of carried away."

"It's okay," he said. "No need to thank me."

"Kind of ruined your evening though, didn't it? Having your date pass out on you."

Jack smiled. "Funny, when I was in high school, it was a fantasy of mine. Then when it happened, all I thought about was getting you home without banging you against anything."

"How did we get back to your car?"

"I carried you over to the other side of the Square, then grabbed a cab up to Iberville."

P.J. tried to raise another smile, without much success. "Oh, god, I feel like such an idiot."

"Don't worry," he said. "Happens to the best of us."

"Didn't seem to happen to you."

Lynch shrugged. "Cast-iron liver?"

"That would worry me."

"Sometimes, it does me. Other times, I don't worry about it."

"By the way," she said. "I hope this never happens again, but if does, feel free to take the dress off next time. The only thing worse than waking up sick and hungover is waking up sick and hungover in the same clothes you had on the night before."

Jack blushed. "Well, I thought about it. I didn't figure we knew each other quite well enough yet."

"I appreciate your Southern gentlemanliness. Thanks for leaving a glass of water and the aspirin by the bed."

"Can I call you when I get back from B.R.?" Jack asked suddenly.

"I'd hoped you would."

■ 163

"Can I kiss you goodbye before I go?"

"You may not want to," she warned. "I haven't brushed my teeth yet."

Jack stepped toward her. "I'll take my chances." He leaned down and gave her a quick peck on the lips. He turned, picked up his bags. "Our first date was a lot of fun. I hope it won't be our last."

"Don't worry."

Lynch walked down the hall, plodding under the weight of the bag and briefcase.

"Jack?"

He stopped, turned his head around to face her. "Yeah?"

"Which one was it?"

"Which one was what?"

"Which one was the alcoholic, your mother or your father?"

Lynch's shoulders tightened visibly under his suitcoat. He pivoted slowly on his right foot to face her squarely. His jaw was set solid, his eyes two dark, burning, bloodshot circles set above purple shadows.

"Both," he answered. He sighed and his face fell almost imperceptibly. "But they're both dead. My father was killed in a wreck when I was three. Drunk, hit a telephone pole. My mother died a couple of months ago."

He hesitated, looked down at the floor. "Finally. They're both dead finally. And I'm free of it."

P.J. grinned, her left incisor shining white in the early morning light streaming in through the hall window.

"You're never free of them. Alcoholic parents never die; they just lie six feet under waiting for you."

He stared at her, his face stone. After a moment, he cleared his throat, then said: "I've got to go. See you."

"Yeah," she said. "See you. Call me when you get back?"

He walked down the hall carrying his burden, his back to her.

"I'll bring a bottle of wine over," he kidded.

She groaned, loudly.

* * *

After the night before, Jack was glad to have the chance to leave town. Part of it was his frustration over not being able to untangle the network of lies that he felt was surrounding the extortion of five million dollars from the First Interstate Bank of Louisiana. He was astounded that the story had not been leaked to the newspapers yet. It seemed almost certain that someone—and Martin Brown was, of course, the most obvious candidate—would have made an anonymous call to either the newspaper or the television stations, if only to cause the bank the most embarrassment possible. It was equally certain that the longer the scandal went unresolved, the greater the chances that it would be brought to light. It was a race, really, and the only way he could win was to undo the damage before it had a chance to compound itself.

But there were other things as well. Lynch had not cried at his mother's funeral; had, in fact, felt more relief than anything else. It was impossible for him to mourn his mother's death. They had been a burden to each other for most of their lives. The two or three times a year they spoke was a strain for both of them. His mother's drinking had plagued his formative years and his early adult years; the physical problems that resulted from her years of abuse had taken an equally dreadful toll on both of them the past decade. He loved her, of course, and understood that her disease was one she could not control. He could forgive her for that. What he could never resolve, though, was the sense that her twisted combination of emotional neediness and emotional abuse was something she could not control as well. He could forgive her drinking; he could neither forgive nor forget all her years of psychic vampirism. It had all come to a head during his doomed first marriage to Katherine Herbert, his college sweetheart who was more like his mother than he ever dared admit to himself. Katherine and his mother hated each other to the bone marrow from the first moment they met. He was forced to make a choice between the two. As any young, normal man would have done, he chose hormones over blood and put distance between himself and his mother.

Katherine and his mother had sized each other up and declared that until the moment death carried them to the other side, they would hate each other. And they had. His mother had never forgiven him his choice, although to hear her tell it, there had never been any bad feeling between any of them to start with and she never understood for a moment why her Jackie quit calling her and writing her regularly, and why he never brought his lovely, successful wife out to California to see her. She had held that illusion until the Alzheimer's or the Karsikoff's Psychosis or the senility or the simple wearing out of brain cells had robbed her of it, and she laid in a nursing-home bed for almost a year unable to remember her Jackie's name or anyone else's.

And now, Jack thought, as he fought the traffic under the interstate bridge on Carrollton Avenue, they were both on the other side. Death had claimed both his mother and his wife, as well as more people in his life than he cared to summarize at that moment, and he was alive and mostly well, still on this side, with the illusion that he carried within him not a trace of survivor's guilt.

He was aware also of a growing loneliness within. Perhaps it was turning forty with not much in the way of resources to pursue the American dream. More likely it was the growing conviction that this was the way life was going to be for him. A forty-year-old man, especially a forty-year-old-man with a lot of mileage on him, was much less willing to admit the possibility of change and the potential of redesigning a life than someone younger. At some point in every man's life, the Popeye Syndrome hits: he looks at himself and says he yams what he yams, and that's all what he yams, with two possible results: either he finds a kind of peace in that, or he goes completely off the deep end.

Jack parked the car in front of Maud's house and took the steps up to the porch two at a time. The curtain was pulled on the door, so he couldn't tell if she was at home. He pushed the doorbell button and heard nothing, so he rapped on the glass.

He stood there waiting, but no response came from inside.

On a hunch, Jack walked around to the left side of the house and down the narrow walkway between Maud's house and the one next door.

"Maud," he called so as not to startle her.

"Yeah, I'm back here."

He turned the corner. Maud was seated in a wicker chair next to her garden, a cup of coffee in one hand, a stack of mail in her lap. She wore the same jeans she had on the other night, as well as a new blouse. It appeared, Lynch thought, that Maud Pelletier had given up shabby housedresses.

"Don't get up," he said.

"Okay," she smiled, looking up from an open letter. "I won't."

"How are you, dear?" he said, leaning down and giving her a no more than friendly peck on the cheek.

"Fine. Can I offer you some coffee?"

"No, I don't have a lot of time. I'm on my way out of town."

"Oh, dear. Does this mean we won't see you again for months?"

Jack laughed. "Not this time. I'm on my way to B.R. to do a little digging."

"Digging, huh?"

"Yeah, and I just wanted to give you this," he said. He dug around in his pocket and pulled out a spare keyring. "Here's a key to the office for you. There are three keys, actually. This one gets in the building after hours. These two get you in the front door of the office and into my own office."

"Okay. When do you want me to start?"

"The phone's been turned on. You can start moving your stuff down there today if you want. If that's not cool, move in tomorrow. But I'd like to start getting the phones covered sometime tomorrow."

"No problem. I'll go in today."

"Thanks." He handed her the keyring. She held it up, studied it.

"What's the fourth key for?"

"It's an extra key to my apartment, just in case you or anybody else ever needs to get in."

She eyed him curiously, perhaps laced with considerable suspicion. "Why would I need a key to your apartment?"

"It's not like that, Maud. You're my best friend. Hell, maybe my only friend. I don't have anybody else to give a spare key to."

Her expression softened. "Okay. I'll take good care of it."

He fished a card out of his pocket and fumbled with a pen. "Here are the new phone numbers as well."

She took the card and slipped it into the shirt pocket of the blouse. "You be careful up there in Baton Rouge," she said.

"I might be back tonight. If it's not too late, I'll call you. Otherwise, see you in the office tomorrow."

"I'll be there."

"Listen, I gotta run. You take care, my dear."

Jack walked over and bent down to her, then gave her another casual cheek brush. "Be good," he said.

"Oh, I always am. That's part of my problem. I always am."

▪ CHAPTER 20 ▪

Louisiana Lottery Commission read the gold and black decal above the immense dark wooden doors. And below that, in smaller gold letters: Andover Brouchard, Chairman.

Jack Lynch pushed the door open and walked into a large carpeted lobby under a high ceiling in the Louisiana State Capitol, or as it was called locally, "the house that Huey built."

"Good afternoon," a middle-aged woman in a stiff blue dress and gold necklace said. "May I help you?"

"Hi," Jack said. "My name's Jack Lynch and I'm a freelance writer from New Orleans. I'm doing an article for *Gaming Industry News* on the lottery and I could use a little help."

The woman eyed him carefully, then decided he looked scruffy enough to actually be a freelance writer.

"Please have a seat, Mr. Lynch," she instructed. "I'll see if Mr. Cole can talk to you."

"Great."

Lynch sat on a brown leather sofa that must have set the taxpayers back enough to feed a family of four for a month. The receptionist's desk was a massive, ornately carved oak piece. He wondered what the boss's looked like.

The state of Louisiana may be poor, he thought, *but it'll never be tacky.*

"Mr. Cole will see you," the woman announced, pointing

toward a hall that went down through two glass doors. "He's our public information officer. Third door on the right."

Jack walked through the double doors and down the hall. An open door, third down on the right, led into a small, windowless office crowded with books, magazines, and the kind of desk issued a minor and insignificant bureaucrat. Even the receptionist's was bigger.

"Jack Lynch from New Orleans, Mr. Cole," he said brightly, extending a hand. Bert Cole looked like the kind of man who'd rather be a novelist or a great journalist, only he'd had too many kids too early in life and now couldn't afford to walk out on the kind of gig that offered the benefits and security of a civil service job. He was pale from lack of sun, wore thick glasses, and even though he was clearly younger than Lynch, was already exhibiting the stoop of an over-burdened drone.

"Please, Mr. Lynch, call me Bert," he offered, standing up and taking Jack's hand. "What can I do for you today?"

"I'm doing a piece for *Gaming Industry News.*" Lynch took a seat as Bert settled back into his own chair. "I could use a little background on the Lottery, especially the men and support staff on the Commission. I could also use some information on the company that's actually going to be running the Lottery. What was it, the Gaming Corporation of America?"

"GCA. Sure, that's no problem. In fact, I've got a press package prepared that should have everything you need."

"Will it include some extensive background on the commissioners? I'd like for our readers to really get to know these guys, to get an idea of where they're coming from, how they envision the Lottery helping the state. Real positive piece, you know."

"Well, it depends on what you call extensive. But we've prepared a packet that I think will answer almost all your questions. And I'll be happy to answer anything not covered by the press kit."

"Great," Lynch said, opening a notebook. He scribbled down a few meaningless notes just to look like a reporter.

"By the way, what is *Gaming Industry News*? I've been around this business awhile and I've never heard of it."

The reason for that, Lynch thought, was that he had taken great pains to make sure no such publication existed. The last thing he needed was some government flack calling to check his credentials.

"It's a newsletter, really. Not a magazine. Not yet. Sold through subscription only. Very expensive. I don't have a sample copy on me, but tell you what. I'll have one sent to you as soon as I get back to my office."

"Where's it published?" Cole asked. "Where are their offices?"

"North Dakota," Lynch said off the top of his head.

"Oh, I see. Well, the North Dakotans are very interested in gaming these days. What with the Indian tribes and all."

Lynch had no idea what the man was talking about, but shook his head intelligently all the same. "If I could get a copy of that press kit."

"Oh, sure. I'll have Rosemary get you one." He picked up the phone and spoke into it. Lynch glanced around the man's office. A few trophy plaques hung on the wall, the kind professionals award each other because nobody in the real world gives a damn who wrote the best story on agricultural production to come out of Northeast Louisiana since 1954. There was a picture of Cole as well, standing in the background as three fat cigar chompers shook hands with the Governor while pretending to slap him on the back. Bert Cole, Lynch realized, was the kind of man who would spend his life in the background making pictures like this possible for other people. No one would ever slap his back or put him center focus in a picture. He was perennially and forever a flack, the kind of man who took menial requests from the higher-ups and executed them among the higher-paid.

Lynch felt briefly sorry for him, until he realized that he had spent the better part of his adult life performing the same duties. The thought gave him a pang.

"Okay, Mr. Lynch," Bert Cole said, "Rosemary will have

your press kit ready outside. Please, take one of my cards and call me if you need anything else."

Lynch stood up, determined to say something to this man that might brighten his day.

"Please Bert, call me Jack. I really appreciate all your help. It must be kind of rough for you having to fend off the press and protect the big guys. Looks like you're doing a hell of a job."

"I appreciate that," Bert said, smiling. "I really do. And you call me any time you need anything, you hear?"

"Sure, Bert," Lynch said, backing out the door. "You knock 'em dead, now."

"You, too, buddy." The happier Bert got, the thicker his drawl became. If Jack wasn't careful, he'd get an invitation to dinner, to meet the wife and kids, and admire Bert's hunting dogs.

Lynch left the Louisiana Lottery Commission offices with a wave of nausea spreading over him, and the feeling that he'd just made a friend.

"The computer's very easy to use," the young woman clerk said, leaning over Jack and pointing to a row of keys across the top of the keyboard. "It's all menu-driven. Just hit the 'F10' key to start and follow the instructions. If you need help, hit the 'F1' key or come get me."

"Thanks. I really appreciate it."

"And anything that comes up in these records is public information," she added. "Hit 'F5' to get a printout. You can pick up your printout off that printer right down there. Each page costs fifty cents."

Lynch scribbled down notes so he wouldn't forget which F key to punch, and when.

He was the only person at a row of computer terminals in the search room at the secretary of state's office. He had before him the stack of papers from the Louisiana Lottery Commission P.R. flack and an open notebook. Jack Lynch knew as much about computers as he did about flying a space shuttle, but figured if there was anything delicate about the system, the clerk would have warned him. He held a breath, then slowly let it out as he hit the 'F10' key on the top row of buttons as if it were a trigger. The green screen flickered, then came to life.

WELCOME TO THE
LOUISIANA SECRETARY OF STATE
CORPORATE RESEARCH RECORDS
FOR HELP, PRESS F1
TO PRINT ANY PAGE, PRESS F5
TO CONTINUE, PRESS (ENTER)

Lynch scanned the keyboard and found the ENTER key. The screen went blank for a moment, then filled again with green letters.

LOUISIANA SECRETARY OF STATE
CORPORATE RESEARCH RECORDS
MAIN MENU
NAME SEARCH - F2   OFFICERS - F3
TAX STATUS - F4   CHARTER - F6
STOCK./OFF CHAIN SEARCH   - F7
ANNUAL REPORT CROSS-REF NO.   - F8

TO MAKE SELECTION, PRESS FUNCTION
TO LEAVE THIS MENU, PRESS < ESC >
FOR HELP, PRESS F1

Lynch pressed F2. A prompt read: ENTER NAME, THEN PRESS < ENTER >

Lynch typed "Gaming Corporation Of America" and pressed the ENTER key. The computer blinked: SEARCHING—PLEASE WAIT.

Ten seconds later, the screen jumped to life with information. Jack pressed in close to the fuzzy green letters. The Gaming Corporation of America was located in Metairie, Louisiana, a New Orleans bedroom community. The address was familiar; one of the myriad of office buildings on Causeway Boulevard near the lake.

Lynch read on. Terry Hanover was chairman of the board

and president of the company. The corporation had been founded only nine months earlier. There were six major stockholders; two, besides Terry, had the last name Hanover. There were 500,000 shares outstanding in the company. The officers and major stockholders held all but 75,000 shares. Lynch guessed these shares were spread around among employees and other family members.

A sub-menu below the information explained that Jack could access other information on the company by hitting one of the function keys. He hit "F5" first to print the information on this screen and heard a whirring sound as the file was successfully sent to the laser printer at the other end of the room.

"Look at me," he whispered. "I'm computing."

He hit another key to bring up the files on the officers and major stockholders. Disclosure rules, Lynch knew, required that background information on the officers and directors, as well as major stockholders, be filed with the application for corporate charter.

He watched as line after line of green jetted across the screen. Terry Hanover was a graduate of what was then called Louisiana State University in New Orleans, Lynch saw. Now it was just the University of New Orleans, and Hanover got his bachelor's degree in industrial engineering there in 1976, then an M.B.A. in 1988.

"Not bad," Lynch whispered. The other two Hanovers were equally well educated, one with a degree in computer science, the other with a bachelor's and master's in electrical engineering.

The list of officers, directors, and stockholders rolled across the screen until Lynch's eyes got tired of following. He pressed the button to send the files to the printers, then brought up another menu. As long as he was getting information, he thought, he may as well collect it all. The final menu choice was to get a cross-reference number to request a copy of the latest annual report from the secretary of state's office. That choice gave nothing; the Gaming Corporation of America was too young to have filed its first annual report.

Jack went to the printer and retrieved his stack of pages.

What else was available, he wondered. So far, the trip had been a waste. All he was doing was collecting a bunch of paper and running up expenses for Carlton Smith and the bank. He took the papers back to his seat and plopped down. What could he find in the seemingly endless stream of computer printout, line after line, page after page? He kept saying to himself that there had to be something, there had to be. But what? And the other voice inside him kept telling him he was wasting his time, that he was going after something that simply did not exist.

For the time being, Lynch was willing to ignore that voice. He didn't see any alternative. There was nothing else to go on.

He turned back to the printouts. He opened the press kit on the Louisiana Lottery Commission. Surely, he thought, no one would be so obvious as to be on the Commission and involved in GCA at the same time. There would have to be some way to disguise the connection, to hide the thread.

The two stacks of information had no names in common. It appeared from what Lynch could tell that the Gaming Corporation of America had played fair and square, had submitted the best proposal and won the contract. Everything was on the up and up, no influence bought, no favors traded, no graft allowed. Play fair now, boys, with the tax-payer's money. They're trusting you.

Right, Lynch thought, *and maybe the Tooth Fairy and Santa Claus will be appointed to the Commission as well.*

Jack rubbed his tired eyes. He hadn't had enough sleep. That, combined with too much to drink the night before and the long drive to Baton Rouge, left him sleepy and fuzzy.

I'm not thinking hard enough, he scolded himself. *C'mon, dammit. Think! What other ways are out there?*

Lynch pressed the button labelled Esc a few times. At that moment, he wished he could find a little escape himself. The screen went blank, then exploded once again in green with the main menu:

LOUISIANA SECRETARY OF STATE
CORPORATE RESEARCH RECORDS

```
                    MAIN MENU
         NAME SEARCH - F2    OFFICERS - F3
         TAX STATUS - F4    CHARTER - F6
         STOCK./OFF CHAIN SEARCH    - F7
         ANNUAL REPORT CROSS-REF NO.   - F8

         TO MAKE SELECTION, PRESS FUNCTION
         TO LEAVE THIS MENU, PRESS  < ESC >
               FOR HELP, PRESS F1
```

Lynch looked at his choices. "What is a 'Stock./Off Chain Search?' " he muttered. "What the hell, go for it. . . ."

He pressed F7. A moment's wait, and then the computer spoke again:

```
         ENTER NAME < LAST, FIRST >  THEN
       < ENTER >  FOR GLOBAL RECORD SEARCH.
```

Lynch typed in the name "Hanover, Terry." He hit the Enter key and waited.

When the computer responded, Lynch's eyes widened and his mouth opened involuntarily. Terry Hanover, it seemed, had quite a business career going.

CHAPTER 21

Development Data Systems, Inc.; MicroData Enterprises, Ltd.; The Jackson Square Corporation; Medical Data Systems, Inc.; Express Data Associates, Inc.; Data Corporation of America; CompuCare Associates, Ltd.—

The list went on another few lines, and these were just the Louisiana corporations. According to the computer, Terry Hanover was also a director or major shareholder in another half dozen companies out of state.

"Jesus," Lynch whispered. "This guy has to be some kind of freaking tycoon or something."

All the companies worked in some aspect of the computer industry as well. Shades of Ross Perot. . . .

How was it, Jack wondered, that he'd never heard of Terry Hanover. He prided himself on knowing the movers and shakers in New Orleans; his years at the bank had put him in close contact with most of them, and those he never met, he knew about. But Terry Hanover was different. To begin with, judging from his college graduation dates, he was still fairly young. To have a finger in that many different pies required a lot of stroke, the kind of stroke that takes more years than Terry Hanover could possibly have accumulated.

Or maybe, Lynch thought, Hanover wasn't the mover and shaker he appeared to be. Any clown with a few bucks, a lawyer, and a mailing address could form a corporation.

Before the shakeout of the eighties and early nineties, the streets had been full of guys who looked great on paper but couldn't make a car payment.

But still, to have formed a company that was impressive enough to land the management contract for a state-owned lottery that would be grossing in the hundreds of millions was quite a coup. Lynch was looking forward to meeting this Terry Hanover one day. But for now, he realized that the Louisiana secretary of state's computer had opened up a whole new trail for him. Lynch glanced down at his watch; it was already three in the afternoon. There wasn't much chance Lynch would get it all done before the offices closed at 4:30. He'd have to find a hotel room, then come back tomorrow.

After all, he had to gather and print out information on every company that every stockholder, officer, and director of the Gaming Corporation of America had anything to do with. There was a thread to be followed here; Jack Lynch only hoped it would lead him somewhere worthwhile.

There had been the promise of a hefty retainer and a decent expense account from Jack Lynch's newest client, but so far he hadn't seen any of it. He decided prudently that since he was covering this one with his own nearly maxed-out VISA, he'd find the nearest cheap motel, rather than a Hyatt or Marriott.

"Yessir, we have a single for twenty-one ninety-five," the brown-skinned, black mustached clerk said.

"I'll take it." Lynch reached for the key before the man changed his mind.

The room was small—cinderblock painted in a disgusting hue of swimming-pool green—but clean. Lynch switched on the evening news and settled back on the bed with his open briefcase in front of him. He loosened his tie and rolled up his sleeves, then fluffed the pillow behind his head. Before the network news was halfway over, Jack Lynch had drifted into an uneasy, unsettled sleep.

Two hours later, Lynch awoke in a cold sweat, his arms

locked rock-hard at his side, his teeth sore from grinding in his sleep. The dream had returned, although he was unable to remember all but the most vague images.

It was dark, always dark. And always there was a woman, a different woman every time, but always a woman. Tonight, it had been Sally again, his murdered fiancée. There were cars, and dark, hulking forms coming at them between the cars. All the cars were the same, and they were arranged in a way that created a kind of maze. And he and Sally ran between the cars, first one way, then another, with the forms chasing them all the while. Each time it seemed they were about to escape, a form jumped out between the cars and blocked them.

Her hand was tiny in his. She panted as they ran; she grunted as he jerked her faster, to try and get away, to escape. Only there was no escape. And the shapes came at them in the dark from all sides now, and he was down on the asphalt, the asphalt that was still hot from the day's sunshine and gritty with tiny pieces of gravel. The men start kicking them and he drops her hand, the blows to his gut and his head fierce, powerful, blunt. But for some reason or other, not painful. It is as if he is numb everywhere, cannot feel the impact of shoe leather on ribs anymore, the scrape of heel on face. The men kick so fast, so hard, they have to reach out with their massive arms and their ham hands and balance themselves on the roofs of the cars.

Jack, on the ground, reaches for Sally. But a boot comes down on him again. They are kicking her as well, and with each kick, she gets pushed farther and farther away. She reaches for him, vainly, her thin white arms almost glowing in the darkness beneath the eerie streetlights.

He opens his mouth, tries to scream to her, but no sound comes out. He pulls himself up on all fours, the kicks in his gut now helping him up, and he starts for her. Suddenly, the biggest hulking dark form of all is in front of him and the man leans down, close in Jack's face, and whispers something Jack cannot hear. But in the twisted logic that is dream-logic, Jack knows it is something dreadful. He knows she is gone.

He knows he will not see her again. He tries to push past the man, but he is too big. He steps in front of Jack and blocks his view of Sally. Jack panics, tries to stand up. The huge man's foot comes off the ground, catching Jack beneath the chin. His head snaps back; he falls over and begins spiralling downward. He raises his head off the asphalt one last time, looks between the man's legs. Sally is gone. She is nowhere. Jack starts to scream, but again, nothing comes out, and he closes his eyes and begins the deep spiral into black. . . .

Jack Lynch shot up out of bed, drenched in sweat, shaking. *This,* he thinks, *was a bad one.* The first one in a while. A bad one.

He got to his feet unsteadily and walked over to a bureau in the hotel room where his bag sat unopened. He flicked the silver catches on both sides, opened the lid and leaned it against the wall behind the bureau. He pulled two neatly folded shirts out of the way and retrieved a bottle of Dewar's.

Two shrink-wrapped plastic glasses sat on a tray on the bathroom vanity. Lynch tore the wrapping off one, then poured two fingers of the amber liquid. He ran the tap for a moment, then filled the glass with cold water.

Jack took a long slug of the drink, the chemical warmth radiating down the back of his throat and glowing to a lump in his stomach. He stared into the bathroom mirror as he stood there, the wrinkled, sweaty shirt hanging off him sloppily, great dark circles under his eyes.

He was tired, weary to the point of dropping. He felt as if his feet were so heavy he could barely lift them. He pulled his cigarette pack out of his coat jacket and lit one. He'd been trying, with some success, to cut down lately. In fact, this was only his fourth or fifth of the day, but it was a necessary one. As necessary a one as the drink, given the dream he'd just had.

It had been over two years since Sally's death. He'd been warned that it might take at least that long to recover, to work through the grief. For much of the past months, he had walked around in a kind of daze, going through the day-to-day motions of working, eating, and all the daily, tedious rituals that comprise much of life.

He missed her still, always would, but it was not as if every day was agony, every moment an ache. Life went on, he kept telling himself, and in fact, he did have many of the same reactions to people, to life, that he'd always had. He thought of P.J. Campbell, an attractive, intelligent woman who seemed to see something in him, and who seemed, at least, to be willing to look further. He saw in the mirror a weary man roaring headlong into middle-age, but he saw that because he was comparing himself to the Jack Lynch that existed twenty years ago, the Jack Lynch who could go days without sleep, work constantly, play hard, never slow down, never let the mental processes go dull around the edges.

That Jack Lynch was gone forever. He mourned that Jack Lynch, as all people mourn at least some part of the person they were in youth. But other people looking at the middle-aged Jack Lynch saw something entirely different. To outsiders, he was a thin, dark, well-dressed man whose face was beginning to take on "character." He seldom smiled, but when he did, his smile was bright, with an unmistakable charm to it. His eyes, though tired, still sparkled with life and would even be thought his most attractive feature by some.

Lynch steadied his nerves and finished the cigarette. He had been so engrossed in his work that he had skipped lunch. The scotch on an empty stomach had given him the faintest trace of a buzz. He knew it was time to eat.

Jack loaded his stack of papers into his briefcase—reading material for another dinner spent alone—and set off in search of a decent restaurant.

By noon the next day, Jack had spent nearly fifty dollars on copies. It would take him the better part of a day just to read and organize the information he'd obtained. As he walked to his car, he decided that this would be a good project for Maud to take over. After all, she had to be bored with watching the silent phone and opening the junk mail.

The northern sky was clouding over; Lynch decided to leave the top up on the drive back to New Orleans. He left the capitol grounds and took the shortest route to the loop, then got onto I-10 in sight of Tiger Stadium. The long drive stretched ahead of him, with only the high-pitched whine of the engine to keep him company.

Time and distance went by quickly. His thoughts wandered aimlessly, drifting without connection from one subject to another. He fantasized scenarios of how someone in the data processing division of the First Interstate Bank of Louisiana might have been behind the successful extortion. He turned each thread, each possible story line, over in his mind until they all blended together in a muddle. He had only gone to Baton Rouge in the first place because of some vague hunch that something about Harold Gupton—and he wasn't sure what—stank. Gupton was the director of one of the largest computer networks in the state, and a consulting member of the Louisiana Lottery. No one would know better than he how important it was to keep the shine on both institutions as clean and free of blemish as possible. And no one would know better than he how vulnerable that made everything. Whoever the extortionist, the software bomber, was, he had perfect timing.

Lynch slapped the steering wheel as he came within sight of the city. "No, dammit, it's too big a coincidence," he said out loud over the blast of wind and engine noise. "Just too damn big a coincidence."

Maud Pelletier was arranging flowers when Jack opened the door to his office. She had brought a standing floor lamp from home, a small area rug, and had somehow managed to turn the spartan furnishings of the office into something warm and cheery.

"Look at this place," Lynch said. "This is great."

Maud turned, smiled at him. "You like it?"

"It's wonderful!" Lynch threw his coat across a chair and laid his briefcase on her desk.

"I always could make chicken salad out of chicken poop," she offered.

"A good skill in this day and age. Any mail?"

"No. A couple of phone calls, though. Carlton Smith wants you to call him. And some fellow named Rapid Edward, whoever that is."

Lynch laughed. "Fast Eddie. He's going to be doing a little work for me on the side."

Maud plucked a couple of pink telephone messages off her desk and handed them to Jack. "He said he'd call back. He didn't leave a number."

"Eddie doesn't have a phone in his office. He's a little inaccessible, unless you know where to find him."

"You have any luck up in B.R.?" Maud sat down in her chair. She was wearing what looked like a new dress.

"Maybe. I'm going to get you to help me out on some of it. I've got a bag full of papers to go through."

"Sure. Beats sitting around here waiting for the phones to ring."

Jack leaned over and opened his briefcase, then took out a pile of printouts nearly two inches thick.

"Good heavens," she said. "You get all that up in Baton Rouge?"

"Yeah, it turns out that the fellow who's head of the company that's going to run the Louisiana Lottery has his finger in about two dozen other pies as well."

"That doesn't surprise me," Maud said. "I wouldn't think the state would award that contract to small fry."

"Agreed. But what I'm looking for is some connection between a fellow named Harold Gupton and the head of GCA."

"GCA?"

"The Gaming Corporation of America," Lynch answered. "They're going to run the lottery. Fellow named Terry Hanover is the president, founder, chairman of the board, head poobah."

"So's who's Harold Gupton?"

"He's head of the data processing division at the bank. He's also head of the advisory committee that recommended Terry Hanover's company get the contract to run the lottery."

"Ahh, so you smell a rat?" Maud took the loose stack of papers and jogged them into a neat pile on her desk.

"Well, let's say the foul stench of business as usual is beginning to waft through my window."

"This is all very neat and pretty," Maud said. "But what's any of it got to do with this little extortion problem the bank's got?"

"That's just it, my darling. It's all too damn neat and pretty. Any other time, the bank would have gone after the bloodsucker with both barrels. But there's so much at stake here. Like Carlton said, it's better to lose five big ones than to get a hundred million worth of bad publicity. Whatever happens with the Louisiana Lottery, it's got to have at least the perception of being a square game."

"Even if it's not."

"Oh, hell, Maud, you know it's not. You expect a fair amount of graft and corruption. Comes with the lease. But if people think the integrity of the system itself isn't what it's supposed to be, they'll go back to playing street-corner numbers. And the state will go down the toilet."

Maud shook her head. "How did we get in this mess?"

"Welcome to the nineties, darling. The age of diminished expectations." Lynch picked up his briefcase and disappeared into his office. "We're on our way to becoming the world's most technologically advanced Third World nation."

Lynch fumbled with his cigarette pack while cradling the phone between his left shoulder and ear.

"Hello, Jack. How's it going?" Carlton asked.

"Fine. I just got back from B.R. Have you still got an account with Disclosure?"

"I don't in my office, but the bank does. The terminal's down in the Trust Department."

"I'd go through the SEC, but there's not time. Can you run me the data on some out-of-state companies?"

"Of course. Let me get a pen."

Lynch pulled his notebook out of his briefcase and opened on the desk in front of him. He couldn't help but notice that the scarred and scuffed surface of the old wooden desk had been polished to a bright shine. *Maud,* he thought, *is a treasure.*

"Okay, go."

"First one's in Delaware," Lynch said.

"That figures."

"Dedicated Data Systems, Inc. Terry Hanover's on the board of directors. I need the rest of the officers and directors as well."

"This is a publicly traded corporation?"

"I don't know," Lynch answered.

"If it was publicly traded, I could also get you compensation numbers from the database."

"May as well try."

"What's the next one?"

"Another Delaware, Electronic Data Transfer Associates."

"Jesus, where'd they get a name like that?"

"They're all like that, Carlton. This guy Terry Hanover breeds computer companies like you or I would raise Black Labs."

"I remember reading his resume and background information when we were in negotiations on the line of credit, but I don't remember it being this extensive."

"Maybe he's held something back?"

"Maybe, what's the next one?"

"Only two more. A New York corporation. SYDATA Systems, Inc. And one in Connecticut. Data Products Research Corporation."

"It'll take a few hours to get all this information in." Carlton said after scribbling down the last name.

"And it's going to cost a fortune, I'm afraid."

"Don't worry about that. Whichever way it leads, it's money well spent."

"I'm glad you feel that way, because my next question concerns that very subject."

"You need some money, don't you?"

"You read my mind," Lynch said.

"I'll have a check cut this afternoon. If you don't mind, I'd rather feed you your money in smaller chunks. Easier to cover up, if you know what I mean."

"I don't care if you deliver cash in the middle of the night."

Carlton laughed. "We don't have to go that far."

"There's one more thing, Carlton. And this one's a little touchy."

"Okay."

"You gave me some background on everybody that works in the department. But I need more. Can I have copies of their personnel files."

There was a long moment of silence. "That is touchy, Jack. Personnel's very concerned about privacy issues these days."

"They'll never go any further than you and me."

Carlton sighed. "Are you sure you need them?"

"That's just it," Lynch said. "I won't know if I need them until I get them."

"All right. I'll arrange a discreet photocopying session. But we'd better be careful on this one, Jack. This is pushing the envelope for sure."

"Carlton," Jack said, "that's what envelopes were made for."

■ *CHAPTER 22* ■

You hungry?" Lynch asked as he walked back into the outer office.

Maud was bent over her desk, reading glasses pushed up on the bridge of her nose, studying photocopies. She held a red pen in her right hand, making what seemed to be random circles on pieces of paper as they passed in front of her. Paper was spread all over her desk already. She'd soon need more room.

Jack cleared his throat. "Maud?"

She looked up, startled. "Yes?"

"You hungry?"

"What you got in mind?"

"Actually, I thought I'd run and get us a couple of sandwiches."

"I don't believe I can handle another sack from Bud's Broiler."

"You're never going to let me forget that, are you? All right, how about a shrimp po' boy from the Pearl?"

"Dressed, no tomato," she instructed, bending back to her work. "Fries, too. And a large coke."

Jack stood there staring at her a moment. "Okay," he said. "Why don't I make it my treat."

Maud ignored him, her brow scrunching up as she held a

copy up in each hand, poring over two pieces of paper at once.

"Yeah," he said, pushing the door open. "My treat."

Three hours later, Carlton Smith called with the information Jack had requested on the out-of-state companies.

"I can fax it over to you any time, but there's ten or twelve sheets here."

"I don't have a fax machine, anyway," Lynch admitted, looking at the pile of papers scattered across his desk.

"He doesn't like computers and doesn't have a fax machine," Carlton said. "When are you going to enter the twentieth century, my boy?"

"I had to be dragged kicking and screaming into the nineteenth. Why don't I just walk over and pick them up."

"I'll save you the trouble. I'll messenger them over to you, along with your check. Unless you'd like to have me deposit it directly into your account."

"Are you kidding?" Lynch said. "I wouldn't keep my money in that bank if it was the last coffee can on earth."

"Are you serious?" Carlton asked, surprised.

"Carlton, I didn't even keep my money in that bank back when I worked there."

Carlton laughed so loud Lynch had to pull the phone away from his ear. "Mr. Jennings would have loved that," he said, between laughs.

"I like to think so," Lynch offered.

Carlton rang off. Jack settled back into his chair and stared blankly at the copies in front of him. He heard the scraping of a chair in the outer office, and Maud came in with a yellow legal pad in her hand.

"Okay, here's the chain as best I can put it together," she said. She pulled a chair up to the other side of Jack's desk, and set the pad down between them.

"I've drawn it out. Terry Hanover seems to be a power in at least these twelve companies." Maud pointed out twelve circles she'd drawn on the pad, with the words TERRY HANOVER in caps in the center. "As far as I can tell, he started out with MicroData Enterprises. I can't tell exactly what business they were in, but it had something to do with exporting computers to some Middle Eastern countries. I've gotten that far, at least.

"Then he went into CompuCare Associates and Medical Data Systems. That one's easy, and it makes me want to shoot the guy. Both of those companies are set up to keep track of people with medical problems or a history of suing doctors."

"Great," Lynch said, "so they pull your name up on a screen when you apply for insurance or need a doctor, and if you've got a bad case of chronic litigation, they tell you to hit the road."

"Exactly. Real nice bunch of guys. Working hand-in-hand with the insurance companies to get the troublemakers out of the system."

"I may shoot the sonofabitch myself," Lynch offered.

"Now the Jackson Square Corporation was where Hanover started to get politically connected. By the way, doing a little deduction from his college graduation dates, I'd have to say the guy was no more than about twenty-eight when he started filling in his corporate dancecard."

"Yeah, I saw that," Jack said. "And judging from that, I'd say the guy's maybe thirty-seven, thirty-eight tops now."

"You remember Maynard Broussard?"

"Yeah," Jack said, hesitating. "I think so. Wasn't he Mayor or something back in the sixties."

"Maynard Broussard was as close as we've ever come to having a mayor in New Orleans that was competent and honest. He was one of the reasons we never had any serious burnings down here, not like out in Watts."

"Yeah, but wasn't there some kind of scandal or something toward the end of the administration?"

"It wasn't no scandal. He just quit, that's all. Blew the whole city away. Here he was, the most popular man in office this century. Could'a been elected again by a landslide. Decides to chuck it all. Nobody ever figured out why. At least not for a few years."

"Then what happened?"

"I used to hear at the newspaper that he was a real behind-the-scenes-type powerbroker in the late sixties, early seventies. Then he just kind of faded into the background, got out of politics altogether."

"Let me guess—he started making some serious money."

Maud tapped her pencil on the pad. "Exactly. And he did it all very quietly. Never would allow himself to be interviewed. But he had a lot of money and a lot of power and he was willing to bankroll anything that interested him and had potential."

"And I gather our young friend Mr. Hanover came along at just the right time."

"You're pretty smart, you know that?" she teased. "Look."

Maud pulled one of the photocopies out of the stack. "The Jackson Square Corporation. The company behind the development of most of the nonpublic areas on the riverfront from Cafe du Monde to Audubon Park."

"Jesus, Maud. That's some serious money."

"Serious as a heart attack."

"My guess is that somehow our young Mr. Hanover got the support of Mayor Maynard Broussard and that's when his career really started to take off," Jack said. Maud nodded back eagerly. "Oh, well, everybody needs a mentor."

"But how does this help us find whatever it is you're looking for?" she asked.

Jack leaned back and scraped a hand across his jaw. It was getting late in the afternoon; he needed a shower, a shave, and probably a few good hours sleep.

"Sometimes, Maud, you just got to follow the money. Even if it ain't the right money. Money does two things. It draws more money, and it draws people who like money. Just like flies to syrup. When you find money, you usually find both those things."

Maud looked thoughtfully at him for a moment. "My heavens. Sometimes you're almost profound."

Lynch sat up quickly, trying to raise his energy level by torquing his body, as if to squeeze whatever was left in there out so he could keep going. His effort was interrupted by a loud knock at the door.

"Who could that be?"

"Carlton was having some things messengered over here," Jack answered. "Including a check. Hope that's it."

Maud got up and went into the outer lobby. Jack followed and leaned against the door jamb as she opened the front door.

"Bank messenger, ma'am," a young, freckled man said.

"Thanks," Maud said.

Jack dug in his pocket and pulled out a couple of singles. He walked over to the man and stuck out his hand.

"Thank you, sir," the man said, turning and walking quickly away from the door.

Maud pulled a pair of scissors out of her drawer and slit the large, padded envelope.

"By the way, Maud," Jack said. "The stuff in that envelope's top secret, kind of. I mean, we're really not supposed to have it. The bank could get sued and we'd be in deep fertilizer if anybody found out we had it."

"My, my," Maud said, pulling the stack of papers out of the mailer. "Aren't we being little super spys—"

Her voice stopped as she scanned the first file in front of her. "Jack, is this what I think it is?"

"Personnel files. All the records on everybody down in data processing."

"Holy cow, get this away from me." She dropped the stack on the desk and backed away as if it were poisonous. "What in heavens name are you doing with that stuff?"

"Trying to find connections," Jack answered. "Nobody knows we have those files, and nobody ever *will* know. They don't leave this office except with me, and they're under lock and key any time we're not using them. Got it?"

"Yeah. Oh, look," Maud said, pulling a sealed white envelope out of the padded bag. "This must be your check."

Jack took it from her, ripped open the envelope, and smiled. "Twenty-five hundred," he said. "That'll get us through a couple of weeks, anyway."

"There was a pair of keys taped inside one of the drawers of my desk," Maud said, crossing behind her desk and pulling the center drawer open. "Maybe they fit something."

She pulled two small chrome keys out from under a strip of yellowed cellophane tape. "Let's try this."

Maud fit the key in the lock of the bottom, left-hand drawer of her desk and turned. "It works. These kind of locks are a joke, though."

"It's the best we can do for now," Jack said. "You take one key, give me the other. I'm not going to be needing the personnel files until later. I figure I'll stay late tonight, try to get a handle on this stuff. Right now, I think I'll run down to the bank and stick this check in."

"Okay," Maud said. "I'll stay here and keep working on the corporate trail. We've got a long way to go to really figure out Terry Hanover."

"Thanks," Jack said. "It's nearly quitting time now. If I'm not back when you leave, just lock up."

Maud grinned at him impatiently. "Really? I thought I'd leave everything open with a sign that says 'Free Stuff' taped on the door."

Outside, the late afternoon buzz of pedestrian and car traffic was a constant din and blur of movement. In his fatigue and his preoccupation, Lynch paid little attention to his surroundings as he wove his way in and out of the jostling crowds on Canal Street. There was a branch of his bank five blocks down toward the river and a block or so off Canal away from the Quarter.

From inside the Quarter, four or five blocks up Royal Street, he could hear the quick, brassy sound of a street jazz band as the musicians enthralled tourists and collected donations inside an open banjo case. This band was sophisticated and good, with the clear tinkling of a piano cutting through the horns and banjo. It amazed Lynch that street musicians would actually haul around an upright piano on a wheeled pallet from corner to corner. It was either a testament to dedication or a sorry comment on the number of regular gigs available.

The sky was unusually clear for a late spring afternoon. He would have expected rain by now, but none was on the horizon. A blend of automobile exhaust, cooking fumes, and the aroma of rotting garbage assaulted his senses.

Jack shook his head, forced his thoughts back to reality as he walked. Slowly, he was building connections. There was no way to know where they would lead, but the connections were there.

He stopped on the way back to his office and picked up another sandwich for dinner and a bottle of soda. With the heat and the long day he'd had, a couple of bottles of beer would have been a welcome relief. But he wanted to keep himself as sharp as possible for his work.

It was just after 5:30 when he got back to the Audubon Building. The security guard at the front desk was wrapping up his paperwork as Jack entered the building against the outgoing tide of tired workers.

"Working late tonight?" the guard asked.

"Yeah, playing catch-up."

"Aw, man," the guard smiled. "That's rough."

"Tell me about it," Jack said as the elevator door slid shut.

Maud was already gone. The files from Baton Rouge and Disclosure were in two neat stacks on his desk. A scribbled note lay on top of the center pile.

"I didn't get a chance to go through much of this," the note read. "But I'll pick it up tomorrow. Don't stay too late—Maud."

The personnel files could stay locked up for the time being; there were close to a hundred other pages that could occupy his night. Lynch took off his jacket, loosened his tie even further, and rolled up his shirt sleeves. He unwrapped his second shrimp po' boy of the day and laid it out on the greasy wax paper, then popped the top on a sweaty can of Barq's root beer. He relaxed behind his desk, glad to be alone with his work, and bit the corner off the sandwich and took a long gulp of the drink. It was good, he thought, to be home.

Four hours later, his eyes were heavy and drooping with exhaustion. Night had long since set in, and only the eerie, orange ambient light of Canal Street shone through his un-curtained windows. Paper was spread over every inch of his desk, along with page after page of scribbled handwritten notes on yellow legal pad. Dark circles spread out under his bloodshot eyes as he struggled to keep the words in focus. He knew that he was going to have to quit soon; in his state, if there was anything there to find, he might not notice.

There was one more company printout to go through. Jack racked the sheets into a neat pile and moved his desklamp a couple of inches closer. He squinted his eyes to focus and noticed the faint glow of a headache growing behind his forehead.

Visual Imaging Technologies, Inc., of Teaneck, New Jersey: the company grossed $22 million the past year, was eight years old, employed forty-two people. It specialized in high-tech medical imaging devices: MRIs, CAT scans, and the like.

"Jeez," Lynch muttered, "maybe Hanover's changing careers. Moving out of health care fraud and into lottery fraud."

He became silent as he read on. The company history section revealed that Terry Hanover was one of the founders, and had been on the board of directors for its entire existence. He was also the largest shareholder, owning not quite 800,000 shares in the company.

The latest annual report figures were as dry and dull as the rest of the report, but the picture it painted was just like the others. On paper, anyway, Terry Hanover looked very impressive. Lynch still couldn't figure out why he'd never heard of the man, his only explanation being that in this day and age, wealth was something best enjoyed quietly unless one had a Donald Trumplike pathological need for attention. And it was clear that Terry Hanover had no such need.

Jack was about to let it go, when he came to the last section, which detailed the other major company sharehold-ers and the directors. His eyes ran over it once, stopped, widened, then came back and read the whole section over again. Jack Lynch all but broke out laughing. There it was, hidden in the small print. It's always, he thought, buried in the small print, the last line in a section of eight-point type set solid, on a fuzzy printout uncovered late at night in bad light with a pair of tired eyes.

"H. Gupton," the line read, "240,000 shares."

Jack slammed his right fist into his left open palm. "Pow!" he yelled. "Nailed you, you son of a bitch!!"

▪ CHAPTER 23 ▪

This wasn't like finding the perp in a mugging or a street-corner shootout over a dope deal gone sour. The Mel Gibsons and the Clint Eastwoods went after those guys, and they got the glamour and the glory and the girls.

This was different. The evidence in this kind of crime wasn't a fingerprint or a ballistics test; it was some obscure line buried in a million other obscure lines in a stack of computer printout a mile high. The Dirty Harrys of this world were balding accountants and thick-waisted auditors with smudged glasses and fingers grimy from pencil lead, and eyes gone fuzzy from years of staring at computer screens. Yet the auditors and the accountants probably protected the populace as much or more than the tough guys with the guns and the sexy jawlines and the come-ons.

Lynch was no lawyer, but he knew enough about conflict-of-interest law to know that the undisclosed corporate connection between Terry Hanover and Harold Gupton was a heavy-duty violation. It had never been reported in the paper, and certainly wasn't in the package of material he'd gotten from the Lottery Commission. The man who essentially makes the decision—for it was clear to Lynch now that the Commission had simply rubber-stamped Harold Gupton's recommendation—about who's going to run a state-wide lottery owns a big chunk of stock in a company owned by a man who's going to be awarded the contract.

No, it just doesn't work that way, Lynch said to himself. You can't freaking do that. It ain't kosher.

It also wasn't the software bomber, but it was something. Lynch felt, for the first time since he'd come back to New Orleans and gotten involved in this mess, that he was accomplishing something. There was a connection; he'd known it all along. And he'd gone after it and chased it down until he had his jaws around its neck.

His heart raced, and he was suddenly wide awake.

But what next? Jack stood up, stretched, trying to clear his mind. The first thing, he thought, was to have a look at Harold Gupton's personnel file. He walked into the darkened outer office, switched on the light, and opened the drawer to Maud's desk.

Gupton's was the one on top. The photocopied pages of the file were stapled together. Jack took the pile back into his office and settled into his chair.

Harold Gupton was born in 1949, he saw, which made him only forty-four. He looked a lot older than that, Lynch thought. Closer to fifty. But it was the place of birth that got him: Paterson, New Jersey, just up the road from Teaneck.

"Well, well, well," Lynch said out loud. "What do you want to bet Terry Hanover's from that stretch of the woods as well?" And, he thought, given that Hanover's age was somewhere around forty, these two guys could have been contemporaries.

Jack remembered that Hanover had also gone to school in New Orleans, some twenty years or so earlier. He wondered if Gupton had been in New Orleans then as well.

Lynch thumbed through more of the file. The third sheet down was Gupton's photocopied resume.

Across the top of the resume was typeset: Harold Gupton, 2833 Meadowdale Drive, Metairie, Louisiana. Below that, the employment section detailed Gupton's career history. He had come to New Orleans seven years earlier, from a job as the director of data processing for Applied Innovations Technology, Incorporated in Clifton, New Jersey.

"Applied Innovations," Lynch muttered, dropping Gupton's file and fumbling through another pile of papers. He picked up the stack from Disclosure and nervously flipped through it.

"Damn, that's it," he said out loud. "Jesus, the S.O.B. used to work for Hanover!"

Harold Gupton had at one time worked for Terry Hanover, they had probably grown up within earshot of each other, and they now held stock in at least one company together. And Harold Gupton had recommended that Terry Hanover's new company, with no track record and no experience in running a gaming operation, be given the contract to run the Louisiana Lottery. And the Lottery Commission had awarded it to him, no questions asked.

One thing led to another, which led to another, which led to another, and on and on, with no regard for conflict of interest rules or appearances of impropriety. And, Lynch wondered, what if it was more than the undue exercise of influence? What if bribe money had exchanged hands?

Jack fumbled through Gupton's personnel file again. He felt like a Peeping Tom as he dug through to Gupton's salary history. He had taken the job for only $62,000 seven years earlier. It must have been a shock to him to discover how low salaries were in the deep south compared to New Jersey. But then again, the money goes a lot further down here. Gupton's present salary was $72,865. Lynch didn't put a calculator to it, but it looked to him like Gupton had gotten the standard bank salary increases of three to six percent each year. Enough to afford a decent house in the suburbs, out in the nouveau riche section of Metairie, but not enough to live in any real style.

Jack fingered the file. Near the end was a change of address form. It had been filed fourteen months earlier, about the time Gupton had been appointed to the advisory committee of the Louisiana Lottery Commission.

Gupton's new address was 896 Lakefront Drive in New Orleans. He was living on the lakefront now, in a part of town where the cheap homes ran two-hundred thousand on up. Jack's ex-wife's family had lived out there, and he knew

Gupton's address wasn't in the poor section of the lakefront. If anything, Gupton's house would have run closer to three, maybe four hundred thousand.

Harold Gupton had quietly taken a big step up in lifestyle, all about the same time he got connected with the Lottery Commission, at about the same time he recommended that a buddy of his be allowed to run the whole show.

How convenient, Lynch thought.

The night air had cooled and Esplanade Avenue was virtually free of traffic as Lynch sailed through the light at North Broad. He'd pulled the top down before leaving downtown. He felt invigorated, awake, alive, and even a bit frightened.

What if someone finds out I know?

He thought briefly of passing right by his apartment house, cutting left at City Park, and buzzing out Wisner Boulevard to the lake. There was a section that went along Bayou St. John that was two lanes wide in the same direction, with little traffic this time of night and few stoplights. He could wind the car out, let the wind tear through him like a cleansing hurricane and blast the cobwebs away for good.

His apartment house was two blocks away. He held up his arm in the dim glow of the dashboard lights: 11:35. He really ought to go home, get a decent night's sleep. But his heart was beating too fast. For the first time in weeks, he felt excitement. Sleep was a long way off tonight.

The car approached the decision point. Just as he reached the corner of Mystery and Esplanade, he looked up to his apartment. His lights were off, but P.J.'s were on.

Lynch slowed the car and turned left, bringing it to a stop on the thin layer of gravel next to the storm drains.

He got out, raised the top and latched it, then pulled his overnight bag out of the trunk. With his briefcase in one hand, his bag in the other, and a coat thrown over his shoulders, Lynch crossed the front lawn and climbed the stairs to the porch.

Standing still on the porch, without the grinding whine of the car engine to keep him awake and the wind to slap at him continuously, he felt for the first time since his discovery the weight of his fatigue. It was as if as soon as he slowed down, it all caught up with him. He wearily trudged up the stairs and to his apartment. Across the hall, light peeked out from under P.J.'s door.

He stopped, hesitated for a moment, then turned the key. The hall light flooded the darkness, illuminating the drabness of his home. Jack Lynch had always been the kind of man who never paid much attention to his surroundings. It was a place to go at the end of the day, a repository for his belongings. But now, as he felt himself sliding headlong and alone into middle age, the monotonous and dreary quality of his space seemed to sap the energy out of him.

The tediousness exaggerated his weariness, made his footsteps heavier than usual. He went through the apartment, switching on every light, and turned on the FM alarm radio by his bed. The answering machine by his bedside telephone sat unblinking. He was relieved to have no calls to return. He opened the French doors onto the gallery to let in fresh air.

His spirits lifted in a few moments. He found two bottles of beer in the refrigerator and opened one, then carried it back into his bedroom and plopped the overnighter onto the bed. He unzipped it and removed his clothes, his dirty underwear and socks from the night before wadded into the bottom of the bag. Lynch always travelled light; he unpacked in less than two minutes.

He pulled his tie off, briefly debated stepping into the shower, then decided it was too late. The noise might wake the neighbors.

He changed into a pair of running shorts and a T-shirt, then went into his living room and dug through an unpacked carton of paperbacks for reading material. Behind him, there was a light knock at the front door.

Jack stopped, turned and stared at the door as if by doing so, he could see through it. He stood up, went to the door and opened it.

"Hi," P.J. said. "You're home."

"Yeah," Jack said. "C'mon in."

They spoke in low tones, as if afraid of being caught sneaking out of their rooms after hours. He held the door for her. She stepped in, almost sheepishly, and stood there in an old pair of jeans and a pearl-buttoned, flowered blouse. Her hair was loose, combed back over her ears, and she had scrubbed the day's makeup off her face.

"I know it's late," she said. "I just thought I'd say hi."

"I'm glad you did. I would have knocked on your door, but I didn't know whether you were getting ready for bed or what."

"How was your trip to Baton Rouge?"

"Fine. I got everything I needed and then some. But I got back late this morning and went straight to my office. Been there ever since."

"My goodness, long day."

"Yeah. Can I get you a beer, P.J.? Or maybe something else, although I'm afraid the menu here at Chez Lynch is a little bare."

"No, I'm fine. I just, well, really, I was a little worried about you. You seemed upset when you left yesterday morning."

"Would you like to sit down?" he asked. She nodded and he motioned her over to a chair. He sat on the couch, an orange crate full of records on the floor between them.

"I certainly wasn't upset at you," he said. "At myself more than anything else."

Lynch pulled his legs up and sat cross-legged on the couch. He set the beer bottle down on the floor.

"When I didn't hear from you, I. . . . Well, as long as everything's okay," P.J. said. She reached across and laid her hand on his. She squeezed it gently, her touch cool and soft to him. He rolled his hand over under hers and opened his palm, then took her hand in his.

"Mind if I join you over there?" she asked.

"Sure," Lynch said, an edge to his voice. "I mean, no. Of course not, please. . . ."

P.J. crossed around in front of his scuffed coffee table and sat on his old couch. As she sat down, the worn springs creaked and gave way; she rolled toward him.

"I'm sorry," he said. "This couch is about as old as I am."

"Yeah, right." She smiled at him, teasing. "I'll bet you had it custom built that way so all your dates would roll into your arms."

He brought his arm around the back of the couch and laid it on her shoulders. She felt warm, electric, beneath his touch. His heart began to beat faster and he was worried that the rumbling in his gut might become loud enough to hear.

"I'm really glad to see you," he said softly. "I started to call you from Baton Rouge last night."

"Why didn't you?"

"I don't know. Maybe I was afraid you wouldn't want to hear from me."

He unfolded his legs and stretched them out in front of him. She placed her right hand on his knee as he turned toward her, squeezing her gently, gradually closer to him.

"Do people ever get to a point in their lives where they don't have to play those kind of games anymore?" she whispered.

"I doubt it," he said.

"Well, I think it's time we tried. I like you. I don't know you very well, but I like you. I'd like to get to know you better."

"I'd like that too."

P.J. Campbell brought her hand to his cheek and scraped it across the rough stubble on his face. "I probably need to run a razor across my face," he said.

"No, I like it," she whispered again. She pulled him toward her, her lips opening as she brought the two of them together. Lynch enjoyed the feeling of being led through the process. He hadn't expected to find himself so awkward around her. He felt a wave run through him again, for the first time in longer than he cared to think about. She moaned, very low, a deep sound from way down behind her throat, from somewhere way inside her.

He pulled her close now, the two of them pressed together, their arms around each other, their lingering kiss continuing until they needed air. He pulled away slightly, his eyes half-open.

"That's nice," she said plainly, without inflection or exaggeration. "I've been wondering what it would be like to kiss you sober."

Lynch chuckled. "You have a way with words. You should be in public relations."

"Good heavens, no," she said. "I haven't the patience."

"Me either," he said. "Not right now."

He leaned down and kissed her, his hand sliding down to her waist, pulling her even closer to him. They were wrapped around each other now, the energy overtaking them, the thoughts driven from their heads. Jack pulled back from their kiss and dropped his face to her neck, pulling her hair back, kissing the line that ran from her earlobe to her collar bone.

"Oh, my," she whispered.

He ran his lips up and down the line a few times, each time harder, more pressure, and then moved around just to the back of her neck and found himself, without even thinking about it, nipping the skin below the nape of her neck.

She moaned deeper this time, pulled him toward her, moving his hand to her breast. He felt her beneath the flowered blouse, felt her heat and her firmness. His own breath came faster, and he felt himself filling. He ran his tongue around the line just above her collar and stopped at the top of her breastbone. He slowly, tentatively, kissed the skin above her top button.

She leaned down on his bowed head and ran her open mouth, teeth first, across the back of his neck. Something shot through him from the top of his head to his feet, then back again. It was almost painful, impossible to sit still, sweet and delicious and aching and tenacious. He wanted her, was afraid of her, had to have her, felt like screaming and laughing and crying all at once. She raised her lips off his neck, the back of his head planted under her jaw. He brought up his left hand and unbuttoned the top two buttons of her blouse. In the dim light he could see white lace trace a line across the top of her breast. He bent down even further and kissed her, then gently sucked the skin between his lips. Above him, she gasped loudly and backed away from him.

"Oh, my, wait, stop, just a second," she panted.

Jack sat up, looked into her face. P.J. was flushed, the red in her cheeks bright and vibrant. Her eyes had a faintly spacey look to them, as if she had just awakened from a juicy, sensuous dream and wasn't quite back to reality yet.

"You okay?" Jack asked.

"Oh, God, yes, I feel great. You're wonder—, I mean," she stopped to get her breath. "No, this is just fine. I just have a question, that's all."

"Yeah?"

"This is a little embarrassing, sensitive, maybe. But this is the nineties, you know. We all have to be careful."

"Yeah, sure. No problem."

"Do you," she hesitated, her voice dropping, "have any condoms?"

Lynch burst out laughing with delight. He thought she was going to leave. "No, but if you want, I'll crawl on my belly to the K & B to get some."

She giggled. "That won't be necessary. If you don't think it's too forward, I've got some."

"I think it's terribly forward," he said, "and terribly delightful."

"Would you like to adjourn to my apartment."

"I'd love to," he said. "Let's go."

They stood, crossed over to the door. Lynch let the door click to behind him.

P.J. dug through her right front jeans pocket and pulled out a keyring. She inserted a key in the lock, then quietly and quickly opened her door. She stepped in ahead of him, stopped and turned. Lynch pulled her close to him and kissed her quickly.

"C'mon," she said, pulling him into the apartment. "Let's go."

Five hours later, the sun was just rising over the city skyline, the orange peeking over the horizon as if spying on the darkened city in preparation for an assault. The phone in Jack's bedroom rang once, then again. At the second ring, the answering machine picked up.

"Hi, this is Jack," came Jack's electronically reproduced voice. "I can't come to the phone right now. Leave a message at the beep and I'll get back to you as quick as I can."

A moment later, the tone was followed by the anguished voice of Carlton Smith.

"Jack, are you there? Jack? Dammit, I'm sorry to be calling so early, but I've just gotten a call from the director of security at the bank. The NOPD homicide squad called him from the bank. Jack, it's Harold Gupton. He's been murdered. Call me as soon as you get in."

▪ CHAPTER 24 ▪

J ack Lynch opened one eye barely, the inside of his eyelid like sandpaper across the surface of his eye. There were sheets all around him, tangled and bunched between his legs, under his arms and side, around his right foot like a too-tight boot. An alarm clock that wasn't his stared back at him. 7:15, it read.

He lowered his eyelids back to the dark position and let a smile crawl across his dry, cracked lips. Other than that single beer, half of which was still in a bottle on his living room floor, he hadn't had a thing to drink the night before. And he could swear he felt worse—a sleep-starvation hangover.

He suddenly felt the warmth and pressure of something moving against his back. Already half into sleep again, he rolled over toward the warmth, fighting the tangled sheets as he moved. A chaotic, dishevelled mass of black hair fell onto his face. It tickled his nose, sending a shiver down his back.

He groaned, then brought a hand up to wipe her hair out of his face. His groan was answered with another.

"Did the clock go off?" P.J. asked, her voice thick with sleep.

"No, I just woke up," he mumbled.

"What time is it?"

Lynch tried to remember. "Seven-fifteen, I think."

"Oh," she murmured, "it goes off in ten minutes, anyway. Think I'll get up."

He felt her move next to him, then slide away quickly. As she moved, she pulled the sheet with her. The sheet was knotted around between his legs, and as she pulled, it tightened first painfully, then dangerously, into his crotch.

"Dammit," she muttered on the edge of the bed. "I'm caught."

Lynch felt her getting set to yank hard and his eyes flew open.

"Wait a minute!"

"What," she said, whirling around.

He stared at her naked torso, crisscrossed with a red splay of marks from sleeping on the bunched sheets.

"I'm hung," he said.

She leaned down in his face, kissed him full on the lips, then raised back up. "I knew that."

She carefully freed herself of the sheets and walked into the bathroom. Jack was exhausted beyond movement, but as he watched her through cracked eyelids, he felt an involuntary stirring deep within. P.J. Campbell had awakened something in him that he thought gone forever. He reflected back over the last few hours and felt almost a certain pride in being a forty-year-old man who could stay up all night making love.

Not as old as I thought I was. He smiled and buried his head into a pillow, the smell of her hair and the scent of her body wafting up from the cloth.

Then P.J. started the shower, and Jack realized he needed to take care of something else, and fast. He got up, walked over to the bathroom door and gently knocked.

"Yes?" she called.

"Mind if I come in?"

"C'mon."

Jack stepped into the steamy bathroom. The mirror was fogged over, the translucent shower curtain like a thick cloud surrounding her.

"Mind if I—?"

She hesitated, trying to figure out what he meant. "Oh, yeah, go ahead. I'll just stay here behind the curtain."

Jack was too tired to stand, so he allowed himself the luxury of sitting down on the toilet. Through the curtain, he could see the blurry image of her arms raised in the air as she soaped herself.

Jack stood, lowered the lid. "P.J.?"

"Yes?" She stopped in mid-swipe.

"I don't want to be too forward or anything, but how'd you like some company in there?"

She lowered her arms, pulled the rear of the shower curtain back, and looked out at him. "God forbid after last night, you should be too forward. C'mon."

Jack stepped into the hot shower, the spray so hard it felt like needles on his skin.

"You look wonderful," he said, plainly, honestly, over the roar of the shower. "It's been a long time since I've been this happy waking up."

She looked up at him, her soaking hair plastered like a black sheen over the back of her head. "It's been a while for me, too. Thank you for last night. Thank you for this morning."

"Ma'am," Jack said with an exaggerated drawl, "it'uz mah pleasure."

Jack leaned and let the full force of the spray wash over his head. He opened his mouth, letting the shower fill him, swishing the water around to get the foul taste out of his mouth, then letting it run down the sides of his face and body as he stood straight up again.

He took her in his arms and pulled her toward the shower, then kissed her full and long under the spray. He felt her weight easing beneath him, as if she were about to sink to the floor of the tub.

"You okay?" he asked.

Her moan was barely audible over the spray. "I think my knees are giving out."

Jack kissed her again, not as passionately this time. "C'mon, let's soap up and get out. We probably need to be off to work, don't we?"

"Yeah," she said, wrapping her arms around his waist and

staring into his eyes. "But I want to do this again real soon."

"Me, too," he said. His heart clutched in his chest. This was something he never expected. He could have kissed Gus Pelias for throwing him out of the old apartment.

A few minutes later, Jack turned the shower off and stood there dripping in the steam. P.J. had gotten out already, left the bathroom, and was drying off in the bedroom. The door opened.

"Jack?"

"Yes, my dear?" he said happily.

"Here's a towel."

Jack pulled the shower curtain back and caught the thick towel as she tossed it. He wrapped the towel around him, the feel of it on his skin like fur. P.J. had nice things, he'd discovered, and surrounded herself with small luxuries that made life more tolerable a little bit at a time. Most of Jack's towels were bare and thin with age. He lived his life like he took his meals, on a functional basis rooted in daily necessities.

Maybe, he thought as he stood there enjoying the sensations around him, it was time to slow down a bit.

He finished drying himself and walked into the bedroom with the towel wrapped around his waist. P.J. was sitting at the end of the bed, slipping on a pair of shoes and watching a portable television in the corner of the room.

She stood up as he entered. She was wearing a pair of pleated black silk pants and a silk blouse. Her wet hair was brushed back, drying in the morning air.

"Hi," she said. "Hope you don't mind the television. I've developed the habit of watching the morning news shows, since it's been awhile since I've had anyone to talk to in the morning."

"Fine, no problem." He sat on the edge of the bed and she came around in front of him, placing her hands gently on his shoulders.

"How are you, Mr. Lynch?"

"I'm fine, Dr. Campbell," he answered. "Maybe a little shellshocked."

"Me, too. I think this is that awkward moment that people

have when they've spent a very intense time together and know that, at least for awhile, they've got to go their separate ways."

"Yeah." Jack reached out and pulled her to him, his arms around her waist, his head to her side as he tried to avoid getting her blouse wet. "I don't want to get weird on you or anything, but this feels like it's happening too fast."

She hugged him close. "I know." Then she pulled away, smiled. "I hope you don't think I'm a loose woman."

He laughed. "No, of course not. I just, well, as I've gotten older, I can't help but feel more cautious about things."

"Me, too," she said. "I always was cautious, until last night. I don't know what it is. Sometimes, people . . . people become physically aware of each other very quickly. There's no explaining it, no accounting for it. I'm not comfortable with it. But I don't want it to go away."

He pulled back and looked up into her face. "Dr. Campbell, I don't want to fall in love with you."

She blushed slightly. "I think that kind of talk's a little premature, anyway, isn't it?"

"You're right," he said abruptly, standing up and pushing her gently away. He leaned over to his pile of clothes. "Besides, you know what the gypsies say, don't you?"

"What?"

Jack stood back up with a wad of clothes in his hand. "He who confesses first, loses. Ancient gypsy saying."

He headed into the bathroom to get dressed. As he opened the door to step in, he heard the end of a commercial.

"Returning now to our top local stories," the announcer said, "police say they have no clues in last night's murder of First Interstate Bank executive Harold Gupton."

Lynch stopped dead in his tracks, whirled around.

"Jack, I don't want you to—" P.J. said.

"Ssshhhh!" he hissed.

"Investigators say the murder could be either random street crime or a professional hit. The body of the forty-four-year-old executive was found around five-thirty this morning in the rear of the parking lot of the downtown offices of the First Interstate Bank of Louisiana. The body was discovered by a security guard showing up for his morning shift."

"Oh no," Lynch muttered, staring intently at the television. P.J. stared into his face as his eyes visibly darkened, the circles under his eyes growing a deeper purple by the second.

"Gupton had been shot one time in the side of the head as he sat behind the steering wheel of his late-model Lincoln Continental. Police say the weapon was a small-caliber pistol and that there were no signs of a struggle. An autopsy has been scheduled for this afternoon. Funeral services have yet to be arranged."

Lynch let his clothes fall out of his grip onto the floor.

"Jack, what's wrong?" P.J. asked, tension in her voice.

Lynch stood there in shock, his towel unraveling from around his waist and joining the clothes on the floor.

"P.J.," he said, standing naked before her, "I've got to go."

Jack tossed his briefcase and suitcoat into the backseat, then plopped down into the driver's seat. He jammed the key into the ignition and twisted it. The engine made a grinding noise, spun uselessly, then kicked into a high-pitched whirr.

"Dammit," Lynch muttered, twisting the key again. The starter spun, then slipped and whirred again.

"Don't do this to me," Lynch pleaded. "C'mon. . . ."

He frantically pumped the gas pedal, then jerked the key just as his foot was cycling down on the pedal. The engine turned, then lit, and exploded into life, backfiring loud enough to be heard two blocks away. Great clouds of blue-black smoke trailed out behind the Fiat.

"No time to worry about that now," he said out loud, as he jammed the car into gear and let the clutch slip into place.

The car pulled away. Ten minutes later, he pulled to a stop in front of Martin Brown's house.

He had found the message from Carlton on his answering machine, only Carlton wasn't in his office or at home. Jack thought of waking Martin Brown before going out to his house, but then decided it would be better to surprise him.

Jack trotted up to the sidewalk to the Victorian duplex cottage that Martin's wife, Patí, had decorated so charmingly. Pots of white and yellow freesia sat on the porch. The scent made Lynch's head swim. He felt queasy, almost dizzy. Mixed in with the freesia were pots of brilliant red and green impatiens; the blaze of color assaulted his eyes. He wished only for sleep, to fall into deep unconsciousness with P.J. next to him.

He forced those thoughts from his head and pounded on the front door, hard and loud and quick. He wanted Martin Brown up and out of a deep sleep as abruptly and impolitely as possible. If there were any way to shake the cocky young man out of his bad attitude, Jack wanted to find it right at that moment.

There was no sound from inside. Jack pounded again. The glass of the front door shook in its glaze; any harder and he would have shattered it.

"Hold on," a sleepy voice yelled.

Jack banged on the door again, a staccato rhythm against the glass with the knuckle of his right index finger.

"I want you rattled, you sonofabitch," Jack whispered. "Get over here, now."

Martin Brown's footsteps were quick, dull, barefooted thuds on the polished wooden floors. He pulled the curtain off the glass and stared angrily out the window.

"What in the goddamn hell is the matter with—"

"Open the door! Now!" Jack demanded.

Martin fumbled with the lock, then disconnected the door chain. Jack pushed the door open. Martin had to jump back to keep from getting his bare feet mashed by the door.

"What in the hell?"

"Get over here, on the couch." Jack ordered, then slammed the door shut behind him.

Martin scooted over backwards through the living room, then settled back on the couch. "What's going on, man? I was sound fucking asleep in there. . . ."

"Have the police been here?" Jack stood over Martin, threatening him.

"What are you talking about? Why would the police be here?"

"You haven't heard then?"

"Heard what?" Martin demanded.

"What time did you leave the bank last night?"

"What the hell business—"

"Answer my question!" Jack yelled. "What time did you leave the bank?"

"About two A.M.," Martin answered weakly. "Maybe a little later. Reports ran late. Why?"

"Harold Gupton was murdered last night."

Brown's eyes shot open and his jaw dropped. "What? When?"

"Last night, dammit. And his body was found in the back parking lot of the bank. The one the employees use. The one you would have gone out into last night when you clocked out."

"Holy shit. . . ." Martin groaned.

"My thoughts exactly," Lynch said. "Now listen, the police are going to want to talk to you. If they haven't been here yet, they will be. This is important: was Gupton's car in the parking lot when you left last night?"

"I don't know." Martin hesitated, shook his head as if trying to clear the haze away. "I . . . I wasn't paying attention."

"Think, dammit! It was a big Lincoln. It would have been hard to miss. How many cars were in the lot?"

"Well, let me see. There was mine, Jody's Volkswagen, Mark's Toyota station wagon, and Amy's . . . no, wait, Amy's husband came after her last night. There was . . . ." Martin closed his eyes in thought, then reached up and rubbed his temples.

"No," he continued. "It wasn't there. I'm sure of it."

"So when you left at two in the morning, Gupton hadn't gotten there yet. Whoever killed him did it after the late shift left the computer room."

Martin stood. "You think somebody in DP did it?"

"Martin, I'm pretty sure that Harold Gupton was dirty. I don't know how dirty, but I was working on it. Now it's too late. Oh, God, if I'd just been a little quicker. . . ."

"You think he planted the software bomb?"

Jack turned, thinking, staring off into space at some unseen object as he paced the room. "This is too weird, man. Too weird." He brought his left hand up to the bridge of his nose and rubbed it. "There's got to be something I've missed. First the timing of the extortion attempt, now the murder of the man I figured was behind it."

"How was he dirty?"

Jack turned, stared at Martin Brown. "No time for the details now. But I've got a pretty strong hunch he was taking bribes from the company that was awarded the contract to run the state lottery."

Martin Brown stared intently ahead as well, focusing on something midair between himself and Jack Lynch.

"Damn," he said, "that explains the money."

"What money?" Jack demanded.

"You told me to do a little sneaking around. So I ran balance summaries on all the hotshots in the data processing department. I know how much Gupton had in the bank."

Jack looked at Martin in amazement. "My God," he muttered. "How much did he have?"

"Checking account not quite ten grand, another twenty-five in a savings account. Certificates of Deposit worth another hundred."

Lynch crossed his arms and laughed. "Well, the guy had balls. You gotta give him that much. Take a six-figure bribe, then stick it in your bank account."

"I guess he figured nobody'd ever find out," Martin said.

"Of course he figured nobody'd ever find out," Lynch exclaimed. "Nobody *thinks* they'll get caught!"

The two men sat in silence for a moment.

"The next question," Jack said, "is who popped him. Was it somebody trying to cover up the bribe, or was it somebody in on what's beginning to look like an extortion conspiracy? The problem is, you got two separate crimes here."

"Three counting the murder," Martin said.

Lynch turned in his chair and glared at Martin. "Yeah, the murder. That's where you come in."

"Where I come in? Wait a minute, dude, I didn't have nothing to do with that." Brown held his hands out in front of him, palms outward, as if to ward off the suggestion.

"I know you didn't, dammit, but think about it. What's one of the first things I said to you when we first talked about the software bomber?"

"You said it could be me."

"Right," Jack said. "And it still looks that way. When the police get here—and I guarantee you, they will get here—I want you to be very careful what you say to them."

"What's that supposed to mean?" Martin demanded, the sharp edge of arrogance back in his voice.

Jack scowled. "Let me tell you how the police are going to look at this. You're a freaking computer genius, but a frustrated one. You've been in a state of open warfare with your superiors, and they may already suspect you of extorting five million dollars out of the bank. Your boss, whom you have consistently and clearly told everyone you've ever met in your entire life how much you hated, is murdered in the middle of the night not fifty feet from where you're working, probably lured there by a phone call the police are going to assume you made. To top everything off, you're rude, arrogant, cocky and you have a voice that sounds like Sean Penn in *Fast Times At Ridgemont High*."

Jack paused, took a deep breath, then let it out. "This will not endear you to the New Orleans Police."

For the first time, Martin Brown looked scared. "What am I going to do?"

"Did you kill Harold Gupton?"

"No, I didn't."

"Did you extort five million dollars from the First Interstate Bank of Louisiana?"

"No, I did not."

Lynch looked at him, his face relaxing just a bit. "Then just be cool. Beyond cool. Cooperate with the police. Call each one of them 'sir.' Be properly submissive, and control your temper. And if they really start to wear you down, ask—very politely—if you can speak with an attorney. And when they say 'yes,' you are to thank them. Can you do all that?"

Martin scowled. "Fuck, yes, if I have to. Maybe it won't come to that."

"I'm afraid it already has," Lynch said, staring through the front window over Martin's shoulders. "An unmarked police car just pulled up out front."

Martin jumped up and spun around. "Holy shit, what am I gonna do!"

"Just what I told you to do. And for God's sake, calm down."

Martin turned to look at him. "And I'm going to do something I've never done before," Jack continued. "I'm going to go out the back way, through your neighbor's yard, and out the next block. I think it's better if the police don't see me right now."

"You sure that's cool?"

"No, I'm not. But my guts tell me it won't do either of us any good to be seen together. Besides, if they can't ask me any questions, then I don't have to lie to them."

"Okay," Martin said. "I'll stall them as long as I can. Hit the road."

Jack turned, went through the kitchen, and out the back door into the bright sunshine. Martin's short backyard ended in a three-foot fence that bordered the yard of the house behind him. Jack looked around very calmly; there was no one around.

He walked through the backyard, easily climbed over the fence, and trespassed as serenely as possible through a neighbor's backyard, down the driveway, and out onto Pine Street. He walked a couple of blocks toward St. Charles, turned left and walked to Broadway. Once on Broadway, he joined the throng of college students parading around Tulane University's frat row. His breathing came a little easier, but not much.

Not for the first time in his life, Jack Lynch felt like an escaped fugitive.

■ *CHAPTER 25* ■

For the second time in a week, Jack found himself wandering the Tulane University campus. He needed coffee and food, but above all else, he needed a pay phone.

The late-morning swarm of students in the University Center created a continuous murmur of indistinguishable voices. Jack walked up the concrete steps to the Quad entrance, then down the hall, past the cafeteria and bookstore, the information desk, and downstairs to the basement of the Center. He found a bank of pay phones across from the student television station and dug a quarter out of his pocket.

"Carlton Smith, please. Jack Lynch calling."

A moment later, the barely controlled anguish in Carlton Smith's voice came across the line.

"Where have you been?" he demanded.

"I tried to call you," Jack defended himself. "I left a message."

"I know, I don't mean to bark at you. What a day. By the way, aren't you ever home? I called you at dawn this morning. Surely you weren't already at work."

Lynch ignored the question. "Where do the police stand now?"

"They're still asking questions. The only real clue they found was a single cartridge casing in the parking lot. They've identified it as a nine-millimeter, which will probably match the slug they take out of Gupton's skull. Other than that, they don't have much."

"You remember Martin Brown, the lead computer operator?"

"Yes, of course. The young man with the rotten attitude."

"That's him. He's been helping me out on some things. That's just between us and the bedpost, okay? I was over at his house and the cops pulled up to question him. I ducked out the back and cut through somebody's backyard."

"Good heavens, Jack. Do you realize what that would look like if they saw you?"

"It would be worse if they sat me down and started questioning me. Believe me."

"Why? Why would it be worse?"

Jack hesitated. "Carlton, I'm pretty sure that Gupton was dirty. He took a bribe to see that GCA was awarded the state contract. He used to work for Terry Hanover, the guy who founded GCA. He owns stock in another company owned by Hanover."

There was only silence on the phone, for what seemed like forever. "Carlton?"

"My god," Carlton gasped. "And we guaranteed them ten million dollars. Do you have any idea how bad this looks?"

"You'd have to be pretty dumb to miss it. We've got extortion, bribery, and murder all wrapped up in one little computer room. Who says gearheads are boring?"

"Jack, this has got to be taken care of." Carlton's voice was strained, almost choked off. "If a scandal of this magnitude comes to light, the very foundations of the—I don't even want to think about it."

Jack stood silently, the phone like dead weight in his hands.

"What's the next step?" Carlton asked, resigned to turning over responsibility for the entire affair to an exhausted, middle-aged man who didn't get enough sleep the night before.

Jack thought for a moment. "The first thing I've got to do is get something to eat. I'm starving. Then I have to get my car back. It's still parked in front of Martin Brown's house. Then I guess it's back to square one."

"This isn't boosting my confidence, Jack. I'm not feeling better about this."

"I'm sorry, Carlton, it's the best I can do standing in front of a freaking pay phone surrounded by twenty-year-olds. But one thing's for sure; I found a thread to yank on. If I just keep yanking, the whole sweater's going to unravel."

Carlton sighed over the phone. "One thing," he said.

"Yeah?"

"Watch yourself. If whoever's behind this is serious enough to kill once, they won't hesitate to do it twice. I've gotten used to our little conversations. I wouldn't want anything to happen to you."

Jack smiled. "Don't worry. I'm protected by the patron saint of physical cowards."

Maud sat hunched over her desk, clipping the brief article on Harold Gupton's death out of the morning *Times-Picayune*. With deadlines, all they had time to do was get a box on the front page in the last edition. A more extensive account would appear in tomorrow's paper.

"I figured you'd want this," Maud said, handing Jack the article as he shut the door behind him.

"It's really hit the fan over there, Maud." Jack put his briefcase down on the visitor's chair and hung his coat on a wooden coat rack. "Harold Gupton was taking bribes from the company that got the contract to run the lottery. Now he's dead."

"Jack, don't you think you oughta go to the police?"

Jack sat down in the chair, pulled a cigarette out of his pocket. "I can't go yet."

"When you gonna go? When somebody puts a bullet in your head?"

Jack lit the cigarette, drew deeply on it, and glared at Maud through the blue-gray smoke. "I wish you wouldn't say things like that."

"I just worry about you. God knows, somebody's got to."

"I appreciate that, Maud. Any calls today?"

"Yeah, Martin Brown called. Said to tell you everything went okay with the cops and that he'd call you later. And that character Fast Eddie called again."

"He want anything in particular?"

"Said he was just checking in, that you knew where to find him when you needed him."

Jack stretched, blew cigarette smoke toward the ceiling. "He'll be down in the Quarter, making a fortune hustling tourists while the rest of us limp through a day at a time. God, Maud, we're in the wrong business."

"So what are you going to do next?"

Jack sat up in the chair, grabbed his briefcase and pulled it onto his lap. "The only thing I can do," he announced. "Start over."

Hours later, he sat up from where he'd been bent over his desk and massaged his burning eyes. He felt himself buried in paper. If it wasn't Harold Gupton behind the successful extortion attempt, then who could it have been? The more he thought about it, the less likely it seemed that Gupton would have been involved. After all, if he was taking bribe money from the Gaming Corporation of America and Terry Hanover, why risk it by trying to pull another ripoff? The kind of ripoff that was likely to draw down a lot of heat.

Unless, of course, Gupton got greedy. Once a man gets a taste of the good life, it's hard to let go, hard to settle for being just another middle-management drone. Maybe the payoff money just primed the pump; maybe Gupton was going after the big score, was going to lay low for awhile, then resign his position, fly to whatever Southeast Asian bank the five mil wound up in, and retire in just enough high cotton to really enjoy the rest of his life, but not enough to get Interpol on him.

But who killed him? And why? Maybe Gupton burned somebody. Maybe the whole, intricately woven conspiracy fell apart when Gupton got greedy. If he had a partner up front, whom he then tried to cut out of the action, that would be excuse enough to whack somebody, Lynch thought.

Hell, I'd probably kill him myself.

Jack kept coming back to the same question: Who? The why part was easy to surmise, although the inference may or may not have been accurate. But it was enough to get started. He'd been following a blind trail too long. It was time to find some landmarks.

Lynch read each personnel file over again. Kenneth Cook, the chief programmer and bad cop was the logical choice. He was rough around the edges, mean enough to kill somebody, and arrogant enough to think he could get away with it.

Lynch picked up his file. Cook had been with the bank the longest, just over twenty years. Unusual, Jack thought, for a forty-four-year-old man to have earned his twenty-year pin. Cook had graduated from Mississippi State Vocational-Technical Institute in 1972, then gone to work for the bank as a junior computer operator. Not exactly an MIT background, but apparently hard work and perseverance still counted for something. In 1975, Cook became lead operator—the position Martin Brown held now—and a programmer in 1979. In 1986, he became chief programmer, second in command of the department, and had held the position ever since. He'd attended some continuing education courses and seminars, and had gone to various schools offered by the computer manufacturers who'd sold equipment to the bank. He had, on paper at least, been a model, steady employee who would by all accounts stay at the First Interstate Bank of Louisiana for the rest of his working life. He would retire with forty-five or so years under his belt, then go live on the Gulf coast somewhere probably a hundred miles or less from the place where he was born.

It was, Lynch thought, the kind of quiet, desperate life that could turn anyone into a killer.

Buford Adkins was an entirely different story. He was considerably younger than the rest of the department's top management, and had only been with the bank two years. Barely thirty, he had by far the strongest academic credentials. He'd gone to Riverside Academy, an exclusive boys school out in

Chalmette, then on to Tulane for a degree in computer science. He may have been four or five years ahead of Martin Brown in age, but in terms of career advancement, it was no contest.

Adkins was a team player, the kind of jovial, somewhat ineffectual, man who did well in the corporate environment. He would never be top management; he hadn't the shark instinct. But he would be dependable middle-management support who would let his boss have the glory when it was dished out, and would fall on his sword if asked to. He was the kind of fellow who would "fit in;" do the golf thing on weekends, wear the right suits, drive the right car, and be missed when he died of a heart attack at fifty-five. There would be a scholarship fund established by the bank in his name, and his widow would go on to be a classic grandmother to their snotty-nosed grandkids.

Lynch went on to the next file, which belonged to one of the four programmers employed by the bank. It revealed nothing that could be of any use, as did the other three. Each of the programmers had remarkably similar backgrounds, as if cast from the same mold. Lynch knew this was impossible, that people were as varied and unique as their chromosomal markings. But there seemed a sameness about them all that both depressed and frustrated him. After the programmers, there were two junior systems analysts, subordinates to Buford Adkins. Their files could have been, with only a few changes, photocopies of each other.

The largest number of employees in the data processing department were the computer operators themselves, who were the grunts, the gofers, of the data processing world. Their jobs often involved manual labor—hauling carts of magnetic tapes or two-wheelers stacked high with print-outs—so they weren't even required to wear coats and ties to work, nor were they assigned individual desks. When idle, they sat at a large table in the magnetic tape library, a dark cold room that had the feel of a high-tech coal mine, waiting for the next assignment. There were nine operators altogether, and they came from much more varied backgrounds.

Their jobs were considered menial, with a starting pay of only $6.50 an hour, not bad for the South in a deep economic recession, but not the golden road to riches either.

Of the nine computer operators, Martin Brown was the only one who had a college degree. Apparently, the job called for a strong back and an ability to follow instructions more than anything else.

No wonder Brown was pissed all the time. Clearly over-qualified for the job, and on the fast-track to nowhere, it was the kind of situation that could lead the young man to perch atop the building across the street with a 30.06 and a scope and start picking people off one afternoon in the ultimate twentieth-century American expression of frustration.

Jack's chest ached. Perhaps in his two years of self-employment he had become spoiled. He looked back in wonder over his years as a worker bee in the corporate hive. Had he been asleep all those years?

"One thing's for sure," he said out loud. "I'm never going back. I'll starve if I have to."

"You calling me?" Maud said from the outer office. Jack shook his head back to reality.

"No, Maud. Sorry. Just talking to myself."

She stepped into his office with the reports outlining Terry Hanover's web of corporate connections. He hadn't realized she was out there grubbing away as hard as he was.

"This is everything I can put together," she said, searching unsuccessfully for a place on Jack's desk to set the stack down. He reached over and wiped a place on his desk clean.

"Just stick them down there," he said.

"It's four-thirty. I think I might take the streetcar on home."

"Okay, that's fine." Jack rubbed his eyes wearily. "I'll see you tomorrow morning."

"You look like you didn't get too much sleep last night," Maud said, swivelling her hips around and leaning against the front edge of his desk. "Can I ask you a personal question?"

He looked at her quizzically. "Personal? Sure, go ahead."

"You drinking a lot these days?"

He gazed at her stonily for a moment. "No, Maud. I mean,

off and on, maybe. But I, well, last night I had a date with someone."

She smiled at him. "Date, huh? Nice girl?"

"Well, yeah, Maud. She's a nice girl. You think I'd go out with a bad one?"

Maud stood up, straightened her dress, her voice chirping in mock good humor. "I don't know what I think. And if I don't get on my way, it'll be midnight before I get home from the Winn-Dixie."

She started out the door. "Grocery shopping, huh?" Jack said, trying to make friendly small talk.

"Yeah," she said, turning to face him as she slung her bag over her shoulder. "You oughta try it sometime."

"Why? When God gave us perfectly good restaurants?"

Maud opened the office door, the hinges creaking over her voice. "You're hopeless, boy," she said. "Goodnight."

"Goodnight, Maud," he whispered as she shut the door. "And you're right. I probably am hopeless."

When the sun dipped down behind his building and it became hard to read, Jack wearily looked at his watch: 7:15. There were close to 150 pages laying scattered on his desk, each one read and studied several times. If there were answers buried somewhere in this mess, they were too well hidden for him to find tonight. He pulled a small spiral notebook out of his jacket pocket and flipped through until he found the page where he'd scribbled down P.J.'s phone number.

Her phone rang three times before she picked it up.

"Hi," Lynch said, his voice low, smoky.

"Hello," she said. "That's either the sexiest bedroom voice I've ever heard or you're exhausted."

"Mostly exhaustion," he said, stifling a yawn. "Long day."

"Me, too. I thought this day would never end. Guess it's like that when you get three hours' sleep."

"God, did we get that much?"

"Barely."

"P.J., I know things are kind of weird right now. And living across the hall from each other makes things kind of. . . ."

"Kind of what?" she asked after a moment.

"I guess what I'm trying to say is I'd love to see you tonight, but we don't have to see each other every night."

"And there'll be nights when we won't see each other," she said. "There'll be nights when we just need time alone."

"Is tonight one of those nights?"

She hesitated. "No, I don't think so. Although I have to be honest with you, I need a decent night's sleep. And I won't get that if you stay over."

"Should I take that as a compliment?" he asked.

"Please do. We'll just call it an early evening."

"I could stop, pick up a movie. There's a rental store down Canal. I'll pass it on my way home."

"Sure, that'll be great. Have you had dinner?"

"No, can I bring us something?"

"I'm just fixing a big salad. If that's enough for you, join me."

"Great. I'll pick up a bottle of wine as well. Another Chardonnay, maybe?"

"Sounds great. But I'm going to go light tonight. That sleep thing, you know."

"Yeah, me too. I'll be there in a half-hour, maybe forty-five minutes."

"Good. I'll look forward to it."

Her voice was sweet, warm over the phone. Jack hung up, then settled briefly back in his chair. Despite his preoccupation with the software bomber and the murder of Harold Gupton, as well as his sense of being drained of all energy, Jack Lynch felt almost contented, a sensation with which he was profoundly unaccustomed.

Life, he thought, was definitely taking a turn for the better.

■ *CHAPTER 26* ■

Jack wandered through the aisles of his favorite video rental store, overwhelmed by row upon row of videocassette boxes on display. It occurred to him that he had no notion of what kinds of movies P.J. Campbell liked.

Something classy, he thought. Nothing with gratuitous sex or graphic violence, which eliminated about 95 percent of everything on the shelves. Maybe an old film, a classic, although what could he be sure she hadn't seen?

He strolled down the next to the last aisle at the back of the store. He fought the tendency to aimlessly lose himself in the store as he occasionally did at libraries. It would be close to eight before he got over to P.J.'s anyway, and she'd already said she wanted to make it an early night.

Then he saw it. *The Tarnished Angels,* the 1957 Universal-International adaptation of William Faulkner's novel *Pylon.* A largely ignored, black-and-white B masterpiece, it featured one of Rock Hudson's most serious and effective performances. Jack had seen the film once, years ago. The way he stared at Dorothy Malone, Lynch thought, it was hard to believe he was leading an entirely different kind of life.

Jack grabbed the box and headed for the checkout counter. As he wove his way through the crowded store, he cut left to avoid a family of six arguing over which cartoon to rent and headed up the first aisle, past the "A"'s.

He absentmindedly scanned the boxes as he walked, his brain on automatic pilot. He savored the anticipation of seeing her again. An empty videocassette box popped up in the corner of his vision as he walked; Jack stopped abruptly.

What was that? Wait, there was something. . . .

Jack turned, searched out the box that had caught his attention. He ran his eyes across the shelf, unable to recover the brief, fleeting thought that had brought him to such a brusque stop.

There it was: *National Lampoon's Animal House.*

Jack picked up the box, turned it over. Copyright 1978, starring John Belushi, Tim Matheson, John Vernon.

Vernon, Lynch thought. *Vernon. John Vernon played Dean Vernon Wormer.*

Lynch furrowed his brow, struggling to remember the film. He'd seen it fifteen years ago in the theater, caught it occasionally on late-night cable television. But what the hell was it he was trying to remember?

Then it hit him. How could he have forgotten?

The extortionist had demanded an E-mail box: an electronic mailbox in the name of *Vernon Wormer.*

Martin Brown, Lynch remembered, had thought that hilarious, had barely been able to control himself.

Jack folded his hand around the empty cassette box. If P.J. Campbell wanted to call it an early night, maybe he'd stay up and watch a second movie.

"Holy Hannah," Lynch panted, "you're going to kill me."

P.J.'s eyes rolled back in her head. She shook all over, her breath in short gasps, her legs tightening. A loud yelp escaped her lips and she fell forward onto him, exhausted, limp.

Jack lay on his back, dripping wet, unable to draw more than the shallowest of breaths. She was beautiful on top of him, straddling him, her body draped across his in a sweltering heap.

"So much for watching movies," she gasped.

Her hair draped over his face, the fine blackness of it tickling his nose. He brought an arm up and pushed it off, then wrapped his arms around her and held her to him tightly. It had been a long time.

"I'm beat," she said. "I thought moving to New Orleans would be fun, but I never expected this."

Jack lay there silently, feeling himself inside her, her all around him. He squeezed her tightly, and found himself overwhelmed with emotion in a way that he'd never been. A tear rolled out of his right eye, down his cheek to the pillow.

She pushed herself up, raised her head so she could look into his face.

"You're awfully quiet," she said. "Are you all right?"

He pulled her back down, wrapped his arms around her again, would not—could not—let her go.

"What is it?" she whispered.

His chest heaved and a wet sob escaped. He struggled to regain control of himself. "I'm sorry," he apologized.

"What, what are you sorry for?"

"It's just that. . . ." He went silent again, unable to finish his thought.

"Just that what?"

"I never expected this," he whispered. "I've been alone for a long time, and this is just. . . . This is frightening."

She pressed against his face, her lips at his ear. "What scares you, Jack? What is it?"

He laughed, kind of an ironic chuckle. "Boy, talk about breaking the spell. Here we are locked together in this great romantic moment, and I pick now to fall apart on you."

She sat up, her arms extended as she held herself above him. Her eyes were dark, tired, but deep and intense. "You don't have to tell me what frightens you if you don't want to, but for what it's worth, I'm just as scared."

"You are?"

"I think you're right. There's something going on here, and I don't know what it is either. But I'm willing to take it a step at a time. See where it goes."

"Me, too," he said, reaching up and taking her shoulders. She leaned down, kissed him softly, longingly, then leaned back up. "My knees are giving way. If you don't mind, I think I'll stretch out."

"Be my guest," he said.

P.J. eased herself off and settled next to him. He held her close, his arms around her shoulders, her head in the crook of his neck. Bodies intertwining, he thought, looked almost comic, unless yours was one of the bodies in question. Then there was something about it that was as serene and peaceful as anything on earth.

He reached over and lifted his cold wineglass off the nightstand, and raised his head to take a sip.

"Want some?" he asked.

"No, I think I'm falling asleep."

"I've been meaning to ask you something," he said.

"What?" Her voice was growing sleepier by the second.

"Now that we've been, how does one say, 'intimate' twice now, I hope it's not too personal for me to ask you your name."

She sat up in bed, groggy, confused. "What?"

"What's the 'P.J.' stand for?"

She settled back into the pillow. "You don't want to know."

"Sure I do. But I'm not going to pressure you to tell me."

She opened one eye, stared at him through a loose mass of hair that had fallen across her face. "You sure?"

He laughed. "Yes. What's the big deal?"

She gritted her teeth and closed her one open eye. "You have to promise not to laugh."

"I'll do my best."

"That's not exactly a promise."

"Okay, I promise."

She hesitated, then whispered: "Penelope Jean."

"Penelope Jean," he repeated. "Why, that's beautiful. What's the problem? You don't like it?"

"How would you like to be named 'Penelope' in late twentieth-century America? It's a real popular name, right up there with 'Beryl' and 'Elspeth.' "

Jack laughed.

"You promised," she warned.

"I'm not laughing at your name. It's your reaction to it." He hugged her tightly, felt wonderful next to her.

"Well, then," she said. "Let me ask you something."

"Sure."

"Who's Sally?"

He stiffened. "How'd you know about—"

"That first night you stayed over. You were having a nightmare. I woke up. You were sweating, trembling something awful. I shook you, tried to wake you up. Your eyes shot open and you called me Sally."

"I'm sorry," he said. "I don't remember that."

"It was the middle of the night. You dropped back off. You don't have to tell me if you don't want to."

Jack pulled away from her, curled his knees up and rolled over on his hips. He planted his feet firmly on the floor, bent over as if to pray, locked his fingers together and placed his elbows on his knees.

"We used to work together at the bank," he said slowly, his speech halting. "She was my secretary for years. We were always friends, but she got a divorce, then I got divorced. Nothing happened for a couple years, maybe longer. Then, I don't know, it just happened. We started seeing each other in a different way. One thing led to another and. . . ."

"And you got involved," P.J. said, placing a hand on his shoulder. "Those things happen. So what happened to her?"

Jack opened his hands and rubbed his eyes, as if the memory brought him more weariness than anything else. He had been over their last night together more times than he could count. Parts of it were still only shadow, but enough of it remained that he could not shake it or get it out of his mind.

"I got in some trouble," he said. "The bank got involved in a lawsuit and my boss asked me to do some poking around. I guess I stuck my nose in where I shouldn't. One night a couple, three goons jumped me in the parking lot. They weren't going to kill me or anything. If they were going to do that, I wouldn't be here now. But they were going to beat the stew out of me and scare the hell out of me. I was fine with that; I can take a beating if I have to, and I can take having the hell scared out of me.

"It was different with Sally, though. She fought them, fought them like a tigress protecting her cubs. Only it didn't do any good. They killed her."

P.J. gasped and dug her hand into his shoulder. "Good God, Jack."

He sat up straight, turned to face her. "It was a long time ago, P.J." He let his right hand settle into the crook of her left shoulder and rubbed her lightly, distractedly, as if staring into her face somehow put him somewhere else.

"But Jack, you've never gotten over—"

"You do, love. You do get over it. You get up and start each day over again. It's just a weight you carry around with you, like a bad back you can't do anything about, and you just live with it."

"But it'll eat away at you," she said. "If you just let it fester inside you."

He settled back in next to her, threw his arm across her torso, just beneath her breasts, the rhythm of her breathing lifting his arm in a gentle motion. "P.J., that stuff's history. It can't be changed. I'm fine except for the dreams, and I don't have those near as bad as I used to. Maybe I'm mellowing out. What matters now is that we're here, alive, together."

She leaned toward him, kissed him softly on his left cheek, then nuzzled in to him tightly and became silent. They lay there a few minutes longer. He could feel her relaxing in his arms, her breathing growing deeper, the rhythm slower.

"It's nearly ten-thirty," he said, checking out the alarm clock by the side of her bed. "You wanted to call it an early evening. Why don't I head on back to my place."

"Oh," she moaned, "just stay here."

Jack shifted his weight. "Actually, my dear, I've still got a little work to do before bedtime. Why don't I just take off?"

She leaned up on an elbow. "Call me tomorrow?"

"Of course. Listen, Penelope Jean—"

She bared her teeth and growled.

"Okay, P.J.," he said. "I'm crazy about you."

She tucked her fangs back in and smiled gently. "I'm grow-ing rather fond of you myself."

"Good, then I hope you don't mind if I ask you a favor?"

"Sure. What is it?"

"Can I borrow your VCR? Mine got ripped off."

She looked at him questioningly, then waved good-bye to him. By the time he unwired the videocassette recorder and turned her lights off, she was fast asleep.

Jack watched in fascination as the brilliant and doomed Belushi shoved handfuls of mashed potatoes into his mouth, then popped his cheeks like a huge, infected zit. He had forgotten what an outrageous movie it was; the perform-ances by Tim Matheson, John Vernon, Belushi, Stephen Furst, and the rest of the cast captured perfectly the zaniness and carefree chaos that was every adolescent male's fantasy about college life. It was great escape—hilarious, disrespect-ful of authority, filled with shots of property being destroyed and young girls in their underwear; in short, everything a movie should be.

Lynch enjoyed it so much he forgot why he was looking at it. He was tired before, but after another evening with P.J., he was drained to incoherence. The movie flashed by before him, the voices becoming a muddled stream of sound. Jack Lynch relaxed, took the last sip of a scotch and soda, and drifted off to sleep just as Bluto was driving off into the sunset with the prom queen by his side, the caption under the shot identifying him as the future Senator John Blutarsky.

The cassette played itself out and stopped, the images replaced by video snow and hiss. The scratchy buzzing of the television and the white light dancing on his eyelids put Jack deeper and deeper into sleep. He was under now, his sub-conscious mind in control, the dreams playing on the backs of his eyelids like the second half of a double-feature.

He was replaying *Animal House* in his head again, only this time Harold Gupton was Dean Wormer, Kenneth Cook was the awful Neidermeyer, and Martin Brown was Larry Kroger. The faces fit in everywhere, with the Stephen Furst character the only one to retain his real face. But gradually, as the dream went on, his face began to change as well, and in the surreality that exists only in dreams, the face of Stephen Furst as "Flounder" became the face of Buford Adkins.

Jack shot up on the couch, knocking over his glass, melted ice sliding over the floor.

Buford Adkins. Flounder.

This is crazy. Wake up, you idiot! You're having one helluva dream.

But it was no dream. He shook his head groggily, bewildered and disconnected. What the hell? he thought.

He grabbed the remote control and flicked off the television. What was it about the image of Buford Adkins as a character in *National Lampoon's Animal House* that was so startling, so compelling.

Then it hit him: put a few years on Flounder, say, ten, and you'd have Buford Adkins.

Jack turned the lights off throughout his apartment. He was embarrassed at himself; thank heavens P.J. hadn't been here to hear his ramblings. He felt downright delusional.

But somehow, even as he dropped off to sleep for real, he couldn't get the image out of his mind.

▪ CHAPTER 27 ▪

They were on him all night, the images rushing at him, raging through the hours of shallow sleep. He went under obsessed with the extortionist, while the images of the movie flowed together in an endless crazy stream. His murdered fiancée, Sally, charged at him out of the blackness, her face blending like wet paint swirling into P.J.'s. The loose folds of Harold Gupton's tanned, lined face seemed to flap as he ran at him, like some great hound on a rampage.

Finally, mercifully, the clock went off and Jack clawed his way to the surface from one of the most restless, fitful nights he'd had in years. His muscles were sore from tension, the bed linens bunched up in a tight ball, pillows kicked off the bed, nearly across the room.

His head was heavy; a knife-like edge of pain seared up the back of his neck into his skull. He twisted his head around, rubbed the knot of bone above the nape of his neck in a vain attempt to massage the pain away. He groaned like a man who'd just come to after being knocked senseless.

Ten minutes under a hot shower spray, though, and he felt mostly functional. He could remember some of the dreams, knew where a lot of them came from. But much of the night's images remained a mystery to him, as if there were something lying inside him waiting to go off. He wondered what would trigger it, and if he were going crazy.

Losing his mind, he thought, would fit the pattern. Lynch had always felt that sort of thing was genetic in origin; craziness ran in some families like cancer and diabetes, or blue eyes and red hair. He remembered his mother's last few years, his rare conversations with her, the even rarer visits. She hardly knew who she was, let alone who he was. And in her infrequent moments of lucidity, she blamed him for everything. He was a bad son, a failure. Her life had been a waste. It had all been his fault.

He stepped out of the shower without towelling off and dripped water through his apartment as he walked nude into the kitchen. The windows were open, but the branches of the great oaks outside were their fullest green, shielding him from the house across the street. He poured water into the coffeemaker and shakily jammed the basket full of grounds into its slot.

Then he went back in and laid down on his bed until the coffee was made.

Jack started to drift back off to sleep, but fought it off with whatever strength he could muster. It wasn't so much his fear of the dreams coming back as much as it was the sense that if he fell back asleep, he'd be gone for the day. And there was far too much to do for that.

Outside, he heard footsteps on concrete, the clicking of heels staccato along the sidewalk. A car door opened, then shut again. Jack got up and stood at the bedroom window overlooking Mystery Street. Below him, he could barely see P.J.'s bare knees tucked under the steering wheel. He wasn't sure if he'd ever seen her in a dress before; he was too sleepy to recall, and besides, it didn't matter. He watched her in a daze as the car pulled away from the sidewalk.

He poured a tall mug of coffee and lit a cigarette, hoping the combined punch of nicotine and caffeine would bring him to full consciousness. The steaming, black coffee burned down the back of his throat, and the first cloud of thick smoke entering his lungs felt like a hot poker jabbed through his chest. But he was waking up.

By the second cup of coffee, he was dressed, coherent,

feeling as if the sludge he was trudging through now was only ankle-rather than hip-deep. He piled his papers into the battered briefcase, tossed the two rental tapes on top, and threw his jacket over his shoulder.

One advantage to over-sleeping, Jack discovered, was that most of the traffic had already dissipated. He made it to his office in about ten minutes. Maud was pouring water into the top of a coffeemaker as he opened the door.

"Good morning," he said brightly, surprised at the life in his voice.

"You sound chipper this morning."

"Couldn't be happier," he said. "I've got a screwy feeling that I might be on to something."

"What?" she turned quickly. "You've figured this out?"

"Maybe," he answered. "The problem is that I can't figure out how to verify what I'm suspecting."

"That's always the tough part," Maud said. "Anybody can suspect anything."

Jack sat down at his desk, opened his briefcase, and pulled out Buford Adkins personnel file again. For what seemed like the hundredth time, he started from the beginning. Only this time, he focused on where Buford Adkins was when *National Lampoon's Animal House* hit the box office.

"This is crazy," he muttered softly, thumbing through the pages. "I'm outta my mind."

In 1978, Buford Adkins was a junior at Riverside Academy. An impressionable age, especially for a young boy who was a little overweight, probably shy and insecure to begin with. He graduated in 1979, went straight on to college. He was still unmarried, still living in the same town he'd been born in. Probably wondering when life was going to really start for him. . . .

He reached into his side desk drawer and pulled out the Greater New Orleans white pages. He thumbed through until he found the main number of the Ochsner Clinic.

"Ochsner, may I help you?" the operator piped.

"I'm trying to locate Dr. P.J. Campbell. She's a psychiatrist in charge of the substance abuse unit."

"Please hold while I connect you."

Jack sat tapping a pencil against the top of his desk. Maud brought in a cup of coffee and sat it in front of him. "You okay?" she mouthed.

"Yeah, just on hold."

A moment later, a voice came on the line. "Recovery Clinic, this is Sherry. May I help you?"

"Yes, is Dr. Campbell available?"

"May I say who's calling?"

"This is Jack Lynch."

"Okay, Mr. Lynch, please hold."

Jack reached across the desk and grabbed the cup by its hook. The coffee was hot, steaming, black. He raised it to his lips and carefully took a sip.

"Jack!" P.J.'s voice on the phone was bright, cheery.

"Hi, P.J. How are you?"

"Fine. How are you?"

"Great. I hope you don't mind me tracking you down at the clinic."

"I'm flattered you couldn't go a whole day without talking to me."

"Well, I can usually control myself, but this is business."

"Oh," she said. "What's up?"

"I read an article once about how the FBI has a team of analysts and psychiatrists and people like that who can create a description of a criminal by examining the details of the crime."

"Yes, that's the FBI Behavioral Science Unit. They've been very successful in profiling serial killers."

"Can you do that sort of thing with other kinds of crimes? Not murder, I mean."

P.J.'s voice acquired a note of caution. "What are you talking about? Give me some specifics."

"I don't know exactly how much I can tell you. I'm working for a client that's just been the victim of an extortion. A very large sum of money was involved. We think someone on the inside of the company may have been responsible."

"Jack," she hesitated. "That's not really my field."

"Can you give me a little professional speculation here? Unofficially, just background stuff?"

"Well, I'll give it my best shot."

"Great, darling—"

"Hmmm, I like the sound of that. 'Darling.' "

"Me, too. Back to business. The extortion was pulled off by someone dialing into a mainframe computer system, bypassing security, and planting a very sophisticated virus in the computer. It was more than a virus, though. Apparently, it's the high-tech equivalent of a bomb. The 'bomber,' for lack of a better word, left a ransom note demanding money be wired electronically to a secret bank account in Southeast Asia. Doesn't matter where. But if the instructions aren't followed, the bomb goes off, wiping out the mainframe and putting the company out of business. Here's the weird part. The ransom note instructed my client to create an electronic mailbox for a Vernon Wormer."

"Who?" P.J. asked. "God, Jack, this is weird."

"You got that right. Vernon Wormer was a character in the movie *Animal House*. Remember?"

"Wait, yes. I think I saw it. Back in the seventies sometime, wasn't it?"

"1978."

"So you've got a computer hacker who plants a bomb in the software of a computer and has a really wicked, maybe warped is a better word, sense of humor."

"We figured that much already. Can you help us with anything else?"

The phone was silent for perhaps fifteen seconds, which seemed to Lynch like an hour.

"Like I said, love, this really isn't my specialty. But I'll give you a down-and-dirty profile based on just what you've told me. My guess is the person is male and relatively young. That was the kind of movie that appealed to young, immature men, and your bomber would have been probably a teenager when the movie came out. He's remarkably intelligent, but he may or may not be well-educated in the classical sense. He's certainly at least a near-genius when it comes to computers."

"Okay, what else?" Lynch scribbled down notes as she spoke.

"On so little information it's tough to come up with anything solid. So you have to understand this is really guesswork. He's emotionally stunted, probably insecure around women. He's incredibly frustrated, and has a rich fantasy life that's gotten out of hand. Despite his awkwardness around women and in social situations, he's at the core intellectually arrogant and superior. The Vernon Wormer bit proves that. He's not just committing a major crime, he's pulling a putz on top of it. A joke, a prank. He thinks he's funny, and he's so convinced he can get away with it that he's thumbing his nose at you.

"There," she said after a moment's pause. "That help?"

Jack let loose a held-in breath and dropped his pencil. "Jesus, Mary, and Joseph. You got that much from what I told you?"

"Jack, be careful with what I just said. It's only speculation. You didn't give me much to go on. When you catch the guy, let me know if I was on target."

"Yeah," he said, his voice almost shocky. "Okay."

"And Jack, one thing."

"Yeah?"

"The one thing no one can predict is how he'll react when he's cornered. He may fold up and cry like a baby. It may take ten men to hold him down. Don't do anything that would get you hurt. I'd hate that."

Jack grinned. "So would I. I'm having too much fun these days. For the first time in a long time."

"Me, too. Be careful."

"Call you tonight?"

"Please do."

It still wasn't enough to go on. He wished he had the option of checking out more background: college transcripts, credit history, that sort of thing. Martin Brown had gotten Adkins' bank balance, but there was nothing unusual in that. Nothing that would indicate a recent infusion of major wealth.

He picked up the file again. Buford Adkins, Riverside

Academy, Class of 1979. Riverside Academy, a private boy's school, a college preparatory school. Jack had gone to a private school himself; he wondered what kind of hell life at a boy's boarding school was for someone named "Buford."

He stared ahead, focusing on some point halfway through the room, halfway to the ceiling.

Maybe, he thought, that's where the answers—if there were any—lay hidden: Riverside Academy.

It perched on a rise just east of the Chalmette National Military Cemetery in St. Bernard Parish. In years past, that borderline area between Arabi and Chalmette had been considered a day's outing in the country, with much of the land overgrown and swampy enough to be of no great priority on anyone's wish list. But the city was spreading eastward at great speed, and the small towns that had once been "the country" were now bedroom communities, and even the great oaks and cypress and weeping willows were being bulldozed under to make room for apartment complexes and strip malls and convenience stores. The only thing out there that still spoke passionately and truly of times past were the roads. Lynch's already battered car fought bravely to negotiate the potholes and soft shoulders of the crowded, abused roadway.

A small sign on a metal post towered over the-two lane road, and it was almost obscured from view by the mass of Spanish moss that hung down to within a foot or two of the ground. Jack slowed the car, the air brakes of the impatient tractor-trailer behind him hissing like a rowdy dance-hall crowd. He turned onto the pea gravel road that took him up to a brick wall with an ornate, black wrought-iron gate pushed open. Above the gate, more black wrought-iron made an ornate arch with a circle in the middle. Inside the arch was the letter "R" embellished with curves and twists. It reminded Jack of the entrance to Charles Foster Kane's Xanadu.

The gravel road split into a Y, with a large building at the top of a small rise to the left, and several smaller buildings off to the right. A discreet sign, gold letters on black, read: ADMIN-ISTRATION, with an arrow pointing toward the rise. Jack steered the car to the left and proceeded up the hill.

He pulled into a parking spot marked "Visitors" and climbed a flight of concrete steps, then pushed open a massive set of oak doors into the lobby of the administration building. A circular island sat in the center of the room, and inside the waist-high nest was a middle-aged, distinguished-looking woman behind a switchboard, who seemed to be having a great deal of trouble staying awake.

"May I help you?" she asked as Jack approached. Her Southern drawl was pronounced, yet sophisticated, as if she were the mother of one of the school's students doing volunteer work rather than an employee.

"Hi, my name's Jack Lynch. I'm a public relations consultant working for a client who employs one of your graduates. My client has decided to give this person their 'Employee of the Month' award, and I am the one who puts together the newsletter for them. I'm trying to get some background information on the person for my article and thought I'd drop in here and see what I could find."

"Great," the woman said. "The headmaster isn't in right now, but I'm sure our assistant headmistress would be glad to help you. If you'll hold on a moment, I'll call her."

Lynch stood off to one side, wondering if the lie would hold up.

Down the hall, to his left, a wooden door with a frosted glass insert opened. A tall, bespectacled woman with soft salt-and-pepper hair emerged. She walked ramrod straight, with a sureness and solidness that let everyone know this was *her* turf.

"Hello, Mr. Lynch," she said, approaching him with outstretched hand. Her grip was as firm as a man's. "I'm Dr. Bouvier. May I help you?"

Jack repeated his story to her, craning his head slightly upward at an angle to meet her eyes.

"Hmm," she said as he finished. "And who was this student?"

"His name was Buford Adkins. He graduated in 1979."

The woman didn't move a twitch, but her eyes seemed to get heavier in their sockets. "Adkins, eh? Yes, I remember him."

She stood there staring at Jack for a moment, the silence between them unsettling his stomach a moment at a time. "Now tell me, Mr. Lynch," she said. "What is it you really want?"

Jack tried to smile pleasantly, but he realized as her face darkened even more that she wasn't buying a word of it. In fact, he thought, he'd better backstroke quickly or this dowager was going to eat him alive.

"Well?" Dr. Bouvier demanded.

Jack reached up subconsciously and tugged at his tie. He felt the blood rising in his face and wondered if this was the onset of a full-blown anxiety attack.

"Dr. Bouvier, here's my card." Jack reached into his pocket and handed her a business card. "You can call my contact at the bank to verify what I'm saying if you want."

She studied the card. Her expression eased, but just a fraction. "I'm sorry, Mr. Lynch. I don't mean to be rude. It's just that, frankly, Adkins was so singularly unimpressive a young man that it's hard to imagine him getting any kind of award at all. All he cared about here was computers. Computers, computers, computers. . . . That and movies and comic books. It was very tiresome."

Jack bled off a little tension and tried to relax. "Well, Dr. Bouvier, he's turned his adolescent obsessions into a career. He's now the senior systems analyst at the First Interstate Bank of Louisiana."

"Hmm, well, I suppose that the young man has made something out of himself after all. I couldn't be happier. Of course, Mr. Lynch, I can't let you do anything like look at his transcript or his file without his permission."

"This is going to be a surprise," Jack interrupted. "So we really can't ask him for that."

"I understand. However, if you want to go over to the

library, you can take a look at the yearbooks for those years. There will be something in there about him, I'm sure. Especially his senior year. Our graduating classes are so small that each senior gets an entire page in the annual."

Jack thanked the woman politely, relieved to be out of her range. He started toward the front of the building, into the white heat of the afternoon sun, when Dr. Bouvier cleared her throat behind him.

"I'm especially surprised to find that Mr. Adkins has done well in the corporate environment given his behavior here."

Jack turned. "Ma'am?"

She lowered her face, then smiled slyly at him. "Well, I shouldn't tell tales, but Mr. Adkins was one of the more memorable students from that class. But for all the wrong reasons."

"What do you mean?"

She walked toward him, her voice lowering. "Well, I suppose in retrospect, it's funny. But we had just opened our new computer center that year. Mr. Adkins somehow managed to use his student terminal to tap into the school's main computer, the ones where we kept all the academic records."

Jack gulped. "He—?"

"Yes. Of course, he didn't change grades or anything like that. We questioned him very closely. He would have been expelled immediately. What Mr. Adkins did was plant a virus in our computer, one that caused a rather naughty limerick to appear on the screen every morning when we booted up. I don't suppose he'd mind anyone knowing about it now. It does seem funny in memory, although not very funny at the time. Buford had the highest SAT scores in his class, and graduated fifty-first out of a class of fifty-three. He just didn't try very hard."

"Well, ma'am, he's changed his tune. He's trying mighty hard these days."

"And, I gather, succeeding," Dr. Bouvier commented as Jack stepped out of the door.

"Not if I can help it," he whispered.

Jack was surprised to find himself on a bluff overlooking the Mississippi. The river below and away from him for perhaps a half-mile spread lazily out from right to left like a muddy green-brown strip gashed across the landscape. From his right, from upstream toward the city, the white dot of a tugboat pushed a line of rusty barges downstream toward the gulf. The wind was blowing from the south as well, and the faintly chemical smell from the plants across the river in Algiers hit his nostrils.

Jack walked up a long aggregate sidewalk toward the library. He imagined a Confederate artillery squad perched atop the bluff, trying in vain to keep Farragut away from the city. Farragut would sail the Union fleet past those bluffs, then past the levees across from Jackson Square and aim his guns down at the crowds. The world has come so far, Jack thought: now we wage war by pushing buttons, and steal millions without ever seeing a cent of it.

He climbed another set of cracked concrete stairs and pushed a pair of thick plate glass doors into the library. Jack walked up to the main desk and whispered his request to the librarian, along with the fact that Dr. Bouvier had granted permission for him to be there. The librarian whispered instructions back to him; what he wanted was on the second floor. He took the steps two at a time, excited at the prospect of what he hoped to find, and entered the musty, empty room.

Black letters painted on the glass door read: SCHOOL ARCHIVES—REFERENCE ONLY. Inside this room, the neglected, bound copies of senior honors theses, yearbooks, and bound volumes of the school newspaper dating back to the late nineteenth century sat unused and crumbling inside this intellectual crypt. Jack wandered in and out of the stacks until he found the yearbooks, then scanned quickly along the shelf until he came to the 1970s. He pulled out 1976 through 1979, and took them to a seat at a long wooden table.

As he expected, the first three years revealed little besides pictures of the adolescent Buford Adkins. Adkins was a pudgy, pudding-faced young boy with a bad haircut and a slightly-worse-than-average case of teenage acne. He excelled at little, it seemed, but his face showed up in the group photos of the computer club every year, surrounded by rows of other teenaged boys who looked as though they had trouble getting dates on Saturday night.

Jack nervously picked up the volume labelled "1979," with the embossed letters below it that spelled out "Riverside Academy." He flipped through to the section marked "Seniors." The entries were arranged alphabetically; Adkins was first in line. Forever and for all time, the 1979 graduating senior class of Riverside Academy would be met by the goofy smiling face of Buford Adkins every time they opened their yearbooks to reminisce. Below Buford's picture, with the shiny forehead and the roughly airbrushed-out zits, a list of accomplishments summarized his years at the exclusive boys' school:

BUFORD ADKINS
"FLOUNDER"

Wild Man of Adams Dormitory; Future Faber College Graduate; Computer Club, I, II, III, IV; Spanish Club, II, III, IV; Electronics Club, I, II, III, IV; "Toga Parties on the South Lawn"; "Oh boy, this is great. . . ." Planted the Limerick Virus in the School's mainframe.

"Well, Flounder," he whispered, "guess you got bored with being a grown-up. Not too many toga parties in corporate life, eh partner?"

Jack slowly let the covers of the book fall toward each other and close. He wondered if Buford Adkins had booked his flight to the Far East yet.

■ *CHAPTER 28* ■

A chemical truck had overturned and ruptured on the St. Bernard Highway. As Jack pulled out of the school grounds, he noticed traffic backing up just parallel to the railroad, slowing gradually, then coming to a complete stop.

He shut the Fiat down to keep it from overheating. He turned on the radio, switched to the AM band and searched for a traffic report. Within a few minutes, it was clear the stoppage was a serious one. No one was going anywhere for awhile.

If Buford Adkins had killed Gupton, Jack thought, he must be near panic by now. Buford Adkins, the kind of guy who thought nicknames like "Flounder" were cool, couldn't have been a murderer. He was too middle-class, suburban white bread, the kind of man who'd cheat on his taxes and cheat on his wife—when he got one—but when it came to sticking a pistol, a *real* pistol, above a man's left ear and pulling the trigger and feeling the recoil of the weapon as it sprayed blood and bone fragments and goo all over the inside of a car—well, that was an entirely different matter altogether. Jack wondered if he himself could have the *cojones* to do something like that, but then thought that just having balls wasn't the only thing it would take. An alcoholic who goes through his day with an ache in his gut and a longing in his heart for a boilermaker, then goes to bed sober at night had balls. A single mother who got her kids off to school, then trudged into a soul-killing minimum-wage job day after day; she had balls, too.

But to whack a guy you know in a parking lot, a guy who gave you a job, a guy whose office you hung around in and shot the bull with on slow days . . . that took something more, something a lot darker. Something Lynch didn't really want to think about. Something that was a lot darker even than stealing five million dollars anonymously, facelessly, by computer.

Jack ran up the walk, sweat dripping off him, and pounded on Martin Brown's front door. There was no sound from inside. It was nearly three P.M.; surely Martin was awake.

Jack pounded again, rattling the glass in the door like a box of beads. He pressed his face against the glass, straining to look for movement beyond the thin sheer gauze curtain that covered the door. Nothing.

Frustrated, he slammed his fist into the wooden door frame one last time. He stuffed his hands into his pockets and walked to the end of the porch, surveying the neighborhood like it was his own private territory. What next?

There was a clatter behind him as a dazed Martin Brown fumbled with the door lock and opened the door. Jack turned and glared at the young man who stood there in an unbuttoned, dirty pair of jeans and no shirt. Brown's greasy hair hung tangled and knotted over his forehead, and his eyes were thick with sleep.

"Dammit," Brown groaned, "as long as you're around, I'm never going to get a decent night's sleep."

Jack pushed past him into living room. "C'mon in," Martin said, resigned to the intrusion.

"I've got it figured out," Lynch said, turning to face him from the center of the room.

"Got what figured out?"

"I know who the extortionist is."

"The guy who planted the software bomb?" Martin said, consciousness returning to his voice.

"And murdered Harold Gupton."

Brown gulped, then cleared his throat. "Who?"

"Buford Adkins."

Martin's eyes rolled back in his head and a sneer crossed his face. "Oh, Jesus, Lynch. Get real. Buford Adkins wouldn't slap a dog with a rolled-up newspaper."

Jack stepped toward him. "I don't have time to mess with you on this one, Marty. You're either going to help me, or you're not. What's it going to be?"

Martin walked past Jack and sat down on the living room couch. He yawned deeply, his scummy teeth visible from across the room. "Buford Adkins? Are you sure?"

"It's got to be. There's nobody else." Jack told Martin everything he'd found out in the past couple of days.

"It's not much," Martin said when he finished.

"I know that. Not enough to go to the police. Not without something else."

"Like what?"

"I think if I can get him alone, under the right circumstances, I can get him to admit it. If he thinks he's won, if he thinks he can't be caught, then he might be just a little cocky himself. That's where you come in."

"How come every time you use the word 'cocky', I get brought into the conversation?"

Jack sat on the edge of the sofa. "I need you to get him there, late tonight. He'll be off guard. I need to get him somewhere alone, somewhere where he feels safe."

"How about the tape library? There's a table in there; the operators hang out in there when there's nothing going on. It's a good place to hide."

"Will they be in there tonight?"

"I'll fix it so they won't be. Then I can work up some kind of problem with running the nightly reports, something Buford can't fix from home by dialing in. He'll have to come in."

"Once he's in the office, can you get him back in the tape library?"

"Sure," Martin said, rubbing his eyes. "I'll figure out something."

"I don't want you there," Jack said. "He won't say anything unless we're alone."

"How are you going to prove anything?"

"I'll be wired. I've got a pocket tape recorder, voice-activated, real sensitive. If I can get him to talk, the tape will be enough to set the cops on him at least."

Martin turned to Jack. "What if he goes ballistic on you? Like, I mean with a gun or something?"

"He wouldn't have any reason to bring a gun down there, would he?"

"Other than the fact that half the population of this city carries guns with them everywhere they go. . . ."

"I don't think he'll do anything like that. That'll get him caught for sure. My guess is the gun he shot Gupton with is at the bottom of the lake by now."

"Well," Martin said, inhaling deeply and swelling his chest, "I'll be there to back you up. Anything happens, I'll take him down."

It was Lynch's turn to roll his eyes. "Okay, Jack Webb. But would you mind if I brought along somebody else just in case?"

The Vieux Carré crowds were starting to pick up as the clock eased its way toward cocktail hour. A late afternoon shower had drenched the area for ten minutes, the soaked tourists caught unawares, and then just as quickly rolled on. Puddles of water stood on the street now, steam rising slowly from the asphalt.

On foot, Jack cut behind the French Market, crossed North Peters, then went up the back of Cafe du Monde near the public bathrooms, then out onto Decatur and up the steps to the Moonwalk. It was past four; getting late for the day-shift hustlers. If Fast Eddie had scored his quota for the day, he might be settling in front of the TV for the night.

Lynch scanned the area toward Woldenberg Park. The tourists had returned to the concrete walks after the rain, strolling aimlessly in the cool afternoon air. The *Natchez* was docked and preparing for its evening cruise. Everything seemed calm and ordinary to Lynch, as if only he knew the turbulence and violence boiling just beneath the surface.

No sign of Fast Eddie. He began walking quickly toward the bridge, past the fountain and the manicured grass of the park. The wrought iron benches were filled with people taking the early evening air, some skipping out on their offices ahead of time, others simply with nothing better to do. Lynch walked past them intently, surveying the faces one-by-one, looking not only for Fast Eddie, but for anyone wearing that pained and humiliated expression of disbelief that meant they'd just encountered Fast Eddie or one of his colleagues.

The aquarium lay ahead of him, towering over the riverfront in its concrete, tile, and girder architecture. A crowd stood in front, patiently waiting admittance. It wasn't Fast Eddie's style to work the aquarium crowds; security guards tended to be a little quick in running the nickel-and-dime hustlers off, not realizing those nickel-and-dimer's were pulling down about ten bucks an hour more than they were.

Off to his right, a hot dog cart sat shiny and metallic in the sun, hot shafts of blue light reflecting off its polished surface beneath a red and yellow striped umbrella. Jack glanced at it, then turned away. Out of the corner of his eye, he caught a flash of white on black walking up to the cart. The image rushed by in a twinkling and almost didn't register, but then he stopped and turned back to the cart.

Fast Eddie reached into his pocket and pulled out a wad of bills that filled his palm. It had been a good day. He peeled off a single bill and handed it to the guy standing behind the cart with the white paper hat on his head.

Jack followed him briefly as Fast Eddie went off snarfing down the hotdog. He wore a white T-shirt with the colors of the African National Congress emblazoned on the front and back, along with a pair of checked baggy shorts that came to his knees. His Air Jordans were unlaced, the tongues flopping in front, the laces bundled up and shoved inside. Eddie looked around, perusing the crowd, looking for one last potential score before calling it a day.

"Hey, mister," Jack said, walking up behind him. "Betcha I can tell you where you got those shoes."

Eddie turned, a wide grin on his face. "Fast Jack, my man."

Eddie stuck out his palm. Jack Lynch laid an awkward high-five on him, a middle-aged homeboy learning the streets a day at a time. "So wha's happening?" Eddie asked.

"You remember the last time we talked?"

"Fast Eddie remembers everything."

"I had to pay you in advance for a day's work, right?"

"Memory serves me," Eddie said, his face dark ebony stillness, "you made a deposit."

"Well, guy," Lynch said, reaching into his wallet with one hand while bringing his other arm around Fast Eddie's massive shoulders. "I'm here to make another deposit."

CHAPTER 29

There's a silence that settles over the Central Business District at night, after the office workers have gone home and the night people have gone off to more colorful pursuits in the Quarter. There are no crowds on the sidewalks, only people walking nervously up the streets alone, or perhaps in groups of one or two. There's more caution than revelry here, and if New Orleans was the city that care forgot, it became over the past decade the city that care remembered, and came back home to.

The wrought-iron facades of many of the newer buildings, where the architects had tried to capture the flavor and mood of the city as it must have been a hundred years earlier, draped web-like against the buildings above the street. It was neither a place to feel at home nor comfortable.

Jack Lynch spun the Fiat around Lee Circle and came up Carondelet. Two blocks short of the bank, he pulled the car over and parked it. The amber yellow of the sulfurous streetlights cast dim formless shadows over the car as he got out and pulled the top up, then locked the doors.

He wished that he'd had time to go replace the .38 that had been stolen when his old apartment was burglarized. Not that he'd ever want to use it, and not that it even gave him that much comfort to carry it.

He just wished he'd thought of it.

He'd checked in with Maud, but thought it better not to tell her his plans for the evening. There was no point in worrying her. She couldn't be any help to him; he wouldn't allow her to, would never put her in that position. He'd gone home and changed into a pair of jeans and running shoes, along with a light flannel shirt and jacket. The air was still heavy with humidity, and when the temperature dropped at night in the springtime, the chill was penetrating and deep. P.J. hadn't been home yet, so he slipped a note under her door telling her he had to work late and would knock on her door when he got home if her light was still on.

He'd driven down Tulane Avenue and stopped at Bud's Broiler, but for once he couldn't stomach another hamburger and paper pouch full of greasy french fries. He'd ordered a Dixie and sat on one of the picnic tables that served as furnishings at Bud's and sipped the beer slowly. His stomach was knotted up, his usual reaction to anxiety, and he wondered how long it would be before he burned an ulcer in his gut.

He had a feeling this was going to be a long night.

At his office, he'd fished through Maud's desk drawers until he found his portable tape recorder, a fist-sized, expensive Sony that could pick up a whisper from ten feet away. He would carry it in his shirt pocket, and hope that once he and Buford Adkins were alone, the man he had gradually come to believe was both a thief and a murderer would slip and talk too much.

It seemed a remote chance at best, but it was his only trump. If he played it and lost, he was no worse off than he was now. If he didn't play it at all, then Lynch knew that this man would find an excuse to turn in his resignation very shortly, and there would be coffee and cake for him one Friday afternoon as his co-workers said good-bye to him. And then the next day, he would be out at Moissant Field boarding a plane with a passport in his pocket and a smile on his face. Buford Adkins would finally, he thought, be somebody.

It was not that Lynch had any great affection for the First

Interstate Bank of Louisiana, and it certainly wasn't because he felt a deep personal loss at the murder of Harold Gupton. But the man had had a wife and two children; hell, somebody out there had loved him. Better not to ask why. Moral choices and consequences aside, there were two young kids out there—a seven-year-old boy and a nine-year-old girl—who had some hellacious therapy bills in front of them because of what Buford Adkins had done. If for no other reason than that he was intimately acquainted with the pain of grief, Jack Lynch was going to take his shot.

He stepped around the car one last time to make sure it was secure, as secure as a ragtop sitting on a dark, isolated block in an American city could be. He held his wrist up and strained to read his watch in the dim light: 10:25. He and Fast Eddie were supposed to meet in five minutes at the shipping entrance in back of the bank building.

He walked quickly up the block, swiveling his shoulders to loosen the tension in his muscles. Then he cocked his arms at the elbow and stiffly swung them back and forth, as if marching in a military parade. He reached the building and turned right, down the block away from the front entrance on Carondelet. Halfway down the side street block, an alley cut in between the bank building that faced on Carondelet and the building that faced out on St. Charles. Ahead of him, coming from his left to the right, he heard the metallic clattering and electrical popping of the streetcar as it rounded Canal and headed uptown on St. Charles. Jack could smell the burnt ozone from the blue-green sparks.

Ahead of him, the alley lay dark and threatening, illuminated only by a bare light bulb above the bank's loading dock. He *really* wished he'd gotten another pistol now, but it was too late for that. He gritted his teeth, checked all four directions around him, then walked quickly into the alley.

Three concrete steps led up to a metal door next to the loading dock. Jack climbed the steps and stood there, feeling naked under the bare bulb. He raised his jacket sleeve, checked his watch. Martin Brown, he thought, better goddamn well be on time.

He stood there perhaps thirty seconds longer, lost in thought, when the heavy clunking of an industrial slide bolt being pulled jerked him back to the world. The door opened, revealing a thin crack of dim light. Martin Brown stood there, nervously holding the door open.

"Everything okay?" he whispered.

"I can't find Eddie," Jack said in a normal voice.

"Who's Eddie?"

"I'm Eddie," Fast Eddie said, stepping out of the shadows. He had been there the whole time, in a small niche in the brick building across the gravelled alley.

Jack jumped and twisted around. "Damn, Ed, scare the shit out of me, why don'tcha?"

Eddie smiled and climbed the steps to the porch next to Jack. He was wearing black satin jogging pants with thin vertical green and red stripes. A black satin warm-up jacket was zippered halfway up, covering part of his bare chest. Around his neck, a half-dozen gold chains hung glittering in the light.

"Fast Eddie," he said, holding out his hand to Martin. "Glad to meet you."

"Jesus, Eddie," Jack said, checking out the black satin. "What are you, doing a guest spot on 'Soul Train' after this?"

"Ease up, my man," Eddie said, "before somebody breaks a pencil off in that tight ass o' yours. I got a date later, that's okay with you. . . ."

"Hey, you guys gonna stand there, you gonna come in?"

Eddie pulled the door open past Jack and stepped into the building ahead of him. Jack pulled the door to and looked around. Faint lightbulbs lit the loading dock, but just barely. Jack could feel the cold concrete through the soles of his shoes, and the stifling dust clogged his nostrils.

"You call Adkins?" he asked.

"Right before I came down here. He's on his way over."

"What'd you tell him?"

Martin gave him a look that made Jack want to slap him across the back of the head. "I'll try and explain it to you if you want. But I don't think you'd get it."

Jack sighed disgustedly. "Okay, fine. You got the program, though, right?"

"I'm with you," Martin said.

"Let's do it," Fast Eddie added.

Martin led the way back through the loading dock to a heavy metal door that he'd propped open with a stack of computer printout. A long hallway led to another door, which took them down a flight of stairs below ground level.

"This smell's awful," Jack said. "Is everything down here mildewed?"

"Remember, man," Martin said, "this is New Orleans. You go ten feet below the ground, you're in the wet. We run dehumidifiers constantly down here. Doesn't do any good, though."

Another long hall, then through another door into a brightly lit hallway that ran behind the glass-enclosed computer room.

"Here's what I figured in terms of the logistics," Martin said. "This room over here's the decollating room."

"The what?" Eddie asked.

"The place where we get the reports together. Eddie, you go in there and stay out of sight. The other operators are scattered throughout the building, taking care of bullshit that I had to be real creative to make up."

"Okay," Eddie said, pointing. "Through there?"

"Yeah, and when Adkins goes into the tape library, I'll come get you. You and I'll be in the computer room itself, ready to help Jack out if he needs it."

"Yo, gotcha'," Eddie said. He stepped into the doorway of the decollating room and disappeared from sight.

"We don't have a lot of time, do we?" Jack asked.

"Buford lives in an apartment complex out in New Orleans East. No traffic this time of night. Shouldn't take him more'n about twenty-five minutes to get here."

"I'd better get settled."

"Yeah. Listen, there's a fire-alarm in the tape library. If things get out of hand, just slam that bell. All hell'll break loose, but we'll get in there and help you out."

"I hope it doesn't come to that," Jack said.

"Aw, c'mon, we could use the excitement in our dull, dreary lives."

"*You* could use the excitement in *your* dull, dreary life," Jack said as Martin Brown pulled a plastic card out of his wallet and ran it through the slot on an electronic card reader. A light above the glass door changed from red to green and Martin pulled it open.

"After you," he said.

The two walked into the dry, icy air of the computer room. A dull whirring filled their ears, shutting out all other sounds. To his right, Jack saw a bank of mag tape readers and huge metal cabinets, with row after row of smaller metal cabinets with clear plastic domes on the other side of the wall. To his left, a pair of high-speed printers ten feet high sat idle.

"You know what all this stuff is?" Jack asked.

"Naw, dude, I just fake it."

Martin led him past the printers, toward a glass door that looked out on the data processing department offices. A solid wooden door to the left of the glass door was closed. Martin twisted the knob and opened it, then led Jack into the dark narrow room, with rows of magnetic tape reels in white collars hooked onto heavy steel racks covering every wall from floor to ceiling. A long wooden table with a few folding metal chairs sat in the middle, with a green utility cabinet pushed off in the corner out of the way. The room was cramped, cheerless, drab.

"So this is where you guys hang out when things get quiet?"

"Hey, it's home away from home for us. Now you see why every operator in the department's on Prozac."

Jack looked around the room, then turned to Martin. "Marty, I appreciate all your help with this. If it turns out to be nothing, I'll make sure you're protected. Your job'll be safe, anyway."

"Don't worry about it," Martin said. "Besides, I'm going to be turning in my resignation and leaving town soon anyway."

Jack's brow furrowed. "Yeah? How come?"

"Patí left me yesterday. Said she's filing for divorce."

Jack's face fell. "Aw, no, man. Hey, I'm sorry. Really."

Martin raised one corner of his lip in a sneer. "I'm not. It's for the better. We were a bad match. Easy come, easy go."

The two men stood there wordlessly for a second. "Listen, dude," Martin said, opening the door of the tape library. "If you get behind the utility cabinet, he won't be able to see you when he opens the door. Watch y'er ass, okay?"

Jack nodded his head. "You, too."

Martin stepped out into the computer room and pulled the door to behind him. The tape drives spun on endlessly. The brilliant, sterile white light of the computer room hurt his eyes.

He took his place at the console and typed in a few instructions, instructions that would start a job that would tie up the computer for about two minutes. He had the commands typed out on the console, but he didn't hit the key that would start the job.

Outside the computer room, a bank of fluorescent overheads flickered to life. Martin's hand poised midair over the RETURN key on his console. In a moment, Buford Adkins walked into the department wearing a pair of jeans and a Tulane University pullover shirt. Martin's eyes followed him as he walked the length of the computer room, then pulled his card out of his wallet and ran it through the reader. As Adkins entered the computer room, Martin hit the key. The tape drives spun to life.

"Showtime," Martin whispered.

"Okay, Marty," Adkins called jovially from across the room. "What's the big emergency?"

Martin jumped off the elevated part of the floor where the main console stood and stomped over to Adkins in a rage.

"Goddamit! Your people screwed up again and now I'm gonna get my ass chewed for not doing my job!" he screamed, spit flying from his lips.

"Yo, Marty, chill out a minute. What do you mean?" Adkins's voice was typically conciliatory.

"The REM-1200 report bombed out in the middle and just gave me a bunch of gibberish! Goddamit, Buford, every time I have to run that report, something happens. Why can't you people *get it right*?"

"Marty, what're you crawling all over me about it for? Why didn't you call Ken? It's his section, not mine."

"To begin with, I couldn't find Ken. All I got was his answering machine. Secondly, if I get that son of a bitch down here after hours, he's only gonna find some way to blame it on me and I'll just get my bony little ass chewed on again. You see back here, Buford?"

Martin turned, pointed to the seat of his pants. "I got no ass left here. No ass at all. And it's all Ken Cook's fault. Listen, buddy, help me out here, will you?"

Adkins softened. "Sure, Marty. Let me take a look at it."

"The mainframe's tied up right now running the Year-to-Date CD summary. Vice-president Megadeath from Hell wanted it run a week early this quarter."

Adkins squinted his eyes in confusion. "That doesn't make sense. But what the heck, show me the report."

"It's in the tape library," Martin said quietly. "I put it on the conference table. You'll figure it out."

"Sure, fella. No problem. Give me a minute."

As Buford Adkins turned to go into the tape library, Martin Brown walked calmly to the opposite door of the computer room and opened it. As long as Fast Eddie was still in the decollating room, everything was copacetic.

Lynch hoped his heart wouldn't explode right out of his chest. He couldn't decide which was worse: the notion that he'd be alone in a dark room with a murderer, or the thought that he was going to be completely, abysmally humiliated by the ludicrousness of his accusations.

Even through the closed solid door, he could hear Martin Brown screaming in the computer room. He was really pouring it on thick.

Then there was a moment of silence, and the door opened. Hidden in the shadow behind the utility cabinet,

Lynch remained unseen as Adkins walked to the end of the conference table and sat down in front of a pile of computer printout not three feet from where he stood. Adkins's back was to him now as he flipped through the two-inch stack of paper looking for the problem Martin Brown had described.

The only sound was the hiss of cold air entering the room through a vent in the ceiling. Lynch tried not to shudder; the place was as frigid as a meat locker.

"Well, Marty," Buford Adkins said out loud, "I don't see where your problem is. . . ."

Lynch strained his stomach muscles into a knot. "He doesn't have a problem, Buford," he said. "I do."

Adkins jerked around in the chair wild-eyed. "Criminy, you almost gave me a heart attack!"

"I'm sorry," Jack said, stepping out of the shadows and crossing to Adkins's right. He walked up past three chairs and took one in the middle of the table.

"What's going on here?" Adkins demanded. "Who gave you authorization to be in the computer room? Brown's in a lot of trouble if he let you in here."

"Don't blame Martin. He was acting at my instructions."

"Your instructions? Who gave you the authority to give Martin instructions? I'm calling Security." Adkins stood up.

Jack sighed, folded his hands in front of him. The weight of the tiny tape recorder in his shirt pocket felt like an anchor. "I wouldn't do that just yet. Not until we've had a chance to talk, anyway."

Adkins's eyes seemed to focus on a point six inches from the middle of Jack Lynch's chest.

"Why would we have anything to talk about?"

"You fascinate me, Buford. I've been doing some checking on you. You're an interesting man."

Adkins narrowed his eyes suspiciously, then sat back down at the table, his massive forearms, pasty and pale in the harsh fluorescent light, spread across the table.

"What are you talking about? You have no right—"

"Oh, yes, I do, Buford. I was hired by this bank to handle a potential public relations disaster, and I was told I could do just about anything I had to do to protect this bank."

"Including violating my privacy?"

"Yours and everybody else's in this department. . . ." Lynch said.

"I resent the hell out of that," Adkins said. It was the first time Lynch had ever heard the man use an obscenity.

"Don't be too upset," Lynch said. "The stuff I got on you was all flattering. In fact, I can't figure out why you weren't running the department. You're good, Buford. You know what you're doing."

"Which is more than you can say for a lot of the people around here," Adkins grumbled.

"Talent didn't seem to amount to much in this department, did it? Seems like it was mostly politics. Say Ken Cook, for instance. His academic credentials are barely a step up from correspondence school, yet he is your boss. And Gupton, even he was just a manager, right?"

"Not a very good one, either. It's tough to manage people," Adkins said offhandedly, "when you can't look 'em in the face."

"You designed most of the system around here, didn't you?"

Adkins smiled. "The new mainframe came in last year. These bozos around here couldn't find their butts with both hands and an instruction book. It wasn't for me, they'd still be trying to figure out how to boot it up."

Jack smiled back at him, fatigue dulling the edges of his thought. "So you learned it inside and out, better than anyone else."

"Yeah," Adkins said, his voice rising proudly. "It was mine. I could make it hum, make it squeal and jump around in circles. I knew it as well or better than the engineers that designed it."

"It must be frustrating to be that good and have to put up with the kind of bull you had to around here."

Adkins brought his hands together and squeezed them. "I wasn't going to be around here forever."

"Really?"

"I meant, well, in my job. Sooner or later I was going to be running the department. Especially with Gupton gone now."

"Yeah, that's right. Gupton's not a factor any more. But there's Ken Cook."

"Cook's an idiot," Adkins said. "A blowhard. He's Peter Principled out."

"So it was going to be your sandbox," Lynch said slowly. "This is assuming, of course, that you even wanted it."

"What do you mean?" Adkins asked. "Of course, I wanted it."

"Why? Smart fellow like you. You could do better. I really compliment you on the way you made the system work here. It was remarkable. But a fellow with your brains, your drive . . . hell, you could do a lot better. After all, you had the highest SAT scores in your class, right? You're no dummy."

Buford Adkins lifted his heavy eyelids as far as they would go. "How'd you know about that?"

Lynch smiled. "C'mon, Buford. I know a lot about you. I know about the computer club, the SAT scores. I even know about the trouble you got into your senior year. You know, when you sabotaged the computers at school."

Adkins clenched his teeth. "Wait a minute, that wasn't sabotage, it was just—"

"I know, I know," Lynch interrupted. "It was just a prank, a practical joke. Something for them to remember you by, since they'd paid so little attention to you while you were there. You saw the other guys getting the girls. The jocks and the studs. The prizes, the strokes. All the time you were smarter than them. I can understand why you did it . . . Flounder."

Adkins sat still, almost dazed, then shook his head and stared intently at Jack. "What are you getting at?"

"Only that I understand what drove you to it."

"Drove me to what?" he demanded.

"Drove you to salt away five big ones in a Southeast Asian bank. . . ."

"Aw, Christ, you have gone off the deep end." Adkins laughed crudely, uncomfortably.

"C'mon, Flounder, you can level with me." Lynch said.

"Please don't call me Flounder," Adkins said, his voice almost pleading. "I always hated that nickname. Flounder was the loser, the fat guy. I didn't like that nickname. They gave it to me."

Jack jumped up, attacking now. "What I don't understand is why you had to kill Gupton. I know he was on the take from the Gaming Corporation of America. It's not like he was some kind of straight arrow or something. What was it? Was he trying to cut in on you? Or were the two of you in it together?"

"You're crazy," Buford gasped. His eyes, Jack noticed, were filling with tears and his cheeks shook with tension. His fists were clenched at his side.

Jack was poised on the balls of his feet, as if there were enough space in this tiny room for him to run if he had to.

"I figured it out, Flounder. And if I can do it, other people will too. I was just the first. I won't be the last."

Adkins eyes filled completely and two thin streams of liquid ran down the sides of his face. Jack felt sorry for him; he was no killer. Just somebody who made some rotten decisions and got caught in a bad place. But it was too late to do anything about that now.

"What happened, Buford? Why'd you kill him?"

His cheeks glistened now in the dim light. "I'll be thirty years old next month and I'm still a virgin," he said pathetically. "It was my birthday present to myself. It was wonderful, it really was. I created the language when I was in college. Nothing in the world like it. A high-speed burst compiler language. Data transferred at unbelievably high speeds. Instead of hiding the software bomb in the programs, I hid it in a data file."

"A data file?"

"Yeah, I found a bank customer who'd been dead for a year, but who still had an open account. I hid the bomb there instead of in the software itself. I never meant to set it off. I just wanted the money."

"So that's why none of the programmers could find it. You are good, Buford. The best."

"I knew the bank wasn't going to miss five million, not over the long haul. I mean, who's it going to hurt?"

Lynch knew it would hurt a lot of people, but now wasn't

the time to tell Adkins that. "Nobody, but then Gupton. . . ."

Buford rolled his fists into tight balls and slammed them on the desk. His lips trembled; tears fell heavily on the table. "Yeah, Gupton. Here he was, pulling down the big bucks, with everybody bowing and scraping to him. On top of that, everybody knew he was taking money under the table. He almost bragged about it. That's when I decided it was my turn."

"But he was on to you."

"He never did believe it was somebody on the outside, not with the timing and how slick it was. He knew Cook didn't have the smarts to pull something like that off. All along he suspected me or Marty. He confronted me in his office one day, really started squeezing my balls. Said he wasn't going to have his little golden egg ruined by some greedy S.O.B. *junior executive.* That's all any of us were to him: underlings, stooges. . . . We did all the work. He got all the gravy."

"That's corporate America, Buford. That's the way it works. But he wasn't a very nice man. I'll give you that much."

"I told him I'd turn myself in, give him the numbers to recover the money from my bank account. I told him to meet me in the middle of the night, in the parking lot. He said he wasn't going to turn me in. He just wanted the five million, and if I wanted to stay out of jail, I'd let him have it."

"So when you went to meet him that night, you took a gun along, didn't you?"

Adkins put his hands to his face; his shoulders shook as he sobbed into his bare hands. He sniffed, a loud wet snarfle that made Lynch want to gag, then pulled his hands down.

"I didn't mean to kill him. I just wanted to scare him. But he grabbed for the pistol. There was nothing I could do. I swear it."

"I know that, Buford. You didn't mean to kill him. That's going to make it go easier on you."

"What do you mean?" Adkins looked at him, confused and questioning. He sniffed again and ran his bare hand along under his nose.

"Buford, you've got to take responsibility for this, pal."

"You're crazy."

"There's no options here, Buford. Not on this one."

"You're out of your mind. I'm not going to jail! No sir, not me."

He stood up again, his shoulders heaving, his breathing becoming deeper and more rapid. Buford Adkins was slowly working himself into a rage. Control was slipping away.

"Maybe you can work out a deal, serve your time in a camp somewhere," Lynch said, grasping. "You don't have to go to Angola."

This seemed to trigger something even deeper in Adkins.

"Angola? No way, man. I'll die first. Lynch, we can split the money. I'll give you half. I'll give you all of it! But I ain't turning myself in!"

"Then I'm turning you in, Buford. It's the only way, friend. I'm sorry. I really am."

"There's nobody here," Adkins spat. "Nobody heard us. I'll deny everything. You can't prove it. The gun's long gone. Nobody'll believe you."

"No, Buford. But they'll believe this." Lynch reached into his shirt pocket and pulled out the tape recorder. "It's over, pal. Let's call it a night."

He stuffed the recorder back in his pocket. Adkins looked on in horror, his eyes widening as terror seemed to engulf him. He jerked forward on the table, flailing away, trying to grab Jack.

Jack jumped up, backed away from the table, in front of the steel tape rack. "C'mon, Buford, quit that before one of us gets hurt. It won't make any difference anyway. You can't leave the building."

"The hell I can't!" he yelled. He lunged at Jack, his massive right fist flying upwards as he did so. His feet were planted well, and he caught Lynch off guard. All his weight was behind his fist as it shot out and caught Lynch on the left side of his face.

Something cracked and Jack saw a burst of light, then red and blue sparkles as the room began to spin around him. He tried to yell, but nothing came out. A searing, white-hot pain shot through his skull and he felt himself sailing into a deep black hole.

He fell backwards, his weight slamming into the metal rack holding the rows of mag tapes. He pounded against the shelves and fell in a heap. The rack above him swayed back and forth crazily, then let go and fell forward, sending hundreds of tape reels down on him in a heap. Lynch was buried under a pile of reels each nearly two feet in diameter, and two pounds apiece.

Adkins jumped out of the way as the rack fell forward, sliding across the table on his rump just in time. His feet slammed on the linoleum as he fought for traction and ran for the door. His right fist was swelling fast and bleeding.

He ran for the door and jerked it open. A short, stocky black man in black satin and gold stood in front of him. Buford Adkins screamed and raised his fist. The black man ducked, planted his own feet, and caught him in the gut with a full impact uppercut.

Buford Adkins bent over and vomit began to spew out of his mouth. The black man jumped out of the way, got in behind him, then kicked him, hard, in the seat of the pants. Buford crumpled, lying in his own slop, helpless and silently, breathlessly crying.

"Get over there, man," Fast Eddie ordered Martin Brown, pointing at the pile of mag tapes. "Dig him outta that mess."

Brown jumped over the fallen Adkins and scrambled across the table, which had caught the edge of the shelving and was the only thing keeping the heavy steel structure from crushing Jack.

He got himself under the metal, then pushed with all his might. Another set of tapes fell out onto the floor as he lifted the rack back against the wall. He jumped to the floor beside Jack and began pulling tapes off him.

Martin cleared a hole around Jack's head. The whole side of Jack's face was swollen and beginning its long process of discoloration; the capillaries had exploded in his left eye and filled it with blood.

"Man, you look like you got a softball growing out of the side of your head. You all right?"

Lynch tried to focus on the face above him. He was dazed, shocky, and just beginning to hurt *real* bad.

"I t'ink," he mumbled, "ta' sunfabitch bwoke my chaw...."

■ CHAPTER 30 ■

He swam up from deep within himself, toward the tiny sparkles of light that seemed high above him. He spun slowly, dizzy and slightly nauseous, as the surface got nearer and nearer. There was pressure, like ears popping from a change in altitude, only his head was popping everywhere. Not just in his ears. It hurt, but it was a strange kind of hurt, like nothing he'd ever felt before. The sparkles got brighter, more distinct, and then like a skin diver breaking the surface after the deepest dive he'd ever done, with his lungs about to burst and consciousness a touch-and-go proposition, Jack Lynch opened his eyes and saw white everywhere.

He groaned, his head pounding. *Where the hell am I?*

He tried to speak, but couldn't. Something was holding his head clamped shut. He tried to open his mouth, but as soon as his muscles clenched, a pain like a foot-long needle being jammed into the side of his jaw stopped that immediately.

His eyes rolled back in his head and his eyelids fell shut, then cracked open again.

Someone stood above him. Someone he'd never seen before.

"Don't try to talk," the voice said, stern, old. *My God,* he thought, *I'm back in boarding school.*

"Your jaw is wired shut. You cannot open your mouth. Don't even try," the voice instructed again. Jack tried to raise his head. His strength was gone. He settled back into the thick pillow. When he let everything relax and let go, the ache subsided and he was almost comfortable.

"The doctor will be in to talk to you in a few minutes. Until then, you're to lie there quietly. Are you thirsty?"

Jack nodded his head weakly. Thirsty wasn't the word for it.

"All right," the voice said. The stiff white uniform crinkled as the body turned to its left, then came back with a plastic glass and straw. The straw bent at an accordion fold and came toward his mouth.

"Go easy," the voice said. "Don't choke."

His reserves were gone. He barely had strength enough to draw on the straw. A thin stream of tepid water trickled onto his teeth and into his mouth. He moaned. It was wonderful. He ran his tongue along the inside of his mouth, across the back of his teeth. He gently tried to open his mouth. The pain was less this time, but his mouth wasn't going anywhere. It was like a box lid nailed shut.

The body pulled the glass away. "Now just lie here," it said. "Are you up to having a visitor? There's someone outside who'd like to see you."

Jack opened his eyes further and nodded yes.

The body receded toward a door, then disappeared. A moment later, Maud came into the room. She seemed thinner, with great circles under her eyes. He was coming back to consciousness now, beginning to recognize things. Beginning to remember how he got there.

She stood next to his bed, then put out a bony hand and touched his arm. "How you feeling, babe?" she asked softly.

Jack formed his lips into word shapes and whispered without moving his jaw. "Okay," he slurred. "Not hurt too bad."

"Good. You scared the hell out of me. Carlton woke me up at four this morning and said they were fixing to take you into surgery. You know how hard it is to find a cab at four in the morning?" she said lightly.

"Sorry," Jack whispered. "I'll reimburse you."

She laughed. "I'm just kidding." Then her voice turned

serious. "I was just so worried about you. Why do you keep doing this to yourself?"

He started to open his mouth, but pain was becoming a consistent reminder that this was impossible. "Hell, Maud," he said through clamped teeth. "I didn't exactly mean to."

She squeezed his arm. "I know that. I'm just glad it's not any worse than it is."

The door behind her opened and a black-haired young man wearing a lab coat came in. He walked over and stood next to Maud.

"Well, Mr. Lynch, how are you today?"

Jack nodded, tried to smile.

"I'm Doctor Adams. I did the welding job on your mouth this morning. The wires are a little tough to get used to, aren't they?"

Jack nodded again. "Well," Dr. Adams continued, a tired smile crossing his face, "you'll get used to it quick enough. Let me give you the rundown on your injuries, and I think you'll be pleasantly surprised. I suspect right now you feel like you've been run over by a truck."

Jack smiled and whispered through his teeth again. "Big one."

"Believe me, it's not that bad. You've got a bump on the back of your head, but no concussion or brain damage or anything like that. Your X-rays were clean, except for one thing. I could give you all the technical jargon, but basically when that fellow hit you, he dislocated your jaw. We set it and wired it shut. You'll be on a liquid diet, I'm afraid, for a few weeks, depending on how fast you heal. You've got some minor contusions and abrasions all over. Apparently some kind of rack or something fell on you?"

"Tapes," Jack groaned. "Tapes. . . ."

"None of that is of any consequence except you're going to be sore as hell for a few days."

"When can I go home?" Jack murmured through clenched teeth.

Doctor Adams rubbed his stubbled jaw. "Not today, I think. There's not much to worry about, but we did have to put you under to wire your jaw. I'd like to keep you in overnight, see how you feel tomorrow. Make sure your temp stays down, no infection. You feel a little better tomorrow, we'll let you check out."

"Great."

"Meantime, you can have visitors, watch a little tube, kick back. The nurse is going to come by and explain how this business of feeding yourself is going to work the next few weeks. It's not so bad, you'll get used to it. Look at it as a way to lose a little weight."

"There's a silver lining to every cloud," Maud said.

"Doan may me frow up," Jack said, his voice a little stronger.

"I'll see you this afternoon, then again tomorrow morning. Everything looks okay, you're out of here."

"And listen," Maud said, "I'm going on to the office, let you drop back off to sleep. I'll see you this evening, too. Okay?"

Jack reached out, took her hand. "Tanks, Maud."

His eyes were already sliding shut as Maud and Dr. Adams let the door fall closed behind them. He felt himself easing into the swirl again, sleep sweeping over him like a sweet, warm blanket. He drifted in and out, with no notion of time or space. He dreamt a little, only the dreams were softer, less harsh than they'd been in awhile.

He felt something over him, a presence, and awoke to see Carlton Smith standing next to his bed. When his eyes opened, Carlton smiled. "Hello, friend," he said.

Jack raised his arm up weakly from the bed and waved.

"The nurses told me you're going home tomorrow."

"Hope sho'," Jack whispered.

"Mind if I pull up a chair?" Carlton asked. "We've got some things to discuss. If you feel up to it, that is."

"Shure. Help me raise the bed up."

Carlton fumbled below the bed rail and came up with a plastic box with a long cable hanging out of it. Jack took the box from him and studied it, then pushed one of the buttons. The hospital bed whirred, the top half of it cranking into an upright position. In a few moments, Jack got his first glimpse of the hospital room. There were flowers on the window sill, several pots of them. He wondered who sent them.

Carlton pulled a chair up next to the bed. Jack reached over and lifted his glass of water, then took a long gulp through the straw. He was feeling stronger now, the effects of the anesthesia wearing off.

"Carlton," he said, his voice still off. "Real sorry . . . I could have handled this better."

Carlton looked at him, puzzled. "Go on."

"Until last minute . . . wasn't sure if Adkins was the extortionist, if he murdered Gupton. Not enough to go to police. . . ."

Jack rolled his head on the pillow away from Carlton. Now that the reality of his situation had sunk in, he felt as low and dejected as he ever had.

"Know what worst part is?" he asked.

"Tell me," Carlton said.

Jack attempted a snigger, but it came out through his wired jaw more as a wet sigh. "No money. Can't work with jaw wired shut. My face. . . . Jesus, I look like a prizefighter who got dropped in twelve."

"Hell," he continued after a moment, "Bankruptcy court, here I come."

Carlton stared at him silently, studying the swelling and the many colors of Jack Lynch's face. A sickening yellow-green was the most predominant color; it reminded Carlton of a mudcat's belly. Dark red and blacks were in there as well, fighting for attention over the rest of the hues.

"Your face does look like an artist's palette," he said finally.

"Stop trying to cheer me up."

"Well, maybe this will cheer you up, my friend. Things aren't as black as they may seem. To begin with, the police have arrested Buford Adkins for the murder of Harold Gupton. Adkins has fallen apart, confessed to everything. Additionally, he's supplied the District Attorney's office and the police with all the details of his foreign bank account. The bank is already in the process of recovering its money. Furthermore, the D.A.'s office has agreed to our request that charges against Adkins not be pressed on the extortion charge."

"Why?"

"The very same reason we hired you. There is always more money. Lost credibility can never be recovered. Once we explained our situation to the authorities, they agreed to cooperate in keeping this quiet. Besides, it makes their job easier. All they have in front of them is a relatively simple, solved murder, complete with a signed, legal confession. Makes them look very good."

"What about the news media?"

Carlton grinned. "I think that's going to work. To the media, this is great copy. A disgruntled, frustrated corporate employee shoots his boss over problems at work. They won't dig any further."

"Unless Adkins decides to grant an interview. . . ." Jack mumbled.

"Why would he do that? As it stands, the D.A. will probably let him plead to second-degree murder. With good time, he'll be out in what, maybe five years? If his ego gets ahead of his brain and he admits to extortion, the D.A. will just press those charges as well. The more he runs his mouth, the more time he does.

"No," Carlton continued after a moment. "This is all just going to go quietly away. You earned your money this time, Jack."

"Great. Worked out okay then."

Carlton leaned forward, placed his arms on the hospital bed rail. "Not just for the bank. I think you'll see that your situation is not as dire as you thought it was either."

"What you mean?" Jack asked quizzically.

"For starters, the bank will, of course, cover your medical bills, as well as paying your full invoice and expenses for services rendered. But I had a meeting this morning with the chairman of the board of directors and the president of the bank, and we've all agreed that since you were singlehandedly responsible for recovering the five million dollars, a finder's fee was appropriate as well. The Chairman suggested the customary ten percent of any monies recovered."

Jack's eyes widened and he sat up in bed on his haunches. "Holy shit, Carlton, that's a—"

"Yes, it is," Carlton agreed. "But I made the case that this was the absolute bare minimum under the circumstances. I also stated that since it was a bank employee who assaulted you, causing you possibly permanent injury, disability, and loss of livelihood, and that since the assault occurred on bank property, you were at the very least likely to sue us for damages that could run into millions of dollars. Furthermore, any civil lawsuit that results from this unprovoked attack on you by a bank employee will likely divulge in a public forum the reason your services were retained in the first place."

Jack eased back into the pillow, stunned. "What you telling me?" he rasped.

"The president and the chairman agreed with me that if you're willing to enter into a contract with the bank whereby you agree to never publicly divulge any information you know about this affair, and to relieve the bank of any future liability as a result of your injuries, the bank will give you as a reward an additional ten percent of the recovered money."

"Carlton," Jack gasped, "that's . . that's—"

"One million dollars. After you pay your taxes, you'll have enough to live on the rest of your life if you shepherd it well. You've earned it, Jack. You've saved the bank and the state lottery system more than that in potential damages."

Jack Lynch was quiet for what seemed like a long time. "Don't know . . . what to say."

"I understand that it's a lot to think about. You may, in fact, want to consult counsel of your own regarding a lawsuit."

"Carlton," Jack said, his voice low and hushed. "You don't have to buy my silence. You'd have it anyway. You know that."

Carlton's face went dark and severe. He got down in Jack's face, his breath hot, intense.

"Jack Lynch," he ordered, "you must *never* repeat that

again to anyone else as long as you live. Do you understand me?"

"Don't know what to say."

"You don't have to say anything. My staff is drawing up the papers right now. When you get out of here, come to my office and we'll settle everything. I've tried to make the best deal possible for you. A million dollars is not what it used to be, but it's still a lot of money. You can live very well on it for a long time."

Jack eyes glazed over, his face a portrait of shellshock. "I . . . I . . . appreciate this, Carlton," he said, his voice hollow.

The older man stood up, held out his hand and took Jack's. "I'll consider it part of my professional legacy. I'm retiring next month. May as well go out with a bang."

Jack narrowed his eyes, trying to focus on Carlton. "I didn't realize what a good friend I had in you. I do now."

Carlton smiled. "We've even managed to clean up most of the jumble from that demonstration version of the software bomb Adkins set off. Only one problem—an old lady, widow on a pension, lives uptown in a falling down shotgun, rarely more than a couple of hundred dollars in her account. She gets her bank statement. The computer has randomly put over a half-million into her account the day before. Now we can't find her. Accounts closed, her house's empty. No forwarding address."

Jack smiled. "Maybe the old lady got away with it."

"One thing's for sure," Carlton said. "If she got far enough away, we'll never find her. . . ."

The voices over the television were tinny coming through the tiny pillow speaker by his head. Jack was awake now, had been fed, and had waved off his last pain pill an hour earlier. He felt stronger, still in shock, but coming back by the minute.

"I'll take an R," the ditzy blonde squealed.

"There are two Rs," Sajak announced. Vanna swept across the stage in a sequined, cranberry red gown, spinning letters. Lynch had figured out the puzzle four turns ago.

"Buy a vowel, you asshole," he whispered through clenched teeth.

The door opened and P.J. Campbell poked her head in. "Have I come at a bad time?"

Jack hit the mute button on the television. "No, please, c'mon in."

P.J. stepped in, still dressed in her work outfit, a blue skirt, jacket, and a white silk blouse. She was at that moment the most beautiful thing he'd ever seen in his life.

Suddenly, he found himself turning away from her, hiding the left side of his face. She stepped over to the bed, leaned down and kissed him softly on his right side.

"C'mon," she said. "I'm a doctor. I can take it."

She placed her hand on the point of his chin and slowly pulled his head around to face her. "Hmmm, lot's of pretty colors. But I spoke with your physician. He says you're going to live."

"How did you find out?" he asked.

"Your secretary called the landlord, asked him to keep an eye on your apartment. I got home, he mentioned it to me. Needless to say, I panicked and phoned the hospital, then came down here as quickly as I could. Touro's a good place; I'm glad you're here."

Jack reached up and took her hand in his. It was cool, dry.

"Cold hands," he said.

"Happens every time somebody I care about gets the hell beat out of them. Can't help it. Thought I told you to be careful."

"What can I say? I screwed up," he said. He put his hand softly on the back of her neck and pulled her toward his lips.

"You sure this is a good idea?" she asked. "I don't want to do anything that's going to hurt you."

"Don't worry," he said. "I'll take my chances." Jack kissed her softly, for a long time. Her eyes were unfocused, wet, when they pulled apart.

"I'm so sorry this happened to you."

"I'll mend. Need time, that's all. P.J., we've got to talk."

"Okay," she said softly, cautiously.

He settled back into the pillow and stared past her. "I'm scared," he said slowly, haltingly. "I'm forty years old, and I don't seem to be able to make anything work with anybody. Bad dreams. Can't get things out of my mind. Demons and shit. I'm tired, worn down. For the first time in my life, I'm really scared that something's at stake here that I don't understand. Since my mother died, I can't get her out of mind. All the craziness over the years. . . . Hell, I don't even know what I'm talking about. But sometimes, P.J., I get to the point where I can't even *feel* anything anymore. And, Jesus, when I get like that, I drink too much. I don't know whether I'm an alcoholic or not, but I do know that I'm going to be if something doesn't change."

She brought her hand up to his forehead and stroked him gently, then brushed a hank of hair back out of his face.

"I want things to work out for us," Jack continued. "I'm tired of screwing up my life, and tired of screwing other people's lives up as well. You mean a lot to me; I want us to have a chance. But I feel like I need to do some damage control."

She smiled, ran her fingers along his forehead again. "Jack, there aren't any guarantees. You never know if something's going to work out. You do your best, go into it with your eyes open, and you give it your best shot. That's all any of us can do. We can do things to try and gain insight, to reach a better understanding of why this all works the way it does. But ultimately, there are no guarantees. We all have to live with that."

"So you just step off the edge, right? And hope there's a safety net. . . ."

She smiled. "That's about it, buckaroo."

He looked at her intently. "I want some help. Some things have happened, P.J. Lots to tell you about. I've been given a second chance. Real second chance . . . start life over again. I want to do it right this time. Will you help me?"

"Well," she said, "I can't be your therapist and still be your lover. So we have some choices to make, don't we?"

Jack reached over the bed rails, yanked a latch and let the

■ 277

metal drop. Then he wrapped his right arm around her waist, and pulled her up onto the bed on top of him.

"Have you lost your mind?" she asked, giggling.

"All I need is a referral, Dr. Campbell. I wasn't looking to engage you. At least not professionally. . . ."

She kissed him, very softly and carefully around his bruises. Then she raised her head and looked straight into his eyes.

"You know, Jack Lynch, one of the things that keeps us all going is the notion that a little refuge of personal happiness can be carved out of a very lousy world."

Jack pulled her back down on top of him, feeling himself coming alive again, her weight a delicious and wonderful pressure on his tired and battered body.

Personal happiness, he thought, *what a concept. . . .*

■ *EPILOGUE* ■

Trevenia Royale stretched lazily under the warm Caribbean sun and adjusted herself slightly on the chaise lounge. The Costa Rican beach in front of her was as deserted as the lunar landscape, the brilliant white sand as pure and unsullied as innocence itself.

Of course, this stretch of beach would be deserted. After all, she owned it. And it was very private.

A cool breeze blew in from the south, from over the water, against the mountains and back down on her. Her nipples, dark and erect, hardened even further. She reached to the small table that had been set there for her by the servants. She lifted a crystal glass to her lips and downed the last of the sweet, cold liquid. She fished one of the ice cubes out with her long, thin fingers and rubbed it over her chest, over her sternum, on the faint down that lined her stomach. She stared down at her breasts. The doctor had done a fine job. With the face lift, the tucks, and the boob job, she could pass for late forties tops. And with her hair dyed jet black, no one would ever guess that her sixty-eighth birthday was day after tomorrow.

Trevenia dropped the book she was reading in the sand next to her and picked up a small silver bell. She shook it casually, the tinkling of the metal filling the air. Behind her, she heard the scuffling of footsteps in the sand. She smiled as Miguel crossed in front of her, his black pants creased to a razor's edge and his starched white shirt a flurry of ruffles.

"Sí, señora," Miguel said. His skin was the color of seasoned oak, and his black, searing eyes bore out his Indian heritage. Trevenia stared at his broad shoulders, the blood in what she referred to as her "nether regions" pooling, the pressure increasing.

"Una otra marguerita, por favor," she said in her halting Spanish. She was never sure if she got it right, but as long as the servants brought her what she needed and didn't laugh to her face, she didn't give a damn. "Y mas de aceite."

Miguel turned and trotted up the beach toward the house. She turned lazily on her chair and watched him as he ran, his pants stretched across his trim, tight butt.

Trevenia sighed and stretched her arms and legs out, making an X with her body. Relaxed minutes later, she heard the door slam in the cabana, and rolled over on her stomach as Miguel approached. He set the tray down on the small table and offered the glass to her. She took a long sip of the green, syrupy drink, the salt on the rim of the glass a biting complement to the sweetness. The tequila went straight to her head and she settled back face-first into the chaise as Miguel knelt down in the sand next to her.

He shook the plastic bottle and popped the top off it, then poured a dollop into his hands. He rubbed his palms together and started at her shoulders, the smooth, lubricated texture of his hands like velvet on her skin. He rubbed the oil into the crook of her neck, just barely into her hairline, then down her back slowly, a little at a time. Then he poured oil directly out of the bottle onto her hips, his hands rubbing over her bottom first lightly, then with greater pressure, and finally squeezing her so hard, forcing the blood throughout her, that the pain could only be described as exquisite.

Trevenia moaned as his hand slid between her legs, running the oil up into her hair, around her lips, even inside her just a touch. He oiled between her thighs, down the backs of her legs and her calves and then, one at a time, his fingers slid in and out between her toes. Then he leaned over and lifted her right foot until her knee was bent at a right angle.

He bared his teeth, gently stuck her big toe inside his mouth and nipped it.

Trevenia jumped and squealed, then broke into giggles like a schoolgirl. She turned over on her back, his smiling face above her as he stared—no, leered—down at her nude torso. He turned the oil upside down and let the entire bottle pour out on her, then he rubbed it in carefully around her healed stitches, with only the faint pink scars to give her true age away. He gently rubbed oil all over her breasts, massaging her nipples between his thumbs and forefinger. The skin of his hands and her nipples was so dark that when Trevenia relaxed and let her eyes go out of focus, the two forms seemed to blend together into one.

He rubbed down her flat stomach, to the mound of thick hair below her navel. He let his hand slide just over the top of her hair, the sensation electric. Then Miguel ran his hands over her mound with more pressure, his slick hand slithering down between her legs as if on a chute. He gently probed for a moment, then let two fingers slide into her all the way to his hand.

Trevenia moaned and arched her back, her eyes shut, her head shaking from side to side. She sucked in a deep breath, then brought her hands up, grabbed his arms, and pulled them away from her. She couldn't take anymore, not like that.

She let go of his arms and undid the row of mother-of-pearl buttons. She yanked his shirt open, his hairless chest shiny and dark and hard under the cloth. She fumbled with his belt buckle until it gave way, then pulled on his trousers until a button popped and the waistline dropped open.

She looked up into his eyes. "Miguel. . . ." she sighed.

"Señora," he said, lowering his face to meet hers. She opened her mouth to him, his tongue inside her, forcing her open wider still. In front of them, a wave crashed over the beach and rode the sand to the foot of her chair. Miguel pulled away from her. He stood up slowly, the pants tight around him, caught on him.

Trevenia took a deep breath and reached slowly upward. She found the silver catch of the zipper and unlatched it, then lowered it slowly. He wore nothing under the black pants. She pulled the pants apart, and let them drop to his ankles.

Her eyes bulged, and she had a fleeting moment of sweet fear and panic.

"Oh, my goodness," she said, her jaw dropping open.

Life was sweet.